paint my body red

Heidi R. Kling

Entangled Publishing, LLC
2614 South Timberline Road
Suite 109
Fort Collins, CO 80525
Visit our website at www.entangledpublishing.com.

Ember is an imprint of Entangled Publishing, LLC.

ISBN 978-1-68281-0-224

Edited by Heather Howland
Cover design by Louisa Maggio
Cover art from iStock

Manufactured in the United States of America

First Edition November 2015

"At my death paint my body with red paint and plunge it into fresh water to be restored back to life, otherwise my bones will be turned into stone and my joints into flint in my grave, but my spirit will rise."

—Crazy Horse

Chapter One

Now

It's two weeks after high school graduation, and I'm not much more than a monster of madness when my mom drops me off at San Francisco International Airport. It feels more like a life flight than a vacation.

"You don't have to walk me in," I mumble.

It's easier to lose myself in the darkness of my life when I'm alone.

My mother's impeccably manicured hands flutter against my shoulder like she's trying to help me with my bag, so tentatively, she might as well be wearing a HAZMAT suit. She can't wait to get me on that plane.

"I'm eighteen, Mom. I can carry my own bag."

"You'll always be my baby, Paige."

Her baby. Right. Babies are innocent, pure, harmless. I'm the opposite.

The official reason I'm leaving town is to see my sick dad— the father I barely know, the man who hardly knows me—but mom and I both know the real reason I'm being sent away: to avoid being Dead Kid #7. To see if I can be saved.

The dirty secrets we don't talk about—they're the reason I'm leaving. Not the obvious things that everyone else sees: not the yellow tape screaming *caution*, not the blood on the tracks, not the deaths—but everything in between—everything that happened during, before, since. It's the empty space that screams between my ears at night, shrill and violent, lurking beneath the silence. It's his voice—seductive, thrilling, menacing—that haunts me. Ghostly, but permanent. Ty's unescapable threats.

"Seriously," I snap while she hovers, wanting to touch me, wanting to be a good mother. "You don't have to wait with me."

Her eyebrows pinch. She's hurt. I hurt her. Again. She stops reaching and lets her hands fall to her sides. I feel bad for a second, but then I remember why I'm here. Where they are sending me. And most importantly *why*. And I'm angry all over again. At them. At him. At her. But mostly him.

Anger, the second stage of grief. Anger is easier than the suffocating blanket of black I'm treading under. The unrelenting sadness I was drowning in before.

"If you're sure…" She wipes the corner of her eye with her sleeve, streaking the pale yellow cashmere black with mascara.

On the street, taxis whiz by, cars honk. I hug my arms and wince. I wasn't always like this. I wasn't even remotely like this. I was an easy kid. An easy teen. I did what I was told: got good grades, had nice friends, cleared my plate after supper.

I have no idea who I am anymore. The Paige I used to be wouldn't have done any of the things I did.

But I did do them. And I can't take them back.

Above us, the monorail rumbles by, and I jump. Even though it looks like a harmless Disneyland ride, my eyes are glued to the tracks, knowing what it could do. I remember the article I read about the conductor driving the train—how he hears the sound of 400 tons of metal hitting the body off the tracks at 40 mph; how the thud haunts his sleep.

The monorail's speakers warn the passengers in a monotone voice, "Terminal B. Next stop, Terminal B. Stay back from the closing doors. Move away from the tracks."

I feel sick. At least the scream stays trapped in my head.

Mom looks at me like I'm an open wound. "You sure you have your ticket?"

I nod.

"Your ID?"

My wallet is clenched in my sweaty hand.

"A car will be there to pick you up in Wyoming. If you don't see it right away, call me immediately. If you don't have cell reception, use the land line in the gift shop."

"Shouldn't I, like, hail a horse instead?" Sarcastic humor. Another "defense mechanism" I use. Unfortunately, the words come out sounding panicked instead.

Her eyebrow arches.

"It was a joke." And maybe it'll feel like one, eventually.

My mother swallows a deep breath of foggy, smoggy Bay Area air and lets it out slowly in a poof. This is a response I'm used to. Lucky for her, she won't have to deal with me anymore.

The next monorail slows to a stop, hardly making a sound, but I hear horns blasting, distant screams. I see bare feet sticking out of a yellow sheet that looks like a rain slicker.

It isn't raining.

My mother cups my head in her hands, forcing my eyes away from the tracks and onto her. "Stop. Paige, you just have to stop."

Despite the fact that my mother's body language screams don't even try, despite the fact that I know I *need* to go—that there's no way, after everything that's happened, that I can possibly stay—I still want to beg her to let me. I want to dive back into her unbearably perfumed car, have her ruffle my hair, and suggest we have a girls' afternoon of lunch and a matinee like we did before I grew up too fast and she stopped asking. I want to find a reset button on her BMW's dash and start this year over like it's one of Ty's video games instead of my life, because everything about this moment screams Game Over.

With hard edges and perfect hair, she reaches out to hug me. I shrug her off harder than I intend. I can't stand being touched anymore, even by my mom who isn't trying to hurt me.

"Sorry," I say, and I am—for not letting her help me, for not letting her touch me, for leaving her with a mess too big to clean up, and most importantly for the secrets floating around her perfect house, leaving a layer of filth she'll never be able to scrub off.

"It's fine." She shakes her head sadly. "Do you have your pills?"

"Yeah."

"Did you take a Xanax?" She looks around, ensuring our privacy. God forbid some random tourist heading to Alcatraz hears the perfect CEO's daughter is taking medication for anxiety.

"A half, yeah," I lie. I don't want to take my newly prescribed pills. Addiction runs in my family—even the people I'm not biologically related to. That's the last thing I need.

"Maybe you should take a whole one before the flight."

"I'm fine."

She bites her lip. "You don't look fine. You look pale. You didn't eat anything this morning."

"It's not a magic bean, Mom. It's not going to fix anything."

I look down at my shoes. My legs are so thin now they flop over the bench like a stuffed scarecrow's limbs. I lost weight... after. I try to eat, I do, but my appetite is non-existent. I know I'm pale, that my hair is a mess. I know she thinks I've given up, but I haven't. It's the opposite. All I want to do is run. Run away. Run far away. It's that surge of energy that keeps me going.

It's why I agreed to leave.

I tilt my head up and stare into the foggy sky—After spending nearly the entire month in my bedroom staring at the ceiling, being outside is scary enough.

"Seriously, I'm okay, Mom. You don't have to wait with me."

She hesitates. "I do have that meeting with the VCs..."

Venture capitalists. They are to the Silicon Valley what

stockbrokers are to New York City: the money, the big numbers my mother loves chasing. "You don't want to keep VCs waiting," I say.

My mother gestures toward my new designer carry-on suitcase and matching leather laptop bag. "This isn't forever, sweetie. Just until…"

Her words disappear into the mucky sky.

Until it's safe to come home?

Until *I'm* safe to come home?

Until I stop thinking about him?

Until I leave for Wesleyan in the fall?

All around us busy travelers are rushing through the swivel doors into the airport.

"Excuse us," a lady says. She's pushing a stroller carrying a raisin-eating toddler. She glances back at her husband who is wrestling a little boy's backpack onto his small shoulders. He tells him it's his responsibility to carry his own toys onto the plane. He scoffs at the idea and then ends up nodding.

Responsibility. When did I stop claiming it?

My stomach clenches. I can't remember the last time I've eaten, but I might puke right here on the sidewalk. "I need to go," I think I say out loud.

The traffic control lady scoots up behind us dressed in polyester pants and an orange crossing guard vest. She motions for us to get moving, to move the black BMW, engine still running, hazard-lights on, leaning against the red NO STOPPING AT ANYTIME curb.

My mother, who isn't used to others telling her what to do, peers at her over her glasses as if to say, *You ask me to move it before I'm ready, I'll run you over with it.* She follows up the glare with the straight-up-pointy-French-manicure finger, which means, *I'll deal with* you *in a sec.*

"I love you," Mom says, her expression melting some when she faces me. Her icy voice cracks like I'm her broken baby bird leaving the nest. She feels guilty for pushing me out before

I'm ready to fly. But she's going to do it anyway. "Call me if you need anything. I'll come right away."

Uh-huh. Right. "You hate Wyoming. You hate Dad. Besides, you can't leave Phil."

She blinks. A good mom *would* come. She's always wanted to be a good mom, but she was much better at being CEO of an influential start-up and serving her own agenda, whether it was tearing down a large section of our house to make new offices for her and Phil or ripping me out of my dad's arms all those years ago as I cried and screamed.

I'm right—she won't come—but she argues anyway.

"I certainly do not hate your father. Do I find it ironic he's suffering from ALS and not from alcohol-induced liver failure? I do. But most importantly, I love you. Give him my—" Something—guilt?—spider webs across her face as she struggles over what message to convey to my father, the ex-husband she left in an ugly fashion and hasn't seen in years. "Give him my best, okay?"

I can't help defending him. "He's been sober for years, hasn't he? But okay."

Her eyes widen, and I know what she's thinking: *Do you really want to get into anything personal right now?* No. I don't. In fact, that's the last thing I want. I'm not in a place to do any chastising anymore. Not about my father. Not about anything. And though we don't say it out loud, we both know it. I equal parts love and despise her, ironically similar to the way I feel about her stepson.

When she moves in close enough to give me an awkward pat on the back and grazes my cheek with a kiss that feels more like a sting, she smells like taxi exhaust and a new scent I don't recognize. She looks like my mom but smells like a stranger, and I'm certain she feels the same way about me.

Chapter Two

When I arrive at Jackson Hole's pincushion of an airport and stumble down the narrow metal stairs, immediately it hits me, flooding my senses—air so dry and pine fresh it ought to star in its own commercial. After months of holding my breath, stomach clamped awaiting the next disaster, I inhale in quiet desperation as my lungs fill with this once familiar air. Maybe my mother was right. Maybe a fresh start will be the pill that finally works. No one to stress out over, no death, no responsibilities, no one's life to endanger simply by existing— just a couple months of breathing in and out.

I can do that.

I can do that if I can breathe. After years of living at sea level, breathing mountain air feels like sucking air through a straw.

I don't realize I've stopped walking until my suitcase rolls into the back of my calves and tips over. The Grand Tetons unfold before me, cragged and magnificent. The mountain range rears up like a lioness of rock defending her territory. I like that I'm so small in comparison. It'll be easier to disappear this way, pretend I'm not even here. The summer months will slip by, and if I'm still around by September, I'll slip off to college to disappear again.

And the sky above me, the blue, blue, cloudless sky—the color of sapphires—I tilt my head back and just look.

Tourists breeze past me, chattering on their way to their ranch and national park vacations. No one is paying attention to me, and I like that, too. Even though caffeine makes my anxiety worse, when I finally tear my eyes away from the blue sky, I buy a latte at a small stand in the lobby with the intention of drinking it while I wait for my ride. A woman with three carry-ons smashes past me, and before I've taken a sip, the hot liquid splashes all over my black T-shirt. Pissed off, I find some wet-wipes in my bag and mop some of it up, but the shirt is essentially trashed. I can't see my dad after all this time looking like this, so I stumble into the tiny gift shop and flip through the sale rack.

As expected, everything is cheesy tourist junk. I narrow it down to an extra-large blue moose T-shirt with Christmas lights on its antlers that says "Welcome to Moose, Wyoming" which would delight an eight-year-old boy, or an extra-small pink tank top that reads "Cowgirl" in glittery silver letters. I appreciate the irony of the latter as I'm about as much a cowgirl now as I am a pillar of sanity, so I toss it onto the counter.

An old-timer with a big gut tucked into blue jeans and under an even bigger belt buckle makes small talk while giving me my change. "You going to check out Old Faithful while you're here?"

"I doubt it. I'm visiting family," I say vaguely.

"Ah, who?"

I don't want to give an inch of personal information but he's staring at me, waiting. "My dad," I finally say.

"Ah! Who's your old man?"

"You probably don't know him—Gus Mason?"

His face molds into an expression I've seen too many times: a funeral face. I'm confused when he offers up a bleak, "Give him my best."

Uncomfortably done with me, the man shifts his attention

to a customer asking about Old Faithful up in Yellowstone an hour or so from here. She's wondering about the chances of it going haywire and killing everyone in the vicinity. Can't even count on Old Faithful anymore, I guess. You better go home then.

In the bathroom stall, I rip off my wet black T-shirt and shove it into the sticky metal feminine products dispenser. I want to rip off my white city jeans—my bra and panties, too, for that matter—but I don't have replacements for those yet. I remember the man's strange expression when I mentioned my dad. What's his deal? Old enemies? Or is Dad not doing well? Mom would've told me, right?

When I wash my hands, my face in the mirror isn't me anymore than this Cowgirl shirt is me. My once-bright eyes are one-percent milk, and once-silky hair is old straw. I squeeze my cheeks to bring up blood and bite my lips to paint them red.

A half hour later, I'm still waiting at the curb, my arms getting burned in the high altitude sunshine. I don't miss the fog, but the dry heat will take some getting used to. Sweating, I'm about to give up and call the ranch for a ride when I spot a Jeep with Eight Hands Ranch written on the side in bold Western-style black letters sitting in the middle of the small parking lot.

Dad's is called Six Hands Ranch. I wondered if somebody copied it? Might as well go check it out; I have nothing else to do. My nerves shake like a bottle of soda in the hands of a toddler as I get closer. Six has clearly been painted over and replaced by Eight. A bolt of anxiety shoots through my veins, an instinctive cue of something minor meaning something much bigger—the same feeling I got when the gift shop clerk shot me that funeral stare. Something's up.

It's so still and quiet that I don't think anyone is in the driver's seat until I'm almost at the Jeep. The driver's seat is leaned way back, and I'm startled to find a lanky cowboy snoozing away in a pair of country-boy jeans—dirt-stained and well-worn. Above an unbuttoned collar of an equally dirty plaid shirt, a brown riding hat tips over the guy's eyes, exposing the smooth, square jaw of a young cowboy maybe a little older than me. Again I check out the door. EIGHT HANDS RANCH and sure enough it's our family's icon—a silhouette of a mustang rearing up in front of the Grand Tetons.

"Excuse me?" I ask, carefully. My request cracks through my desert of a throat, reminding me I haven't spoken louder than a mumble since I got on the plane.

Instead of jumping up startled, like I would, the cowboy's hand moves slowly toward his hat, which he proceeds to slowly tip up off his chin to his forehead to reveal, like I guessed, maybe a nineteen or twenty-year-old cowboy. His face isn't perfect, but his curious eyes as blue as the wide Wyoming sky and expressive eyebrows immediately draw me in, even in my bitter-numb state. No small task. I blink.

"Well, there you are," he says, in a typical cowboy accent— which sounds more like "there ya' are"—staring at me like I finally turned up in the lost and found bin.

It's been a long time since I've seen a flesh and blood cowboy and the innate mix of casual confidence that seems to come with the title.

"Here I am," I say in a flat voice. I avoid inviting male attention like the plague. "I take it you're my ride?"

Rubbing at his eye with a dirt-stained knuckle, he blinks away his nap. "Sorry about the sleeping, Miss Paige. Long night, even longer day," he says with a little chuckle as if recalling something. He sticks out his hand like I should recognize him. "It's Jake."

Jake.

Doesn't ring a bell, but he looks at me expectantly, like he hears the chimes.

I don't. Doesn't seem to matter, because this Jake is now

wide awake and all smiles, even though I don't accept his hand. He's cheerful. Healthy. Sane. I can tell these three things from a one-minute greeting. What could he tell about me? Hopefully nothing more than I want to reveal. I glance down at my cheesy new tank top, my too-loose pressed two-hundred-dollar jeans, and remember my hollow eyes. What story do I tell? His interested gaze doesn't indicate anything more than Gus's daughter coming home for the summer. If Mom told my dad anything, he either hasn't shared it with this guy or he's a very good actor. I feel a little bit of relief.

"How was your flight?" he asks, dropping his hand without question. I'm grateful for that.

"Fine," I say. I rub my sunburned arms that hang out the sides of my tank top like wet noodles. Why did I buy this revealing tank top? I should've gone for the extra-large cartoon moose shirt. I frown and look down. I hate being so skinny. I used to love food. I once had a ravenous appetite.

Don't look at me, Cowboy Jake.

"Little bumpy coming in?" His friendliness doesn't ease up. Maybe that's part of the job. Being friendly even to rude tourists.

"A little bit."

"Summer storm clouds. Happens every afternoon, as predictable as Old Faithful." He nods with squinty eyes, trying to entertain me.

I smile. I can't help it. "That's funny."

He lifts an eyebrow. "Why's that?"

"Some lady in the gift shop was asking about Old Faithful and said she heard it might go off one day and kill everyone."

Leaning back, he laughs heartily. "Tourists. They even worry on sunny days. These days it's the bison. They seem to be goring tourists more than usual. A foreign kid the other day. Exhange student got too close. They don't understand these are wild animals, and they need to leave them be. Anyhow, glad to see this one is more creative." He's still smiling, shaking his head like those gorging stories are comedy gold. "Old Faithful blowing her top. That'll be the day."

I smile, too. The more normal I appear the greater chance I'll be left alone. Plus, being cold to this warm boy is proving difficult. It's like ignoring a puppy. "So you work for my dad?"

"Happy to report I do. Was me driving his Jeep the giveaway?" He smiles again, teasing.

I shrug, embarrassed, my ears getting hot. *You're adorable, but I can't do adorable cowboy this summer, so let's not banter, Cowboy.*

I need to get on the road, unpack, and shower—and then get on with the hiding away part of the summer.

As if he can read my mind—or is astute enough to read my expression—he nods once. "Well, let's get you on your way, before Gus sends the calvary after me."

Confident, too. And his easy kindness feels like a gift.

Two long legs swing out of the Jeep, and suddenly my suitcase is behind me, the tailgate slams shut, and I'm tucked into the passenger seat next to Jake.

I'd forgotten how a cowboy's energy level flips on a dime. One minute sound asleep, the next a whirl of palpable capability. He reminds me of my dad. My mom, the original energy bunny, seems a sloth by comparison. As if he can read my mind again, he says, "By the way, your mama's called the ranch five times since noon. Suspect you might want to call her upon arrival." His ridiculously blue eyes hang onto mine a moment too long, but then they crinkle around the edges like an inside joke.

"Yeah, she's like that."

He surveys me, narrowing his eyes again, as though he's trying to figure it all out. "Surprised she's willing to part with you for a whole summer," he says, again in a meaningful way, almost like a question, as he revs up the engine.

"You know. I'm an annoying teenager. What mother doesn't want to get rid of her annoying teenager?"

He shrugs and turns down his bottom lip in this funny-cute

way.

"You don't seem annoying to me," Jake says, and I flush again.

I'm not used to boys this nice. Or boys that act like confident men instead of needy a-holes.

"A little ticked off maybe, but not annoying," he finishes.

Ticked off? Who says that? My guts constrict again. I don't want to talk about my mother or home. My answer is a noncommittal shrug, which he seems to accept. I *was* ticked off. I appreciated his transparency.

I remember this refreshing way of cowboy communicating. A comment out there on the breeze — up for the grabbing if you want a bite or not. If not, no one will press you. Maybe this will work out after all. Maybe Wyoming is the perfect place to dodge everything and hole up until I can escape to Wesleyan in August.

"You thirsty?" Before I can answer, Jake reaches a long arm over the seat and digs a Dr. Pepper out of a red-topped cooler. He pops open the top and hands the cold can to me. I haven't had a soda in years, but I appreciate his chivalry. When was the last time a boy opened a drink for me? It seemed like second nature to him, so it wasn't like he thought I couldn't open it myself. He was just being nice. Once again, he reminds me of Dad, and suddenly I'm excited to see my father again. To be back on the ranch. To breathe the clean air that smells like pine and horses and childhood.

Two minutes in his company, and already, Jake is bringing me back to life.

I take a sip, careful to keep it even as Jake revs up the engine and backs out of the parking spot. "Careful there," he says. "Road gets bumpy."

The bubbles spring into my mouth, tumbling down my throat like fire water as we move out of the parking lot and onto the lone highway that snakes away from the town of Jackson up toward Yellowstone.

"So, who are the new hands?" I ask my escort after a few quiet minutes, the sugar and caffeine making me brave.

"Pardon?"

Pardon. I hide my amused smile. It may only be a few states away from California, but Wyoming has always felt like a different planet.

"Eight Hands Ranch? On the side of the Jeep? It's been Six Hands as long as I can remember."

He shoots me a sideways glance, wrinkling his nicely shaped, sunburned nose a bit when he does. "How long has it been since you've talked to him, Miss Paige?"

"It's been a while."

"And I know you haven't been here."

"That's true," I admit, guiltily. I was fourteen the last time I came. I think. Too old for the little-girl-getting-dirty-is-fun ranch hand stuff. I preferred California, or my mom taking me to Europe and Australia and Hawaii in the summers. Even though I hated leaving Dad at first, after a while I got used to it. He and the ranch became the unknown, the strange, the oddity.

"Mm." Jake's jaw tightens.

"What does that mean?"

He glances at me pointedly. "Lot changes in a half dozen years, that's all."

He says it like it's the end of a short story, not the beginning of a new one.

I frown. I don't like his tone or his comment. I don't want any changes. I've come here to hide from life. Period. Even though he's sweet and making me feel more comfortable than I have in a long time, I don't need any wise-for-his-age cowboy prophesizing about change like he's some sage. Maybe I am wrong. Maybe he *won't* mind his business. I examine his profile—His nose is a little crooked, like he's broken it once or twice. How old is he anyway?

It's hard to tell with cowboys. Boys become men here much earlier than they do in the city. One look at those weathered hands, at the way he carries himself—so mature and poised—tells me he's been working for money since the age of twelve, maybe longer.

I can tell he's sizing me up as well by the way he keeps glancing at me with his peripheral vision. He thumbs the steering wheel, intermittently, like he's hearing a drum beat in his head. I want to ask how he knows me, but I don't want to be rude, or frankly give him any more of my thoughts than I already have. I don't want to wonder about this strangely remarkable cowboy.

My hair whips all around my face in the hot wind, so I tie it back with the rubber band around my wrist. I hope my body language gives him the hint that I don't want his attention. I don't want his questions. I don't even want this Dr. Pepper. It's making me feel sick and hyper and frankly, now I have to pee. I hold it in, because asking him to stop would be far too embarrassing and intimate so I watch the miles of pine trees lining the silver creek rush by. One minute passes. Then five. He flips on some music—country, naturally—as we rumble along.

The drive up to Dad's place is about an hour once we hit this dirt road.

The effects of the soda plus the vast sky and endless bright sun wilderness leave me feeling antsy and sticking to the seat, so I fiddle with my sunglasses, my SPF 30 lip-gloss—*The high altitude sunburns, Paige,* Mom's warning—and tiny pieces of paper in my purse.

Finally I can't hold it anymore.

"Can you pull over?"

"Sure thing." He doesn't ask why—he likely knows why. He hands me a package of Kleenex from his glovebox, and I can't help but laugh a little.

Without looking at him, I dash into the scrabble-brush, and after scanning the dirt for snakes or large bugs, I find a decent tree to squat behind. I wipe and then bury the spoiled tissue under a rock.

Jake doesn't say anything when I return.

He just starts the engine and we're off.

Maybe it's the relief, maybe it's the soda, but I suddenly want to talk. "A ranch that's been called one name forever suddenly being called something else? I think it's weird that's all," I say, with a shrug as if our conversation about this hadn't ended many miles back.

He keeps his gaze on the road but adjusts his hat over his eyes, bending the intense sun off the rim. He looks slightly uncomfortable with my question. I sit quietly and wait, knowing he will consider it ruder to ignore me than to answer—even if that answer is something that's not his place to discuss.

"Gus added a couple hands. Sure he'll explain. Changing a ranch's name outright," he glances over at me, before tightening his grip on the steering wheel, "is a different thing all together."

Thing sounds like *thang* out of Cowboy Jake's lips.

I accidentally forget to stop watching him after he's finished his statement. The tanned square of his jaw moves when he swallows. He has a nice profile—strong—his right arm wrangling the steering wheel as the left one rests on the unrolled window, exposing his veiny forearm to even more sun below his rolled up red plaid sleeve.

Stop it, Paige.

I snap back around and face forward. I think about pulling out my phone, but my battery is drained, and I'd have no reception out here anyway. It's so quiet. I'm used to fiddling with electronics, and suddenly there's nothing to do with my hands: no Twitter or Instagram to update. No Facebook to check. No incoming ping of texts and emojis from my friends.

It's just this cute cowboy and me.

I tap my feet on the floor of the cab and watch the dust spiral up from the road and into the topless Jeep. All the while, we ramble toward where my father—the man who used to mean everything to me—is waiting.

That's the main reason I agreed to come to my father's

ranch instead of a health spa for emotionally wayward teens or wherever else Mom and Phil were planning on sending me. I was being sent away for sure, but because he was sick…and because he wouldn't pry, the ranch was the best option. After the dozens of appointments with psychiatrists and psychologists and peer counselors and even a visit to some random priest (we haven't gone to church since I was a little girl living in Jackson), I'm done talking it through.

I never told them the whole truth anyway. I skirted over the stuff I wasn't comfortable with. I strained to be vague. Maybe it's because I grew up here in a place where people respected privacy, encouraged burying secrets under dusty rugs. Or maybe I'm just afraid to face the truth, to accept my role in all of the chaos and pain back home. Afraid the dark secrets will consume me — swallow me whole. Or he'll follow me here, somehow. In my nightmares. In the darkness.

Even in the middle of nowhere, my stepbrother still could find me.

I push back that eerie thought and hug my arms tighter across my chest.

I focus on the feel of hot wind in my hair and on my skin. Welcome the sun.

I listen to Jake ramble on and on about specific tundra we're driving through. He gets more detailed about the bison problem as well as the dying wolf population. I nod, listening. It's all interesting and his voice is oddly soothing, the slow cadence and earnestness — clearly he loves this place — like my dad's was.

"You don't have any trains here, do you?"

"Working railways? Nah. The only train we have goes through Cody. Unless you're talking about a wagon train, and that we have. But usually it's just for tourists trying to reenact the Wild West."

"Good."

"Got something against trains, Cowgirl?"

"Yes."

"I don't care for them much myself. Prefer my old Jeep."

"Why?"

He shrugs good-naturedly. "Perfer to be in the captain's seat."

I chuckle. "Control freak?"

"Just prefer it is all."

"Well, you're a good driver," I say.

"Oh I am, huh?" Grinning, he cranks the wheel to the left, and we swerve. I roll into his shoulder. He laughs as I squeal and then steady myself with a tight grip to the rollbar.

"I take it back!" I yell, and he laughs again, hitting a ditch that sends my head back against the musky cloth seat that smells like a dusty rider crossing a mustard flower meadow. I used to pluck those flowers out of the summer dirt and suck their lemon-flavored juice until my friend told me they were sweet and sour from all the animal pee. I never touched them again.

"Sorry 'bout that, Cowgirl," Jake says, mischieviously. "Never can predict the bumps."

"Very funny. Point made. You're a terrible driver," I say, and he chuckles. Then I ask: "Cowgirl, huh? World's worst cowgirl, maybe. I don't even remember how to get on a horse."

"Oh, we'll remedy that right quick."

"Oh, will we? You're awfully confident."

"You just forgot who you are, that's all." He takes his eyes off the bumpy road and catches mine before looking back to the road again. "Don't worry, you'll remember soon enough."

"I'm many things," I say, sarcastically, "but I'll never again be a cowgirl."

"Never say never," he says.

His words linger in the air, making me suspect he might know more about me than he let on.

Chapter Three

I wasn't expecting this.

The ranch I remember—with its teeming clots of roughnecks tangled up in the mud, kids scurrying about, barbeque wafting hot meat on an open fire, and people—people everywhere: joking, roughhousing, squealing—this isn't that place. As we pull up to the ranch the only sounds I hear are the roar of the Jeep's engine lulling to a halt and a lone horse in the center of a beat-up corral neighing into the dry, soft wind. The quiet is so eerily strange, I half expect tumbleweeds rolling by.

"Where is everybody?" I ask Jake, who, in a flash, has pulled the key from the ignition and is on my side of the Jeep, opening my door for me.

Jake's shoulders soften and a frown crosses his strong brow.

"Where are all the staff and the guests?" I ask. "Oh, are they on an overnight?" Once per ranch stay, some of the cowpokes take guests on a covered wagon ride up to the mountain top overlook where they can wrangle up cows and sleep under the stars.

Jake extends a dirt-stained hand, offering to help me out of the Jeep. I take it but only for a second. His hand is long-fingered and rough but has a soft strength that fits around my smaller hand like a cocoon. I let go as soon as my flip-flops hit the dirt.

That was the longest I'd let anyone touch me since Ty.

Jake glances down at my feet with an amused expression on his face as the dust puffs up around my freshly painted toenails. Mom's send-off: a mother-daughter mani-pedi. A cool eucalyptus towel and a fresh coat of red polish fixes everything, right? Especially when Zen music is playing overhead.

"I don't have any other shoes," I say.

"I didn't say a word," he drawls. "But we can fix that later." He holds my eyes a little too long, and I feel that flush again. He blinks. Did he feel it, too?

I swallow away any inappropriate thoughts.

"At any rate," he says, as if clearing the air, "you better just come on in." He grabs my suitcase out of the back. Flipping it sideways, he tucks it under his arm like it weighs less than a Kleenex box. Like it doesn't have wheels and a handle and was meant to roll wherever you needed to take it.

But still…I can't remember anyone at home ever offering to carry my suitcase. Never mind doing it without asking.

It's a little *too* endearing.

"Thanks," I say, "I can get that." I reach for the suitcase and our fingers brush. Flustered, I pull away. Jake must think I'm nuts.

He glances at my dusty feet again and shoots me an amused look. "What, and risk dirtying up those pretty toes?"

Pretty toes. Is he making fun of me or does he mean it?

Then I realize what I'm standing on.

Circles of mosaic cement lead from the drive to the porch, and the first one is my own. A little girl's handprint, painted blue with a yellow dove in the center: PAIGE AGE SIX. I can't fight the feeling that I'm going to break it, so I step around the other ones until I'm walking over cracks corroding fingers indenting round stone: Papa's, then Gran's, then Uncle Joe's, then Dad's. I stop at Mom's, surprised Dad kept it here: her long-fingered hand in yellow paint, daisy leaves pressed into the palm. I still remember her laughing that day, braids in her hair, yellow paint smeared across her cheek. I remember Dad teasing her for not liking to get dirty, and instead of scowling and snapping at him—that would come later—she just waved his comment away with a smile.

"I apologize for them being so run down," Jake says. "I haven't got to it yet."

I press my palm into hers. Our hands are now the exact same size, and I suddenly miss this version of my mom so much my heart lurches and tears pop into my eyes. I swallow hard, pushing them away. "You're going to fix them up?" I look up at this cowboy now carrying my suitcase over his shoulder like it's a saddle.

"You bet. Do it every year after the snow melts."

I blink.

He doesn't.

"Why?" I ask.

"You don't remember me, do you?"

I'm searching for something recognizable in those ridiculously blue eyes when the heavy wood door swings open and a strange man, thinner, more pale than me, rolls out onto the porch. A button under his right finger propels his wheelchair forward.

Two microphone shaped pieces of black foam hold up his head. Plastic tubing snakes from his neck down his chest, and from that, springs more tubing, thinner lines that disappear under pearl buttons on his red and blue plaid shirt. His legs are what shock me the most. Covered in baggy grey sweats, they look like two floppy seals, dangling on metal footrests.

I suck in a breath. It's not a strange man. It's my…father.

This man, whose facial features resemble my dad's—if you sucked the muscle and blood right from under his skin, if you watered, and then lightened his blue eyes to the shade of an abandoned winter's bird bath, if you took away everything about him that once was, that he used to be—mumbles something incoherent.

I had no idea. I had no idea things were this bad, that he had deteriorated this drastically.

Jake's hand rests on my daddy's shoulder. "He says it's okay, Paige. Don't be scared."

Say something. Move forward.

But I can't move. I can't say anything. I stand there, frozen in place, on Mom's yellow handprint like I'm the one unable to move on my own.

"Hi, Daddy. How…are you?" I say. Choking on my own words, I look to Jake, suddenly understanding everything: the look on the gift shop clerk's face, Jake's comments about the ranch, why this place is a ghost town, Mom's insistence to send me here this summer. "This is why he only emails, never calls? He can't…"

Talk anymore.

I knew he was sick—but it was a long-term disease. The last time I saw him he was still walking, talking. He just had a slight tremor in his hand. That's it. And why isn't he wearing jeans? The only time I've seen my dad in something other than jeans was at Papa's funeral. I latch onto that image, floundering for something to say.

I feel Jake's eyes on me. He doesn't want me to say anything else. I've already said enough. I look back at my dad.

"Thanks for your emails. I'm…it's so good to see you."

My dad might be everything Mom accused him of: neglectful, self-centered, alcoholic—but standing here, one thing is absolutely certain. Whatever my father is, or had been before, I am a terrible daughter.

"Paige." Jake's look tugs on me like I'm a stubborn fish he's trying to drag in. I push back, not wanting to see the truth in his eyes. Not wanting to stand here on this stupid handprint, not wanting to acknowledge this ghost who used to be my dad, or the ghosts that chased me here. I want to disappear. I want to clamber back into the Jeep and get on an airplane heading toward anywhere, but Jake doesn't let me get away. He keeps pulling.

I follow them into the living room where the giant moose head, named Freddie, still hangs over the river rock fireplace. Vaulted ceilings made of huge, heavy beams—strong enough to hold back piles of snow each winter—arch above the L-shaped couch, where Native American stitching tells the long-ago story of a herd of buffalo running across a golden prairie. The same pea-green crochet throw blanket still sprawls over the back.

On the left hand corner of the left hand cushion closest to the door, I plop down, awkwardly. This room used to smell of dust and cigars. One look at the humming machine pulling alongside Dad tells me he isn't smoking anymore. A hint of strawberries in the air replaces the cigar scent; a sterile lemon cleaner smeared on the tree stump coffee table replaces the dust.

Jake speaks to my father in a low, soothing voice as he parks him by the well-worn leather recliner next to the river rock fireplace. Easily lifting my father from his wheelchair, he settles him onto the leather chair like he's a small child. The muscles in Jake's arms don't even strain under the weight. Dad must weigh even less than me.

I yank my silver ring up and down on my middle finger, nervously. Under the silver, a mold-colored ring band stands out against my pale skin. Mom warned me not to buy cheap jewelry, but I couldn't resist it early last year when my friends and I were shopping on the coast. That seems like forever ago.

I glance over at my dad who is staring straight into the unlit fireplace. Jake kneels beside his wheel, confidently busying himself with Dad's tubes and wires like it's second nature. He's saying something to him, something too low for me to hear. Now he's walking over to me.

"Come on into the kitchen and help me get some tea, will you?"

I jump off the couch like its coils sprung me off.

Jake stops short halfway down the dimly lit hallway, and I crash into him in an awkward way that sends unwelcome heat up my arms. He steadies me with a strong hand on my elbow and says in an insistent whisper, "You talk to him, Paige. He can hear you same as I can. His body is fading, but his brain is perfectly intact. You can't have him thinking you're afraid of him, of the way he looks." His eyes dart away before he says, "He's afraid enough as it is."

He loves him. Jake loves my dad. I can tell. Why can't I remember this sweet cowboy? It's like everything good in my memories has been washed away by everything bad at home.

I fight away tears. "I'm sorry. It's...I don't even know him, anymore. Not really."

He shakes away my words like they're ridiculous. "He's your father. Of course you know him." His eyes steady me. Why do they have to be so, so blue? It's like he can see into what's left of my soul and is trying to rescue the remnants.

I suck in a breath. He's standing so close to me. The soothing cadence of his voice makes me feel pangs of emotions I haven't felt in a long time. Safe. Heard.

Why does it have to be so dark in this hallway?

He sucks in a deep breath, as if steadying himself, too. "Don't be sorry, Cowgirl," he says, softly. His words are harsh, but his voice is kind. "And don't make excuses. Not to me, not to yourself. Excuses don't work here on the ranch, remember? Just do better."

Remember.

He knows me. From before.

Something clicks, and just like that I remember him.

The river hole was crowded with kids, some splashing around on the sandy bank, some rock skimming on the silver river. A few of the older boys cast fly rods in a fluid motion that reminded me of the ballet. I wandered from the beach and scampered over rocks to watch them. One of the boys' daddies worked at the ranch, and I recognized the boy as someone who helped lift the bales of hay from the back of the green truck into the barn.

The boy knew how to work like any other ranch hand, but the way he reached back over his left shoulder and cast the fly rod out over the river was a whole different image of loveliness. I was ten years old, and I told him so.

"The ballet?" The boy looked at me like I'd requested he put on a pink tutu and pirouette. I'd meant it as a compliment. Now I was squirming and picking at a scab, feeling all kinds of awkward.

"It's just so pretty." I was too young to even blush.

His blue eyes scrutinized. "You sure you're one of the Mason clan?"

I nodded. "But I don't live here year round."

His eyes lit up with teasing. "Don't have to tell me, Cowgirl."

I didn't like being teased. "I might not live here, but I wish I did."

Now his eyes were curious. "Why don't you then?"

"My mom moved us away two years ago."

"Why so?"

I was a bit embarrassed to tell him why. All the reasons Mom shouted when she and Daddy were arguing.

I want more for her than I had, Gus. It's fine for her to mess around with horses a few weeks out of the summer, but a life on a ranch is no life.

"My mom likes the city," I said.

He caught a bite. Instead of making a production out of it like fishermen in movies, he gently reeled it in. A big one, too. Rainbow trout. It flopped around at the end of that line like nobody's business.

"It's a native," he said, proudly.

"How do you know?"

It squirmed in his hands as he told me how he knew. "The

rainbow is more profound and more beautiful. See, it's darker here, which creates better camouflage in the water. It mimics the granite on the bottom of the stream. Look at the fins on this guy. They're like wings. On planted trout, the fins are stubs on account of their rubbing against the sides of the cement tank all day."

I thought the life of a stocked fish sounded downright awful and told him so.

He seemed to agree, going on with more praise about the natives. "Planted trout are silver, like a salmon. See how strong this guy is? How he's fighting me to get back into that river? This guy's a survivor."

I was confused. "Then why are you still holding him out in our air watching him gasp for breath?"

He glanced at me sideways and, with a spark in his eye, unhooked his mouth. Like a magician tossing a dove into the air, he tossed the native into the rapids. We watched him disappear under the clear water.

"I can't see him anymore!"

"Whaddit I tell you? He's camouflaging right back into the Snake."

"But what are we supposed to eat over the fire tonight?"

"Steak?" he said. "It ain't right to keep a native fish. They work so much harder to survive. They survive the winter, while the plants can't." He scrutinized me. "I'm surprised your daddy didn't tell you any of this."

Daddy sounded like dad-ay from this boy's lips.

"Why?"

And this is why I recognized him from that look on the porch.

On that riverbank seven years ago, twelve-year-old Jake looked at me up from that spinning reel, from winding in that near-transparent fishing line, and drew me right in, too.

"Your daddy's the one that taught me."

Chapter Four

"It's you," I say to Jake, dumbfounded. "The boy I offended by likening his fly fishing to a ballet dance."

"I'm still offended," he says with a grin.

I remember him.

"Wow."

Pause.

"Sorry I didn't recognize you."

"Not a problem," he says. "It's been a long time."

"Why didn't you say something?"

"Wanted to see if you'd figure it out."

I shake my head.

He smiles, pleased with himself. "Now go on in and greet your dad," he says with a slight tip of his head. Out of anyone else's mouth, his words would sound bossy. They aren't. He makes them sound sweet, with just the right push.

"Hi, Dad," I say as I re-enter the room for my retry.

I stand by his chair under the framed panoramic watercolor of the Grand Teton my grandmother painted years ago. I make sure to stand where he can look right at me.

His brain is exactly the same. His brain is exactly the same. His brain is exactly the same.

"I'm so sorry it took so long. For me to come," I say. "I...it's not an excuse. But I didn't know. How sick you were, I mean. No one told me." I'm doing what Jake told me not to—I'm making excuses.

His eyes are watery. Mine are, too.

Tears pool in my eyes, slip down my cheeks. There's no way I can make up for the time we've lost. This is on me. I want to run. Just like I've run from everything the last few months. I want to run more than anything.

But I stay.

Reaching out tentatively, I lay my hand on his. Under my weight, his fingers flutter like a butterfly struggling for flight.

Chapter Five

Nightly supper on the ranch used to be an occasion. Not in the same way a dinner party is back in California where it's more about the age of the French wine and the popularity of the caterers, but an occasion to sit and rest, to be together, and most importantly after a long day, to eat. On the ranch, you work up an authentic, organic hunger unlike any pangs I'd had in the California.

"All that fresh air, kid. Hard work builds up an appetite," Dad would say, patting my tiny back like I was a ranch hand as he strutted through the door at the end of the day. Face flushed with hard sunlight, hands crusted with dirt, he'd lift his hat off his brown cowboy head, set it on the porch swing, and wipe dusty sweat off his brow. I'd pluck a piece of straw off his jeans, and he'd know just what that meant. "I'll be sure to wash up before supper."

Mom didn't like the smell of horses, which was unfortunate since we lived among a thousand head of them. He'd wash. I'd wash. And we'd share a steak. Tender and juicy and marinated to perfection, black grill-lines melted on my tongue, fresh corn on the cob dripped with real butter made from the barn cow's milk, and the biscuits—warm and fluffy and soaked with gravy—were a culinary piece of heaven.

Now he sits beside me at that same weathered farm table, eating blended food through a straw, and I know I'll get nothing down tonight. Jake sits across from me, which at turns flusters and confuses me. Does he always eat with my dad?

Then Dad makes a noise, little more than a moan, and Jake stands up and adjusts the straw in my father's mouth. My father lets out another sigh-like noise, and Jake says, "My pleasure, Chief."

My father's lips turn up in a tiny smile, a quiver really, and I can tell it's a major effort to move at all. I poke at my fried chicken, my mashed potatoes, and my green beans, only taking tiny bites when Jake raises an eyebrow at me.

Anna, the woman who helps my father, comes in from the kitchen wearing a waist-length apron over tight blue jeans. I welcome the distraction. The red nail polish on her fingertips is chipped and worn and matches the hand-embroidered strawberries on her apron. I watch the way her hand curves on my father's shoulder, once so broad and mighty skimming the side of his front door after a day on the ranch, now so frail and bony it looks more like a bird's wing. "You've hardly eaten a thing! Don't you like my cooking?"

"No. I like it." It's just that eating makes me sick.

"We need to fatten you up, Paige, don't we, Gus? You're as skinny as a wild mustang. How do you even have the energy to get from there to here?"

Her hands perch on her ample hips, waiting for an answer. I want to disappear under the table. At home we just pretend I'm eating. Can't we just pretend I'm eating here, too?

"I think she looks fine," Jake says.

Anna grins at him. "You know what they say about California?" she asks mischievously.

"No. What?" Jake asks.

"It's full of nuts and berries."

"I've never heard that," I snap. This Anna person is annoying as shit.

She scratches her nose. "Maybe it's nuts and fruits. Anyway, your old man says it all the time —" She glances at him. "Used to anyway. Now he uses his computer to do his silly talking."

Dad's hand rests on the keyboard. He's talking.

"What did he say?" I lean over to look.

Can't squeeze blood out of a turnip, nor can you squeeze water out of a rock.

Anna laughs. A loud, genuine bellow. "Lot a truth in there, Gus!"

Where there's a will there's a way, he types after.

She laughs again.

To shut her up, I scoop up some potatoes and manage to swallow the spoonful down with a glass of milk. I'm grateful to Jake for sticking up for me, even though it's a total lie. She's paying too close attention to me, this Anna.

For the first time, I legitimately miss my mom. At least she pretends the not-normal is okay and doesn't grill me or put me on the spot. That's what I'm used to—a world of secrets and denial—but here it seems like they are facing Dad's illness head-on, everyone accepting it with grace, even my dad. It's not something I'm used to, and I squirm under the flashlight-in-my-face discomfort.

After I've poked around at the dinner and made sufficient small talk, I excuse myself and do what I do best: I run.

Angry, frustrated tears slip into the wind as I run. I hope I can count on nobody following me. Cowboys have a code: When someone needs a moment, they take a moment. If they want to talk it over later, they're welcome to, but if what you need is quiet, quiet is what you get. At least that's how it used to be. Anna, though? She seems to be all up in my business. Dad, too, with that computer of his, telling Anna this and that. Making jokes about California's nuts and berries? What even was that? Anger over Mom leaving, probably, and taking me. He was always a good ole' boy anyway. So Dad thought I was a nut, a fruit, a berry—a skinny, malnourished one at that. Did they know about my Xanax? Probably. I dig into my pocket and take a half.

When my body calms, so does my brain, and I slow down and watch as dusk settles on the ranch like an encore. I walk and I walk and I notice a sunset explosion of beauty, of reds and gold. A couple of older wranglers setting the horses to hay is a second standing ovation for another perfect day off the grid. The hungry equines snort satisfied noises, scuffing dust into the air with their hooves as I walk past them, past yards of fencing begging for repair, tumbles of scratchy brush, ground critters scrambling to their holes seeking protection against the night, until I come to the red barn. This will do. Actually, this is exactly where I want to be.

I scurry up the ladder to the hayloft, and after blowing away spider webs and moving rusty rakes and boxes, I reveal the trapdoor—the place where I hid my childhood secrets. I fondle the handle on the door, and it creaks open. Inside is a wooden box. I lift its lid, exposing the treasures of my childhood summers, and watch as those treasures of innocence, of an intact girl from a mostly intact family, roll out before me like not a moment has passed.

A blue velvet pouch full of gemstones tumbles into my palm: tigereye, moonstone, and the one I called fire-heart with jade and orange veins, my worry rock moonstone. My faux leather headdress, now dulled with age, beckons me to touch it, and I do, at first with trepidation, its blue, red, yellow feathers now molted, only a few threads on each stem remaining.

Dad and I were in this Girl Scout-esque club together called Indian Princesses when I was little. I was Little Dove and my big, strong, capable father was Chief Big Bear, and it was cheesy in retrospect, yeah, but fun. On those campouts, I ate Pop-Tarts for breakfast, Cheetos for dinner, and didn't have to brush my teeth. Those were the surface things I loved. But the memories that stayed deeply lodged in my chest were the campfires at night, each Little Princess tucked in the strong cavity of their Chief's chest as we rocked back and forth singing old country favorites like "Kumbayah" and "Country Roads," and watched sparks fly up into the darkness. Later, Mom told me my dad was so drunk on that trip that he was howling at the moon, picked a fight, and some of the other dads had to restrain him. I liked my truth better.

I gently set my childhood memories back into the box, worried if they stayed out in the world too long, they'd be crushed. What I'm really looking for I find next. Under the mini treasure chest of fool's gold I panned from the Snake, is my diary.

My therapist back home was always telling me to write it down. If I write it on paper, it may pop the cork off the bottle my chest is holding so tightly closed. If I write it on paper, I might be able to breathe again.

Under the worn velveteen cover, after pages and pages of familiar childhood words, I find a place to finally confess the secrets that have threatened to bubble up since I landed in Wyoming. My California home, the horror stories from there, seem both so very far away and as close as if I were facing them in a cracked mirror. I'm not sure how to date it, to title it. I just know if I don't write them down they'll continue to fester in my gut, slowly poisoning me. And if I'm going to have any chance of starting over—if I have a chance of simply surviving—I have to start distancing myself.

So I simply write *Then*.

Chapter Six

Then

Golden Boy. His real name was Cornell because his parents had big, specific, Cornell plans for him since birth, but everyone called him Golden Boy. Everything about him shone like gold: from the color of his hair reflected in the aqua-pool sun, to the golden palette of his tanned skin, to the gleam of his first place trophies.

Cornell was the first of us to fall, and that may sound melodramatic, but it really was like the crowned prince of school died. Even in retrospect—even after everybody else— his suicide remains the most inexplicable, the most inexcusable, the most painful.

It was just an average school day when The Boy Who Had Everything—a doting perfect girlfriend (swim team Barbie to his water polo playing Ken), straight A's, perfect 2400 SATs— killed himself. Why would he, of all people, jump in front of a commuter train on the way to another perfect school day where he's the most popular guy at school? Where teachers praised him and coaches admired him? Where he was our beloved king?

There were rumors, of course. The most prevalent whispers were he didn't get into his namesake school, and he was worried he'd disappoint his parents. At least, that was the surface of it. If it were even true. College acceptance/rejection season was in full force and everyone was a bigger anxiety ridden mess than usual in our We Breed Champions town—the richest town in a Silicon Valley flowing with gold.

Other rumors circulated, of course. One was that he was secretly pining for his best friend, but Jay had rejected him. That Amanda had been his beard. That he didn't know how to handle the whole complicated mess. But the Cornell theory was the one that stuck. He'd applied for early admission, and he was passed over. His parents' dream was dead and now so was he.

If that was true, I didn't understand it at all.

Why would someone kill themselves over college?

But then again, I was born on a horse ranch in the middle of nowhere. These Silicon Valley ultra high-achiveing "gunner" kids really weren't my people. Even when I pretended they were, I mostly felt like a fish out of water. Partially living, mostly observing. It wasn't until Golden Boy that I was jerked awake. While others seemed to be in a trance of denial and confusion, I started paying attention to everything.

The day leading up to his funeral felt like scratching through a swarm of flies. I could barely push myself through the smothering grief drenching the linoleum floor of our school hallways, and I felt it, too—this thick layer of shock and grief that someone so young, so beautiful, so beloved, could not only die…but kill *himself*. It made no sense and turned the whole of our school from driven, top-tier students into *The Walking Dead*.

His girlfriend, Amanda, made a memorial in front of his locker. A wreath with this year's Polo picture—a perfectly ripped, tanned body in red Speedos, sapphire blue eyes shining from a chiseled yet boyish face, full cherry-red lips pursed seriously for the pose, dangled from the front of a yellow poster board scribbled with red and pink hearts and Xs and Os messages like: *I'll miss you, always. We love you, forever.*

What I told her was how sorry I was. I'd known her since I first moved here. We weren't really close friends, but we were friends. In a breathless panic, she surprised me by saying, "I'm so sorry. I'm so sorry."

"Why are you sorry?"

"I didn't do anything, Paige. I swear. Everything was fine, everything. Those rumors about Jay…they aren't true."

"I'm sure," I said, without certainty. Who knew what was really in someone's heart? "People just want answers, I guess." She looked at me strangely like she wanted to add more, but her mouth clamped shut. "Do you want to talk about it?"

"No. I just…I just feel sick all the time."

"I'm so sorry," I said, because I was. At the time I couldn't imagine going through my life with so much confusion, so much If I Only Could've regret. Now I knew.

Maybe it wasn't just the college thing.

Somehow that seemed too simple. He was a smart kid. Well-rounded. He had to understand life beyond college. Right? He wasn't depressed that anyone knew about. He was always happy, or seemed so, anyway.

I came by later, after the bell rang to draw the blank-eyed cattle into class, when I could be alone and simply wrote, "I'm sorry." Maybe he *was* depressed. Secretly.

I always understood depression to be something lonelier. Something that happened in a dark room. Depressed people on TV ads crept around unkempt bedrooms with bed-head and weepy eyes usually wearing an old bathrobe.

Golden Boy roamed the halls with a ten-thousand-watt toothpaste grin and Abercrombie clothes, high fiving and fist bumping his adoring minions.

Or maybe that was it.

Maybe it was all just *too much*. Maybe being perfect for too long was too much. Being perfect at our school was the goal. Look perfect, act perfect.

When I started at the local elementary school when we first moved here, I found it so odd that everyone had to be included. We couldn't choose the people to play handball with, for instance. Everyone got to play. Everyone had a turn. I thought it was great as a new student — I was instantly included! It wasn't like in Jackson when a new kid came and people were suspicious of him or her for a while and they had to work at making friends. Here there was like a welcoming committee — instant besties! While it felt nice enough, something about it felt disingenuous. Fake. False.

And life continued on like that. No bullying. No excluding. Just this constant climb for success and perfection.

Some of the kids I knew were forced to take the SATs every year since middle school until they got a perfect 2400. The problems at other schools around the country — bullying for sexual orientation or race or anything like that — didn't exist here. If the rumor was true, if he'd fallen for Jay and Jay liked him back, they would've been accepted. We were a big supportive community of sweet kids from seemingly "nice," involved families of overachieving parents who, for the most part, either came here from other countries or scraped their way up from nothing. People who could afford to buy two million dollar homes, many with foreign (China) or local tech (Facebook or Google) cash. And they expected their kids to have the same scrappy attitude and relentless desire for success that they had.

But we were just teenagers.

We wanted to do well, to please, but we also wanted the things other teenagers wanted. The things we saw in movies or on the bits of TV we were allowed to watch when we weren't in our ten-thousand extra-curricular activities: to worry about dances and being socially accepted and discovering our passion.

No one I knew thought about any of that stuff.

Relationships, real ones, were mostly an afterthought.

We pursued straight A's, perfect SATs, and the best portfolio for college.

Maybe Golden Boy was done being Golden.

Otherwise, why would he, with his perfect body and perfect brain pull over, lean his two-thousand-dollar street bike against a chain link fence, and lie on the tracks until a train ran him over?

Because from the outside?

Unlike Ty...unlike me, he had every reason to live.

Chapter Seven

Now

My room is in the main house.

Guests don't sleep here, and by the looks of it, no one has slept in here in quite some time. I am selfishly happy about that.

The wallpaper in The Garden Room is violet and silver with tiny purple flower buds that press out from the wall like they're struggling to bloom. This is the same canopy bed I slept in as a child. The same antique white furniture, the claw-footed dresser, the same stubby nightstands with the same old hardcover versions of *Little House in the Big Woods* and *The Bobbsey Twins* and *Little Women* that creaked a little when I opened them.

When I got back from the barn, everything was quiet. Dad had retired to his quarters on the first floor, and Jake had disappeared to…wherever it is Jake goes. I'm not clear yet on where, exactly, he lives.

Anna, dressed in a strawberry apron, was drying dishes.

I watched her for a second through the doorway, the methodical but comfortable way she ran her hand over the greasy plates, scrubbing bubbles into the air like it was second nature to her. She looked about forty, forty-five maybe. Like I observed earlier with Jake, it's hard to tell the ages of people on the ranch. Exposed to never-ending sun, their skin wrinkled, weathering more quickly than people back home. Then again, the women here don't dye their hair as much, either. They aren't Botox-d and face-lifted. Their skin may look older but their eyes look younger. Years younger.

Before I left the hayloft, I locked my diary away back in the secret trap door. I would never bring it in here. Nobody could ever know those secrets. But writing in the barn got me in the mood to write more.

In this house, I wanted to write my other story. The long-ago story. The one that wasn't all my fault.

I lay my laptop on a lace-edged pillow on my lap, open up a new document, and type, "My daddy is a cowboy, and my mama is a city slicker. There was no way the two of them would work."

I read it again.

And again. Not a bad beginning. I try to type more but nothing comes.

My fingers sit where they are supposed to on the keyboard:

A=left pinkie

S=left ring

D=left eff you

F=left pointer

Space Bar the Thumbs Face Off

J=right pointer

K=right eff you

L=right ring finger (is it even called a ring finger on your right hand?)

;= right pinky. (semi-colon, really?)

But nothing. No mice dancing on glass.

Before, in the barn, the words came so easily.

Now I'm sitting here in this violet and silver bedroom in my childhood sanctuary of imagination, and I can't write anything. I can't start a new story until I finish the first one. So I sneak out of the quiet house, run back to the barn, and spill my guts into that old journal.

Chapter Eight

Then

After the wake, after the perfume-flower rush at Golden Boy's enormous Tudor house, after holding my breath, nodding, repeating over and over again, "I know, it's so sad," to every peer and grown-up there—because it was—I found Ty. Or more specifically, we found each other.

It was more than sad, our new life—it was a nightmare we couldn't wake up from. After flipping off my dress-shoes, after tossing them into manicured bushes, after watching the black heel catch on a branch and hang there, limply, I screamed.

I tilted my head back, looked up into the night and freaking screamed like a werewolf, a lunatic, a banshee.

Ty, my new stepbrother, was the one who found me hysterical on my bed. Ty, who unlike the rest of my senior class, enjoyed the more "average teenage" parts of life: drinking, drugs, tattoos. At the time, I barely knew more than what I'd learned during dinner table talk—they were from Brooklyn, his father and my mother were very much in love, and he was a complete and utter asshole.

"I'm a horrible person," I said, smearing tears off my face like jacked-up windshield wipers.

His normally cocky, above-it-all face winced. "Why would

you say that?"

"Because I'm wondering why he did it. There has to be a better reason than not getting accepted into Cornell. Tonight at the wake I was just watching his father. I thought, did he beat him? Did he threaten him to be so perfect and that's why he was? And I was watching Amanda, too. *Was* she his beard? Was their perfect relationship fake from the get-go? Was he afraid to come out of the closet? I used to be so jealous of her, Ty. She always had the boyfriends and the perfect hair. You know she grew boobs before the rest of us and would brag about it?"

Ty laughed wryly. "You watch too much TV."

"It's not funny. I'm a terrible person to be wondering these things at his *funeral*. A boy is dead. A nice, popular, smart boy. I mean we worked on our Ohlone project together in fourth grade when I just moved here and knew no one. He was so nice. This isn't a stranger, but I feel this weird detachment of wondering why instead of just…grieving and crying and wearing those golden ribbons like the other girls are." I pulled on my shirt where a golden ribbon should be.

Ty scoffed. "I'm not wearing a stupid ribbon, either. Am I a terrible person? You're completely overthinking this."

"Am I? I don't know. I see the looks on everyone's faces, and people aren't just sad…they're scared."

"They're probably relieved they have one less guy to compete with."

I blinked. "That was a terrible thing to say."

"Fuck you," he said with a snort.

"Fuck you back," I said, pissed. Who the hell was he to talk to me like that? And to make fun of the dead? Awful. Ty was awful. Why'd I let him in here?

But instead of getting angry back, he palmed his chest and gasped. "Did you just CURSE? I'm telling *Mom*."

That was our one joke. The "Mom" and "Dad" we used ironically in passing.

"Tell *Mom* to get more toilet paper."

"Tell *Dad* to move his tennis racket out of the hall."

I'd always been curious about Ty. Since our parents' whirlwind dating (they met online on one of those weird websites) and then my stepdad's cross-country move to meet her spun into a quickie marriage before I could catch my breath. It all happened so fast I barely had time to question it, never mind complain. And Mom seemed happy. For the first time in forever she actually smiled. And laughed. And sometimes stopped working long enough to actually enjoy a meal. So I went along with it, not wanting to pop her bubble.

When Ty moved in with us a few months ago, I tried to get to know him, but he wasn't much of a conversationalist. He answered and then disappeared into his room. He was tall. He'd obviously just had a growth spurt because his dad was always commenting on it. He moved in a slightly loose way—a boy uncomfortable in his own bones. Lots of ducks and sideways gestures as he slunk around the house. Like he was trying to be invisible. His dad once referred to him as "The Invisible Man." "I saw you more when you lived in Brooklyn," Phil had joked, and Ty looked at him funny.

At the time, Ty spoke mostly in mumbles.

I think he hated his dad, but he never shared that, not with me anyway.

His dad was fine. My stepdad, I should say. He was a nerdy tech sort who clearly adored my gorgeous mom. He sprang up every morning making her coffee and bringing it to her in bed like he won the lottery.

But Cornell's death sparked something in both Ty and me. Ty was taller, darker—he looked more like the mom I saw in a photo on his desk. She'd stayed in New York where she ran her own private practice. He didn't say he missed her, but the photo did. He was polite with my mom, but distant, like he was with me.

Maybe we needed to bond with someone and it was just… proximity. But suddenly it was like he could see me and I could see him and then we were laughing. Well, I was sort of choking and making this awful high-pitched hyena sound—further proof of my descending from banshees.

His dark blue suit was too big for his narrow shoulders and hung on him like he was a kid playing dress-up. His tie was loose. Tugging his fingers through his dark hair, I noticed Ty was oddly good-looking. Not in a perfect Golden Boy way, but in an interesting way. He had an edge to him. Dark. Dark hair, tan skin. The whiff of secrets that was further enhanced by his light green eyes, the only trait he seemed to inherit from his father.

Ty was an anomaly at our School for Perfect Children.

This shrug of indifference that made girls watch him in the hallway, wonder about him as he fiddled at his locker, as he walked by, usually alone. He smoked outside by the 7-11 after school. I never told on him, and maybe he appreciated that. Maybe that's why he talked to me. He didn't have many friends, a group of skater guys he ate lunch with, but didn't really socialize with them on the weekends or hang out with them after school all that often. He always said he was too big of a dick to keep friends around for long. But since he was funny, they put up with him.

At home, he was mostly on his computer or lying on his bed thumbing to the beat of whatever he was listening to on his earbuds. It was like part of him still lived in New York. His body was here but going through the motions. His eyes reminded me of a cat. Or maybe it was just his demeanor. They always had this slightly aloof, faraway look to them. We had a little of that in common, I guess.

Girls asked me about him a lot. His aloofness both confused and intrigued them. When my friends spent the night, they'd linger outside his closed door wondering what he was up to. He pretty much ignored us all. He didn't do more than glance at my friends, even the really good-looking ones. When he started paying attention to me, I chalked it up to boredom. Or maybe the stuff with Golden Boy was bothering him as much as it bothered me?

Ty was a mystery to most. I had to admit, even though he lived down the hall, he was mostly a mystery to me, too.

A lone purple petal rested on his shoulder. It was so weird. Where had it come from, this purple petal on my hard stepbrother? I brushed it off with a graze of my fingers. He twitched when we touched. I frowned, a little confused both by why I did it and his reaction.

Past him, the mirror reminded me my cheeks were smeared with mascara. Loose hairs stuck out from my bun like popped wire. My lipstick smeared red.

"Jesus. I look like Bette Davis in that freaky old movie."

His cat eyes never left mine. "You know who Bette Davis is?"

"Yeah. My dad and I used to watch old movies all the time."

"On that ranch?"

"Yeah. On his VCR." I laughed.

"Ain't no shame. Bette Davis is hot." That's when he reached out and brushed the pad of his thumb across my cheekbone. I saw him doing this in my reflection. I felt him doing it all over.

I didn't pull away. His touch felt cool and exciting. Like his thumb was asking if I wanted more. If he should turn up the heat so I would be more comfortable.

I didn't want to be alone. He knew who Bette Davis was. We had something in common other than our parents being married to each other.

My forehead moved into the hollow of his chest, my skin against the scratchy navy blue wool suit, and I couldn't see myself in the mirror anymore.

Later I realized he'd talked about Bette Davis in the present tense, even though the old movie actress had been dead for years.

Chapter Nine

Now

"Mornin'," Jake says with a tap of his hat, and I chastise the icy walls for thawing a bit at the sound of him snapping his whip over the horses in the corral, at the thunder of hooves pounding the dirt.

Nothing should make me feel pleasure anymore—not this scene lifted straight out of a postcard, not the Palominos' and Pintos' and Appaloosas' manes dancing in the breeze, and especially not the view of the cowboy in the center of it all.

"Morning," I say. I avoid his eyes and, instead, stare down at the black flip-flops standing on the second rung of chipped fence; my pedicure now looks as mangled as my mind. Jake's "Yeehaw" noise is a concentrated version that hits the air with a punch, "Y-A-h!" and the horses immediately respond. After piling a mix of alfalfa and hay into the feeder, he saunters toward me.

"When are the guests arriving?" I ask.

He blinks. "You still don't get it, do you?"

I don't want to state the obvious. That unless he tells me something, I have no way of knowing it. Dad can't talk and Anna doesn't like me. Jake is it. He's my lifeline. He must read that in my expression because his jaw loosens.

He leans his arms over the fence in a way only a cowboy can pull off and says, "Unless we can get this place into shape by next season's start, we have to close the ranch for tourists."

"What?" I'm shocked. Close the ranch?

"We're closing the—"

"No. I heard you. I just can't believe—The place doesn't look that bad."

Jake's shrug is more like an I'm Too Polite to Argue With the Boss's Daughter than an agreement. *It doesn't look great like it used to, but isn't it fixable?*

"Sure the fences need a little bit of mending and the road could use some improvements, but overall it looks pretty much the same as…"

Before.

You haven't been here in years, Paige. You don't know shit.

Jake's head tilts away from me. All I see is the rim of his hat when I hear his question, "You see Anna up in the house?"

"Strawberry Apron Anna?"

He sticks a piece of straw in his mouth. It hangs out of the corner like an olden day movie star, which immediately reminds me of Ty and Bette Davis, and a rush of guilt and pain overwhelms me. "Well, Anna and I are it, as far as help goes."

"What?" I'm remembering a scene from *Butch Cassidy*—Paul Newman sucking on straw like that. We used to watch that all the time, Dad and I. I wonder if he still has it. Maybe we can watch it later.

He looks up, still chewing. "Me and her…we're it."

I blink. Focus. "I can't believe that. Dad used to have a huge amount of help here, full staff."

He shrugs again.

"But when?"

This time he doesn't look away. His eyes lock on mine. They're the color of a blue, blue sky, cracking open and letting rain fall. "A couple years back."

Another thing Mom didn't tell me.

It was more than just my father's deterioration. It was the ranch's, too. All that's left of his legacy, of our family's legacy, is disappearing along with him.

"How much is left?" I hate to ask.

"Money wise? Not sure. Anna takes care of that end of things."

Anna again.

I narrow my eyes. "What, exactly, is Anna's relationship to my father?"

"You don't know about Anna, either?"

That's it.

My voice tumbles out like a growl. Like a scream, it roars up from my insides and suddenly my words are everywhere, filling this corral. "No, *Jake*. I don't know about Anna. I didn't even know my father was in a wheelchair, okay? My mom didn't tell me a damn thing about it. I knew he had a terminal disease that was getting worse. My dad himself wrote me telling me not to bother visiting. He was too busy with appointments and ranch details and said that I should have a nice summer in Europe, blah blah. And in the end? It was all just bullshit. He's dy…" I can't say it. I groan away the lump and focus on what I *can* say. "And now his ranch is falling apart, too."

Jake's jaw tightens, but he rests his hand on my shoulder. I'm too upset to shy away from his touch. I let it ground me like his words, his voice. "I'm doing my best to stop that from happening."

The morning sun is already noon-hot. It beats against his arms, exposed at the rolled-up sleeves. I dig my knuckle hard into my eye, in an effort to avoid sinking into them.

Do not look at him like that. Do not let him comfort you. They are dead. You are alive. You escaped for now. It doesn't mean you deserve comfort.

I stare right into the punishing sun. "You know why I came here, Jake?"

Everything turns white.

"A bit." Then, "Stop looking into the sun. You'll go blind."

I do as he says and turn away.

"What do you know?" I ask softly. Hoping it's not a lot. Cringing, I wait in a pause so long, I open my eyes to see if he's still there. My spotty peripheral vision sees his shadow spit the chewed-up straw onto the dirt. It crumbles under the heel of his boot until it's just grit, reminding me of Elena's ripped up rejection notice from Harvard that turned to a glue-y mess in her mother's sink. Elena. The second. I haven't thought of her since I left California.

"Enough," he says.

Shit.

"Paige." He says my name like, what? Like he wants to help?

He knows. If not about Ty, he knows something. He knows about the trains?

"I have to go," I say, shakily. I can feel his eyes on my back as I run away. My hands are shaking so hard as I scurry up the ladder in the barn, and my words come out wobbly on the page. But I have to write it down.

Chapter Ten

Then

"Hey!" I said.

Spotting my friends was easy. We always sat on the same table under the oak tree in the quad.

"Hey!" Lucy waved. "We got you a latte."

I kissed her cheek and swept the hot to-go cup out of her outstretched hand. "You are a life saver, Luce. Seriously. Top notch."

"You're welcome."

I took a sip. The burning hot, non-fat sweetness coursed down my throat. In an instant, my synapses fired more accurately.

"Seriously," I said, pointing at the cup of heaven, "if I attempted the test without this, I would fail miserably."

"You? Failing? I doubt that," Elena said, with a half-smile that could be interpreted in many ways, none of them kind. "Have you ever scored below an A+ in your life?"

"Sure. I didn't used to get that good of grades. I used to run around my ranch at home all the time."

"Ranch?" Elena cocked an eyebrow. "Oh, right. I forgot, you come from the country."

"She's been here since elementary school, though," Luce said, defending me.

"And it doesn't make my mom any less of a perfectionist," I added. "She's obsessed with me going to business school like she did."

"My mom, too," Luce said. "If I don't get into medical school, she'll die. I got an A- and was grounded for a semester. You remember that, Paige, in 7th grade?"

"Yes. It was horrible," I agreed, remembering. "You had to skip the spring dance and do an extra hour of violin."

"My mother wouldn't let me go to bed until I'd practiced for three hours instead of two. Because certainly I'll be a violinist at Carnegie Hall one day." She laughed wryly.

"Of course!" I said, laughing, too.

As much as Luce tried to blow it off, the pressure her parents put on her had taken its toll. I worried about her. Since elementary school, she'd had a full day of regular school, plus four hours of Chinese school, then homework, and then violin. She wasn't allowed to have play dates, so the only time I saw her socially was school functions. When those were taken away, we only had "brunch" at school or lunch. It sucked eggs. But Luce was still one of my best friends. She was worth the small amount of time we had together. My friends were always telling me I didn't get the pressure. And it was true. My mom expected me to get good grades but it was more a, "try your best" than a, "straight A's or get locked out of the house!" which was what seemed to be the case with Luce and Elena. Another one of our friends, a guy, was beaten if he didn't get straight A's. BEATEN. It was mindboggling. Why didn't anyone call CPS on these abusive assholes?

Lucy scooted over for me. I cuddled in next to her and nuzzled my head into her shoulder.

"Pet, pet," she said. I made a purring noise.

Since her parents moved here from Brooklyn via Hong Kong via London via France, Lucy had been my best friend. Her worldliness earned her immediate street cred with me. She claimed her genius was due to her schooling abroad, but I didn't believe that. She was born with an exceptionally brilliant brain and a generous heart to match.

Elena glared at us. She didn't get our friendship. "You two are crazy."

"Whatever. Find your own girlfriend," I said, jokingly, but Lucy didn't laugh. She stopped playing with me and sat up as if Elena's look jerked her back straight.

"Katy Perry, your break is almost up," Suri said from my phone.

"Thanks, girl."

"You're welcome, Katy Perry."

"Why do you do that?" Elena said. "It's so lame."

"I think it's funny," Luce said.

I smiled. "And *that* is why we're friends."

I chugged down the rest of the coffee while Elena regained Lucy's attention with Advanced Chem talk.

Elena was Lucy's other best friend. Equally brilliant academically, Elena used her powers for evil. Couldn't blame her really. Her parents were brutal. She wasn't allowed to go to dances, watch TV, or date. They had one shared computer in the kitchen, which her extremely traditional mom monitored to make sure she was doing schoolwork only. The one time I'd been to her house, her 8th grade party, I noted the crazy amount of Harvard posters wallpapering her room. She'd bragged that she had absolutely no intention of pleasing her parents once she escaped her home prison "lock down" and was accepted into Harvard. "It's going to be all about the boys and all about the booze," she said, but I didn't believe it. Elena said a lot of shit. Mostly to impress Luce.

"Let me see your phone," Elena said to Lucy.

Lucy handed her iPhone over.

Elena's forehead wrinkled as she scrutinized her Friends list, reading their updates like it was BBC news.

I was sick of Elena hogging her, taking advantage of her. "Your mom still won't let you get your own phone?"

Elena looked up at me with cold eyes. "Why would you ask me something you already know the answer to?"

"Paige," Lucy said, a pleading tone in her voice that made me even angrier.

"What? I'm just asking."

Her eyes were all freaked out. I wasn't going to back down this time. I pounced back, adrenaline rushing through my core.

"Don't you think it's slightly obnoxious to bogart Luce's phone all the time just to check Facebook? Why don't you go to the library or something?"

She stood up, facing me. "Why don't you," she paused, "fuck off." Her long black hair hung in one straight sheet.

"Fine." I stood up, slinging my purse back over my shoulder. "Thanks for the latte, Luce. I'll call you later. You know. From my phone."

I was being a bitch, but I didn't care. Luce was my best friend. I was sick of sharing her. Since Golden Boy's suicide, I was jumpier than usual, more irritable, less able to take things in stride. I found myself sticking up for things I normally wouldn't and spending more and more time with my stepbrother.

Something about his built-in anger felt comforting.

He already was the way I felt now. My friends' and classmates' drive for straight A's and the perfect college seemed tainted. It's like Cornell's death, his *blood*, was spilled for a worthless pursuit, and suddenly I didn't want to do homework. I didn't want to look in the mailbox to see which college I was accepted to.

I wanted to lie in the grass and get lost in the clouds.

"Bye," Luce said. She waved at me limply, looking from me back to Elena back to me.

I sighed. I was trying to stick up for Luce, and now she was the one that was hurt.

"Sorry, Elena," I said. I couldn't upset Luce. "That was rude of me. I'm just…worried about my test."

"I'm sure you are. A lot rides on this test." Elena's icy

expression cracked and a tiny smile replaced her glare. "Not that your aim is even marginally as high as mine—I mean, anyone can get into a tiny liberal arts college if your parents have money and connections. Where did your mom go again? Brown? I'm sure that will be no problem, but still."

Mocking my college plans. Mocking my future. My face burned with anger. Again. I hated Elena. And she'd just picked the wrong time to fuck with me. "You know what the difference is between me and you?"

"Our hair color?" she said with mock enthusiasm like a kindergartner at a spelling bee.

"Haha. No. If I don't get into Harvard, I won't jump in front of a flipping train over it."

Elena's face turned ashen.

"I can't believe you said that," Lucy said. Her voice was small but sharp as it pinged through my chest.

"Sorry," I said. I couldn't believe I did, either. "I didn't mean it like that. I just meant…"

"Yeah. Whatever."

They looked at me like I was the devil incarnate.

"I'm just saying there's more to life than where you get into college." I tried to scramble out of the crumbling hole I pushed myself into but there was no chance. Elena held the rope and Luce was standing beside her.

"Maybe for you. Your brother gets it. Why don't you ask him? Why don't you ask Ty?"

Got what? Avoiding their eyes, I pleaded, "Really, I'm sorry. Can you just forget I said it?"

Chapter Eleven

Now

Someone is rattling around in the office.

Anna stressing out over piles of bills she isn't sure how to pay, probably. I can hear her muffled voice arguing with an insurance company on the phone. Anna, Dad's employee, is doing this? Why? This should be my mother's job. That's what For Better or For Worse means, right?

But who am I to talk? I was the queen of running away from my problems.

If I'm going to survive here, I have to try and change that. I head out to the corral to look for Jake, to apologize for going off on him earlier. It's the least I can do, only he isn't in the barn and he isn't in the corral. He isn't in the house, either. I'm getting more disappointed at every turn. My slightly optimistic mood leaks slowly out of me, a pinprick to an already faltering balloon, and by the time I run down the road and see him getting into his Jeep, this version of pleasant Paige is nearly deflated.

"Hey!" I yell after him, probably too loudly, too intense.

Naturally, he looks up startled, and I immediately want to retry my approach.

"Jake?" I try again, calmer.

"Yep. Here I am," he says stoically.

"Where are you going?"

He shrugs. "Out."

"Out?" My pulse speeds up. "You're leaving me here alone?"

"You run off all the time," he says, flatly. Another shrug as he steps into the stable and smoothly tosses a saddle into the back of his Jeep with such grace and ease it's like it's a pillow's weight instead of fifty pounds of hard leather. Then, just as naturally, but with a red-streak of defiance, he strides along the side, before hopping into the driver's seat. The key dangles in the ignition, but he doesn't start it up right away. I see my window and jump.

"Where are you going?"

"It's Friday night," he says as if that's an answer.

"That's not a destination."

"You're a quick one."

"I'm trying to apologize and you aren't making this easy!" I blurt out.

"Ah." His eyes lighten and he leans back, enjoying this. "So this is you apologizing?"

"Yes. I mean. I'm sorry. For earlier, okay? I was being… unreasonable."

"Okay."

"Okay?"

"Okay. I accept your apology."

"Oh."

My face heats up. His hand doesn't move any closer to that key. He's still looking at me.

"So," I say, "do you mean, out-out. Like out on the town? But you'll be back, right? Where are you going again?"

Out on the town? Who says that?

"You're relentless," he observes. But the corners of his mouth rise a bit and suddenly I'm dying to see that smile. To be forgiven. "If you must know, I'm off to rodeo."

I feel my eyes widen and the corners of my mouth rise

sarcastically. "Seriously? To rodeo? Like it's a verb?"

He frowns, shaking his head like I'm the most exasperating thing he's set eyes on. I blew it and I know it immediately. "I'll see ya, Paige."

In a fluid, flawless motion, he turns on the engine and lays his right arm across the dirty cloth seat in the cab. Cranking his neck in the same direction as his arm, he watches the road behind him as he backs up. Fast. Rocks spewing all over the road.

"When?" I call after him.

When he doesn't stop to answer me—because of course he can't hear me—I chase his truck down the driveway, rocks and pebbles and dirt flying around me like I'm cruising through an asteroid shower. I'm completely over the top and I know it. I'm literally chasing him down the road. A virtual stranger. But I need to try again. Make him hear me. I really am sorry about before.

Finally, it rolls to a stop. I run to his open window and see myself in his eyes: worse than the fallen-away cowgirl he thought I was—a hot mess who brought her problems onto a ranch filled with enough problems already. He sighs, barely looking up at me. "What?"

"When are you coming back?"

"Tonight. Or tomorrow. Depends. Why the sudden curiosity?" He's frowning now. Unamused.

Jesus, Paige. Turn around and go back inside.

But I can't. I can't spend another night inside that suffocating house filled with the ghosts of a happier time. Or at least a manageable time. When I'm alone, all I do is write in my journal, which brings up the horrors of home and gives me nightmares all night until I wake up screaming. I can't face that tonight. My sanity is slipping away faster than I can grasp on to it. Maybe I'm projecting, but Jake and his steady, steadfast strength—or maybe just all he represents—is the only thing grounding me to reality. Either way, I have to try.

"Can I come with you?"

The next ten seconds last a lifetime. I stand my ground and wait.

Finally he says in a voice neither mean nor kind, just sort of purposefully, excruciatingly vague, "That depends on you changing up your opinion of rodeo 'tween now and the next time you ask."

He drives off. Not as fast this time. Not angry, but still, he drives away leaving me standing in the gravel, wondering why, if my plan was to spend the summer alone, this makes me so unhappy.

After the last of his Jeep's dust settles, I head back to the barn and crack open my journal. It's either this, or gasping for air back in the house. I can't handle that right now. I can't face this either, but writing it down helps make sense of it. And I have to start trying or I'll end up like them.

Chapter Twelve

Then

Ty found me by my locker. I hadn't even seen him approach. The Invisible Boy. "What's up, Sis?"

"Not much. School, school and more school. I'm starting to hate it."

"Aha!" He leans against the orange metal in his ironic T-shirt, jean jacket, and skinny jeans. Attire you don't see much around our campus. We're more of a sporty university sweatshirts and sweater sets crowd. "You're starting to see the light then."

"What?"

"School has always sucked dick. You were drinking the same Kool-aid as your friends until that kid died."

"What Kool-aid? I hate Kool-aid." I wanted to change the subject. The mention of Cornell made me feel like I swallowed battery acid. Amanda wandered around the halls like a ghost. She looked so empty without Cornell by her side. Her hand, once held by his, fell limply to her side. The crowds around her started to fall away. Being around a depressed person was depressing. Amanda used to be Golden. Now she was ash.

"The whole Once You Get Into The Perfect College Wasting Your Teen Years Studying Unnecessary Shit while Mastering Ten

Extra-Curriculars You'll Never Use Again Will All Be Worth It Kool-Aid."

"I'm starting to see the light, then?" I suggested.

"I suspect so."

He watched me intently. Scrutinizing. Ty played with the yarn around his wrist.

"I think Elena hates me," I confessed.

"Of course she hates you. You represent everything she wishes she had."

"What I have? What do *I* have?"

"Freedom. Choices. Need I go on?"

"You've drank from the Fountain of Deep Thoughts today, I see."

Ty shrugged and picked at something on his plaid jacket sleeve. "Don't listen to me. I'm a dark mutherfucker. Go back to your Yale shirt-ed pals and study for the SATs on your way to tennis team. I won't stop you." He held his hands up, smirking and walking backward in that wobbling way of his.

"Have fun with your stoner friends." And then I smiled. "Bro."

"Oh, you can bet I will."

Ty turned his baseball cap around and flashed me a backwards wave. I watched him disappear down the breezeway.

The next day at lunch, I hear about it from Elena.

"I saw you with your stepbrother yesterday," she noted with the knowing glare of a hipster TV show detective. "At the lockers."

"Yeah. So?" I tense up, ready to deny-deny-deny.

"So, you have something to tell us?" My reaction made her smirk. "A little *Flowers in the Attic* stuff going on?"

Lucy's jaw dropped. "Elena!"

"What are you implying?"

"Just saying, a hot boy and a desperate girl living under the same roof? Recipe for romance, that's all."

"He's her stepbrother, Elena!" Good old Luce. Always so

decent and kind.

"I'm just saying Paige should be careful, that's all. You know what they say about dancing with the devil." Elena did this part sneer, part eye roll thing that, if I wasn't getting so upset, would've been impressive.

"Uh. No?" I replied.

Dramatic pause and then Elena skewered me onto a sharpened kabob. "Soon you become him."

"My stepbrother may be a well-documented asshole, but he certainly isn't the devil. And last time I checked? I didn't see any horns. Unless you see some?" I shook my head toward Elena, pointing to two points of my frontal lobe with a nervous psychotic laugh.

Luce's eyes widened with concern. Elena sat back, smug. Like she was right about me all along. Maybe I shouldn't have done the horn thing. Was I acting like Ty? Was I dancing with the devil?

"What do you know about Ty other than…from me?" I pressed.

"Don't you know? You're his *sister*. You should know everything," Elena pressed back.

"*Step*sister. And no. My parents didn't tell me anything about him."

"Well, for one thing he was kicked out of private school on the East Coast for drugs and alcohol." Elena leaned forward, conspiringly. "For another?" She paused for dramatic effect before lowering her voice to a whisper. "I heard he date raped a girl at a party."

My blood caught fire. The latte churned in my belly. "Are you serious?"

"Dead."

I blinked. "Did the girl press charges?"

"I heard his dad paid her off. Settled out of court."

"His dad. My stepdad?" I was horrified. This couldn't be true. No way would my mom move an accused rapist into our house.

"Your stepdad. Yes." Elena looked so pleased with my upset reaction, I wanted to smack her.

"You had no idea about this, Paige?" Lucy asked, nervously. "Dang, and I thought *my* parents kept me in the dark about their dirty little secrets."

If I stayed any longer, I'd have spewed my lukewarm latte all over the picnic table. "I...need to go. Don't tell anyone about that stuff, okay?" I looked at Elena, sarcasm and bravado stricken from my affect. "I need to talk to my mom."

"Paige. Everyone knows it's true. How do you think *we* know?"

Rumors. Gossip. I scratched my cheek a little too hard. Rumors, that's all.

Like the swirl of lies that surrounded Golden Boy that ultimately led to his demise. The rumors that made him choose facing the tracks instead of the hallways of school. "Didn't you learn anything from what happened to Cornell?" I raised my voice and the kids at the tables next to us glanced over. "This isn't a game. Rumors at our school kill people. Don't say anything else about my brother." I glared at her and she winced. I lowered my voice and through blurry eyes, threatened her. "I mean it, Elena."

"Mom?" I called out when I got home from tennis practice. I had to find out ASAP about Ty, even if it was an uncomfortable thing to talk about.

"Yeah, sweetie—in the kitchen, but I'm just heading out, what is it?"

My mother was in her camel-colored Burberry jacket, pressed white slacks, and heels. Her briefcase rested on the granite counter, and she was typing frantically into her newest model iPhone. This wasn't the best time, but I had to know.

"I heard something today at school about Ty."

She arched an eyebrow but didn't stop texting. "What was it?"

"Something…bad. About his past."

She set the phone facedown on the counter with a *clink*. Then she slowly ran her tongue over her bottom red lip. She was thinking about how to answer. She did this when I was nine and asked if Santa was real. I knew she was about to lie.

"He was accused of something none too…pleasant…but it wasn't true." She said the last part adamantly. She was the judge. The verdict was clear.

"How do you know?"

"Because Phil told me it wasn't."

"And you believe him?" I pressed.

"I believe my husband, yes."

"But believing him means he believed Ty?"

Mom sighed and wiggled her eyeballs around a little, searching for the classiest way to state the unclassy. It was also the wiggle move she did when we discussed condoms. And periods. Her mother never discussed this stuff with her, so she made herself be open with me about it, but still I could tell it made her extremely uncomfortable. Mom was prim and proper and a good girl to the core. The rotten apple of me fell very far from that tree.

"This girl was…how should I put it? Not from the *best family*. She…made her self very *available* to boys, if you know what I mean by that? She was drinking. Heavily. She didn't make the best choices."

"Mom! That's victim blaming," I said, completely disgusted with her.

"There's no victim. I just told you Ty did nothing wrong."

"Jesus, Mom. You think you'd have some female solidarity here."

"Watch your language! Listen, Paige, I know it's a disturbing *event*…I'm not even sure how you heard about it," she said, irritation filling her voice. "But if rumors about your brother are going around school, we will find out who started them and get a cease and desist."

"Stepbrother. And "event"? It's called rape. It's very serious and very real. Besides, I don't think even you can cease and desist rumors."

CEO Mom thought she could cease and desist anything because her high powered team of copyright attorneys kept their tech products safe from imitators, hackers, and the like. Clearly, she had *no* idea how high school worked.

Clucking, she told me we'd talk about it later...but she never brought it up again. I pressed; she pushed away. Rejected. Ignored. Eventually I just stopped bringing it up. Mom could put up firewalls that not even the most experienced hacker could break through.

I was more careful around Ty, though.

I studied him the way I studied Cornell's family and friends after the funeral.

I thought I was beginning to know him, and I felt this sort of kinship with him. I had to learn the truth. Had he raped a girl in Brooklyn? Was this possibly the reason he and his father moved out here so suddenly? If she knew about these accusations, how could my mother marry a man and bring his son, an accused rapist, into our home when she had a teenage daughter of her own?

Things were crazy...and they were about to get crazier.

After the regrettable closeness of that post-funeral moment, I kept my distance from Ty. But in the duration of those two months, something happened.

Something we probably should've predicted, but that no one saw coming.

Chapter Thirteen

Now

Dinner, for the third time that first week, is fried chicken, mashed potatoes, green beans, and dinner rolls that smell amazing, but per usual, I don't feel like eating. I'm getting better at it, though, and am starting to fill out in places that were previously skin painted over bones. I have more energy. The ranch fundamentals: sleep, work, food, rinse, repeat is working. Even if I don't mentally feel better, I'm physically stronger, which makes my mind clearer, the downside of which makes the past events even scarier to revisit. Studying the broken pieces of the puzzle for the first time—with clarity, and starting at the very beginning—makes me wonder if I was thinking at all.

Per usual, Anna fusses over my father, wiping the corner of his mouth with a strawberry printed towel, murmuring in his ear in a soothing voice.

"Your dad wants to know if you had a good day today," Anna says to me.

"Sure," I say. I shrug like Jake in the Jeep.

Dad is slurping green liquid from a straw and stops. He mutters, "You okay?" I'm surprised I understand him.

I might be a disaster, but he's the one sitting in the wheelchair drinking from a straw. I need to get over myself. Think about the past only when I'm writing it. Focusing on the now is better.

"I'm fine," I say.

"What do you do out in that old barn?" Anna asks.

I almost spit out my milk. "Barn?" Was she spying on me?

"Sure. I see you head over there all the time. What's in there?"

She's like Jake—direct voice, direct words, and direct eye contact. She doesn't mean anything more than she says, and she asks what she wants to know.

They're both looking at me now.

It's not fair, even slightly, and I damn Jake for ditching me, even though logically he didn't ditch me at all. He never invited me into his world, I just showed up at his door.

Anna hands me a glass of water, and I take a sip. "Some things from when Dad and I were in this club together. Indian Princesses. Remember that, Dad?"

He sort of smiles. "He does," Anna says. I want to press a button that will shoot her down a trap, and have Mom pop back up to make Dad's head tilt straight on his neck again, fill out those baggy sweatpants with strong muscle, make him smile like before, wide and real.

"I found my old headdress. And some of my rocks and fool's gold." *And my old journal where I'm burying my secrets.*

He mutters something and Anna says, "He's never let anyone up in that old loft except you."

"Thank you," I say. "I like spending time up there."

We're all quiet for a bit. Then, Anna excuses herself and my father. She has to help him use the restroom.

"Goodnight, Daddy," I say.

His eyes meet mine and it's so painful that I tear mine away.

The next thing I know I'm holding a flashlight and running through the ranch in the dark and scrambling up that old ladder because I have something to say, and if I don't say it this second, I'll explode.

Chapter Fourteen

Then

After she received her rejection letter to her number one school of choice, Snarky Elena, frenemy #1, killed herself, leaving a suicide note...of the grisliest proportions.

She took the kitchen scissors to a Harvard pendant, thrashing it like a black bear would a salmon, and then slit her wrists with the same scissors in the bathtub.

When her mother got home from the farmer's market with bundles of organic produce, she found slivers of crimson felt spread across her kitchen counters, on her imported tile floor. The water in the stainless steel sink was running; a glop of drippy inked paper clogged the drain. Molted and in the consistency of kindergarten glue, the only sentence she could still make out was, "Unfortunately, we don't have a spot for you this year."

Elena didn't cut herself deeply enough, because she wasn't even close to dying. So, blood dripping from her wrists, and dressed only in a Harvard sweatshirt, she walked to the tracks two blocks from her house and stood there until the same train that ran over Cornell a month before ended her life.

Elena's suicide was more dramatic and gruesome than Golden Boy's.

It was as disturbing as it was surreal. Like it was happening to someone in Paris or in Toyko or in an independent movie, because it couldn't be happening again at my school. It couldn't be someone I knew. No. It couldn't be someone I disliked.

Guilt and confusion and shock consumed me. I watched it all unfold like it was happening to someone else. But not Lucy. She was devastated. Cried uncontrollably for days and days. Nothing helped. And since she knew I never liked Elena, there was nothing I could do or say to make her feel better. She was a nice person? She wasn't. I'm sure she didn't mean to ruin her parents' life? She did. I'm sure she could take it back if she could? I knew she wouldn't. I was angry with her. Angry with her for hurting the people who loved her. I was useless for comfort.

I went to the funeral with Ty who, ironically, was asked to sing. Before our eyes, the boy Elena coined the "devil" transformed into an angel. He had a luminous, edgy voice, and the limply confident presence of a budding rock star. Before that moment, I'd only heard him in the shower, and that was skewed by water. I shouldn't be pausing in the hallway to admire my stepbrother's throaty songbird sound, anyway, so I never paused too long.

Everyone was always telling him he looked like one, though—a rock god—with his moody demeanor, affinity for illegal drugs, and general shitty attitude. He enjoyed egging them on. Last week he showed me the sleeve of tattoos he got in Santa Cruz—an upside down angel falling from heaven with a sword in its side. At the time I didn't realize how prophetic it was. It was chilling to know the image hiding underneath the button-down shirt at Elena's funeral.

That day, sitting in the church after what I'd said to Elena a few weeks before, I felt guilty as hell. Could I have contributed to her decision somehow? Why on earth would she kill herself over a college acceptance?

Elena and Luce were right.

I didn't get it.

It was as inexplicable a thought process as killing yourself over accidentally getting the wrong order at a restaurant, and in such a violent, "fuck you" way, too. Slicing up her wrists, slicing up the Harvard pennants. She knew she'd be found on the tracks in only her underwear and a thrashed sweatshirt bearing her parents' dream for her.

It was downright chilling. Nobody else felt the way I did, though, so I kept my thoughts close to my chest. Everyone else was uttering the usual things: she was "depressed", etc. I don't know though. I think she was angry. Angry and without any outlets to voice just how very angry she was at life, at her parents, at her circumstances. It was tragic, and it was horribly disturbing.

Luce again told me I just didn't get it. Ty did, too. "You want to be a writer," Luce said. "It doesn't matter what school you go to."

That hurt, but she had a point. I applied to only small liberal arts colleges with writing programs, and I didn't much care which one I got into. That was the truth of me. Maybe I lacked ambition? I don't know. I didn't push her on it. I didn't defend myself. How could I? Her friend had just died. But I could not understand Elena's truth.

I slunk down in the hard-backed pew and studied the hymnals while the priest talked, and before my brother was asked to take the stage.

Ty wasn't friends with Elena. But his father knew her parents.

When Ty stood up to sing "Hallelujah," the one that makes

even the hardened among us burst into chills, a calm washed over me akin to sinking into a bubble bath. Ty transcended Ty then, and I couldn't help but think, *You were wrong about him, Elena. Can you hear him singing at your funeral? Hitting all the notes beautifully? How Could He Hurt a Girl? No, not this boy with the voice of an angel.* It made me open my heart to him and close it once and for all for her.

He was nice to me. She treated me like shit.

She was dead. He was alive. Very much alive.

A dead girl warned me. She warned me, and I didn't listen.

Chapter Fifteen

Now

I jerk awake, sweaty, screaming.

I see Elena's eyes judging me. Calling Ty the devil, and coining me the same. I see Ty with horns. With smoke coming from his nose and hooves as he shifts into one of Jake's killer bison, charging me, and throwing me into the air, while Lucy looks on sobbing.

I can't sleep in the dark, not anymore, so the hall light illuminates the sleeping violets on my walls, creating creepy shadows and images. I shudder, burying myself farther under the covers, but it doesn't help. I'm chilled to the bone.

When my heart rate slows with deep, steady breaths, I wander into the kitchen and open the fridge. White light pools onto the dark floor.

The house is still and quiet. No hum of Dad's machines, no pitter-patter of Anna going about her business.

I look at the phone, and in my nightmare it rings. Not just a ring, but a shrill warning of an approaching train. Head beams flood the tracks, and he screams and I scream because I'm too late. I'm always too late.

I wake up sobbing alone in my room. Again sweating and chilled to the bone, but this time I'm actually awake.

This happens night after night after night.

A never-ending nightmare I'm afraid I'll never wake up from. And it's getting harder to keep the nightmares separate from reality.

Chapter Sixteen

The weekend drags on and on.

This must be what rehab is like. Eat, sleep, write, repeat—all soaked in an anxious, unbearable quiet.

After choking down three square meals, and playing a few rounds of a chess game on the computer, alone as always, Dad goes off to take his nap, and I wander around the property alone.

Small, rustic—and now rather decrepit—cabins nestle behind the ranch—where the guests used to stay. I assume one of which is where Jake lives, but there is no sign of his Jeep. I want to peek in the windows, but in case he's home I don't want him to call the sheriff on his boss's crazy daughter, or worse, shoot me thinking I'm an intruder. This is the Wild West after all. People carry guns here the way they carry yoga mats at home.

On the way back to the house, I stop at the stables and watch this gorgeous, skittish horse loping around the corral like a swarm of bees is chasing it. It looks at me with wild, threatening eyes. "Easy," I say, "I get it. You want to be alone."

Eventually, I wander back up to the silent house, which smells like dust and the leftover roasted turkey we had for lunch. Bored and antsy, I scrounge around Dad's kitchen. I spot a bowl of apples.

Hmm.

I grab one and head back to the corral.

The horse is still at it. Loping, scratching, neighing into the hot afternoon air. "What is your deal?" I ask.

Still loping around, the horse stops, scratching at the dust and glaring at me.

I hold out the gift. "Apple?" I ask, with a generous head tilt. "I come in peace. Want it?"

She hoofs at the dirt, her eyes all rage and fire. She reminds me of Ty when I asked him about that girl, when he called Elena a bitch—so mad at the world, he was even angry with the dead. What had happened to this beautiful horse to piss her off so badly? I had no doubt that if I wasn't behind this fence, she'd trample me and likely enjoy it.

"Here," I say. "Take it."

She won't give an inch.

"Fine. I get that, too." So I toss it into the corral and it rolls until coming to a dust puff stop in the center of the ring. She eyes it but doesn't approach it or sniff it out until I understand that I'm way up in her personal space and take a few steps back. Still she doesn't budge. "Fine. You hate me. I get that, too. But you should still take the apple. An apple is an apple no matter who gives it to you."

Her ear twitches like she understands.

I head up to the porch and plop down into the swing. The hard wood doesn't hurt my butt as badly now that I put some meat back on it with Anna's cooking.

I swing gently on the porch, watching the stubborn horse inch toward the apple like it's a grenade she expects to go off.

I smile when she finally takes it.

She chomps at it, nuzzling it with her nose and then flings it through the air before scooping it up again.

Hilarious.

I swing back and forth languidly, watching this fascinating creature. When Jake gets back, I'll ask about her. Why she's here, and most importantly, what's got her so pissed off at the world?

She smacks around the apple for a while, getting some nibbles before what looks like swallowing it whole. "Well played," I say, waving from the deck.

She snorts and turns away, which amuses me. Goofing around with this horse is the highlight of my weekend, by a lot. Finally, when the sweat is pooling in my bra—it's got to be at least 98 in the shade—I retreat back into the cool dark house, down the cool dark, hallways.

Back in my room, I flip open my laptop and stare at the blank screen for what seems like hours.

It's funny, when I write in that old diary the words just flow, but like the horse and that apple, this screen and I can't find a way to get along.

After a while I give up—nothing about the internet interests me anymore, not Facebook, not Twitter, none of it. I don't want to know what the kids at home are up to. And I don't care about celebrities and their bad grammar tweets. Besides, even if I did care, Dad's service is so batshit bad, it would barely come in anyway.

So I take all the clothes out of my suitcase, lay them on the lacy quilt on my bed, refold them, and then, instead of placing them in the drawers like a normal person would, place them back neatly in my suitcase. I'm not ready to make this ranch home again. The idea of a quick stay, a vacation, is more settling on my nerves. If I have to leave in a split second, I can.

Stir crazy, I wander around the house some more.

It's so quiet—eerily so. How long is Dad going to sleep?

While I wait for him to wake up, I watch the horse some more. She looks up at me with a little less anger in her eyes. She liked the apple.

When Dad wakes up, I ask him if he wants to play a few rounds of computer poker. We used to play regular poker all the time. He taught me all kinds of card games: Go Fish morphed to hearts morphed to pitch morphed to poker. I learned quickly, not only tricks of playing a hand well, but the usefulness of a poker face.

Good thing this isn't real money, kid, you'd be broke, he types.

"Ha!" I say. "That's the pot calling the kettle black."

You remember all my sayings, he types. *I like that.*

"How could I forget?"

As much as I enjoy our time together and appreciate the fact that Anna leaves me mostly alone to bond with Dad, by Sunday morning, I can't take the quiet stillness of the ranch for another second.

"Can I take the truck into town today?" I ask over breakfast of fried eggs, crunchy bacon—Dad must've told Anna I like mine well-done—home-fried potatoes, and thick white freshly baked toast with butter and strawberry jam (no wonder I'm packing on the pounds). I haven't driven since I arrived. I feel like getting out, exploring town a bit on my own. Maybe I'll wander into Jake who I haven't seen since he left for rodeo Friday evening.

Anna looks at Dad. He mumbles something to her.

"I'll be happy to take you," Anna says. "I have to get some supplies anyhow. What are you looking for?"

"Oh, it's okay, I can drive myself. I'm looking for some new jeans maybe. A couple shirts? None of my things feel right here."

I'm wearing the sparkly Cowgirl shirt again. Anna glances down at it and back to my face. "That's not from home now, is it?"

I laugh. "No."

Dad smiles a bit, too.

"The airport gift shop," I confess, lamely, remembering the zombie state I was in when I arrived. Mentally I'm not feeling that much better, but just the fact that I have an appetite, am getting more sleep, and am physically healthy is going a long way.

"Thought it looked familiar," Anna says. "The color is good on you."

I'm not sure if she didn't hear me say I'd like to drive myself or she just wanted to go into town, but she stays in group-activity mode, "We'll stop at the boot depot and fit you for some real shoes. You might want to do some riding while you're here and what you have on is not going to cut it."

Her eyebrow lifts as she glances down at my flip-flops. "Okay," I say, thinking about the horse I gave half of my apple to yesterday—and wondering if I can get up the nerve to ask Jake if I can ride her. "Who will take care of Dad while we're gone?"

"He'll come along. We'll take the van."

"Oh, good."

We can play poker on my phone on the way, he types.

"Not a chance. I'll need cash to pay for new boots," I say. I'm forcing the light-hearted conversation. It's still so unbearable for me to see him in this state, but if I act weird, it makes him more uncomfortable, which, in turn, makes me even more uncomfortable, and it's a double-edged sword of awful.

So when he types a smiley face on his computer, I lean over him and type a wink. Nothing says light-hearted more than an emoticon wink.

It works. And soon, we're on our way. The ranch has a van that is wheelchair equipped for Dad. I fumble around trying to appear useful as Anna gets him ready. He wheels himself down the ramp that is now outfitted on the porch.

The day is gorgeous and spread out before us like a panoramic painting: blue sky as far as the eye can see, hawks soaring overhead, squirrels scampering over rocks, the air smelling of pine and clarity.

It's so quiet. All I can hear is the wind whistling through the trees. It will be nice to get into town and be around some people.

Subconsciously, I glance down the driveway looking for

Jake's Jeep.

"He won't be back till Monday."

Caught.

"Oh," I say. "I wasn't…"

The brilliant mind reader kindly doesn't challenge my lie. She knows I'm thinking about him, though, so I might as well ask. "Does he live in one of those cabins on the property?"

"Jake? Sure does. He's been living here since he graduated high school. Easier to have him close."

Should I ask which cabin? *No. No. Don't ask. Why would you need to know that?*

Again, as if she can read my mind, Anna answers my question. "His is the one closest to the river. When he was moving in, I said it's the longest walk to the house, but he said he prefers the peace and quiet." She shrugs. "He used to like to get to the good fish before the other hands. That's not so much a problem anymore."

"Yeah," I say. That sounded like Jake—both the Jake I met as a kid, and the sane, balanced person I'm getting to know now. Too bad he thinks I'm a crazy person.

I'm riding shotgun, but then, once we get to the stop sign, I switch so I can sit by Dad. His chair is in the second row, locked into a device keeping him still and safe.

We bounce along the road, and I alternately joke around and fuss over him.

"Don't mind him," Anna says. "He's fine."

"You sure? Because all of these bumps…won't they loosen up his tubes or anything?"

"They're in there pretty good," she says. "Don't annoy him or he won't treat us to lunch." She winks at Dad in the rearview mirror.

"Fine, fine." I squeeze Dad's hand.

It's quiet for a few minutes before I ask. "Did his dad work on the ranch before? I think I remember him from when I was a kid."

Anna knows exactly whom I'm asking about.

"Sure did. Good man, his daddy. Was killed when Jake was a boy."

"Oh my god. How?"

"Rodeo. Bull accident. He was one of the best in Jackson. Tragic shame."

Shaking her head, Anna lifts her hand from the wheel and does the sign of the cross. Out of habit, I do, too, even though, outside of funerals, I haven't gone to church in forever.

"Poor Jake. That's so sad."

No wonder he's so caring with Dad. It made so much sense now, what he said about my dad telling him stories, mentoring him. Teaching him how to let the wild trout go. Now he's teaching him how to run the ranch. Boy to man—he practically raised him. And did a damn good job of it, too.

"His mama took it really hard. Turned to the drink, bless her heart. Jake got himself into a bit of trouble, too, without parents looking after him, and your daddy here, out of respect for Jake Senior, took Jake under his wing and looked after him."

All this new information about Jake has me reeling. He isn't as simple as I thought. His life isn't as black and white. Where is his mom now? Is she sober or still drinking? Does Jake have a relationship with her at all? My mouth opens to ask a follow up question, or ten, but Anna flips on a local radio station. Country music strums into the van through archaic speakers on the dash, and I clamp my lips closed, taking this as her non-subtle way of telling me she's done talking. She hums along, quietly at first, and then bursts into full-on song.

I listen for a minute before I say, "You have a great voice."

"Thank you," she says, confidently accepting the compliment. I like that she doesn't deny it with mock humility the way some people tend to do. Instead, she keeps on singing. When the song ends and an ad replaces it, she flips the radio off.

"Did you ever try to do anything with it?" I ask. "Pursue a singing career or something?"

At that, she bursts out laughing. "No."

"Why not?"

"I'm quite satisfied with what I'm doing here with your daddy, Paige."

"Really?"

"Yes. Really." Her voice sharpens. She glances back to see if Dad heard. His eyes are closed but I'm not sure if he's listening or not.

"Sorry," I say. "I didn't mean to imply you aren't happy on the ranch. I meant, you know, earlier in life. I know people way less talented than you who try out for *American Idol* and *The Voice* and stuff." I pick at the sparkles on my tank top.

She pushes the dial on the radio again. Another country song pops on, this one a scratchy male voice.

"Who is this singing?" She is so good to Dad, I feel like I need to give her more of a chance. Get to know her better at least.

"Not sure. Probably someone who went on *American Idol* or *The Voice* or one of those shows," she says with a snarky lilt to her voice.

"You have those shows here?"

"Paige, we own a ranch, we don't live in the Dark Ages. We did get a DVD player a few years back. A major improvement. Course he made me buy all his favorites for that machine, and then they invented Blu-ray."

"At home, everyone streams everything."

"Streams?"

"Netflix and stuff?" I try.

"Don't know it."

"And you probably don't need to."

She shrugs and I smile to myself, looking out the window. She's sort of the perfect match for my dad, and I'm glad he's found her.

Ten minutes and as many miles rumble by as I stare out the open window, chin resting on folded arms. I watch my reflection in the side mirror as places zip by behind us. My hair whips around my face. It already seems dryer from high-altitude sun, a shade lighter. Without makeup, my eyes peering through the strips of tumbling hair look quieter, softer, my skin a shade darker, too. My face isn't so gaunt; even though I've only been here a bit over a week, my cheeks are filling out from the hearty ranch food, the good milk, the nine-hour sleeps, and the fresh air. If I had stayed at home, nothing would've changed. I'd be lying on my bed staring up at the ceiling...or worse.

When she speaks again, her voice startles me. "Why is it always so hard for you city slickers to understand? You don't have to be chasing something in order to be happy."

Chapter Seventeen

Jackson Hole's downtown looks like an Old West movie colliding with an upscale tourist destination, which is essentially what it is. Thai restaurants, fancy salons, and boutiques blend easily with authentic steak houses and Western saloons.

Anna pulls the van into an open handicapped parking spot next to a wooden planked sidewalk. I jump out and wait by the side of the van while Dad's lowered on a metal platform onto the sidewalk.

"We always park here. Great height to unload Gus," Anna says, cheerfully.

"What can I do to help?" I ask.

"Just don't get in my way," she says with a wink.

Does that mean she isn't cross with me anymore?

"Hey, Paige? We're glad you're here."

Her words stop me in my tracks. I think I mutter thank you, but I turn my face away from hers, stare instead into a closed store window at a wood carved Native American greeting me with his open palm. I blink away a grateful tear before turning around and following my dad and Anna.

After a long lunch at a smoke-filled steak house with a blasting jukebox and a waitress that looked like she walked off the set of an indie film, I excuse myself and head outside.

I turn on my cell phone for the first time in what feels like forever. Sure enough, I have reception in town. Three bars of it.

I dial my mother's number.

"Paige! Finally! I've left you dozens of messages!"

I hold the phone away from my ear, push speaker, and talk into that instead. "Sorry. I have horrible reception at the ranch. This is my first time in town since I got here."

She sighs. "You could use the landline. Or email."

True.

"I'm glad to hear your voice, finally. How are you?"

"I'm okay."

"Good, good."

Not knowing what to say next, I stare at the shops lining the street. Anna said most people go to church Sunday morning, and then they spend the rest of the day with their families. Church. I know like three people total who still go to church. Only the one steak house is open for lunch, one clothing store, and a couple of brunch places. I hang my ankles over the steps, studying the webs cracking through my blue leather boots.

I agreed to the ankle ones, even though the high ones did look sort of cool. I considered the red ones, but Anna and Dad said I looked better in blue.

"Mom?"

"I'm here, Paige."

I look around to make sure nobody is listening. "What do Dad and Anna and Jake know about me? About what happened?"

"Who is Jake?"

"He works for Dad, he picked me up at the airport."

"Well, I don't know him, so as far as I know, he knows what Anna told him."

"So you know Anna?"

"Not personally, but I spoke with her on the phone to arrange your visit. Since she actually answers the landline at the ranch"—insert innuendo—"I've talked to her several times since you've arrived."

"Mom! You pretended not to know I was okay."

"You think I'm going to be completely out of touch with your well-being, Paige? You weren't answering your cell, so of course I called Anna. We talk daily."

I hate the thought of them discussing me like I'm some little kid. Matching her fiery tone, I snap, "So you knew about Dad and didn't tell me."

"What do you mean by that?"

"You knew he couldn't talk? You knew he was in a wheelchair? Mom, he is breathing with a respirator!"

"Yes."

I click my heels together. "How could you not tell me?"

"You knew he was sick, Paige. You knew he wasn't getting better."

"That's no excuse! Mom, I had no idea he was this bad! We're downtown and we drove here in a van equipped for wheelchairs. He can't even talk. I can't understand him. How could you not at least warn me?"

She's quiet for a second. Then she says in this horrible filled-with-truth voice, "I had to get you out of town, get you somewhere safe, away from here where you'd have people to look after you…"

Jake. Anna. Dad.

"And," her voice softens with guilt, "I was afraid you wouldn't have agreed to go if you knew how bad it was."

My throat burns. "That's not fair."

"Think about me being here, Paige. Here without you." Her voice cracks. I don't want her to cry. I'd rather her be mean, feisty. Vulnerable, undone mom slays me. "Do you think that's fair?"

"No," I admit.

The mess I left her is even bigger than mine.

Chapter Eighteen

Then

"It might be my fault," I confessed to Ty.

"What?" he asked casually, as if I hadn't been ignoring him for two months, ever since I heard the terrible rumor about him.

"Elena."

Ty, splayed against the giant couch in the den, arms folded behind his head like wings, studied me. I thought about what Elena called him—the Devil. That I was Dancing with the Devil, and here he was splayed out like an angel. Truth was I missed him. I missed our talks. I missed the way he seemed to understand me in a way no one else did. It was stupid to reengage after hearing the rumors, but I didn't care. Not anymore. She was gone now. Devil be damned.

"Why would you think that?" His voice was sardonic and annoyed, but not judge-y. Not of me, anyway.

"I said something really horrible to her."

"What'd you say?"

I filled him in about my comment about jumping in front of a train.

"Paige, not trying to be a dick here, but do you really think someone would kill themselves because some girl made a bitchy comment?"

"But the train, Ty, I basically said if you don't get into college you'll kill yourself—and then she—" I tried to swallow but couldn't. "Maybe, did I give her the idea?"

I buried my face in the extra-stuffed pillow. It smelled like his hair gel. A smell I was starting to not hate. I tossed it away. I had to remind myself that he was dangerous, that he was my stepbrother. I stepped up to go, but I couldn't stop watching him play this game. Ever since the funeral, I made sure I was home when he was showering. He was like clockwork with his shower: after school, but before dinner. He said his mom, before she left, was into the family coming to the dinner table in top form. It was a tradition he continued still, even though my mom and his dad didn't care if I showed up to the table in pajamas. We only ate together maybe once a week anyway, and that was just delivery on paper plates. Who had time for a family dinner? Ty did. He wanted to anyway.

So I'd stand outside in the hall and listen to him sing. Some of the songs I didn't recognize. Did he make them up or were they just obscure? When the water turned off, I'd bolt back to my room, carefully shutting the door.

Ty shifted, switching on a dystopian motorcycle game on the flat screen TV. His character weaved in and out of traffic. Once in a while he'd get mowed down but his alter ego—a guy with jet-black hair wearing a red-hot racing outfit—didn't care. He would dissolve into a series of cloudy dots before coming back together, whole, and getting back on his bike.

"Paige, I love ya, you know that."

His voice and his words startled me. I stiffened.

"But sometimes you humor yourself into thinking you are the planet everyone orbits around." He turned his head, catching my eye. "Though in certain instances you might be correct."

A flush crawled up my neck. Did he mean him and me? No. How could he?

If he noticed my discomfort, he didn't let on. He spoke in a clear, comforting tone. "But Elena? No way. That was so much deeper than some frenemy making a flippant comment. She didn't like you because she was jealous you and Luce were so close. She wouldn't like you no matter what you said or didn't say. I think she pretty much hated white girls in general."

"Really?"

"Totally."

When had Ty gained this astute perspective about girlfriend dynamics?

His thumb pushed the red button, his back jerking as he shot things.

"Elena was just one of those," he said, tilting his whole body as if he was really driving the bike.

"Those?"

He glanced up at me again before returning his full attention to the game.

Red Hot Motorcycle Guy jumped off an iceberg.

"You know, *gunners*. All she cared about was the next move. She didn't live in the present at all. That's why she didn't care who she hurt. She was totally jacked psychologically. Her mom was a nutjob, and her dad was barely better. They've been pushing her since she was a toddler to be perfect. Under that kind of pressure, even the hardest nut will crack."

It was the most thoughtful and observant thing I'd ever heard him say. I wanted to hear more so I pressed him on it.

"She never learned to think for herself. She was the parrot of her parents. She didn't get that this life was real. That this life was all she had. This was it. It was always, 'When I get out of high school. When I get out of my parents' house.' If she got accepted into Harvard, it would have been more of that same shit, 'When I get accepted into med school,' and then 'When I get accepted into residency,' then 'When I'm attending at Harvard,' then…blah blah."

"How do you know?"

"My dad was trying to get me to date her when I first got here. I went out with her once but we didn't hit it off. She was so cold. I prefer my girls a little warmer." He glanced at me, his eyes lingering a moment too long. "And my mom," he said, his eyes clouding a bit, "she was totally like that. Eyes on the prize always." He tapped on his controls. "Never on today." He pointed to the wood floor. "This day."

"Is that why…?"

"She didn't care that my dad left and that I moved out here with him? Probably." He shrugged. "Her patients and extended family were always more important than us. She said my dad didn't get it."

Ty didn't move here because of a girl. He moved here because he wasn't close with his mother. Elena hated Ty because he didn't like her. She was lying about him. I *knew* it.

He blinked. His lashes were so dark and long, waving over his green eyes. "When my dad met your mom, everything changed for him."

"Elena said some…terrible things about you."

"Oh, I'm sure she did."

He said it spitefully, but I had to know. If Ty wasn't a rapist, I could still listen to him sing. We could still be friends.

"It was something bad, Ty. Really bad. About a girl and a party…"

His eyes hardened. "Elena was a lying bitch."

"Ty. You shouldn't speak that way about the dead."

I said it in a whisper, like she could hear me, and even though I'd been thinking similar things, it didn't feel right to think them out loud.

"Think she's listening? Doubt it. Her karma's just reversed. She's pretty much hosed."

"Do you believe that? I'm not very religious."

"Lucky you."

I was losing hold of this conversation, and I was already competing with the video game. "So it's not true?"

"No, it is. Suicide put her spiritual clock in reverse. It's the murder of self. And she thought not getting into Harvard was bad."

"I'm talking about the…incident in Brooklyn."

I couldn't even say it.

Just say it. The rape. The rape in Brooklyn.

He glanced up at me, his eyes rapidly blinking. Was that a sign of a liar? Erratic blinking? Clearly he was growing increasingly irritable with my questioning. It was the last thing he wanted to talk about. Of course it was. But if he wasn't guilty, why not just deny it right away so we could move past it?

"Did I date rape some slut at a party?" he snapped. "No, I did not." His expression shifted. "I did have sex with her though, and she *had* been drinking. Did she consent? Did she say, 'Yes, I will have sex with you, Ty'? No, of course not. Does anyone ever actually have that conversation? 'Excuse me, Miss. Would you like to come under my covers and engage in sexual intercourse with me?' 'Why yes, I would. Thank you very much for asking.' 'Shall I remove your panties now?' 'Sure! Now is a good time. Thanks for checking in.'"

He crossed his eyes and made me snort. I shouldn't laugh. Nothing about this was funny. Why was I laughing? Ty both horrified and intrigued me. The devil angel sharing my roof.

"Has anyone asked you that, Sis? Seriously?"

I blushed.

"See? No. If the mood is right, you both get it and you go for it. So no I didn't have her written consent, but I'm not Bill Fucking Cosby. I didn't drug her, and I didn't get her drunk in order to have sex with her. We had just met, we were partying, and we hooked up. The end."

His body tensed as he roared his animated self through the Arctic, blasting everything that got in his way. I stayed quiet so he'd keep talking.

"And as far as Elena goes, I guess she figured without Harvard, without her carefully parentally planned micro future?" He glanced over at me to make an impact. "Game over," he said, just as Ty's alter ego skidded out and exploded into orange flames.

I didn't talk to Ty much after that, but it was pretty obvious the dog-eared and highlighted paperback of *The Virgin Suicides* I found on my bed was a twisted sort of gift from him. After tossing it aside, thoroughly creeped out for a week or so, I picked it up and stayed up all night reading the engrossing story of five teenaged sisters growing up in the suburbs with absurdly religious, overprotective parents who won't give them an ounce of freedom they crave. One girl goes through a period of rebellion, sleeping with the hot boy at school, but when he abandons her, the sisters all kill themselves in grotesque ways (oven, hanging, carbon monoxide, pills).

The story is narrated by their neighbor boys, now grown men, who remain in awe of the beautiful trapped girls.

Beautiful and trapped teens.

Like the train kids.

Like us.

The boys in the story are confused by their group suicide, but as I read the lovely prose, I understood it. Death was the ultimate fuck you to the parents, especially the mother. Death was their ultimate freedom.

It was the most disturbingly brilliant and scary book I'd ever read.

"Now do you understand Elena a bit more?" A scribbled note from my stepbrother splayed out in his bold writing on the last page.

I did.

And I was horrified that I did.

Chapter Nineteen

Now

After Mom admitted she knew about Dad, everything went to hell. I yelled, she yelled, then she was crying, and then we were both crying. I ended up hanging up on her and feeling like absolute crap for doing so. I hated that she was right. I hated that the person I was at home wouldn't have come to see Dad if I knew how sick he was, how bad it was. How close to death—especially after everything else that happened. I couldn't have done it. I'd rather have gone anywhere than face him sick like this.

Dad and Anna eventually find me sitting next to the van, pretending to be talking to a friend when they return.

"Everything okay, Paige?" Anna asks.

"Yeah," I say, avoiding her eyes.

On the long drive back to the ranch, we listen to cowboys bemoaning the fact that they lost their girls to liquor and other men, to women threatening their guys—if they should cheat again—that they'd find their tires slit and their heads dented with crowbars. Maybe the whole theory about cowboys' reticence was that they got their feelings out in their songs and that's why they didn't have to talk everything to death in real time.

Jake's Jeep is in the driveway when we get back, and I cling to the sight like a life raft. But I'm surprised to find another vehicle parked in front of the ranch, and even more surprised to see, standing beside the opulent, gold, high-end pickup truck, an overweight white guy with an oversized belt buckle leering at the ranch house like a lion outside a canary cage.

"Who is that?" I ask, instantly repulsed.

Anna frowns. "I forgot he was coming today." She glances back at Dad, an apologetic look crossing her face. "He's here to look at the property."

A creepy feeling builds in the pit of my gut. "Why?"

"He's interested in buying it."

"Buying it! The ranch isn't for sale. Is it?" I touch her arm. "Wait, is the ranch for sale?"

She doesn't answer me. Instead she goes about her routine of pressing the button, waiting for the metal ramp to lower Dad onto his property. I jump out of the car, lightning-fast like Jake, and follow the two of them to greet this slimy guy.

Instead of getting out a rifle and demanding he leave the property like I wish she would, Anna offers her hand. He shakes it, and they start talking about the ranch: the acreage, the cattle, the horses—the barn.

"Dad," I say, "the ranch isn't for sale." I squat down next to him, pressing my palm into his knee. "We aren't selling the ranch, right?"

"May have to." Jake appears, virtually out of nowhere, as if he hasn't been AWOL for two days.

"Why? You said we just had to fix it up. I know we're running out of money, but…selling the ranch?"

We follow my father up the ramp into the house. Jake talks to my father who wheels himself down the hall toward his office, then pulls me aside by my elbow.

"This isn't the time to make a scene," Jake says in a low, harsh voice.

I pull my elbow loose from his grip. "I wasn't making a scene. Where have you been all weekend anyway?"

"Why do you care?"

"I care."

Oh God, did I just admit I cared about Jake?

"You have a funny way of showing it."

We have no time to argue.

Jake shuts the door, spins on his heels, and says to me, "That man out there might be the one to get us out of the red here, Paige. He is an investor. You asking all kinds of questions and causing problems is going to make him roll that fancy truck of his right on down the drive." He points to further express his point, which makes me want to slug him.

"I thought he was here to buy it."

Jake shakes his head. "You don't need to assume things here. If you want to know, ask."

"If he's an investor, why didn't he greet my father? Why is he dealing directly with Anna?"

"Has it dawned on you how hard this is for Gus? Not only is he trapped in that wheelchair all day, drinking from a straw like a baby, but this place that he loves, that his family has owned for generations, is in jeopardy"—he glances down the hall, where we have a partial view of Dad's wheels at the office desk—"because of his health bills. His life was a train wreck, Paige, way before—"

"I showed up, right? Showed up to make everything worse?"

He avoids my eyes. "I didn't say that."

"You didn't have to. And I'm adjusting to all of this as fast as I can. It's not exactly easy." My throat catches around the words. He clears his before speaking again.

"I didn't mean that the way it came out, but look—come two weeks you'll be packing up that fancy suitcase of yours and catching a plane outta here." He gestures the other way this time, pointing in the direction of the window to the sky. "Leaving us with all of this." His voice is a rough whisper as he closes the distance between us, and I suck in a breath. "Stuck with piles of medical bills we can't pay and a man we're not always sure we're doing right by. We're doing our best here, but please, from now on, leave the business side of things to me and Anna, and keep those sorts of opinions to yourself."

He is so hotheaded. He makes me crazy. "A) My suitcase isn't fancy, and B) I know it probably looks like I don't care because I haven't been here in years, but this is my family's ranch. And I do care. I care that it's falling apart, and I care that we can't afford it. My daddy inherited it from his daddy who inherited from his and even during the depression they figured out a way to keep it from going under water. My point is, I'm not going to sit by and let you sell it to that creeper out there without a fight."

His hands rest on the front of his hips, fingers pointing straight down. "How do you know he's a creeper? What does that mean anyhow?"

"Just a vibe I get. Were you listening to what I was saying?"

"A vibe?" He shakes his head again. "Yes, I heard you, but this is business, Paige, and last I heard you're off to college in August and once you go, you're out of this 'fight' no matter how well and good your intentions are. You'll be off and we could be here, stuck without any potential buyers if you chase this guy off before knowing the whole story."

I wasn't going to let that happen to Eight Hands Ranch. Or to Jake. To Anna. Especially not to Dad. "I'm not leaving until we have a plan to save the ranch."

"Great. If you got any bright ideas, let's hear them." Hands on hips, he stands there. "Because outside of investors like Reverend Hal out there, I'm fresh outta ideas."

"I—I don't have anything right now, but I'll think of something."

"Well, while you're thinking of something, I'm going to go ahead and save our ranch, if that's okay with you?"

He flings the door open, forcing in bright, brutal sun. I grab his forearm and yank him back through, kicking the door shut and snuffing the light until we're, once again, alone in the hallway's shadows. He's startled—by my strength or tenacity, I'm not sure which. I stand on my tiptoes, and his face is inches from mine. "Wait, Jake. Don't do it. Please don't sell him the ranch. It's all…it's all I have left."

"Hey, hey, now."

I hope he doesn't notice the tears that spring into my eyes. His comforting tone makes me uneasy. "Why do you keep saying 'our,' anyway? Last time I checked, you aren't family, Jake."

My words were quiet but I can see they sting like his stung me.

He glances down at my fingers wrapped tightly around his flesh before looking back into my eyes, and his are round with surprise. When he speaks again, his voice is softer, almost guilty, but he's still mad, and he has something to say. "Day you arrived in that pink spangled Cowgirl shirt of yours, you asked me about the Eight Hands in the name of our ranch. How they changed from six? Well. Guess who the other two hands are?"

"I have no idea."

He cocks his head, blue eyes piercing into mine.

Now I do.

You, I think. *You and Anna.*

I don't even have to say it.

I don't need to ask why.

They care about this place. Mom sure didn't and before I got here, I didn't give a shit about it either, so Dad gave parts he loved to people who did.

"Yeah, that's right." He nods. "We're equal owners. All this?" He sticks out his thumb, gesturing toward the beautiful acres of golden fields tucked between grand mountains. Then I feel it land on my forearm. "If I ask that guy to take off, the ranch is all our problem. You get that, Paige?"

"I know about your dad, Jake, what happened to him? Anna told me."

Frowning, he avoids my eyes. Clenches his jaw.

I swallow, clutching hold of his belt loop, and I don't even look away when his eyes go wide. I lean into him. I can't help it. I can't fight it. "I get it."

Chapter Twenty

Then

After Elena, everything at school was sort of quiet — zombie teens at school, going through our zombie motions, until another boy jumped in front of the train.

This time at twilight, a sophomore, on his way home from volunteering at a soup kitchen downtown (another volunteer item for future college applications!), who, rumor had it, was mid-mental breakdown over SATs studying and extra-curriculars.

Then a week later, there was another one. Another Asian boy, a junior, very well-liked. Apparently he thought he shamed his parents about something school-related and decided to jump in front of a train instead of face their disappointment.

This was the fourth death by suicide.

The fourth death by train.

Parents were flipping out. Cornell was a fluke. Elena was a sad copycat. But the third and the fourth — both Asian boys — and the school was in chaos, drenched in fear that someone they knew, or worse, them, would be next.

Officially, the worry was the taboo of suicide had been lifted and now my peers were choosing the physical pain of trains and razor blades over dealing with the emotional pain of disappointment and heartache. We were being trained to be perfect. We didn't know how to handle disappointment. Or failure. We weren't taught resilience. So on the tracks waiting for the commuter train to barrel into him at fifty miles an hour, instead of sucking it up and being resilient like my dad was being with his horrendous ALS, this other kid jumped in front of the train.

ENOUGH IS ENOUGH read the local headlines.

Parents raised a " coalition of the willing"—willing to sit from dusk till long after dark along the tracks, lined up on either side, stuffed into REI chairs, wiggling uncomfortably in metal frames, as they dug deeper and deeper into the bloodstained dirt.

Cradling carafes of customized and made-to-order free trade coffee, their anxious eyes skimmed back and forth from the path behind the tracks, back to their Arts & Leisure sections of the *New York Times*, back to the tracks. They waited. Watched and waited under the intense fluorescent spotlight the police put up, their artificial moon.

The farther I was away from that home, the clearer I understood how insane it all was. We were teenagers. Why were we taking college classes in high school? Why were we spending endless hours studying at home and in the library instead of attending football games and rallies and dances?

Our reality was *nothing* like theirs.

After the first, after the hoopla surrounding Cornell and then Elena, they tried the minimalist approach. Less is more. Or, in this case, less is less. It was a bit like my mother's "If I don't believe it, it didn't happen" approach to life. All the while my fellow mice continued their studies, dancing on their glass stages. The teachers focused on keeping us alive instead of wondering why the others were dead, lest they be partially to blame.

I learned later this was the first stage of grief: Denial.

Tick tick tick tick.

My English teacher, Mr. T, pulled me aside after class. All the teachers acted as therapists now. Checking in with us about our grief, our stress levels. Today was my turn.

"My mother went back to school after she had me, business school, and she paid her own way. My dad is a cowboy. He lives in Wyoming. I don't really care that much which college I get accepted to as long as it's…."

Far Away from Here. He looked at me weird so I took it a step further.

"I got accepted to Wesleyan. They have a decent creative writing program and that's what I want to do, so…"

Still he stared. Listening.

"Look, even if I hadn't gotten in, my mother threw out all of our disposable razors—much to my stepfather's chagrin—so you don't have to worry about that, either."

Mr. T looked uncomfortable, but then, after taking another sip of his water, smiled as if he could feel his pay raise. Above and Beyond his job responsibilities. Like he'd achieved the highly esteemed position of Mentor. Truth was, I did want him to be my mentor. Just not an emotional one.

"That's wonderful about Wesleyan. It's a fine liberal arts education. How is your creative writing project going?" he asked.

"Good. I mean. Okay. I'm having a hard time getting started. I feel so…distracted all the time."

"There's a lot going on here. Sometimes I find that's the best time to write. When there's so much going on around you that only words on a page can help you find order in the chaos."

"That makes sense."

"Glad something does," he said, looking like his dog just died.

Chapter Twenty-One

Now

After almost three weeks together, we've all fallen into a quiet routine that seems to work for us. We have this old green Ford pick-up that I drive around the property, stopping at feed barns while Jake jumps out, loads the alfalfa, then tosses it over into the feed tanks for the horses. The cows mostly feed on grass, but sometimes we stop and feed them, too. We talk and joke and Jake points out things here and there as we drive along.

The other half of my day revolves around feeding and taking care of Dad. I've started to do a little bit of it, mostly giving him blended meals from a spoon or a straw during supper time. He isn't comfortable with me doing the more private details, like taking him to the bathroom or cleaning him — those fall to Anna — but I'm fine with the meals.

I used to do this with you, he typed to me, later, referencing baby food. *It looks like we've come full circle, kid.*

I faked a smile, but when biting my lip didn't work, I excused myself and cried in the bathroom. When I got back, Jake patted my hand under the table, and I didn't pull away. He's still pretty much a stranger on paper — other than fishing with him when we were kids, we've only known each other a few weeks. But we had an immediate connection that first day when he picked me up in his Jeep, and it's starting to flesh out into a quiet, enthralled understanding I'm beginning to count on more than I want to admit.

I'm still feeling the connection as Jake and I sway gently on the porch swing, watching lightning tear across the sky. Thick streams of relentless rain pound the dirt. Thunder strikes so loudly it vibrates the porch, the swing, our spines. I jump and spill the tea I'm drinking all over my shirt.

Wordlessly, Jake hands me a red throw blanket to mop it up.

"Clearly, we've angered the gods," he says, and it both terrifies and delights me that he says *we*.

"This is amazing. We don't have storms like this in California."

"I hear it doesn't rain at all in California."

"True. The drought is bad. All our pretty green lawns have turned to desert plants. It's sort of depressing."

The crisp air feels like a cool shower, without the biting discomfort. We watch the grey streaks of rain bring up the scent of wet hay. I drink Anna's iced tea. Jake drinks his Diet Dr. Pepper. He drinks it all day long—can after can—which is likely why he has so much damn energy all the time, and I tell him so.

"Nah, I have so much energy because of all this." He gestures to the land and sky and everything else in front of us.

I smile. "Storms invigorate you, eh? Finally, the secret of Jake."

"That and my constant supply of soda pop."

Soda pop. Ha.

Since our argument the day Reverend Hal came by, Jake and I have been fine. Better than fine. We're partners. He looks out appreciatively over Eight Hands Ranch. I appreciate it more each day, too. Appreciate him, appreciate Anna.

I haven't asked specifically what Anna's relationship is to Dad, but now that I know she's a part owner of the failing ranch, I know she's more to him than just an assistant. Just as Jake is more to him than simply a ranch hand.

They are his family, and they're becoming mine as well.

"It's terrible for you, you know, " I say. "All that caffeine and dye. You should switch to tea. If I lived here year round, I'd make you switch."

Anna got me hooked on the stuff. She serves it up cold with a thick, fresh lemon wedge and a couple of perfectly baked chocolate chip cookies: chewy on the inside, crunchy on the out. Between the Diet Dr. Pepper, tea, and chocolate chunks, we're pretty much caffeined out 24/7. It helps with the slog of everything else, electrifying the heavy sadness that surrounds us. Gives us strength to combat the darkness.

"What dye?" He frowns with suspicion. "Besides you'd never live here year round, Cowgirl."

"Who says I wouldn't?"

"I know you. You'd never leave the city."

"Not true."

But it was true. I couldn't imagine the winters here. The solitude. As awful as this last year was, I miss ordering take-out. I miss the wide array of restaurants—any ethnicity I wanted, anytime—I miss the buzz of the creative minds in the valley. The hustle.

When I don't add anything else to my "not true", he repeats his question about the dyes.

"Caramel coloring for one," I say. "Never mind the amount of sugar. Did you know one soda has the equivalent of nine and one quarter teaspoons? Not to mention the high fructose corn syrup."

"That's why I drink diet," he says, wagging the can in front of my face.

"Diet is even worse. Aspartame causes brain tumors."

"Yeah, well, we all gotta die sometime."

I frown. "Don't say that."

"It's true. Look at old Gus in there. You think he ever would've thought he'd contract a rare disease? Anna could get cancer. Hell, we could get struck by lightning and fry right here on the porch."

"That makes me feel better."

"I'm just saying, we all have our vices, and this is mine."

He shakes the can again, his eyes wild from the caffeine. It's nearly empty, and I hear the liquid gunk swish around in the can.

"I guess you're right. But it doesn't feel like you'll ever die. You're invincible, or something."

He scoffs. "Invincible? No. Just lucky, that's all."

His blue, blue eyes flash, holding my whole world steady. We're sitting very close to each other on the swing. Each clash of thunder sent me scooting a little closer to him. Blushing, I cut the eye contact and look down, mumbling something about how hot it is. "The weather, I mean," I say, and he chuckles, like he knows my reaction to his eyes on mine have nothing to do with the temperature in the air.

"Let's hope your luck helps us come up with an idea to save the ranch," I say as a way to cover my reaction.

His jaw clenches as he takes in the wide expanse of our falling-apart home again. Always watching and noticing, he points across the valley. "Look at that."

"Wow," I whisper. As if painted by the hand of Zeus himself, white stripes pierce the clouds and zigzag over the Tetons. The entire sky is like a painting: grays and blues and whites. "That doesn't even look real."

"That's why we don't need all those gadgets you guys have in the city. We have *this*."

I feel him breathe in the vibration of the swing, and my breath catches up with his. If we can't be physically together, we can breathe together. In and out. Our feet rest near each others, gently pressing the swing back and forth, back and forth. I press my hand down on the narrow space between us on the hard wood of the swing. The painted wood is hot against my palm. If he just set his hand on mine like he did that one time during dinner, would that be so bad?

Yes.

Yes, it would be. But the fact that I longed for touch, human touch, *his* touch—meant something. I was doing better. The ranch was helping. He was helping.

"Maybe we can start a YouFundIt," I suggest.

"What's that?"

"It's something people do on social media. You get a cause and then raise money for that cause."

"Random people donate?"

"Yeah."

"Why?"

"I don't know. They get excited about the idea, I guess," I say.

"Don't they have stuff going on in their own lives they have to spend money on?"

"Probably. Or maybe not? I don't know. I never really thought about it before."

Suddenly the crowdsourcing idea did sound weird. But it worked. I knew lots of people who raised money for women's business projects in developing countries, indie films, even books this way.

"I wouldn't want to be indebted to any strangers like that."

Cowboy Jake being Cowboy Jake. Had I really expected a different reaction?

Smiling, I just nod. Explaining the tech capital of the world and bitcoins and start-ups to someone who had never lived twenty miles outside where he was born was pointless. Maybe crowdfunding was, too. I don't know.

"It was just an idea," I say.

"I'm not faulting your ideas, Paige. I like your brain. It's always running." His fingers draw circles next to my forehead like a helicopter propeller.

"Running away, maybe. It's my flaw. Like you said."

He shrugs, his form of an apology. "I was just mad. Besides I run, too. It's easier to run sometimes. But that's not what I mean here. I mean running. Charging. Working on overtime. I look at you sometimes and I can tell you're thinking about something."

"Really?"

"Yep."

"You look at me?" I ask.

"Sure."

Jake notices me like I notice him. And admits it.

We sit for a while watching the storm. I stare at Jake's dusty boots and suddenly they're all I want to see for the rest of my life. Jake's dusty boots beside mine.

And for a second I let myself want.

For a second I let myself long for Jake.

Maybe he feels it, too, the buzz between us as real as lightning in the summer sky because he tilts his body a little into mine, not so close that we are touching, but just enough to let me know he might be thinking that way about me as well.

Chapter Twenty-Two

Then

I decided to give Ty the benefit of the doubt. I needed someone to talk to, someone that understood, and that was Ty. Luce had a mental breakdown and got early acceptance to Princeton and left without even saying goodbye. I couldn't relate to the crying, hugging classmates, to the crying/hugging teachers. I felt like an alien on a strange, depressing planet.

I needed another alien.

I needed Ty.

And as much as I hated to admit it, I missed him.

We were just starting to get chatty again—slugging each other in the hallway, meeting eyes over takeout with Mom and Phil at dinner—when Elliot happened.

Elliot was the fifth.

And for Ty, Elliot was the worst.

It happened in mid-May when we thought our string of suicides was over. When the volunteer parents who made up the coalition of the willing started to peter off—heading back to tone their million-dollar bodies with pre-dawn Pilates, early-morning meetings, fair-trade coffee with angel investors, and kale smoothies with venture capitalists looking for the Next Big Thing.

Ty and Elliot were on the same Little League team—the Cardinals, he reminded me after—when they were in second grade back in Brooklyn. He relocated a few years before Ty. There's a continual Harvard-Stanford shuffle that goes on between university scholars. Ty told me Elliot was a quiet, unassuming kid with an amazing knack for hitting doubles. Because he was small, the other team would come in closer when he was up, then, when he'd bang that shit out of the ballpark, they'd scramble like eggs in a blender to catch his heat.

Ty played a mean shortstop with Elliot manning first base. They'd work together, scrawny Ty scooping up the ball and tossing it underhand to Elliot who'd nail the kid out at first. They'd high five after, chase each other around the play structure, and sneak a second bag of Doritos at snack time.

Ty moved up to machine pitch after that year but Elliot's parents pulled him out. He had to adjust his schedule to make room for things that mattered more than baseball. Like violin lessons and tutoring.

Ty was thrilled to run into him again last year when he moved to California, but they didn't have a connection anymore. They had nothing in common, and Elliot blew him off when he tried to get together. "I have to study," he always said.

Ty thought Elliot looked at him like he was a bad influence. Someone who would suck him down to the sewer, keep him from his dreams—like those confident spring days when nothing could come between them but a ball that the two of them, together, could tackle easily.

By the time Elliot stood on the train tracks, he and Ty weren't even communicating anymore, other than a half-hearted wave in the hallway. But his death hit Ty so hard I didn't think he'd ever recover.

After school, instead of playing video games or bantering with me in the kitchen, Ty would lie on his blue comforter and toss his old baseball against the wall, over and over and over, until a day became a week and a week a month.

"Ty," I asked, knocking softly on the open door frame, "Can I come in?"

His room stunk the way the inside of a closed trunk does.

Thunk. Thunk. Thunk.

His Little League uniform was flat on his desk, hand pressed like he'd run his palm over the size 8 T-shirt over and over again. His tiny white uniform pants, still with faded grass stains on the knees, lay next to it. And next to them, red knee-high socks.

His hat, a small red cap with a Cardinal on it, was resting on his head, bill pointed backward. He'd unhooked the back to make it fit, but it was still way too small.

Ty looked like a crazy person sitting there surrounded by his childhood things.

"I don't care," he said.

"Yes, you do."

I shut the door behind us. Pushed in the lock with my thumb. "Ty."

I sat next to him and felt the bed shift.

His eyes were red and puffy and broke my heart into a million pieces.

"What can I do?" I asked.

"Get me a time machine. Let me go back. Let me go back and make his parents stop being such assholes. Let him continue with baseball, the one thing he loved, instead of forcing him down a road he had no interest in going down. You have a time machine, *Sis*?"

His voice had an angry edge to it, the *Sis* oozed with sarcasm. It was just a mask.

"I wish I did."

Thunk. Thunk.

"Why'd you want to help me anyway? I'm a rapist remember?" He spat that last bit.

"Ty."

"What? You believed them! You know you did. You probably

still do."

"I live down the hall from you. I have every right to be scared."

That stopped him. His glare faded into pure horror. His eyes filled with tears. "You think I'd hurt you, Paige?"

"No. I mean, I don't know. After the last time…"

"FUCK. THIS. WORLD."

He didn't ask me to leave. So I stayed.

"His dad's a fucking asshole is what he is." Ty continued to toss the ball against the wall while he ranted. "He works, what? Eleven, twelve hours a day at that crazy place? Even when we were kids, he never took the time to play catch with Elliot. It was the coach who invested in him, recognized his talent. You know I was there when that sonofabitch talked to Coach and told him Elliot wouldn't be coming back next year, wouldn't be moving on with the rest of us, and Elliot just had to stand there, taking it? He didn't say a word. He wasn't even breathing."

"What did you do?"

"I laid into him! I begged him to let him go on with us. We were a team. We've been at it since T-ball. Saturdays at the park and Sundays at the batting cages, it was what we did. It was what we loved. Who we were."

"What happened?"

"He told me to mind my own business. What will Elliot do, become a pro-baseball player? They expected things from him."

Thunk. Thunk.

"That sucks."

He scowled at the wall. "It doesn't suck. Missing a green light sucks. That was fucking insane is what it was. You don't tell an eight-year-old kid they have to be pro-anything. A pro-baseball player? What the fuck? It's for fun. We were KIDS. Sometimes I fucking hate all these so-called 'successful' motherfuckers who rob their children's childhoods for some blank canvas future. That's what's happening, you know? In their attempt to secure these 'successful futures', they are quite literally killing their children."

He stood up. He shoved his closet open and grabbed a baseball bat. He started swinging it around the room. I backed up against the closet and spoke in a quiet voice reserved for... God, I didn't remember the last time I used it. Probably when my dad was drunk and we were in Wyoming. I shivered at the thought.

"You know why I didn't go to his funeral, Paige? You know why I didn't get up on the altar like I did at Elena's and sing for my friend?" Ty stared darkly into my soul. I sucked in a breath. He was holding the bat up above his head. One false move and I could be dead. I could be next.

"Because you'd kill his dad if you had?" I said, my voice barely above a whisper.

He looked at me then as if he was seeing me for the first time.

"No. *Jesus.* You think I want to go to jail for life? No fucking way." He glanced at the bat like he just noticed he was holding it up in a threatening matter. He tossed it gently on the bed and approached me, slowly, purposefully, like a tiger. "I'd tell him, 'You did this.'" He shook his finger in my face. "'Elliot didn't kill himself. You did. Nine years ago. Because he was a strong-ass kid. It just took this long to make his heart stop. And Elliot was such a sweet guy, he wouldn't want to hurt his father's feelings.'"

After that moment, I knew Ty was capable of pretty much anything. He was both an angel and a devil. The problem was, I had no idea of my role—who I was to him, or which persona he was to me—but the room was thick with passion and pain, and it was only a matter of time until my curiosity would win, and I'd make myself find out.

Chapter Twenty-Three

Now

After chores, dinner, and watching old movies with my dad, Anna and I move out onto the porch, watching the sun pour down onto the corral in front of us, baking the previously wet dirt into cracked cake. When I feel the tension in the air shift from a casual break to a more formal conversation, I ask, "Where's Jake?"

This is my new stand-by for when the anxiety rises from my stomach to my chest and threatens to pour out of me in the form of a tantrum or tears—I'm never sure which. Even if Jake and I aren't actively involved in a conversation, just being around his cool confidence while he works is so calming. I like to know he's nearby.

"Getting the horses ready."

"For what?"

She takes a long sip out of a tall, strawberry-decorated glass. She peers at me over the lip. "For our overnight."

My pulse races. "Overnight, like overnight-overnight?"

"What else would overnight mean? Tanya, our friend from town, is coming to sit with your daddy, and we're going to fetch a herd of cattle that have been grazing over the mountain."

"We?"

"You, me, and Jake."

Thunk. My heart. Not unlike the sound of Ty's baseball hitting that wall. "Oh."

Jake and me on an overnight? Just the three of us for 24 hours? At night. Over. Night. Stars. Sleeping bags.

Panic mode. "I can't go. I have too much…writing to do."

"You don't write. You just sit there and stare at that screen."

Crap.

"That's called writer's block, and it's very normal — I hear — and anyway, I'm writing somewhere else. Not that it… besides, I don't think we should up and leave dad with this Tanya, this stranger."

"Him and Tanya get along just fine."

"Why can't the two of you just go?"

"We could. But we want you to come along."

The way she says it is strange. Anna and Jake worship at the Church of Personal Space.

Then it dawns on me. "You don't want to leave me alone."

"Your mother asked that we don't."

"Is that why Jake hangs around? You're paying him to babysit me?"

"Jake? No. Jake does what he wants. If he's hanging around you, that's on his own accord."

I feel stupid. And stupidly relieved. I look away so she can't see the relief spilling all over my face.

"What exactly does my mom think I'll do?" I ask.

Anna takes a long sip of tea. Her ice cubes clink around in her tall glass. She doesn't need to answer, and it was dumb of me to ask anyway. What did I want, her to actually say it? That I was on suicide watch? That I was sent here because they suspected I'd be next?

We exchange a knowing look and I realize there's no point in arguing I could stay home alone. I didn't even want to stay home alone. I'd way rather be with Anna and Jake, though I hated to admit it. Anna is now part of the Coalition of the

Willing—except she rides a horse instead of an REI chair. "Fine. When do we go?"

"Day after tomorrow at sunrise, which means you better get your butt in a saddle today."

Subtle.

Truth is, I love horses—used to anyway. For years riding was my favorite thing in the entire world. I missed horses so much when mom first took me away from the ranch. Missed their smell, the feel of their racing pulse, and their sweaty coat after a long ride. I even missed scooping the poop (though I wouldn't admit that at the time).

Now I'm here. I'm back.

Everything is different. *I'm* different. Rearranged completely. But that…reverence and affection I used to have for the four-legged almost mythological creatures of my childhood is bubbling up again, despite myself. I've been eying that golden-red horse. Sharing apples with her in the same manner I did that first day. Admiring her strength and wild beauty, mostly from afar. Hell, she doesn't want much to do with me, but who could blame her? I feel a sort of kinship with her. Like me, she's trapped and mad as hell about it.

I know I can't ride her. She isn't tame.

But there are others. Why hadn't I asked to ride?

I knew why. It's because *they* can't. All those once-healthy bodies of my peers reduced to ash, melted to bits of bone. Their futures resting in engraved urns of wood, of metal, of cast iron, ceramic, glass—on their parents' mantels. And soon, my dad's may be resting on mine. Their right to do the things they love was stolen from them way too soon. So why should that right be mine?

Chapter Twenty-Four

Then

"It wasn't just his father's fault," Ty said, like I was a priest and our dim, modern living room was a confessional. Our parents were out at a charity dinner, ironically for Teen Suicide Prevention.

They were wearing black tie attire.

Five teenagers were buried in the dirt.

We were sitting on opposite sides of the couch, soaking in the tension. I was still scared of him—unsure, yet sure at the same time. Sure he wouldn't hurt me. Something about him was a little lost boy. He was a problem to solve. A mystery—and I craved the revealing chapter.

"No?"

"No. It was mine, too. I shouldn't have let the baseball thing come between us. We still could have hung out."

"Ty."

"What?"

"You said something really smart to me when I said the same thing to you about Elena."

He looked almost hopeful for a second. "Which was?"

"You think someone would kill themselves over something as minor as a comment made by a sort of friend?"

His eyes flared. "Don't compare Elliot to Elena. She was a selfish bitch."

"A *dead* selfish bitch," I lamely corrected him. "And Elliot *used* to be your friend. Past tense. You need to think rationally about this. Do you think you could have stopped him from dying if you still played ball together?"

"Yes."

"But…how?"

"You kill yourself if you give up hope. Paige, he had no hope. In ball, you always have hope. There's always another game, another season, another exciting thing around the next corner."

"Ty. You haven't played ball since second grade, either."

"So?"

"So."

I didn't want to fill in the blanks here. He was alive. He had the wherewithal to move on to the next day. It had nothing to do with baseball or sports or him.

I told him what he told me. "This is bigger than you, Ty."

I thought he'd listened, but the next morning an article in the paper said renowned heart surgeon Dr. Lu's BMW had his windows busted out in the hospital's parking garage.

I looked for Ty's baseball bat in his room.

I checked it for shards of glass.

But it'd been carefully polished, preserved, and placed next to the rest of his memoirs from his young days at the ballpark. Days when he thought, probably incorrectly, that his life was perfect, that Elliot's life had limitless potential.

That they'd both go pro together one day.

Now I had proof Ty was more devil than angel.

And still, I didn't stay away.

Chapter Twenty-Five

Now

By the time I stumble into the stable area, Jake is readying an old gelding.

"I'm impressed," he says, a wry look on his face.

"With what?"

I take another sip of cowboy coffee Anna handed me as she shoved me out the door, half comatose, five minutes ago at 5:25 a.m.

"You got out of bed."

"Haha," I said. "I didn't think it was exactly optional."

"Wasn't. Still." He grinned. "I'm impressed."

"Well, thank you."

"Well, you're welcome."

His look makes me wonder how in the world I'll make it through an overnight with this blue-eyed cowboy.

I pat the horse's big spotted ass and redirect the conversation. "Who's this?"

"Ole' Blue."

"What about that one?" I say, gesturing to my red-gold beauty in the corral, angrily dashing back and forth like a bee is in her bridal.

Jake makes this laugh-snort sound and shakes his head.

"What?"

"She's not even broke."

I shrug.

"Do you remember *anything* about riding, Cowgirl?"

"It's just like getting back on a horse, I hear."

"Haha," he mimics. He readies the saddle, the bridle, and the bit. Yanks on this, adjusts that. Leans his shoulder into the horse.

He explains how to adjust the bridle, pull in the reins. Adjust the bit. Cowboys are the kind of teachers who show you something once and expect you to have it down. I figured Jake would be the same way. That if I don't understand something, he'd expect me to speak up and ask. In this specific case I didn't need to be shown anything. I remembered clearly, but I could tell he was getting a little pleasure in showing me what to do. "Here you go," he says, tapping the top of my boot. "Put your foot here, and hop on up."

"I remember how to get on a horse, Jake."

"Uh-huh," he mutters.

"What? I do. It's not like it's something you forget."

"You wanted to get up on a wild 'stang your first time back out. Don't take this the wrong way, Cowgirl, but let me take the lead when it comes to the horses. You break your back, Anna breaks my face."

"Duly noted."

Jake's face was perfectly imperfect. It was becoming the image I saw every time I closed my eyes, the image of something good in my messed-up world, and it would be a damn shame if harm came to it. Especially of the Anna variety. I bet she packs a mean punch.

I grip the horn with both hands. Slivers of dirt and sweat rub off on my palms as I place my left heel into the stirrup and heave myself up and onto the saddle.

"Toes up in the stirrups, good," Jake says. "Heels down."

"Got it."

"Well, why aren't you doing it, then?" He lifts my foot gently into the stirrup, and adjusts it the way he sees fit. "Might as well get it right out the gate."

He meets my eyes, talking about more than a stirrup, I think.

I blink. "That's not as easy as the cliché makes it sound."

I adjust my ankle in the metal as he directs me to.

"Better," he says.

He takes the lead rope, a rich blue color, and leads me out of the corral.

"Where's your mount?" I ask.

He smiles then. I'm not sure if it's because of the word itself or the fact that I know it. "I'm not going with you."

"I thought we were all going?"

"This is your practice ride, Cowgirl. Find your sea legs again."

My heart seizes, and I inadvertently yank on the reins. The horse whinnies and rears back its head. Jake touches the horse's face to calm it down. "Hey, easy, there, old man. Ease up on the reins, Paige. Listen, you'll be fine. Just hug the reins in tight when you want him to stop but keep them loose as he walks along. Blue here is an old guy. He's not up for more than a walk anyhow. Stick to the trail loop and—"

"Jake. I haven't been on a horse in years. What if—"

"Don't worry. If you ain't back in a half hour, I'll come for you. I have to finish getting the supplies ready for the trip. Ready the other horses."

The graying gelding with the coarse white mane sneezes. At least I think it was a sneeze; it may have been a protest. Then, he shakes his head again when I pull the reins back.

"It'll be fun." He takes my hand and readjusts it on the reins. "Not so tight. Here like this." He twists his hand around the thin straps of leather, shows me, and then wraps my fingers around the soft leather the right way. "Like you're holding an ice cream cone, see? Let a bit of it fall over like this."

About six inches of thin leather flapped over the side, dusting against my tight fist. "I think mine's dripping."

"You got it, then."

"But, Jake," I say, nervously. "I think Anna meant for you

to come along."

"If Anna'd meant for me to go along, Anna'd told me to go along. Now get," he says, with a slap on the gelding's butt. "I got stuff to do. Don't look back, Paige, look on ahead."

Blue breaks into this awkward trot-walk thing and I pull back on the reins. "Jake?"

"Let him know who's in charge. Keep the reins in tight, but not too tight. Keep your eyes on the trail and you'll be fine."

"What if we get lost?"

"Sometimes you got to do stuff that scares you, Paige. That's how you know you're alive," he calls to me in the wind.

Jake is right about Ole' Blue.

He is as unmotivated as all get out, and after that initial burst of energy, I can barely keep him going. At every green bush, he sticks out his velvety nose, opens those huge chompers, and goes to town. I have to yank his neck back every few feet to keep him on the trail. I feel right up here, though. Natural. Like after a rainy suburban winter, getting back on my bike on that first sunny day and just riding and riding with nothing but the wind in my hair and a song in my head.

I remember this trail.

It's the loop-de-loop beginner trail. The one the Kids' Club would go on at the ranch. After a bit, I even remember this old horse. He was younger then, obviously, but always a calm one. Good with kids—gentle.

We mosey along for a while in this routine that reminds me of mine and Anna's: a quiet understanding that we were stuck with each other, so we best just get along.

Critters crackle through the bushes, a chipmunk spins circles in the dirt, and a huge osprey appears out of nowhere, diving toward a small lake, hunting for his breakfast as songbirds twitter their morning tunes.

Other than the creatures, the only noise is the breath of the horse, the sound of his hooves on the hard-dirt trail, and the heart in my chest adjusting to being alone.

"I see you survived," Jake says, with a wry smile as we mosey back into the corral maybe twenty minutes later. My gelding heads straight for the large trough. When he lowers his head to lap up the water, I lean forward, too. "Ole' Blue," he says with appreciation for the horse. "She treated you all right, didn't she?"

"Indeed," I say. "We got along fine. Can I get down now?"

"Sure enough."

This time he reaches out and offers me a hand, and I accept it, swinging my leg over and landing with a *thump* on the dirt. His hands fall on either side of my waist, steadying me. My right hand on that hard-soft spot between his chest and shoulder.

"Oh," I say. If we were somewhere else, if we were somebody else, we could be dancing. My body tenses up, and he quickly lets go, wiping his palms on his cowboy pants.

"So how was it?" he asks, to fill the space with something other than our closeness.

"Good," I say. "Fine," I say. But was anything fine?

Nodding, like he knows it's not fine, but knows it's definitely something, he lifts off his hat, scratches a fake itch, and puts it back on.

I like the way his hands feel on me, that's obvious. Denying it is a fool's game, but I can't get close to Jake like this. I'm not ready. I may never be ready again. How was I going to handle the overnight?

"You'll be ready in a half hour then?"

"Sure," I say. "I'll just run in and say bye to my dad."

"Hm." He examines me the way he did when we first met by his Jeep.

"What?"

"Think there might be hope for you after all," he says and laughs when I slug him.

Chapter Twenty-Six

"How you feeling, Cowgirl?" Jake asks me half an hour later, on the dot.

"Like I should've stuck to saying goodbye to Dad instead of stopping by my room," I mutter as I hoist my body weight onto the horn and, after securing my right foot in the stirrup, deftly swing my other leg over. "My bed is way more comfortable than this saddle."

Jake pats the horse's rear and half smiles.

Don't flirt with him.

Don't flirt with Jake.

Don't.

Just do not. And don't wonder what he does at night, either, because that's none of your damn business.

With new resolve, I face forward and study the back of Anna's jacket. It is fringed suede, long and thick, like something she ripped off the set of *Dances With Wolves*. One half of me wants to take a picture, text it to Ty, with those mocking words. The other half of me wants to cling to sanity, to stop thinking about Ty, so instead I watch the fringes sway under a near-morning sky so bright with a mix of pink hints of sun and pinpricks of stars that I want to follow her forever.

We don't stop until long after dawn. I don't have my phone.

I don't have a watch. I completely rely on the two of them for everything.

"Time for grub," Jake says. His horse stops, then Anna's, then mine sort of sticks his face into her horse's tail and then lurches back, and I think I'll slide down his neck when he plunges his face into a bush.

"Pull back on his reins, Paige. Knock it off, Blue," Jake says. He hops off his mount and winds the reins casually around his wrist before handing them to Anna. Then he grabs Blue's bridle and lifts his head, gently.

I shield my eyes. "He's old. He probably shouldn't be walking this much."

"Why don't you step down and give him a break then?" Jakes says, teasing, offering his hand to me.

"Sheesh," I say.

Chuckling under his breath he mutters, "You'll be a waddy yet."

"What's a waddy?"

"You'll know when you are one, Cowgirl."

"It does take some getting used to. I'm glad you made me go this morning."

"See? Besides, you're doing fine. Don't be so hard on yourself." Jake wraps the reins and ties him to a tree. "I'll get him a drink."

The sun is blinding, but sure enough, Jake fills a water bucket and ties it to Blue's bridle. "You hungry?" he asks when he's done. "Day one breakfast is always the best. We can't keep the bacon and eggs fresh far after that."

"Bacon and eggs, for real?"

"Sure. Why not?"

"If y'all don't need me, I think I'll mosey up the trail and see what's what," Anna says, and both Jake and I look up, startled at the sound of her voice. I had forgotten she was there. We meet eyes and laugh.

"Sure thing. Breakfast up in fifteen minutes or so," Jake says.

I shift back and forth on my legs as I watch him cook. Cracking the brown eggs on a piece of granite, and splitting the yolk and runny white over the heavy skillet. He makes the fire in, like, seconds, and won't accept any help from me.

The bacon sizzles next to the eggs, mixing with the fresh scent of pine trees and dust, and man, it's just about the best thing I've ever smelled in my life. My belly rumbles as I sit across from him on a rock, and while I finish wiping every last bit of egg off my camping plate, *he* watches *me,* chewing on a piece of straw in an amused way that tells me he has absolutely no idea who I am or what I'm capable of. Anna comes back in time for breakfast and eats heartily. We clean up, and then we're back up on our mounts. We talk about this and that. Sometimes we're quiet. Jake points out an eagle soaring over the tippy tops of pine trees.

We stop again a couple hours later, and I'm grateful for the change up.

I excuse myself to go to the bathroom in the forest, reminding me of that first day here when I dashed from Jake's Jeep into the woods. I drip some of the Purell in my pocket onto my palms after, and when I rejoin them, Anna hands me a sandwich: peanut butter and jelly on Wonder Bread. Jake is leaning against a tree like he's a freaking model for some western magazine, piece of hay sticking out of his mouth and everything. When he catches me looking, he half-smiles and stares down at his scuffed up boots.

Those dusty boots.

I make it a point to remember to take a picture of them when we get back to the ranch, but then I remind myself the Golden Rule of this overnight:

Don't engage. No flirting. Flirting leads to disaster.

While he works, settling in the horses, I think about the wide blue sky that seems to go on for days, the tangle of dried brush, Old Blue and the swish of his tail as he bats off annoying flies. Anything to keep my mind off of Jake's charms.

After lunch and clean up, we don't stop the horses again until dusk, and we're next to a small lake shaped like an almost full moon.

The sunset sky is pink and orange and blue and quite literally the most beautiful thing I've ever seen. "Wow," I say. I wander down to the water's edge alone. The lake is so still—a mirror, a slate of glass. A bird glides over it, skimming its talons on the water, and I'm surprised it doesn't leave a scratch when it lifts off again.

"Nice, isn't it?" Jake says from behind me.

"Incredible," I say. "It's like it's…untouched. That sounds stupid."

"Not at all. It is, practically. Your dad owns this land. No one comes up here but us, and we leave it as we found it."

"That doesn't seem right though, does it? For this beauty to go to waste?"

His nose wrinkles. "Just because the tourists aren't here making home movies they're never going to watch again, doesn't mean it's going to waste."

"I don't mean tourists."

"What do you mean?"

"I'm not sure yet." I pull my eyes from the pinks and the lavenders and look at Jake. "Who told you that, your daddy?"

"Indeed he did, and he's not the only one."

I wait a bit, taking it all in. The scenery, the feelings. Him. "Thanks, Jake."

"For what?"

"For bringing me out here. You didn't have to, did you?"

He chews his straw some more before he says, "'Spose we could've found someone to babysit you down there for the night."

I elbow him in the ribs and he ducks out of the way. "I don't need a babysitter."

His eyes skim over me. "You certainly do not," he says like he appreciates what he sees. Like he means it. "I'm glad we brought you up, anyhow," he says. "It's nice having you along."

"It's nice being along," I say, because it's true. It is. And it's not flirting to tell the truth.

Supper is a can of beans split three ways. Jake heats them in the same pan he used for eggs this morning (there's a little yellow scruff of residue as a reminder) over an open fire and under a gathering of stars so bright we don't need more than a lantern propped on a log to see what we're doing.

We eat quietly. The beans taste smoky, like this morning's bacon.

Jake's rock is slightly in front of mine and to the left, so while I eat, I study his profile. The way his wavy hair is bent in at the top. Hat head. Cowboy hat head. He wolfs his food down like it's his last meal and then wipes his mouth with the bottom of his sleeve. I love how he eats. I love how he does everything. Quick. Efficient. Gets it done. Even when I was a little girl, I always stood back, watching before diving in. When the other kids would cannonball into the swimming hole, I'd hold back, contemplating what would happen if I jumped. What if it was too cold and I screamed, embarrassing myself? What if I rubbed up against a fish, or God forbid, a snake? There are river snakes out here. Everybody'd wave me in at first, but then forget about me because they'd be so busy having fun. Not thinking about having fun, just having fun.

Jake twitches a bit as if my stare sparks genuine fire into his skin, or maybe he's just swiping at a bug? Either way, he glances at me sidelong with an amused frown as if he feels my inner commentary.

Later, I stand back and watch Jake and Anna roll out their sleeping bags. Anna finds a patch of grassy dirt under a tree and is careful about how she lays hers down. Jake is deliberate, too, about this decision, the way he is about everything. He glances up at the stars, studies the distance to the fire, and presses the heel of his boot onto the ground.

With a quick flick, he unties the rope around the bag, and with another one, flips it onto the ground. There are two blankets in there, turns out, and a sleeping bag. He smooths the blankets one on top of the other and when I think his next move is going to be kicking off his boots and lying down, he turns to me and says, "It's not the Ritz, City Slicker, but you should be comfortable."

"That's for me?"

"Yep."

"Thanks," I say.

"You're welcome. Come on now." He pats the ground. "Try it out for size. I checked the dirt for rocks, but sometimes the ones you can't see are the sharpest."

Again with meaning more than he says. "That sounds comfy."

"Not so sharp that you feel it. Won't keep you up, but in the morning you're all sore and when you look around, you find a bruise," Jake says.

Anna is busy with her pile still, adjusting her lantern, messing with the horses. I love the space Anna gives me, gives us, to just be.

"Know what I mean?" Jake asks.

"Yeah, I know what you mean." I smile. He's so damn cute.

"So make sure it's all smooth before you close your eyes."

I sit down and sort of wiggle around.

"Okay?"

"Yeah, it's good. Thanks."

"Sure?" He's looking at me, and I want him to keep looking at me but I need him to go away. I need him to stop that.

"Yep. Thanks."

"You said that already." His eyes grin.

"What?"

"Thanks," Jake says. "You've already thanked me. Couple times even."

"I guess I'm just not that used to people doing all this stuff for me. Stuff like this, anyway."

"All I did was roll a sleep sack on the dirt, Cowgirl."

"If you say so," I say.

But the way his eyes shine through the dark, he's pleased I noticed.

We chat a little bit, then Anna says goodnight and curls into her bed under the stars. It's only after she turns over, that Jake rolls out his bed, a precise distance from mine, maybe four feet away, close enough to be close but not close enough to be too close.

Soon Jake is lying on his back, next to me, his cowboy hat tipped over his face. His boots are lined up neatly at the foot of his sack, and it's like I stumbled upon him on a movie set.

As if he can feel my gaze, he lifts his hat off his eyes and we exchange a smile.

"Goodnight, Cowgirl."

"I have a name you know," I say, propping up on my elbow.

"I know," he says. He holds my gaze for a moment before disappearing under his hat.

"Good night, Jake."

I want to scoot closer to him. If I stretch my arm and reach out my hand, I can touch him. But I can't touch Jake. Touching Jake would lead to other things.

His face may be hiding under that cowboy hat, but I can feel he's thinking about me, too. It's that thing you only understand once you've experienced it — this pull. This slow, throbbing beat deep inside, like music only you and the person you're drawn to can hear. It plays. It plays loudly, but I do my best to silence it. Cool it down. Ignore it.

A few minutes later I can hear Jake's quiet breathing — even and methodical.

Once it's safe, once I know he's asleep, I watch him for a long time: the rise and fall of his beautiful chest — the simplicity of his beating heart.

Chapter Twenty-Seven

Then

After Elliot, Ty never fully recovered.

Neither did the school.

Or the community. There was no more pretending this wasn't a full-fledged epidemic.

The Coalition of the Willing was baffled. And exhausted. They couldn't sit on the tracks 24 hours a day. When the police jumped into action and placed a new chain link fence with wrappings of barbed wire that looked like bales of hay on top, huge signs that read, "Need Help?" With an 800 number written next to it for the desperate. And for the easily scared off, another sign read: FINE up to $1,000 for playing on or around the tracks. I read them over and over again.

The taboo had been lifted. My peers were taking a permanent exit from childhood and it wasn't into adulthood.

The whole thing was both horrifying and bewildering. I started having panic attacks. I'd have them at school. I'd have them at home. Mom took me to my pediatrician who sent me to a Child and Adolescent Psychiatrist. It was all too much, the therapist told me. So many kids from my school were coming, one after the other. "This time of your life is already so full of uncertainty with applying to colleges, with planning to move away from home—and then all this grief on top of it?" She looked sad for me. She prescribed me an anti-depressant and Xanax for anxiety to be used "When needed."

I didn't get it. I was all set for college. I was accepted to four of my six top choices—and planned on attending Wesleyan on the East Coast. It was Mom's alma mater, and I know this sounds lame as hell, but it reminded me of one of the small, liberal arts colleges on some of the TV dramas I liked. Where the girl crushes on her creative writing professor, and her slutty roommate with a heart-of-gold transforms into her BFF. That's what I wanted: pea coats and steaming mugs of coffee and icy roads. I wanted something new, far away from here.

So I wasn't worried about college per se or even leaving my mom. Since leaving the ranch as a kid, my life hadn't felt grounded, so I didn't have that "I never want to leave my childhood bedroom" thing because I'd already faced that pain. But I was worried about Ty. And getting out of town…well…at all. It was like our class was cursed. Game over. The End.

Our new routine at home and at school was one of polite, dispassionate existence. Scared to rattle anyone, scared to offend, scared to breathe lest they dive in front of a train or overdose on one of their newly prescribed bottles of antidepressants at a party.

It was after one of these long, May days of walking on eggshells at school and jumping at the sight of our own shadows, that we watched the stupidest movie on "family night." After, Ty watched me brush my teeth.

He was wearing his Batman pajamas and a white t-shirt that was tight over his arms. When he lifted them up to stretch, his palms held the sides of the bathroom doorway and his shirt lifted slightly at his belly exposing his belly button. I was thinking, *When did Ty get so hot?*

"Want to check out this crazy Funny or Die video?" he asked.

"Where are the parents?"

"In bed."

Their bedroom was downstairs. Ours were up.

"Are they asleep?"

"I just checked. Yeah."

He just checked?

Why would he need to check?

Chills ran up my torso, but they weren't the bad kind. The space between where he was standing in the doorway and where I was standing over the sink shrunk to nothing. In his eyes, in his voice, I read everything I felt.

Why would our parents need to be asleep for me to go into his room to watch a video?

Right.

"I'll be right there." *Fuck it*, I thought. I was sick of being so...careful. Just once, for one night, I'd let the eggshells crack. What's the worst that could happen?

He nodded, and I kicked the door closed.

I splashed more water on my face. I didn't have to pinch my cheeks to give them color. I didn't recognize myself in the mirror, these bright, hot eyes. This flushed face. I was wearing a white tank top and boy boxer shorts. Why had I felt it was okay to walk in front of him in these? Because our parents got married last year after dating for 6 months?

He was still a teenage boy.

I was still a teenage girl.

I knocked lightly on his door.

"Ty."

"Yeah?" he said, watching me. His gaze ran down my chest, my stomach, down my legs, and I felt it as if his look were his fingertips.

"Um. Your computer isn't open."

He sauntered across the room toward me. He ran his fingers down my naked shoulder slowly, down my forearm, my wrist, my hand. He weaved his fingers through mine and held on tight, so tight. Then, with his other arm, he pulled me into him. I tilted my head back and let my lips meet his with a fiery hunger I didn't know I had in me. My arms flew around his neck and held on tight. His tongue was a crazy thing, digging into my mouth, tugging on my lips. If he were anyone else I would've backed away, but I just let him get crazy, and I shoved him back on that blue comforter and dug into him as he dug into me. With his remote control buried under his pillow he turned up his music to full blast, and we took our rage and frustration and grief and confusion out on each other.

"Do you…have a condom?" I asked.

"Seriously?"

"Well."

I looked down at my tank top, torn, his boxers, half-off.

We were both sweaty and drunk and crazed.

Wasn't sex the obvious next step?

"I don't."

I pulled my shorts back on and stumbled backwards toward the door.

"Where are you going?"

"To get one."

"You have condoms in your room?" he asked, amused.

"Ty, shit, shh."

"Sorry." But he didn't look sorry.

"I figured *you* would."

"Why?"

"Well, you're the one who invited me in."

His eyes sparked. "To watch a video."

"Oh yeah, right. I'll be right back. Hold tight."

I slipped through the dark hall into my room and headed to the top drawer of my nightstand where I kept a little jeweled box filled with Just In Case condoms from Mom.

I'd never done it before.

Ty had. At least once that I knew of. I paused. My head was buzzing pretty badly. Was this the best idea? No, of course not—this was the *worst* idea. But I saw him lying there, and I wanted to be there, too. I wanted Ty, and I was sick of being careful, sick of being numb, sick of being scared: to hell with it.

I grabbed two, sticking them in the elastic waistband of my boxer shorts.

"Got them," I said when I got back to his room, waving them like candy.

"Two? Ambitious, aren't we?" His voice was so sweet in the shadows, and he kissed so well and I couldn't wait to get back to the soft of his skin and the hard of his muscles. I had no idea what this next step would be like, but I could imagine, in my slightly delirious state, that it would be something.

He moved around in the dark, awkwardly for a moment. "Let me help you."

I did.

He was on me in seconds and I opened up my legs to him. The weight of him and everything sinking in…it didn't hurt the way Elena said it would, it was more like an elastic rubber band snapping, and after all the hurt, it felt good. Like scratching an itch too hard, until it was raw.

He moaned. On top of me, his face and lips crushed the side of my neck.

In an instant, he was sound asleep and I was as squirrely as forever.

Where was the fire?

Was that it? Really? I was still so amped up. That couldn't be it.

"Ty. Ty?"

"Hmm," he mumbled, his face in my hair. That was it. He wasn't waking up.

Chapter Twenty-Eight

Now

I stay up way too late watching Jake sleep and then buried in my sleeping bag writing in my journal. When I wake up, squinty eyed and foul-mouthed, I think I'm seeing things when I catch Jake watching me.

"Well, good morning," he says in this slow, heart-melting voice that erases everything else on my mind.

Damn.

"Hi," I say.

"You gonna get up some time this decade or should we just let the cows meander over to the next mountain and disappoint the heck out of your daddy?"

"Oh, shoot. Sorry." I pop up so fast, my ankles catch in my sleeping bag. Jake reaches out, and I sort of fall forward in an awkward heap, right into his arms.

He helps me out of the sack. "Make sure you aren't available for the July 4th sack races, okay?"

"Ha. I'm a ringer, you know," I say, an embarrassed flush crawling up my cheeks.

Jake's gaze falls to a book on the ground. "What's this?"

The book.

My diary.

"Nothing. Just…"

I scoop it up and tuck it quickly into my knapsack. Jesus.

"Is that a diary?"

"No."

He grins. "Were you writing about me?"

"Uh." I wish. I wish my diary was all about Jake. Meeting him. Re-meeting him. I could describe the mountain. The sounds. The smells. I could talk forever about the way my stomach feels when we lock eyes. Or how the sound of my name on his lips makes me feel safe in the way I haven't in maybe forever.

But that isn't this journal.

And he can't see it.

Ever.

"It's just…some stuff I'm working through." There. It's not a lie. It's not even a half-truth. It's the full truth. "And no you can't read it."

"Fair enough." He wipes his palms on his dusty jeans and that's it. "Saved you some grub. Anna, of course, wanted to leave without you—she's such a workaholic—but I convinced her not to leave you behind."

His eyes twinkle.

Smiling, I get on with the leftover beans and mush in the crisp mountain morning air.

"Cows. Everywhere," I say in a monotonic voice.

Jake laughs. "Yep."

White and brown, spotted and not—all lazily munching grass on the top of a hill like it's their minimum wage job and their manager is out of town.

A couple look up, bored, when they see us before bending back to the ground. The rest don't even bother. Like they see people all the time, when I know they haven't for at least six months.

I say my thoughts out loud, then add, "It's like they're thinking,

'Oh, it's just you guys,'" I deadpan, and Anna and Jake laugh.

"They aren't the most emotive creatures," Anna says.

"But damn, do they taste good over a hot fire."

"Jake!"

It's been a good morning, light, easy—shocking after the unlight and unfunny entries scribbled in my journal under the stars last night. As hard as it is to conjure up the memories, it's like the more I write, the less weight presses on my chest. The sharper the words, the more my gut knots unloosen. Well, first they pull tighter and tighter, but then after? It's less. The beginning of that space where you finally get the knot to begin its slow untangle. If that makes sense.

Anyway, I'm getting used to the saddle. In fact, when we take breaks for lunch and to give our mounts a drink in the creek, I miss it. The feel of it, the soothing sway, the rhythm, even the irritating rub of leather against my inner thighs. My butt aches, but it feels good. Like after exercising. I used to feel that way after running on the beach. I haven't done that for a while. Maybe after this trip, I'll see if Jake wants to go on a hike. That might feel good. Walking straight up the mountain.

I talk to Blue while we walk, pat his sweaty neck, give him an apple. I notice he isn't stopping to nibble on bushes anymore and tell Jake.

"He's getting used to you," he says. "He's trying to make you happy."

"I love him," I say.

"Love?" His eyes open wide with curious amusement.

"What? He's a good peep."

Instead of making fun of me, he grins wide and real, and I do the same back before thinking I don't really love that gelding. I love this feeling—the hot sun on my back melting into my dirty plaid shirt. It's been so long since I've had a genuinely good day, and I never want it to end.

Chapter Twenty-Nine

Then

After that first time, Ty came into my room every night for a week. It got better each time, the sex part. He lasted longer, anyway, and didn't always fall asleep right after. We had a consistent plan. We'd brush our teeth, and wash our faces, and get into our PJs. After his dad and my mom were fully quiet, after the *tip tip tip* of their laptops had come to a complete stop. We had a code. Two light knocks.

He'd slip in, and he'd lock my door behind him.

We always kept the lights off and had a plan in case one of the parents knocked. If God forbid the smoke alarm went off, if the phone rang with an emergency, and we were interrupted. He would dive onto the floor and roll under the bed.

In the dark, no one would know.

I wanted him, wanted him badly, and sometimes over and over again. In the dark, I could pretend he was real—that he was my boyfriend, not my stepbrother. That we went to a normal high school where the whole class graduated, where we attended dances instead of funerals. In the dark, I could pretend he was someone else, that I was someone else, or that we were someplace else, together.

"I love you," Ty said after, his nose in my hair, breathing

heat onto the back of my neck.

"You do?" I flinched away from him. I knew he liked me, but love. No. Ty couldn't love me. Not like that. "Why?"

"I don't know." He frowns. "I just do. You don't have to be mean about it."

I rolled over. This was not good. This wasn't what I wanted.

"What's wrong?" he asked, propped up on an elbow.

"Nothing."

"Don't lie. What's wrong?" His voice cracked. "Don't you love me?"

"Ty. Of course. I love...being with you like this, but it's wrong—so, so wrong on so many levels. And there are other girls, Ty. Appropriate girls who aren't your stepsister."

"You're the one I want."

I stared at him over my shoulder.

"What? Don't look at me like that. You're the one I want."

"Why? Because it's wrong? Because you shouldn't?"

I swallowed. Why did Ty want me? Why would he love me?

"Why would you think that? No. I want you because I want *you*. I love you because I love *you*."

I'd heard that before. Dad loved my mom once, too, and we all knew how that ended.

"You don't even know me," I protested lamely.

"That's not true. Why would you say that, Paige?"

Disgusted with myself, disgusted with Ty for being so emotional all of a sudden, I rolled off the bed and pulled on my panties. I told him I had to go to the bathroom. I locked the door and peed. Then, like I always did after, I used a half dozen Wet Ones and wiped the area where he had been even though we always used condoms, and then took a long, hot shower. He didn't like me for me. He liked me because what we were doing was bad and he was hurting and he needed to feel again. That's why I was doing it, and I wouldn't accept anything different from him. As much as I liked Ty, things were getting too crazy. I needed to end it before someone else got hurt.

Chapter Thirty

Now

That night we eat more beans.

Anna boils some water, and we drink hot cocoa out of tin cups that I recognize from childhood. "I wish my dad were here," I say.

Anna and Jake nod. They get it. They do, too, and in a lot of ways they miss him more than I do because they knew him recently. They knew him strong and fit and able, and they know him now. They're the ones watching him disappear before their eyes, helpless to stop it, like one of those nightmares where you try to run and your feet are glued to the ground. And I understand that helplessness, because it happened to me with Ty.

When we finish sipping the cocoa, we lean back on our still-rolled bedrolls and look up at the stars poking through the night. We're listening to the crackling of the fire, snuggling against its heat, when Anna starts humming an old ranch song. As if on cue, Jake pulls a harmonica out of his breast pocket and I sing along, too, this sad, mourning hymn that none of us planned.

Jake abruptly pulls the harmonica from his lips and looks at me with soft, worried eyes. Anna is, too. "What?" I ask.

"You're crying," Anna says.

"What?"

I touch my cheeks, and they're all wet.

I hear the crack in my voice and hiccup and realize she's right. It's too much rehashing all these memories about Ty and now being up here on this mountain where I used to come with Dad. It's all too much. Before, I was able to bury it away, hide it under the numbness, conceal it with my hunger pains from not eating, but now I'm healthy and my mind is as clear as the lake at sunset and I can feel it all, feel everything, and it's the freaking worst.

Anna puts her arm around my trembling, no — convulsing — body and holds me in the crook of her arm. Her plaid shirt and suede jacket smell like my dad — smell just like my childhood. "I'm sorry I'm sorry I'm sorry," I say over and over and over, "I'm so sorry," and she rocks me against her and says in a whisper, "It's okay, everything's going to be okay."

I open my swollen eyes, and over her shoulder, I see Jake watching me. I don't want to look away this time, I don't want to hide from his concern, from his warmth — so I don't.

But I should.

Chapter Thirty-One

Then

"Come on, please," he said.

He was begging.

"I don't feel like it," I said.

"Why not? Did I do something wrong?"

"Yes. You're my stepbrother." *You are a possible date rapist. You don't love me, not really. We're just having guilt-sex because we're still alive.* But if I said all that he'd flip out, or he'd cry and tell me over and over that he was innocent and then start talking about Elliot, and not to be selfish. I didn't want to be insensitive, but I just couldn't do that whole ride tonight.

"I was your stepbrother the other times, too."

"Ty. We can't do this anymore." *I don't want you. I don't want this. It's done.*

"Can I still stay in here?"

My stomach flinched. "Why?"

"I don't want to be alone."

"You can stay, Ty, but I think this better be the last time."

If he heard me, he didn't answer. If he heard me, he didn't agree, because in the middle of the night I woke up with him on top of me. And even though I shoved him off once I realized what was happening, it was already too late.

Chapter Thirty-Two

Now

I sit there after, legs dangling over the granite edge of the cliff, hovering over a deep, black valley — a wide expanse far below me.

If I just moved a few inches forward, that'd be it for me.

Going, going, gone.

Paige, gone, like they are gone.

Why did they do it? What made them stay on the tracks instead of jumping off at the last second? What made Elena slice into her skin, and dripping blood, walk to the tracks? She had to have reached for a towel to stop the bleeding. She must've tickled her phone screen, considering calling 911 and rescuing herself from this useless death. Why didn't she?

Why did I choose to stay on the mountain instead of slipping off into the abyss?

What made the difference between choosing to die and deciding to live?

Was it the weight of sadness that buckled them over and dragged them away from all sane, rational thoughts with an anchor of hopelessness so intense they just gave up fighting? Or was it one day? One night, a night like this one, where a shocking feeling of happiness washed over them, reminding them how sucky life usually is? How hard, how almost impossible it is to cling to the beautiful moments that keep us alive? Keep us fighting through those dark times when those moments are few and far between?

I don't have any answers.

The more I think about it, the fewer answers I have.

Seeing Dad in that chair, fighting so badly to live, to do anything to talk, to breathe on his own, to be able to squeeze the fingers of the woman he loves, to hug his only child, to pat Jake's back when he wants to tell him how proud he is of something—it makes me think they just didn't know better. That they'd lost sight of the wide expanse of life, how the fact that, no matter what their families and friends said, no matter how much pressure, getting into a certain college is only an inkling of a hint of their futures.

If they could be under the stars…if they could realize how very small we are in the grand scheme of things, how we're unlimited potential packed under a thin layer of skin and it's up to us to fight for a piece in all of this wonder…

I know depression is real. That mental illness exists, and some can only fight the darkness for so long until they succumb to it. I get that. But this—the "contagious," copycat suicides—is not that. It's not. It's something else.

It's a ticket off the fast track.

Jumping in front of a train is a ticket out.

I scoot back, way back—a safe distance—suddenly shivering at the close proximity to the cliff and how stupid it is to be on that ledge. Especially in this current mindframe. Mom was right to send me here.

But she was wrong to drag me away from the ranch to a place where people forget what's important, what truly matters, or, more accurately, a place where *I* forgot what was important to *me*. Maybe all that stuff is important to Mom. She wasn't happy here. Here was her misery. But it's not mine. Home was suffocating. Here, I'm free.

I'm listening to the cows graze and thinking all these jumbles of things and then he's next to me, still hot from the close proximity to the campfire. Smelling of its oaky smoke. Like usual, he's chewing on a piece of straw.

"Just wanted to see if you were okay," Jake says.

"Thanks."

"There you go again. You don't have to thank me for checking up on you."

"What should I say?" I swipe at my wet cheek, not wanting him to see anymore of my tears.

"Sometimes you don't have to say anything at all."

I turn to him. "I'm not a cowgirl, Jake. I'm not like you guys."

"No one said you should be." Pause. "What happened back there?"

"It's going to sound stupid to say it out loud."

"Doubt that," he said, leaning into me.

Tilting my chin toward the ground, I lean away. "I—I was happy."

Jake puts his arm around me, and with his other hand, gives me a handkerchief. I blow my nose in it and apologize all over again.

"Now what are you so sorry about? Snuffing up the handkerchief I offered you? If I wanted it to stay clean, I'd stick it in a frame and hang it over my bed."

I can't help but smile. "How high up are we?"

He gives me another squeeze and I feel better. He lets me go and leans back into the dirt, on his hands. I can't see the muscles in his arms but I know they're there, holding him up. "Pretty high."

I blink, looking into the midnight abyss. "If I tell you what happened, you'll hate me."

"I doubt that."

I swallow and scratch at the dirt.

"Look, I get that something bad went down at school, Paige. I get that your dad is dying. I get that the ranch is falling apart and we're scrambling and you're away from home. But I also know that part of you, the part of you that left this place behind, is beginning to find it again. This land"—he stabs at the dirt—"these animals—this is your blood. I remember that hotheaded girl down at the fishing hole and she's still in there. Whatever happened in California is back in California. You have another chance here. Here with us."

It is more than he's ever said at once. It's smart and true and mirrors exactly what I was thinking before he walked up.

I tip my head back, gaze into the endless sky, the countless stars—How can I begin to explain to Jake what I can't understand myself?

"Come here." He lies back and pats the spot where his shoulder meets his chest. I curl into him, and he holds me close with a strong arm so warm, so alive, that I can't help but close my eyes. I breathe in the campfire and his cowboy wisdom and let myself hope he's right. He doesn't try to kiss me. He doesn't take my hand. He doesn't ask for something I'm not ready to give.

Instead he offers exactly what I need.

Chapter Thirty-Three

The next day I'm feeling better, and Jake and Anna teach me how to wrangle cows.

It's like that movie *City Slickers*. We even have a special "Yahoo" cattle call. Jake is awesome, of course. The cows respond to him so easily. Anna, too. I surprise myself by not being half bad, either, some of my earlier skills as a kid falling back into place. I lope after them, raise my arm in the air, give the rope a little spin, and toss it. Half the time it makes its mark, and I jump off my horse and secure the rope on the neck of a partially annoyed cow. All he wants to do is get back to eating. I'm in his way.

"Told ya you were a natural, Cowgirl," Jake says with a little wink from the top of his ride. I grin, and then dodge his eyes. We don't mention last night, but then again why would we ruin it by discussing it? Discussing it would make it real, and real doesn't work. Real doesn't last.

But he knows, and I know how I stayed in Jake's arms for a long time by that ledge.

After a while, with me still in the crook of his arm, he told me stories about the ranch and my dad. Funny stories, light stories, stories that made my heart hurt in the best way. I'd never heard him talk that much. I never had someone work so hard to make me feel better without wanting something back in return.

He reached for my hand on our way back—"Can't see all the rocks on the trail, wouldn't want you to trip"—and I let him take it. I wound my fingers through his, and we didn't talk anymore. We just walked. Walked and were. And when we got back to the campfire all that was left were embers flickering off a charbroiled log and a sleeping Anna. I looked down at our entwined fingers and said, "When we get back, if you still want to know, I'll tell you. I'll tell you everything."

"Only if you want to."

"I'm afraid—you won't think the same of me if you know, Jake. I don't think I could handle that right now."

The last embers of the fire painted his skin with golden light. "Nah," he says in a voice that made me believe him. "If you haven't noticed, I have a weakness for cowgirls."

Chapter Thirty-Four

Then

*D*ance with me.
      No. Ty—knock it off.
Come on, Paige-y…
No.

He was drunk, of course. No wonder everyone believed the date rape rumor. His behavior did little to discount it, and after our last night together I had no doubt he was guilty.

This whole event made me sick. It was prom…sort of. They were going to cancel it. But decided we should have it, just downplay it on account of all the tragedy. Instead of renting a glamorous ballroom, it was held in our gym. Instead of mandatory dates and gorgeous dresses and tuxes, we could wear what we wanted. It was like an anti-prom, and like most things last spring, it sucked. Yet I was there anyway, an active participant.

I was standing with a group of my friends on one side of the gym, leaning against the painted wall mural of our giant mascot who looked way more menacing than our sports teams, when he sauntered over in his baggy jeans, button up shirt, and dark glasses.

Above us, paper vines dangled from the rafters. Stuffed giraffes and apes and panda bears lined the perimeters. A strobe light flashed in our eyes.

"Why are you wearing those?" I asked, gesturing to his glasses. "How can you even see?"

"I can see just fine."

Flicking his glasses on top of his head, he shot me a knowing look.

"Ty, stop." I squirmed away from his skimming eyes, which ran down my chest, landing smack in the middle of my cleavage.

"If not now, later then," he said, breathing boozy breath into my ear.

I shook off hot chills, and hoped the cold shoulder would work.

"See you later, ladies," he oozed, before walking off in a smirk-faux huff.

This acquaintance of mine, Sara, surprised me by saying, "Is it hard having such a hot stepbrother?"

He left me clammy, spent, stressed. "I haven't noticed." I used to think he was attractive, but now he made me sick.

She watched him walk away. "Then you need your eyes checked. Or your mojo."

"Gross."

"Well, it's obvious he's into you."

"Come on, no, he's not." *Next subject please.*

"Paige, please. There's something about him, creepy rumors aside. He's sexy. What was he whispering to you?"

"Nothing."

"Do you think those rumors are true? You know, about the date rape? You live with him. Has he ever, you know, tried anything?"

"Oh my god, of course not. He's my stepbrother."

"*Flowers in the Attic* did it, and they were legit siblings."

"Okay. Can we change the subject please?"

Bile rose in my gut. My heart raced, and I felt like I was going to pass out. "I need to go to the bathroom."

Sarah's smirk matched Ty's when she looked at this other

girl, Keoni, for confirmation. Believe me. I would've loved to have grabbed them by the elbows, yanked them into the girls' bathroom, and confessed everything. Guilt, pleasure, pain, embarrassment—talk about what happened the other night. How I never knew I could feel so many mixed emotions for a person at once. How he equally repulsed and compelled me. How I both needed and was repelled by his touch.

But what if they knew? The truth? The *real* truth. And it spread around? I'd be so embarrassed, so ashamed. To be attracted to your stepbrother is bad enough, but to actually act on that attraction? Having sex with him? Especially someone who already had nasty rumors tied to him that I was pretty sure were true? I was way over my head and I was sinking fast. That had to be taboo in pretty much every culture. Then again, breaking cultural taboos seemed to be our school's theme. What would another one hurt?

I sighed, disgusted with myself.

"You're not going to the bathroom. You're going to catch up with your brother, aren't you?" Keoni said. She wasn't being mean; she was joking. They weren't mean girls. Neither of them had ever had a boyfriend. They didn't even know what they were saying.

I had to get their minds off Ty and me. A shaky laugh escaped my lips, grateful for the shame-hiding darkness. "Hey, Matt Jansen looks pretty hot tonight."

Keoni's black bob moved when she nodded. "He was in Chess Club with me in sixth grade. I always volunteered to be his partner, but I don't think he knows I exist."

"Why don't you ask him to dance, K?"

"No. Way. He's so popular."

I searched the strobe-lit space for Ty.

"Why don't *you* ask him, Paige?"

I didn't see Ty, but that didn't mean he wasn't there. In the crowd. Watching me. Checking to see if I was looking for him.

I spotted him sitting up high in the bleachers watching me.

I needed to prove to my friends there wasn't anything going on between Ty and me. Prove to Ty he couldn't control me. Didn't own me. Couldn't manipulate me or embarrass me in front of my friends.

"Fine," I said.

Matt Jansen was standing with a couple of his friends by the snack table. I didn't really think he was hot. Matt wasn't my type. Nice enough, sure, good looking enough, but nothing between us chemistry wise. But when he caught my eye as I checked him out, he set across the waxy gym floor with a curious eyebrow lift.

"Don't look now but he's coming over here."

"Cool," I said.

Matt was a water polo player, same as Cornell. His blond hair, green eyes, and confident body language screeched "player". Rumor had it he'd screwed the entire cheerleading squad. Twice.

"Hey, Paige," he said. Now Matt was strobe shadows in the dark.

"Hey, Matt," I said.

"I like your dress."

I glanced down at my strapless baby doll dress, my strappy heels.

"Thanks. I like your…" I scanned down over his popped collar polo shirt, tan pants, and shiny white — "shoes," I finished.

"Oh, these old things?"

Wing tips.

Matt also golfed professionally on the weekends and had since he was six. Once in fourth grade I remember him telling me he wasn't allowed to climb trees because an injury could "ruin his golf game."

He was essentially the opposite of my type.

But the simple fact that Matt wasn't Ty made him worthy of tonight's attentions. So when he cocked his head and asked, "Want to dance?" it was easy to reply, "Sure. Why the hell not?"

I ended up in the back of Matt's car.

It was the last place I wanted to be, but I had to prove to Ty and my friends that there was nothing going on. I had to prove to Ty that I wasn't his. He couldn't demand anything of me. He couldn't have sex with me when I was asleep.

Ty was still sitting on the top row of the bleachers when, hand in hand, we left the dance. He watched us, glaring.

Matt had a flask, and I leaned back against the leather seat and took a huge gulp. It burned my throat like hellfire. I liked the burn, liked the way it numbed me. Made me wade half in and half outside this horrific reality. Matt's eyes were red, watery, his smile as weak as my convictions were strong.

"The dance was kind of weird wasn't it, considering all that's going on?"

His comment surprised me. I thought it'd be more like, "Ready to do it?" More like Ty. He was all I knew.

"The school dance committee thought it would be a good thing. Normalizing."

"Do you think it was normalizing?"

He was tipsy. Vulnerable. He wanted to chat, bond even.

I didn't. I took another chug from the flask. Vodka?

"Cornell was a good friend of mine." Pause. "God." He ran his hands through his thick chlorine-blond hair. "I can barely say his name without feeling sick. I just don't understand why he did it? Sure, he had girlfriend troubles and parent issues, but who doesn't? That's just life…high school LIFE, you know? I just…I miss him. And putting a bunch of stuffed monkeys around isn't going to change that. Isn't going to make that go away, you know?"

"I'm sorry," I said.

My head was light. Reality drifted away.

"Yeah, so am I," he said. His green eyes filled with tears. "You're smart, Paige. You're one of the few girls here who is both smart and hot. You know that's a rare combination. And you seem really cool, too, and funny…I like that…"

Matt was also drunk. He must have pre-partied pretty hard.

"Thanks," I said. I eyed the door handle. I could still get out of this. Go back to the gym, find my friends, go home.

No, this was better. If I did it with this daft water polo player, I would erase the evidence of Ty. The trails he left all over my body like snail slime. The ones that made me sick with guilt, like every bit of pleasure we stole in the beginning was bought with the blood of our classmates, and now that he wasn't accepting no for an answer, had birthed my shame. I couldn't live like that anymore.

This water polo playing guy I'd known for most of my life but didn't really know at all, slumped into my side and nibbled drunkenly on my ear.

I took another gulp out of the flask.

"Did you lose any friends?" His voice was wet and needy.

"Not really," I said.

"You're lucky."

"I guess."

"I wasn't so lucky." He talked and talked and talked while he awkwardly fondled my chest. The alcohol was catching up to me. Soon, I was so drunk the car spun upside-down and flipped even though we hadn't moved out of the parking spot. My head bobbed as I struggled to see straight. Tried to listen.

"You're a mess," I slurred. "A confused mess. Don't worry, we're all a confused mess."

"Why did they pick a jungle theme for prom? Why not ocean or fantasy land or New York, New York? It's a metaphor, right? It's a JUNGLE OUT THERE. Right? *Right?*"

Maybe I should tell him about Ty. Tell him that he raped me in my sleep. That I wanted him before, but now I want to toss him onto his bed and pour lighter fluid all over him and burn him down and the house, too. That Ty's the only person that understands the banshee part of me howling into the night. This horrible boy that I used to desire and now detest. That I stood outside my mom's door, crying, with my hand limply shaped like one about to knock, but couldn't do it, because what in the world would I say? *I've been having sex with Ty, but when I decided to stop, he didn't want to?* I could've, yes, but she wouldn't have done anything. She would have either ignored me, pretended she hadn't heard me, or sent me off somewhere. I couldn't leave. I had to graduate from school. In the end, I peeled off my bed sheets, stormed down the stairs, and shoved them into the backyard garbage bin.

Kids were dying. My sordid sexual relationship with my stepbrother wasn't death.

But I didn't say anything to the polo player. I sat there, nodding, while he rambled on and on. When I couldn't listen to that kid for a second more, I grabbed his hand and stuck it all the way down my shirt. I needed to get on with this and get home.

His response was immediate.

He struggled into a condom and climbed on top of me. While we were sort of doing it—I couldn't feel much down there on his end, which confirmed the rumors I'd heard—I stared over his shoulder at the heels of his scuffed white dress shoes, his golfing wing tips, resting neatly on the backseat floor and thought about how, as a kid, he should've opted for tree climbing over golf. How his shoes needed a good cleaning.

A s promised, later that night, Ty came to my room.
He stumbled into my room, drunk, wobbling like the freaking Scarecrow after Dorothy freed him from the stand, a monologue on his lips.

This time I'm ready.

"You just don't get it, Paige. I'm sorry about last night but I've lost everything…everyone is gone and it's that sound of the train whistles and the horns and the screams, and it's all I hear over and over and over in my head. The only time I don't hear it is when I'm in here, in here with you, and only then it stops for even a few minutes"—he held out his hands for emphasis—"and I get that you think I'm pathetic, and I know I shouldn't be in here and I feel pathetic, too, I do, I do. Don't you think I can't see how you see me, how you look at me? But when I'm with you, it's the only time I don't hear the horns and the screams."

"Ty, you are a liar. You are a date rapist. I never should have gotten involved with you."

"No. No. Don't say that."

"It's true and you know it. Get out of my room or I'll tell my mom, Ty. I swear. I'll scream."

"I can't see you with other guys like that." He moaned into the darkness. "Please don't do that to me again. I don't know what I'll do if I see you with him again. Please, Paigy, please."

"Get out of my room and go to sleep, Ty. I'll sleep with whomever I wish. We're done."

Chapter Thirty-Five

Now

B right lights, screaming train whistles, and drunken breath on my face roar through this nightmare of darkness, and I'm screaming. But it isn't a train or Ty that rips me from my dreams—it's Jake, gently shaking me awake. Because I'm too delirious to stop myself, I throw my arms around his neck and he holds me like that, soft but strong, on top of my sleeping bag until I'm not scared anymore.

"Thanks, Jake," I whisper into his neck after a while. "I'm okay now."

"One of these days you're going to stop thanking me," he says back, low and weighty, before tucking a piece of my hair, damp with sweat, behind my ear. He may have even kissed my cheek, but that would be too sweet and perfect for even a dream to muster.

T he ride back to the ranch is relaxing and slow. Anna rides in front, and Jake and I lag behind, chatting, mostly side-by-side. He points out various things on the trail. An eagle's nest clustered in the top of a tall pine, erosion from last winter's storm, one of his favorite fishing holes. He doesn't ask me anything about home, honoring what I said last night, and I appreciate that he doesn't push.

We stop for lunch, and he spreads peanut butter between two pieces of wheat bread. "Want jelly?" he asks.

"Sure, if you have some."

Nodding, he opens a little packet with his teeth and squeezes the purple blob onto the creamy peanut butter. "Unfortunately, it's the packaged stuff."

"It's fine. Every day can't be an Anna Original. You brought wheat bread?" I observe with a surprised grin.

"I did. You don't like the white stuff, health nut," he teases.

"That's so sweet."

He wrinkles his nose, blowing it off like it's nothing. "You know what they say about California…"

But it *is* something. He was thinking about me, and not just in the *How Are You?* kind of way, but also in the *I Listen To What You Want, I Pay Attention To What You Need* way, which makes me feel light.

"Did you run this store-bought grape jelly by Anna?"

"Huh?"

"Well, the mere fact that it's not strawberry could offend her."

He laughs and leans in, breathing lightly in my ear. "Between you and me, I'm getting damn sick of strawberry."

Our eyes meet and we laugh.

"What are you two giggling about?" Anna tosses us a harsh look but her eyes are light.

"Nothing," we say in unison. Then laugh some more.

When we get back, Dad is sitting at the kitchen table having his smoothie with the aid. After initial greetings, he types, *Looks like you three had a good camp out?*

"We did," I say, and tell him all about it.

After, he types, *It makes me happy to see you happy.*

I look up at Jake, who is a big part of the reason I'm so

happy, and guilt rattles through me.

I shouldn't be happy, not with him suffering so badly. Not with…

Dad notices my uneasiness and types, *It's okay to smile, Paige. You've always had a beautiful smile.*

"Thanks, Dad," I say. Then I notice a page opened in the Jackson Hole Gazette. "What's this?"

I scan the words.

TENTATIVE ENTRY FEES

Bareback Riding…………..$50

Saddle Bronco Riding………$50

Bull Riding………………….$50

Mini Bulls…………….$25

4D Barrel Racing………..$30

Pee Wee Barrels……..$10

Calf Roping………..$35

Breakaway…………$30

Team Roping

#1……………$40

#8……………$25

Mutton Busting…….$10

"Jake? What's this?" I follow him into the kitchen and set the flyer down on the counter. While I'm waiting for his answer, I pour myself coffee, choosing, from the neatly lined up rack, a navy blue mug with GOD BLESS COWBOYS written in bold text. Jake opens the fridge and pops open a cold can of Diet Dr. Pepper.

"Rodeo entry fees."

"Oh."

"The real prize money is in the bulls," Jake says into his already halfway empty, sloshing can.

I remember what Anna told me about the way Jake's dad died.

"Bareback and saddle isn't as dangerous, Jake, and the money is still good," Anna says from the other end of the kitchen where she's tossing dirty clothes from our camping bags into the washing machine.

"Not good enough."

"It will have to be."

"What are you guys talking about?" I can't help asking.

"The entry application for Nationals. Jake wants to ride the bulls. We both know it's too dangerous."

"The money is good, Paige," he says to me, ignoring Anna.

"Saving the ranch kind of good?"

He smiles a bit, turning to Anna. "She gets it."

"That's because she doesn't understand the danger the way you and I do. The way you and I *should*." Anna wipes her palms on her apron, looking at him pointedly.

"Jake rodeos already, doesn't he? That's what he said anyway."

"He rides wild bucks, like that Maverick we have out in the corral now. It's still dangerous, but not as dangerous as the bulls."

They named that gorgeous, fiery horse *Maverick*? Ugh. "What's the difference in prize money?"

"Depends on which round we get to," Jake says. "Could be enough."

"Enough to save the ranch?"

"Could be. If we can talk Anna here into letting me enter."

"Why does..." I stop myself before Anna's eyes do.

She answers anyway. "We're family. We have to agree on this kind of thing. We promised Jake's mama, after what happened to his daddy, no more bulls."

Jake grits his teeth and flashes Anna an annoyed look, shaking his head a little like that was a ridiculous thing to promise. "Wish you'd stop using that as an excuse."

To break the tension I say, "I used to barrel rope when I was a kid. It was fun. We had a little practice space outside in the corral. Remember, Daddy?" I cross back over to the circular table and sit down next to him.

You were great, he types. Jake and Anna join us around the table, Jake's chair scratching the linoleum when he scoots in.

"Maybe I can enter something," I say, mostly to get Anna and Jake off the obviously tender subject of bulls.

That would take a lot of practice, Dad types.

"Jake can help me," I blurt out. "You *can* help me, right, Jake?"

Jake meets my eyes over the lip of his can to see if I'm being serious. When he sees that I am, he nods.

"On Maverick?" I ask, still hating the name.

"The mustang you've been giving apples to all week?"

Anna sighs. "Is that where my apples been disappearing to? And I was all set to make apple pie, too."

Jake and I exchange a smile. The shadows from a moment ago vanish. "Well, one of my goals this week is to start breaking her in. But I don't know if she'll be ready to enter rodeo. Or if you'll be ready to ride."

"I'm getting pretty comfortable on Blue."

"Sure, but comparing Blue to that 'stang is like comparing Anna's apple pie to jalapeño peppers. She's got bite in her."

"I want to try."

"Well, there ain't no harm in you watching," he says, looking to Anna for approval. She nods, shrugs, and wanders back into the kitchen mumbling about stolen apples and stubborn cowboys under her breath.

The horse Jake wants to break is anything but fragile. Golden red and strong, with a white mark on her forehead that sets her apart, she is completely different than Old Blue. Her eyes are wild, her body lithe and muscular in a way that tells me she only eats enough to keep her strong. When Jake quietly approaches her, the wild horse paws at the dirt, and blows air through her nostrils so hard I can almost see the smoke. She paws at the dirt again, looking at Jake like she's going to pierce a hole in his chest if he makes the wrong move.

Jake stops and, while he slowly winds a thick blue rope around his forearm, he carefully avoids eye contact with the frantic animal, making a *shhh, shhh, shhh* noise. After a while, Maverick's hooves stop beating the dirt. The breaths through her nose are more natural and less erratic.

With his head down, Jake inches closer. Maverick lets Jake get close enough to reach out his palm and offer it up for a sniff. The horse snorts up Jake's scent and instead of nudging into him like she would if this were a movie and not real life, Maverick neighs angrily into the air. Tossing her head back, she recoils.

Chapter Thirty-Six

The next day he tries again.

"She just needs to get used to me is all," he says in his ever-optimistic way after she chases him out of her corral. Jake narrowly escapes her wrath by leaping over the fence and crashing into me, sending us both tumbling to the dirt.

Maverick catches my eye and from the looks of hers, she's laughing at us.

"Maybe she doesn't like you because you gave her a boy's name." I don't take my eyes off the horse. It's hard to stop looking at such a fine creature.

Jake snorts, still sore from this loss. "Maverick's a fine name."

"Not for a girl."

"She's not a girl. She's a mare. And she's half mustang. This is a wild horse and a good thing, too."

"Because she's so easy to train?"

My tease is met with a cocked eyebrow.

"No, smarty pants, because a lot of cowboys name their mares boys' names. You have a better one for her?"

Cupping my face in my hands, I study her white mark on her forehead; it looks like a broken wing.

"Scout."

"Scout?" He nods. "I had a mare named Scout once. That's

a good name."

"Glad you like it."

"How'd you think of that?"

"Her mark looks like a broken wing, which made me think of a mockingbird—you know, Harper Lee—so obvious deduction is Scout."

"Your brain must be an interesting place to reside."

"Interesting is one word to describe it," I say wryly, and he laughs. "So give it a try. See if she likes you more with her new and improved name."

He tries.

First he circles, the slow approach. Dirt scratches into the air, warm, nose huffs irritation, ending, again, with a furtive dismissal as Scout chases Jake out of her zone. He does this dive roll over the fence, landing on his ass in the dirt. Jake throws his hands in the air. "Don't know what I'm doing wrong."

I'm thoroughly amused as I offer him a hand up. "Is this the first horse who's rejected you, Jake?"

"Yes, as a matter of fact, she is."

"Well, you haven't earned her affection yet. That's all."

"Oh, really. You want to give it a try then, hot shot? Be my guest." He hands me the rope. It's boa constrictor thick.

"Sure, why not?" I know she's not going to hurt me. She wouldn't have hurt Jake either—she just wanted to scare him out of her area.

"Just stay back. Stay calm," he advises unnecessarily. "That sound I was making, it's also how you soothe a crying baby. Do it over and over again. *Shhh. Shhh. Shhh.*"

Right. His lips are all puckered, and it's halfway between hilarious and hot and then I'm practicing too, *Shhh. Shhh. Shhh. Shhh.* Scout's looking at me like I'm nuts.

"Don't make eye contact with her. You don't want to make her think you're challenging her. Approach slowly."

Cautiously, I climb over the fence, keeping my eye on him without making eye contact with Scout.

Her energy changes when I enter the corral. She bends her head down and kicks at the dirt, it sputters into the air as she snorts and grinds. I glance over at Jake for guidance. What if I was wrong? Am I fast enough to get over the fence in time if she charges?

His nod is reassuring. "It's okay. Slowly."

I stop for a second, keeping my gaze on her hooves, avoiding her eyes. *Shhh, shhh,* I say, while Scout adjusts to my being here.

Then I take another step forward.

And another.

In the noonday heat, I circle her, ever so cautiously, keeping her tensely muscled frame in my peripheral vision. I step inside as I circle slowly so she won't know how close I'm actually getting.

I'm close.

And then I'm right there beside her.

"Easy, easy," I say, quietly. "Easy, girl." I hold out my palm and let her sniff my skin. I don't touch her. I don't look directly into them, but I can see her eyes are fiery, and I know our newfound intimacy will be short-lived if I push too much too soon.

Chapter Thirty-Seven

Then

I think a lot about secrets.

How everyone has them: Elena and Golden Boy and Elliot and Ty and me. Mom. How we keep our true feelings buried so deeply beneath the surface no one knows what we're feeling or thinking until it's too late to help. To make them see through the junk to find the treasure.

I tried to make Ty see we could be there for each other without doing that with each other. He didn't see it the same way.

"Next group, come with us," said the counselor at the doorway. We left homeroom in groups of four to go to school board assigned trauma therapy.

Since Ty was in my homeroom and sat next to me, naturally we were in the same group. In a sterile room with chain hotel style art on the walls, we sat around one of those round tables with the fake wood tops that smelled like someone recently sprayed it down with an antibacterial spray.

The chairs were metal folding chairs and I thought about the gum and who knows what else that lurked under the clean surface.

"How are you all feeling?" the counselor, Mr. Fenrick,

asked. He leaned in, and the bald spot on the top of his head glowed like it'd also been rubbed to shine. But his question shone through kind, brown eyes.

"Okay," one girl, Rachel said.

"Fine," one boy, A.J., said.

"Shitty," my brother, Ty, said.

Instead of correcting him for vulgar language, the man in the shirt and tie leaned in and said, "Thanks for being honest. How so?"

"I feel like I'm trapped in a video game with no exit."

"Hmm. And how does that make you feel?"

"Shitty."

"Right."

"Ty," I said, quietly. I was hoping this would be an in-and-out kind of thing. We were all required to attend group therapy once a week now. Check in, in case we were thinking about checking out.

"What?" he glared at me before turning back toward the counselor.

"What about the rest of you? Paige? Can you relate to what Tyler is saying?"

"Sure, but I wouldn't say it like that."

"Yes, well everyone expresses themselves in different ways."

Yeah, like some of us show up drunk night after night banging on their sisters' doors, while some of us turn up the volume so loud on their iPods, we'll probably have irreversible hearing damage later in life.

"How would *you* say it?" He cocked his head. His eyes were warm and open. Was that something he trained in? Listening? It made me uncomfortable, all this focused listening.

My household existed in short sentences of declaration and question. "Who wants Thai food?" and "Did you take the trash out?" and "I'll be home after you're asleep. Don't forget to lock up." There wasn't a lot of eye contact.

I squirmed in the metal chair.

"Things aren't great. We've had multiple suicides at our school that are supposedly contagious, only there is no antidote or serum or vaccine to prevent us from catching it. And we're all aware how ridiculous that sounds. I mean, I'm aware and I'm the one saying it. How could something like wanting to end your life be contagious? It isn't a runny nose. It's your life. What Ty said makes sense, it does feel like being trapped in a video game."

"But do you see an exit?"

I shrugged. "There's always an exit."

"Thank you, Paige. You're right in feeling like there is no rhyme or reason to it. Sometimes, people are looking for a way out. A way out of their misery, and so when one person makes a tragic mistake and commits suicide, it opens the flood gates, releases the taboo, so to speak, and that is why others follow."

This made sense. But.

"So they were already planning to kill themselves and one of us actually going through with it gave them the green light? I don't buy that."

I didn't buy that.

I couldn't buy that.

So many of us were that miserable?

Was *I* that miserable?

I looked at my tablemates. Rachel with the same bob cut she'd been sporting since the fifth grade. Her whole routine of matching socks with her Polo shirt and white tennis shoes that looked so clean she must have twenty pairs. The handle of her tennis racket stuck out of her light blue backpack. She probably had practice after school.

Did she want to die? If so, how? And when? On the court? During a match? After?

What about A.J. with his curly black hair, brown eyes, checkered-hipster shirt, and hipster glasses? He was fumbling with ear buds dangling out of his white painter pants. He just wanted to get back to his music. His scruffy black and white

Vans tapping on the floor told me he was listening to music in his head.

Did he want to die?

No.

No way.

Or did he?

The counselor addressed Ty again.

"Granted I haven't played video games since I was a kid"—Mr. Fenrick looked about forty-five—"but after we won one round we just went to the next level."

"If you don't get killed."

"Right. Which I did many times," he kind of joked, but it fell flat. "What I'd like you guys to do for me this week is to visualize instead of the game ending, advancing to the next level. Moving on. Moving forward. I'd like you to write up different endings. Be as creative as you like."

"Will we get extra credit?" Tennis Rachel asked.

"Sure. So can you do that?"

We needed to move forward. Move on. From each other.

When I thought about what the counselor said, an alternate ending to my video game, this is what I saw.

A computerized image of me running one way.

Ty running another.

A clean split.

I said this to Ty after school when he was playing video games and I was watching him from the wood floor of our entryway.

He didn't look up at me.

"You enjoyed our little visit with the shrink, then?" he asked.

"I found it helpful, yeah."

"As helpful as sleeping with that douchebag water polo player after the dance?"

So he wasn't *that* drunk.

"It's none of your business what I do."

He made this sort of snorting noise. "You just did it to make me jealous."

On the flat screen, overly bloated soldiers exploded. Blood splattered. Heavy artillery. Gushing arteries. *Boom. Boom!*

"No, I didn't."

"Uh-huh. Because you're usually really into douchebag water polo players. They're *exactly* your type."

"What is this?" I grimaced at the realistic graphic violence on the screen. "It's disgusting."

"It's fun. Want to play?"

"No."

"Oh, come on, don't be such a buzzkill."

I sat next to him and he handed me a controller.

"I get to pick my own soldier."

"Go ahead."

He clicked back to the menu screen. My choices were a beefcake marine named Buzz who looked like an even more bloated version of the one who just exploded, a tall, redhead aptly named Red, and a shapely woman with a full head of bleach blonde hair named Goldie.

"This is so sexist. Like she'd be able to run around like that shooting people with her boobs falling out of her uniform."

"Are you kidding? She's hot."

"Well, she might be HOT, but what she's outfitted in isn't PRACTICAL. For war or any other activity."

Ty deadpanned, "This is a futuristic world of zombies and mayhem. Practicality isn't the number one concern. Staying alive is the goal."

"Still," I said.

Even though our subject matter was ridiculous, it was nice talking like this. Almost like things were normal again, but his voice had an edge to it, and I kept my guardrails up.

"Put your machine gun where your mouth is, then." His eyes were bright, challenging.

"Lovely, Ty."

"You know what I mean."

"Fine. I think I will." I matched his tone.

If we were going to move on, move forward, we had to get back to doing normal brother and sister things.

Sitting on the floor.

Playing video games.

Normal.

I chose Goldie and she/we proceeded to kill zombies like a freaking maniac. By the time it was over, I was all amped up, there were zombie bodies everywhere, and my zombody count was at 147.

"Is this what you meant by moving on? Letting me be killed by zombies?" Ty asked.

"I didn't…oh." My stepbrother naturally chose Buzz, and there he was, dead, in a heap of zombies, brain partially eaten.

"Sorry," I said, sheepishly. "You almost made it to the safety zone."

"Almost," he said. "Only works in horseshoes and hand grenades."

"I'm pretty sure that's not at all how that saying goes."

"And I'm pretty sure you know that you didn't have to go off with Matt in order to make me want you."

"That's not why I did it, Ty."

"Who cares why you did it? I noticed. The end. Now do you want to reboot and play again or what?"

Did I want to reboot and play again?

No. I was trying to be friends. I was trying to be stepbrother and stepsister. Sitting on the floor in front of a stupid video game was how all this started and it made sense that this is where it would end. At least in my mind.

Maybe it was his voice. Maybe it was the darkness in his eyes. Maybe it was my behavior last night, first at the dance, lying to my friends, and then going off with a boy I wasn't even slightly attracted to.

None of this I wanted.

Not even remotely.

And something shifted in me. I couldn't worry about Ty's feelings anymore. If he was going to hate me forever, so be it.

Chapter Thirty-Eight

Now

I'm right back out there the next morning.

Scout looks up at me from her alfalfa with an expression of part curiosity, part recollection, but nothing about her says she's about to submit.

I appreciate her honesty.

Climbing onto the lower rung of the splintered fence, I lean back, stretching my arms. My head falls back and I watch the sky while she eats. Then, hoping that she's freshly full from alfalfa and a healthy slurp of fresh water, I approach her.

It's easier this time. She doesn't paw at the dirt as I move closer and closer.

My heart races as I reach out my palm, but instead of rearing up and beating me to death with her powerful hooves, she nuzzles her velveteen nose into my hand. I reach into my pocket and pull out a handful of sweet feed—a mix of oats, corn, and syrup—which she gobbles up. When I dig for another handful and offer it up, she graciously accepts. We do this dance for a while and instead of avoiding my eyes, instead of me avoiding hers—we look at each other. Really look. It's spontaneous and slightly mad but I know what I want. I know exactly what to do—how to fix everything. I run into the house and announce,

"I'm entering the rodeo and I'm going to ride Scout!"

Anna is mid-coffee sip and sort of sputters out the hot liquid, mopping it up with a hand-embroidered napkin and looking at me like Scout had that first day with a mix of contempt and curiosity.

"I must not have heard you correctly. You didn't just say you were planning on entering Scout in the rodeo?"

"I did."

"What? How?" Anna speechless is a new thing. She looks up at Jake who sort of shrugs, like, hear her out.

"She likes me. Ask Jake. She lets me approach her and doesn't kick me, or," I make eye contact with Jake, "chase me out of the corral, like she does with some people."

"Hey now, you want me on your side or not?"

I grin over at him.

"Eating sweet feed out of your hand is not the same as performing in a stadium with hundreds of noisy cow folks looking on. You know what you'd have to do? It's breaking her in. She'll buck you off. She doesn't want to be ridden," Anna says.

I shrug. "Then she can buck me off."

"Paige." Anna sighs. Her tone with Jake is irritable, too. "Jake? Jump in anytime."

"Scout does seem a bit taken by Paige," he says, purposefully. The straw sticking out from his lips again. "She won't let me get anywhere near her, and she is the mare I was planning on competing."

"You'll help me then, Jake?"

"Do I have a choice?" His tone is wry, perhaps for Anna's sake, but he doesn't hide the spark in his eye over this new challenge of breaking in both the city slicker and the mare.

I grin, clasping my hands together. "It's settled then. How do I sign up?"

Anna sighs, tapping the side of her skull. "It's your head, kid. But you need to get your daddy to approve before I'll even consider it."

Chapter Thirty-Nine

I knock lightly on Daddy's door.

He's sitting in his chair facing out the window when I tentatively approach.

When I don't see him for a couple hours and get caught up in something else, I sometimes forget he's sick. I see him, the old him, everywhere on the ranch—tilting his cowboy hat into the sky, riding across the dirt—in all my memories. But then I see the new him again, and it hits me as hard as it did the first day on the ranch when he wheeled onto the porch, transformed, fading, and each day fading more.

The hum of his respirator is the only sound in the wide expanse of bedroom he used to share with my mom. It's so different than the room she shares with Ty's father in California. His bed is the same handmade knotty pine. Even the bedspread and pillow shams are the same, baby blue gingham.

Mom's bed at home is glossy silver. On her wall hangs three framed pen and ink drawings of Chinese symbols. On her armoire sits a simple bamboo plant.

I can't even imagine her in this room now, but I blink and there she is, sitting with Dad in bed, reading the newspaper and drinking coffee. They're laughing about something I'm saying.

I'm eight and big toothed, with skinny legs not yet used to my growth spurt, and I'm standing at the base of their bed, begging Dad to take me fishing.

"Let your daddy rest a bit, Paige."

"What kind of cowboy says no to a fishing offer from a pretty lady?" Dad says, shooting me a wink. He hops out of bed and pulls on his jeans.

"But this is your day to sleep in," Mom says.

"I'll sleep when I'm dead," he says. "And I'll see *you* later," he tells her in a voice that makes eight-year-old me think yuck, but damn if I wouldn't beg to hear it now. To see her respond, with a smile so bright and full of love, "Have fun you two! And bring home some trout big enough for supper!"

Now Dad sits quietly staring out the window.

I swallow hard. It's not getting easier.

I touch his shoulder and sit in the high-backed chair next to him where Mom would be if she were here.

"Daddy? I have an idea. And before you say no, please hear me out."

His watery eyes rest on mine. There's a bit of crust in the right one. I move for the hand towel Anna keeps over his chair to wipe it off, but stop. Retreat. I'll tell Anna about it later. She doesn't want me doing any of Dad's basic care. That it would be too humiliating for him, she says. I disagree. I'm here, why can't I help? But I honor what she wants. What he wants. I do my best to act like a normal daughter. Daughters don't wipe their father's sticky eyes. Maybe they do in an ideal world, but this isn't an ideal world. Whatever. I pick my battles. I clear my throat to pick one now.

"Dad, I'd really love to try to ride that mustang—we call her Scout now—I'd love to try to ride her in the bareback competition...i-if it's okay with you."

His eyes twitch, his version of widening.

I swallow. "Yeah, I know. It sounds a little crazy, but I think I can do it. She's really taken to me. Even Jake says so. If I work hard, I could get her to let me ride her and…"

I stop talking as I watch his fingers move over the device in his keyboard that gives him words.

Bareback is a whole different story, Paige, sweetheart. She'll buck you clear off.

"I don't think so, Daddy. I want to try."

No. You'll get killed, or worse, end up like me.

I blink. "Being like you isn't worse than being dead. Don't say that."

He doesn't answer. Does he mean that? Does he want to die? Does he really think that would be better?

I'm grateful for each sunrise and each sunset, he types.

"Me, too," I say, and I am. "I want to try. I really want to try."

Proud of you, Paige. But let's try and think of something else, okay?

In my daydream, instead of closing his eyes to the hum of his respirator as the sun shines yellow stripes on his baggy gray sweat pants, Dad leaps up, grabs my hand with his left hand and his tackle box with his right, and together we take a dusty walk to the creek. In the new morning sun, we brainstorm ideas together, smart and brave.

In real life, I lean in close, my forehead on his arm, and I hope he changes his mind as we talk in this new way.

Chapter Forty

Then

The following week, the five of us sat around the same table in the same exceedingly uncomfortable chairs. It was Ty's turn to talk.

"I have another problem in addition to the video game one," he said.

"Oh?" The counselor leaned forward, actively listening.

"Yes. I'm in love with someone. A girl. But she isn't in love with me."

"The trials and tribulations of young love," Mr. Fenrick said like he was teaching a Shakespeare class. I groaned and slunk lower in my chair. "Is this girl your girlfriend?"

He cocked an eyebrow in my direction. "Not exactly."

Melt floor. Cave in. Earthquake?

"Well, does she reciprocate your feelings?"

Oh. God.

"At first, yes. But now she's just a tease. You know those types."

Mr. Fenrick frowned. Took off his glasses, and leaned in. "Not necessarily. What do you mean by that?"

"You know, leading you on, then backing off when things get heated."

He was such an asshole. My fists clenched under the table. Heat crawled from my thighs to my belly where it turned into bile.

"Sounds like she's changed her mind. As a young, responsible man, you need to respect that."

"Exactly," I said out loud.

The other students looked confused. Ty tipped back his chair so far I thought he would fall backwards. I hoped he'd fall backwards and split his head.

"Mr. Fenrick?" I said. "I—we…I mean, can I be excused? I need to use the restroom."

I gathered up my stuff and fled. I ran into the bathroom and turned on the water. I splashed my face. When I looked up, Ty's image joined me in the mirror. With a yelp, I jumped.

I spun around. "Are you insane? What are you doing in here?"

"We need to talk."

"No." I poked his chest. "You need to listen. You have to leave me alone. You have to stop thinking about me. What was your plan back there, huh? To out us to Mr. Fenrick—to the whole school? Don't we have enough problems without bringing our personal issues to the public?"

"Maybe." He stared at me with this horrible intensity. *Blink, Ty, blink.* He didn't blink. "I don't know."

I swallowed. He was crazy. This was dangerous and getting worse by the day. When I tried to push past him, he pressed a hand on either side of the wet sink, trapping me. "Let me go, Ty."

"No. You'll run off and you won't listen to me. What happened the other night…I shouldn't have done it. I thought you wanted to. You let me sleep in there and you smelled so good and once we started you seemed to like it."

"I said no, Ty! I pushed you off. If you weren't my stepbrother, if I didn't want anyone finding out about us, you'd be in JAIL for that."

His face was inches from mine when he growled, "Right. Who'd believe you?"

"You're insane."

"You're the one putting me there."

His face was contorted like a psychotic character in a film—angry one second, despondent and pathetic the next. Did he honestly think he'd done nothing wrong? I stopped. "Putting you there? Ty." I glanced at the door to make sure no one was coming in. "I ended things between us. I'm trying to do the right thing."

I grabbed his forearms, pushed at them.

"The right thing for you, maybe. What about the right thing for me?"

"I cannot be the right thing for you." I squeezed his arms harder, tried to shove them out of the way. He held tight—his muscle tensing under my touch. "Ty, move."

"No. I'm not going to let you run away from me. I know you want this as much as I do. Remember. *Remember* how good we are together."

He tried to kiss me. I recoiled and slapped his cheek. Hard. Then shoved him so hard he fell back into the mirror. I ran out of the bathroom, ran down the open corridors. When I couldn't run anymore, I slowed to a brisk walk, my heart pounding. Trembling, I got out my phone, dialed my mom's number. Got her voicemail and hung up again. I thought I could control this. I thought I could control Ty. I couldn't.

He followed me off campus. Down the sidewalks. All the way home. We didn't speak until we were a couple blocks away from anyone who might have overheard.

"I'm sorry. Wait up. Paige, I'm sorry."

"Get away from me, Ty!" I fumbled with the house key. But what would going inside do? He'd follow me in and harass me there. Or attack me.

"I only want you."

I shook my head so hard my brain rattled. "That's crazy talk."

"It's true." He grabbed my wrist.

"Ty. You have to stop this or…"

"Or what? You'll tell your mom? You'll tell your dad? You'd never." He was smiling now, in this weird challenging way that made me want to kill him.

"Leave me alone," I said. "You're s-scaring me."

His eyes changed from hostile to desperate as quick as an afternoon storm. He slumped down on our front porch. Head hanging down, he tugged his fingers through his hair. "What if I wasn't your stepbrother? Would that make a difference?" His eyes were hopeful.

"Not after what happened the other night and just now in the bathroom. No."

His eyes narrowed. "I said I was sorry about that."

I looked at him. I looked at his too-big designer pants, his backward baseball cap, his two-hundred-dollar sunglasses, his sloppy come-hither grin and sarcastic quips he hid behind. Trappings. Like those glue traps people put out to catch mice and rats, leaving them to starve to death, never able to reach the glob of rotten cheese that had lured them there in the first place.

I was the mouse in Ty's trap and I had no idea how to get out.

Chapter Forty-One

Now

Whether it's bareback or saddled, I'm determined to ride Scout without breaking her.

I hate that phrase—breaking—and, as we approach the corral, I tell Jake so.

"Can't we think of a term that doesn't sound so forceful and violent? I don't want to crush her spirit. I don't want to make her do something against her will."

"It's just a word."

"So is murder and r…" I start to say rape, but can't. "Anyway. You know what I mean."

He frowns. "Breaking a horse isn't like rape or murder. Aren't you being a bit hypocritical here, anyway? On one hand, you're trying to get her to trust you while on the other, you've devised grand plans to trick her into rodeo."

"That's not the same thing!"

"Still. Coercion."

I fold my arms. "Is it coercion to get a dog to sit? Or come when they're called? No, it's training. *Training.* That works."

"Sweet feed coercion," he says, teasing me, but I don't want to be teased about this.

I turn my back on Jake and slowly approach Scout. She's

tentative at first, but after a few sniffs in the air tell her what she's going to get if she comes to say hi, she eagerly fills the space between us and laps up the handfuls of sweet feed from my cupped palms. But when I try to put the rope bridle over her neck, she rears away from me, backing off.

"It's okay, girl. It's just a little rope. It's not going to hurt you."

I approach her slowly, bridle tightly gripped in my fist. I see the conflict in her eyes; she wants the feed but not the rope.

She wants me but not my tool.

She's not weak.

She's not willing to break her will for a bit of dessert or a scratch behind the ears.

"Okay, girl," I say. I stop. "It's okay. It doesn't matter."

I toss the halter onto the dirt and then take a step closer and let her lap up the oats, anyway.

"At this rate, you'll have her in full saddle cutting cattle in no time," Jake calls over the fence rail.

"Scout and I are going to get this done, you'll see. But I'm going to do it my way."

"I don't doubt it," he says, exactly like he means it.

We take a break from the scorching heat, and over lemonade on the porch swing, we discuss our various options.

"My dad isn't thrilled with the idea of me trying the bareback thing," I say, "but I think I can convince him."

"From the looks of it, neither is Scout," he says with an eyebrow raise. "You planning on convincing her any time soon?"

I make a face. "It'll take some time. She doesn't trust me yet. She thinks I'll jump on her back and scare the bejesus out of her like I heard *some* cowboy around here did."

"Just doing my job," he says with a grin.

"Well, baby steps."

He takes off his hat and runs a hand through his hair. "Even if things don't work out with Scout, cutting would make the most sense for you. We'll bring some calves down from the herd on the hill. A few that ain't burned up…"

"Burned up?" That's an odd expression. I imagine a pile of calves on a bonfire. Not a pleasant thought.

"Used up—you know, used to people—so they'll still be spooked by you and Scout. We'll need another for the event, too. I can herd hold but we'll need another turn back person…"

"Slow down, cowboy. You're losing me here."

"Sorry," he laughs. "I tend to forget how rookie you are. You used to know this stuff. Don't you remember any of it?"

"Not really."

"Well," he scratches his head, thinking. "I got a DVD we can watch together which will explain it better."

"Ooh, a DVD. Do they still make those?"

He cocks an eyebrow. "Making fun of me, Cowgirl?"

Damn it. Why does he have to be so cute? "Haha, sort of. No one at home watches DVDs anymore. It's all streaming and Netflix and…" And I'd already had this conversation with Anna. "Never mind."

"Well, if you want to learn your stuff, you better get on board with our ancient Wyoming technology. Don't worry. Our TV is actually in color." He sips at his lemonade. It must be killing him to drink something other than Diet Dr. Pepper. "Have you ever ridden freestyle? I doubt your dad would've let you do that when you were little, but you never know."

"No. I tried once but fell off." I laugh at the memory. "I was pretty wild back then. Constantly dirty. My mom had to wrestle me into the tub at night."

"Well, you'd better get used to that all over again if you're gonna give this a try."

"That's fine." I've certainly lived through worse than getting dirty. "I want to try."

Nodding, he takes a long drink of lemonade from the strawberry print tumbler. I guess that's the end of that. Wanting to try is enough for Jake. I'm feeling proud, and a little nervous—what am I getting myself into?—when he says, "You know how Indians used to break the wild mustangs?"

"Native Americans or East Indians?"

He looks at me blankly. "They took them down to the creek, set them in the middle of the water, then jumped on their backs. The mustangs buck like crazy, but because they have nowhere to run, if you get thrown, you end up with a mouth full of water and wet boots instead of dead."

"That sounds fun. Is that your plan?" I ask.

"Nah." He waves his hand in the air. "I like getting tossed onto the hard dirt. Builds grit."

"Grit and a broken coccyx I'd imagine."

We both laugh and then are quiet for a minute. The swing creaks when it rocks back and forth.

"So, if we try this cutting thing, you'll be there with me?" I ask, softly.

"Sure," he says. "Of course."

I'm about to thank him, but since he's always giving me a hard time about that, I stare into my lemonade. I shake the glass around, listening to ice cubes clink against each other and hiss in the sweet juice.

"Barrel racing is another one," he says, and I'm grateful for the change of subject. "But takes the training I don't think we have time for. The deadline to enter rodeo is next week."

"I'll do whatever you think will give us the best chance of winning the prize money."

His long legs bend over the swing. His palms spread across the thighs of his dirty blue jeans. "This is an interesting change, you actually taking my advice."

"This is different. This is about saving the ranch."

"Ah." He's still looking down, but I can see his mouth turn up into a half smile as the heels of his boots gently rise and set on the wood of the porch moving along the smooth rhythm of the swing, of our conversation. When the swing stops, he looks at me dead on. "You got a lot of gumption here, Paige, but remember. Even if we train hard—and believe me, we will—we'll be competing against folks who've trained their whole lives. Authentic rodeo folks. Genuine cowgirls. I don't want you to be disappointed if we don't win this thing first time out the gate."

I smile. "Once upon a time I was a genuine cowgirl, remember? And at this point, losing isn't an option." My throat swells with the need for him to understand the importance of this. "You told me to come up with a plan, and this is what I came up with. It has to work."

Then Jake's hand is on my thigh, lightly, gently, but there.

As if on cue, Anna wheels Daddy onto the porch. Jake's hand flies, spooked, off my leg. He jumps up, and the absence of his weight on the swing causes it to swing sideways and some of my lemonade to swish out onto my shirt. Terrific.

Anna grabs one of the hand towels she keeps draped over the back of Dad's chair and pats down my chest. Even better. Why does spilling drinks on myself, of all things, have to become a trend?

"It's okay," I say, leaping away.

Jake leans against the porch rail, looking like he's about to start laughing, his lanky body, like his words, filling up so much space with seemingly such little effort. Did Anna see his hand on my thigh? Was she listening to our conversation, or does she just have incredibly bad timing? Was he planning on just a supportive pat or would it have lingered there if we hadn't been interrupted?

"How was your nap, Daddy?"

He nods a little, which means okay.

Then he types.

You remember how to cut, Paige. Jake will show you any parts you don't. Jake here is the next best thing to your old man.

I smile and nod. I know he is.

I squeeze his hand. "But will Scout be ready in time? I couldn't even get the rope harness on her this morning, let alone try the saddle yet. And like Jake was just talking to me about"—before the whole hand-on-leg thing—"cutting takes skill."

Dad's face is still. I wish he could talk. Wish like hell I could hear his voice again—his *real* voice telling me what to do in low, precise steps.

Just like riding a bike, Paige, you'll remember as soon as you get back on.

"Well, let's hope I don't have to get thrown again to re-learn that lesson."

Chapter Forty-Two

After dinner, Jake feeds the horses and then announces he's heading into town for supplies. "We're all out of bacon. I'm heading into town. Need anything?" he asks. I shake my head, grateful for his asking. I'm standing on the rung of the corral fence, simply grateful I made it *to* this fence. To this day when so many of my peers didn't. The more I think about what happened, the more memories I relive, the more surprised I am that I'm here at all. As proud as I am, it's unnerving.

I grab a couple handfuls of sweet feed and enter the corral. Seeing Scout will help calm me. But Scout isn't there. And the gate's open.

"Scout!" I run into her stable. She's not there, either.

I sprint into the house, but decide against yelling in case Dad is asleep. Anna. Where is Anna? She isn't in the kitchen or in the living room dog-earing one of her *Flea Market Craft* magazines circa 1984, either. Crap.

Down the dark hallway, I notice Dad's door is open a crack. I don't knock and enter. Instead, I look through the crack and see Anna sitting in the floral-patterned chair I was sitting in earlier. She is talking to Dad in a low voice. Her hand is on his leg.

Recoiling, I backtrack down the hallway. I don't want to

bother them or bug Jake with this either. His cell won't have service on the dirt road anyway. Besides, it was probably me who left the gate open after our walk. I have to find her myself.

Back in the entryway, I throw on Jake's duster—I'm not sure how long I'll be gone, and after the sun sets, it gets cold fast in the mountains—tuck a flashlight into the deep pocket, and set out to look for her.

I'm about a mile up the dirt road, dusk casting long silvery shadows on the rock and dust, when I hear rustling in the creek.

My first thought is *mountain lion*.

Aside from the flashlight—which I guess I could whack over the animal's head, but that's about it—I'm unarmed. I'm starting to freak, flashlight out and shakily aimed, when I hear the rustling again and a familiar whinny.

"Scout!" I call into the darkness. "Is that you, girl?"

The weeds are tall, and I'm careful not to step in a snake or gopher hole on the way down the steep hill. The sun has long set by the time I find her taking a drink out of the stream.

"Hey, you," I say.

She looks up at me like, *Oh, hey you, back*, and keeps drinking.

"What are you doing down here? Come on, we have to get back. There could be mountain lions or bears."

Ignoring me, she continues to drink, like she's thinking, *I'm tougher than any creature out here anyway. What do I have to worry about?*

The creek is wide and clear, like a river, but it's moving slowly. Clear water breaks over smooth granite boulders, gurgling softly.

Jake's words ring in my head: *Indians used to break horses in the creek.*

She's not exactly in the creek right now, but one side is all muddy grass slopes and the other side is water. Infinitely less dangerous than what Jake tried again and again, mounting her in the corral in the heat of the day over hard, potentially spine-shattering dirt.

"Hey, girl," I say in a soothing voice. "You know your little adventure here? Well, how'd you like to make it even more fun?"

She looks up at me and lets me approach. Her nose nestles into Jake's duster, nudging for sweet feed. I scratch her ears as her face presses into my chest.

With my arm wrapped around her velvet head, I tell her what's up in my calmest voice. "I want to try something, and I don't want you to be scared. It's not a super big deal. I'm going to hop up on your back, and we'll just see what happens, okay?"

I scratch behind her ear. The last thing I want to do is scare her, or worse, lose the trust I've worked so hard to gain. I want it to be okay with her.

How can I make her understand, though?

Sometimes you got to do stuff that scares you, Paige. That's how you know you're alive.

Jake's voice again.

So while she's eating out of my hand, I hop onto a boulder, grab a handful of her mane, and with all of my abdominal strength, heave my leg over her back, clutch her neck, and hold on for dear life.

Her back rears, and I grip her neck harder as she bucks again. Then she plunges forward in a gallop-like move that almost shakes me loose and throws me all the way to the left. I haul myself back to her middle, trying to regain equilibrium, but before I'm centered, she rears again, hard and fast. My teeth crash into each other, rattling my brain, and…I'm wet? My eyes fly open, expecting the creek to be maybe knee deep, but it's up to Scout's thighs. She jerks to the right, whinnying into the sky as she finally cuts me loose. Flying into darkness, I think, *This is it. I'm dead*, and in the bright sparks above me, I don't see stars—

I see the headlights of a screaming train.

Chapter Forty-Three

"Paige? Paige?"

I'm drowning or dead. Am I dead? I hit my head on a rock, and I'm on the bottom of the creek. Through foggy water I see a face, or the sky, or a blur of blue stars. I reach out and up. Strain toward the light. "She's coming to."

I recognize his voice, and I lurch toward it with everything I have. I don't want to drown. I want to be pulled up into the air.

I gasp and my head shudders. I feel his hand on mine. "Paige? Can you hear me?"

I nod and hooves pound against my skull.

The blur of blue isn't stars; it's Jake's blue eyes.

"Oh, thank God." Anna's voice. "Paige, where does it hurt, honey?"

I moan.

"What'd she say?"

Jake chuckles. "I think she said everywhere."

"She's okay," Anna says. "She's okay." I think she says it a couple more times, but it hurts my ears to listen. Hurts my brain to translate. Hurts my back to move.

"Can you move your legs?"

I try to move my left leg. My toe wiggles.

"What about your right?"

It hurts. It hurts. But I can move it.

"Her legs are fine," Jake says, pressing my muscles with his fingertips. "Fingers? Wiggle your fingers, Paige."

I lift my fingers up and press against his palm. He's checking to see if I'm paralyzed.

"Lie back down."

Jake's big hand holds my head up and then gently sets it down on something soft. His jacket, his other jacket—I ruined his duster. Now I'm shaking. My head hurts. Everything hurts. Scout! Where is she?

"We found you on this river bed."

"I tried to…like the Native Americans."

Jake gets it right away. "You tried to ride Scout?"

I nod.

"And she tossed you," Jake says, matter-of-factly.

"Scout must've drug her out of the creek," Anna said. "She was out cold when we got here and her clothes are all wet, so it must've happened in the creek."

"Wouldn't hurt me," I manage to mumble through the nails hammering into my skull.

"Well, she meant to buck you off or you wouldn't be lying here. But no, she didn't mean to hurt you. She led us here." Jake's voice, his words as soothing as the flannel of his coat under my bruised head, as sweet as his fingers brushing the sticky hair off my cheek. "She led us to you."

When I wake up again, I squint at the wall, trying to clue together where I am.

Lavender-flower wallpaper.

Antique nightstand.

The hum of familiar and unfamiliar voices.

I'm in my room at the ranch. How long have I been asleep? I pick at the puzzle pieces of words from my visitors. A doctor is here. "Looks like the concussion is pretty bad, but apart from some minor bruising she's not in that bad of shape. I don't think we need to hospitalize her."

"Gus wants to know if she needs an MRI or CAT scan?"

"I don't think so. She's alert. Her pupils look fine. And she was speaking to you after she came to, right?"

"That's correct." Jake's voice. He's here, too. They're all gathered around my bed and I'm utterly embarrassed. Why did I think I could just jump on Scout like that? And that it would end in, what? Us trotting back into her corral all heroic like Tristan Ludlow in *Legends of the Fall*, my mom's favorite movie from the 90s?

The doctor asks me a few questions. They decide someone should wake me up every hour during the night. Jake offers to sit up with me and after some arguments, Anna and Dad agree. Anna stays with Dad—she watches him already. And now Jake's watching me.

For a while I'm quiet. My head pounds less from the medicine they gave me. A Vicodin I think. I swallowed a horse pill.

I must drift off because when I wake again, Jake's sitting next to me, his hand on my shoulder. I'm so glad it's there, and I hope it stays.

"Hi," I say. There's a scared tremble to my voice, like it's daring me to speak.

"Hi."

It's hard to read his expression. I have to ask.

"Are you mad at me?"

He nods but his eyes are light. "You scared me," he says quietly. His thumb rubs circles on my shoulder, like warm little suns.

I wonder if he'll warn me again about the dangers of bareback or going off alone, and instead he surprises me. He leans forward and kisses me lightly on the lips and sort of lingers there. I suck in a breath and reach for his hand. He takes it like he's not surprised in the least. He drags his thumb up and down mine, first on the top and then the soft underside. Then all four of his fingers drift between mine, softly, slowly like they're asking mine to dance. My fingers follow his lead — they hear the same music — and he sits with me like that in this quiet stillness until I drift off again.

I wake up in a cold sweat, struggling to breathe.

I'm underwater.

No.

I'm on the tracks.

No.

I'm on the tracks underwater, and I'm screaming but no one hears me. Then I hear a voice. It's Ty's, and he's angry. He says I don't deserve them. I don't deserve a second chance. Jake fades into focus, replacing Ty's ghost. He's reading in the floral chair in the corner. He tosses down the book, and rushes to my side. I throw my arms around his neck and I'm not sure what I say, but he strokes my hair and says *shhh shhh shhh*. He crawls into the bed next to me, and I bury my face in his neck and then against his chest as he holds me tight, hoping he's not the dream. Hoping he's real.

Chapter Forty-Four

When I wake up again I'm alone, and the absence of Jake's little suns is chilled dreariness even though bright sun is streaming through the curtains. I'm fuzzy in the brain from my concussion, angsty from the nightmare, and looped up from the drugs. Did I dream he was here holding me?

I didn't dream the kiss.

I didn't dream the little suns he rubbed on my shoulder.

I didn't dream up Jake, or Anna, or Dad.

Maybe I don't deserve them watching over me like angels, but here they are.

In my swollen-brained state, the wallpaper flowers bud and blossom and bloom.

Chapter Forty-Five

They make me stay in bed two full weeks. I get up only to eat and shower and go to the bathroom. I get a lot of pep talks from Anna and Dad (via the computer), but not Jake. Jake, instead of joking around in his usual confident way, treats me like I'm a robin's egg. He's kind. He's careful. He sits on the side of my bed and we play hearts. And we talk. We *really* talk.

He tells me about his family, about his dad a little bit, about his mom. I can see that he's worried. I can feel that he's getting close, maybe too close, to me. And that worries me. I'm leaving soon. This was supposed to be my stopover between lives, the place to try and pull the pieces of my life back together. It wasn't supposed to be a place to build a new life. And the fact that that's what's happening scares me. I'm feeling things I can't control. Things I can't predict. People care about me here. *Really* care—and it scares the shit out of me.

Now we're arguing about the upcoming rodeo—I'm Team Yay, he's Team Nay—and it's stressing me out worse than the concussion.

"Jake, we can still enter—"

"No. You heard Doc Rhodes. You have a bad concussion. If you get another concussion within three months, you could get permanent brain damage."

"I already have permanent brain damage."

"Not funny."

"It kind of is?"

He frowns. "Since I already registered you…"

"Right. Excellent!"

"You aren't competing. Not with that head."

"But, Jake, I—"

Instead of arguing with me, he shifts the subject. "You seem okay, so I'm going to head on into town. We need more eggs and alfalfa."

"We need more me entering the rodeo for sure."

Finger waggling, he says, "Remember when we were camping and I said you'd be a waddy someday. Well. This is waddy behavior at its finest. Stubborn, saddle-driven, crazy-ass waddy behavior."

But he doesn't look mad—he looks proud. He kisses my forehead and the tip of my nose, and now I'm certain he kissed me the other night.

I scoot up in bed. "You're the one who told me to do something each day that'd scare me. That's how I'll know I'm alive, right?"

He stops in the doorway and turns around. "I didn't mean jump on Scout in the dark in a creek."

"I want to feel alive so badly."

It's barely a whisper, this truth, but I go ahead and confess it. After so much numbness, I have an inkling of what living feels like again. Now it's *all* I want—to capture that feeling and keep it. I'm not going to give it up. I'm not going to give any of this up: not Scout, not the chance to save the ranch and help my daddy, not Jake—not any of it. I'll fight if I have to.

"You are your daddy's daughter," Jake says, and with a waddy smile, slips out, leaving me to my plans.

Chapter Forty-Six

The first time I'm allowed outside, I go straight to Scout.

Of course, we're in the middle of an afternoon thunderstorm—we get those in the summer months—so I have to walk through hot rain, streaming down from the angry sky, to get anywhere.

She's hanging out in the shelter of her corral. "Nice weather we're having, huh?" I nuzzle into her warm face, and she nuzzles back, grunting a horse hello.

"Not that you deserve this after you landed me two weeks in bed and almost blew my shot at entering us in the rodeo, but here you go."

She gratefully gobbles up the granola mix in my palm, then nudges into my chest, like she knows that's exactly what I need, like she's sorry she hurt me. I give her a cuddle back, hugging her beautiful head, scratching her behind her ears the way she likes.

"Heard you rescued me, girl," I say. "I suppose a thank you is in order."

She nudges into me again, smacking her toothy lips.

"And I'm not trying to rub it in, but if you hadn't bucked me off, you wouldn't have had to rescue me in the first place."

She eyes me like, *Uh-huh. If you hadn't have jumped on my*

back, I wouldn't have had to buck you, and the rescue would be moot.

"Touché."

We stay there together and watch the silver rain pound the red dirt. Breathing in the new-rain, I think how happy I am to be alive.

We wait for the rain to stop. The showers are fast and furious, and I love the sound of water pounding dirt. While we wait, I think. I remember. And then the storm clouds clear morphing from an angry God's revenge into a gentle pastel sunset. I don't know if I believe in God, but this is so lovely and magical, this shift in nature, that I take it as a sign from something. Or someone.

I want to ride her again.

I want to ride her so badly.

The evening is now a perfect mix of orange sky sunset and freshly cleansed glow.

I want to ride her so badly it *burns*.

I grab another handful of sweet feed, hold it out in front of her, and lead her toward the step stool next to the fence. When she's close enough, I climb up to the top of the step stool. She's busy eating out of my left hand when I swing my right leg up and over her back. She twitches, backs up a bit, but doesn't toss me. She's still eating out of my hand and I'm leaning all the way over her neck now, petting her and doing Jake's *Shhh, Shhh,* followed by an almost whispered, "Good girl, Scout. Atta-girl. *Shhh. Shhh.*" When the feed runs out, she jerks her head back and looks at me like I would a kid jumping on my back — not in a mean way, but curious, like, *What are you doing back there?*

I keep up the soothing voice.

Shhh. Shhh.

I stroke her velvety skin.

She neighs.

Shhh. Shhh.

And then she surprises me.

She takes off.

I didn't shut the gate when I entered. It was pouring down so hard, I tucked my head and ran for shelter. My bad, because now she's bolting clear out of it. Leaning forward, I grip her mane for dear life. I squeeze my thighs around her middle to keep me on as she gallops straight up the central dirt road we rode on our camping trip. Dirt flies everywhere, hooves pound wet rock, wind zips my hair—and her mane—into my mouth, and it's exhilarating, like flying on land. Even though I'm scared to death, it's exactly what I want, exactly what I need.

I lean into the rhythm of her strong body as we push through the wet mountain air and pound up the trail, trees and brush and all forms of logical decisions whizzing by. She runs and runs and runs like she needs it, too, and when she finally stops, it's not because I want to, it's because she does. She's exhausted. We're miles from home when, panting and sweaty, she drops her head and starts munching on a bush. I slip off her wet back and nearly fall to the ground. I can barely stand after holding onto Scout with my inner thighs. Bareback is a whole new adventure.

My heart pounds a million miles an hour. I try to take a step, but my legs are wobbly and uncertain.

Scout turns her head from the bush and looks at me like, *Well,* you're *the one who hopped on my back again, girl. What'd you expect?*

"Anna's going to have a field day with this one," I groan, happily.

And I swear to all things holy, it looks like Scout nods in agreement.

Chapter Forty-Seven

It's long after dark by the time I make it back to the house. Anna and Jake are outside calling my name, shining flashlights into the darkness.

"Right here," I say. I try to flatten the excitement out of my voice, but it doesn't quite work. I'm positively giddy that Scout let me ride her. That I'm not hurt. That I found my way back in the dark in one piece.

Jake and Anna run up to me, and Jake grips my arm and moves in like he's going to hug me but Anna beats him to it, pulling me into her arms with a hard squeeze. "Are you okay? What happened? We were worried sick."

"Sorry. I was…well, I was feeding her, and then I thought, okay, what the heck, I'll give it a try, and well, she took off out the gate—I held on and she didn't try to buck me and we ended up miles away before she finally stopped."

Jake's eyes are smiling as he shakes his head, unable to conceal he's at least a little proud of me. Anna, however, is a different story. The creases deepen between her eyebrows.

"Well, where is she?"

"Up on the mountain. She wouldn't come back with me."

"We'll deal with her later. Come on inside. It's cold—the storm, I was worried you were caught up in it—and you look a fright walking around in the dark all chilled! Riding in the dark." Anna storms back to the house, expecting us to follow, still mumbling.

We do, but slowly.

I grab the elbow of Jake's rough jacket, and pull him back. "She let me ride her, Jake! It was amazing! She didn't try to buck me off or anything. It was like nothing I've ever experienced."

"Genuine cowgirl, huh?"

I beam. "Getting there."

"All right, Cowgirl. Time to face the music," he says wryly, but he puts his arm around me and gives me a squeeze. The wool of his coat smells like all the good in the world: horses, mountain air, and Jake—freshly in from the rain.

When we walk through the door, Anna is still loudly listing my crimes, stomping around in the kitchen, banging something together. Coffee and sandwiches, I hope—if she's feeding me, she can't be that mad, can she? When she re-enters the room with a tray of sandwiches and coffee (yes!), she points at a chair for me to sit, and then, after pouring me some hot coffee, sits herself. Arms crossed, she finally demands in the eerily calm voice of a judge, "Explain why you thought riding an untamed 'stang in the dark—again—was a smart choice."

"Sorry. I have no excuse. I wanted to see her. I'd been cooped up inside for so long—I know, also my fault—but we were hanging out, watching the rain. And then the rain stopped. And the sunset was just gorgeous, and well, I guess I wanted to ride her. She was antsy from the storm, and she let me, so I did."

I eye the sandwiches. The turkey and lettuce and tomato falling out of the thick, homemade bread. My stomach growls. She pushes one toward me, and while I listen to her lecture, gobble it up.

"Didn't you learn anything from being in bed a full two weeks? Thank goodness your father is sleeping."

I wipe tomato juice off my chin. "You didn't tell him? Phew."

"And worry him sick? The last couple weeks he barely

left your side. Once we can forgive, but twice makes me think something else is going on here."

"Like what?" My heart is still pounding with adrenaline. I wish Anna would leave so I could pull Jake into a dark corner and regale him with my tale. It's clear my excitement over riding Scout is only feeding Anna's fury. I want to enjoy this triumph. It worked. We connected, finally.

"Like" — she glances first at Jake — "maybe you *want* to get hurt."

That stops me. My chest falls. I put what's left of my sandwich down. "I don't…I don't want to get hurt."

"Then why else would you keep riding a horse who doesn't want to be ridden?"

Anna's face is red. I've never seen her angry like this. And upset. And worried. Her face is a mirror of my mother's at SFO the day she dropped me off. I didn't want to scare my mom then. And I don't want to scare Anna now.

"I'm sorry I scared you, " I start to say. I want to explain, that this was the opposite of wanting to be hurt. I don't want to die. I want to live! But she interrupts me before I have a chance to explain.

"Sorry. Yeah, I've heard that before." She leans forward, eyes intense. "You know what is keeping your father alive, sitting in that chair, eating baby food? You. You being here." She smacks the strawberry tablecloth with her palm. "It's true. Before you came — and I'm sorry if this is blunt, but truth often is — he was thinking of pulling the plug, being done with the machines and — "

"Anna," Jake warns.

He scoots his chair closer to mine, pressing his upper arm against mine for support. A move that is both secretive and strong. I appreciate it so much.

Jake? My eyes ask and he nods with a sad shrug, a confirmation, and a truth.

"You being here, Paige. You on this ranch?" Anna taps the

table. "It changed his mind. It's making him come back to life again. To use the rest of his days the best he can."

"This isn't true," I say, shaking my head. "He loves you. He loves Jake. He wants to live for you."

Anna shakes her head. "You know how hard it is for him to wake up every day and not be able to use his hands? To be unable to form a sentence or use the bathroom? He's a cowboy, Paige. He was brave and he did his best, but he was just done. And what I don't think you understand, maybe because of what you went through in California—and believe me, I know it was a lot. A whole hell of a lot more than anyone your age should have to go through—but Paige, honey, you don't have much time left with him. You're his daughter. Do you think the two of us even compare? You need to stop thinking of yourself and stop beating yourself up about what happened back home and think of him when you make these choices. Your daddy, who has loved you all your life, who would do anything to be able to walk across the room again, to hold you in his arms. Never mind get back on a horse."

Dad was ready to cut off his ventilator and feeding tube and what, just wait to die? My being here gave him the will to live? Well, then I better freaking live.

No wonder Jake and Anna were so shaken up when I was hurt.

And then a horrific thought. A sentence that once I think it tumbles over and over in my shaken brain. *The whole of my life is centered around death.* No matter what I do to try and escape it, I can't. It follows me everywhere. My chest is heavy with sadness—a dull, never-ending ache I finally thought I was escaping. I swipe a hot tear off my cheek and try to swallow the others away. Why do I even try?

I look down at my hands. They suddenly look so small. "I need to learn to ride Scout to save the ranch."

"There are other ways," Anna says.

"There's not," I say. "He can't lose the ranch, Anna. *We*

can't lose the ranch."

Jake sets his hand on mine, and when I look up at the two of them, they are all blurry because my eyes are full of tears.

"So you think Scout's still up on the mountain, then?" Jake asks.

I nod. "I wanted to stay the night up there with her, but I figured you'd be worried."

"Figured we'd be worried? Paige, that's what I'm talking about. We were *sick* with worry…" Anna says. "After all you've been through. I don't want to get into all that right now, but you…Paige. We *have* to worry about you."

That hits me like a crash to the hard dirt. They *have* to worry about me? I don't want their pity. Back in California, I was ignored. My mother was too busy for my problems. She was too disinterested to care, and even when she did care, she didn't know *how* to care. I'm not used to this.

I squirm in my chair. Even Jake's warm hand is starting to feel like a too-thick blanket, smothering and hot, and I want to throw it off me. But I don't have to. He scoots his chair back and moves to the doorway, slipping into Dad's old plaid jacket.

"Where are you going?"

"To get Scout."

I stand back up. "I'm coming too, then." No way am I staying here with angry Anna. Horrible news bearing Anna. I don't want to be in the house at all.

"No. Go on and clean up and get some rest," he says to me. But then he mumbles to Anna in words I can barely make out, "Hope she didn't take back with her herd."

"Her herd?"

Anna rubs the worry lines between her eyebrows. "Oh, god. I hope not."

"What herd?" I ask.

"You didn't tell her yet about Scout's lineage?" Anna asks Jake.

"Nope," he says, putting on his riding gloves.

"What? Come on, you two have been keeping secrets from me since I got here. Please just tell me."

Anna looks at me pointedly, like I'm one to talk about secrets.

I avoid her eyes. I'm torn between wanting to melt through the floor to avoid the Ty talk and pushing further on the Scout lineage business when Jake, still standing at the closed door in his cowboy hat and long, dark brown coat, says the words that make me want to throw my arms around him and keep him forever. "I'll fill her in on the way up the mountain. Grab your coat, City Slicker."

"Really?"

"You're the one that lost her, makes sense you're the one who should find her."

I mouth, *Thank you.* He nods. I slip into my coat and follow him out before Anna can stop me.

In the darkness, Jake and I saddle up Blue and Thunderbolt, and, with headlamps strapped to our foreheads, we follow little pools of light as well as the moonlight up the mountain. The crickets chirp through the dry night air.

"Scout's mom is Luna, our prize-winning mare," he says after a while. His even voice cuts through the night, calming me immediately. I take a deep breath and cling to his voice.

"She was a champion cutter a few years ago," he continues. "One day, when your dad was first diagnosed, we were all in town at the doctor's office—clearly our brains weren't with the horses because we had so much other stuff on our minds—and we forgot Luna was in heat. When we got back to the ranch, the corral had been knocked over and Luna was gone."

"Gone? Did someone steal her?"

"Something like that." Jake's voice smiles in the darkness. "Eloped more like it."

"I don't get it."

"You see," Jake, says in his drawl, "one of the wild mustangs your dad kept for the government—on the top acreage near where we camped out?—well, he wanted to get at Ole' Luna so bad, he tore down the corral fence and somehow convinced her to run away with him."

"That was...ballsy."

"That's one way of putting it." I hear his smile again. "Anyhow, mustangs are known for that sort of thing. So when we finally caught up with her, she was grazing in a field with their herd. She came back home with us reluctantly. Eleven months later, your Scout was born."

Your Scout. Riding side by side in the dark like this makes it so easy to talk. We lumber along and Jake talks. I could listen to Jake talk forever.

"Good news for their filly is that a lot of show horses are inbred now. Breeding with their cousins and aunties and the grandfathers you name it, and they have to be put down a lot of the time. Scout here is half mustang. She's half prize-winning mare. There's a fire inside her and a winner in there, too. That's why we were so disappointed she couldn't be rode. Why I kept trying."

"I'm still trying. She let me ride her, Jake. Me. The fact that she let me mount her like that was a big step in the right direction. It could keep Daddy fighting. Keep him alive, you know?"

Jake knows immediately what I'm referring to.

"You don't need to pay any mind to what Anna said back there. She's just worried about him." I can see his profile in the dark. He turns to look at me. "Worried about you."

I scowl at him. "You don't have to protect me or make excuses for Anna. I'm a big girl and have a pretty decent bullshit detector. Anna speaks her mind, and it's usually the truth. She was telling me the truth back there."

"Those parts of it, that he was planning on giving up *are* true, yes, but most Lou Gehrig's patients don't go to the length he does to stay alive. When they stop eating on their own, they often just…let nature take its course."

"They give up?" That's so awful, I can barely take it.

"More like they can't afford to stay alive. You have any idea how much these machines cost? Or what a full time caregiver would? If we didn't have Anna, we'd be looking at a whole other situation."

"But I'm here. I could do what Anna's doing, if they'd let me try."

"We didn't know you were coming. That you'd come. He didn't know."

"What I don't get…" Tipping my head back, I swallow the infinite stars. "…is why no one told me."

"We tried to."

"You should've tried harder. Made me listen."

"You didn't return our calls. Your mom is impossible to tie down to a phone conversation…"

"She's more of an…electronic communicator." I laugh, although nothing about it is actually funny.

"More like a robot," Jake says, which makes me laugh some more. "How could she not care about the man she was married to for years?"

"She cares in her own way."

"Huh?"

"It's complicated."

He adjusts his hat. "A way I don't understand then."

"Things are different where we are. People don't care about the things you do here."

"Like what? Like *dying relatives*? What human being doesn't care about that?"

"Have you ever been so caught up in something, like training for the rodeo, for instance, that it's all you think about morning, noon, and night? You go to sleep thinking about it and you wake up thinking about it until it consumes you into neglecting the things that *should* be consuming you?"

He shrugs. "I guess."

"Well, that's how she is about her career. That's how my stepdad is, too. When they aren't at work, they are on their computers 24/7. After we left the ranch, it was like she wanted to shake off everything she was here in Wyoming. She never tells people she's from here. I don't know. Maybe my dad hurt her too much…"

"I can't see Gus hurting anyone, but he does go through his periods…"

"Periods?"

"Yeah, where…well, I don't know if you want to hear all this."

"It's fine. What?"

"He'd be fine and then he'd just sort of shut down. Drink more. Drink during the day. I'd be looking for him and catch him sitting in his den with the shades drawn just looking out at space. I'd pick up his empty bottles, toss them out. Sometimes it got pretty bad."

"How so?"

Jake is quiet. We ride along in the dark.

"Jake? Tell me."

"I'd worry about him is all. But then spring would come and he'd be out scraping the horse droppings and cooking up bacon again, and it was like it never happened."

"Yeah, whenever my mom rants about Dad, it's always about his dark spells, his drinking. She wanted him to get help for depression, but I guess he sloughed it off. It was one of their huge problems."

"Was he like that when you were a kid?"

I frown. "I've never really thought about it. But now that you ask, yeah. I remember him making pancakes and laughing and running around with me on his back. Then I remember him sort of…disappearing for a while. Mom would usually take me to California or Hawaii or New York City when that happened. A couple weeks later he'd be okay. All sorry and the house full of flowers, and they'd dance to country music. One time we started looking at houses in California and just didn't come back. "

"That's seems so unsettling."

"Yeah. It was. I haven't thought about all of that in years."

Jake's silhouette moves languidly on the horse. "Weird how stuff we forget is just sitting there the whole time, waiting to be drawn back out."

"Seriously." Again, it's like wiping off the foggy mirror and facing my past head-on.

"So I guess he got worse as the years went on. That's probably why my mom didn't want me to visit. She never knew how he'd be."

"Sounds like she was protecting you."

Some of my past anger fades into appreciation. Mom might not be perfect, but she wanted to do what was best for me, back then, anyway. Maybe even now. Maybe that's why she dropped me off at the airport. She knew I needed this. That coming to the ranch might be the best place for me. "Yeah, I guess so."

"Maybe your daddy tried his best, too? Even back then?" Jake suggests.

I nod in the dark. "Maybe we all do," I say.

Chapter Forty-Eight

We ride along in a still sort of sadness before I say, "Back at home this kind of normal doesn't exist. It's life in the Silicon Valley: start-ups and venture capitalists and New Innovative—you know, leaving your mark, the next mountain to climb, the vast importance of acing this test or winning this meet or adding this volunteer job to get into that school to get into that internship to get that job..." I flashed on Ty and what he said about his mom. And Elena.

That was me before, too. Before all the deaths screeched my ambition to a halt. I wasn't just scared to make the next step—I was scared to move at all. Scared to breathe for fear I'd be next.

"That makes more sense then," he interrupts.

"What?"

"The way you are about entering this rodeo. You're dedicated, but it's not just that. It seems like you're all about the end game. The win instead of the experience."

"That's..." I frown, taken aback. "...Is that true?"

His shadow shrugs.

"There's nothing wrong with wanting to win."

But even as I say it, I know I don't believe it's the whole truth. Kids at home wanted to win so badly they lost it all. On their way to the top they fell and lost everything.

"The first time you tried, you were in bed two weeks. Tonight you were lucky."

It was easier being honest in the dark. "As much as you guys think I have a death wish, I don't. And it's not just about the win. I promise. I thought I was living in California, but I wasn't. I was in constant motion but that isn't the same as feeling alive. This. The way I feel when I'm with Scout, the way I feel in the morning looking at the eagles in the sky...the way I feel when I'm with..."

You. I look at him, and he catches my eye. He knows exactly what I'm thinking. I don't look away or hide from it. How can you hide from something so true? He doesn't look away, either, and I keep talking.

"Before at home I was stagnating. I was surviving. Barely. I wasn't even eating. You know I wasn't even hungry? Here I'm starving...all the time. Surviving isn't the same as living, Jake. You know that. You *told* me that, so don't ask me to stop now."

"I'm glad you're happy here. I just don't want you to get hurt again."

"I don't want me to get hurt either. And now I'm sick over my dad wanting to die before I got here. What if I hadn't come? I almost didn't. I wouldn't have if circumstances weren't so bad there that I didn't have another choice. I can't even think about that right now." I take a deep breath. The headlamp only shines light on what was directly in front of my horse's steps, nothing farther.

The crickets do their thing.

The wind does its dance.

And we do ours.

"Do I look different now, Jake? From when we were kids?"

I see the two of us at the fishing hole: Me in pigtails. Him mop-haired in ripped blue jeans and a red flannel shirt. He pretends to study me in the darkness. "You look the same."

"So do you. But everything else is different."

"Then we've got to change the things we can."

"And the things we can't?"

It's a beat before he answers, and I'm afraid to hear it.

"The things we can't, well, I reckon we gotta let those go."

We don't say anything else, not with words anyway, until we make the final ascent through the mountain pass and arrive on top. They talk about views being breathtaking, and this view feels like a punch of beauty square in the chest. Glowing illumination. The hovering Grand Tetons look close enough to touch. The full moon casts a broad light off the rocky cliffs flooding the meadow, reminding me of lights on a football field.

But the most breathtaking thing is the way Jake is looking at me.

A smile plays on his mouth as he concedes with a happy sigh. "Maybe if you could get her to wear the bridle…"

Yes! If I weren't on top of this horse, I'd throw my arms around his neck and hope he'd swing me around.

"Jake, thank you! But remember, she doesn't like all that stuff. She wants to be free. If we could just…"

"Sometimes we have to do stuff we don't like to get to the good parts."

I raise an eyebrow. His message is clear as the night sky.

"But listen," he goes on. "If she still won't take to it, there's a competition in rodeo. It's relatively new. A champion rodeo rider, Stacey Westfall, coined it when she won the 2006 Championship. It's called 'Freestyle Without a Bridle.'" He scans my face for a read before continuing. "If you're up for trying it again once we get her back into the ring, we could give that a thought."

"Is there prize money involved?"

"You bet there is. But there's also a fair amount of danger."

"Will you help me?"

"Of course."

I start to say something else but my words are lost under a bang of thunder so loud, Ole' Blue rears up with a startled whinny. Jake reaches over, from his horse, grabbing my reins, but I'm not stable. I'm slipping off the side like in the creek. Jake hops off his horse and stops my fall, but Blue lurches again and I catapult onto him. We land hard in a tangle of brush. Jake breaks most of my fall, catching my elbow, but my hip hits the dirt while my face lands in his chest, his protective arm around my head, the other hand bracing the fall against the dirt and bush.

"You okay?" he asks into my face.

"Yeah, are you?"

"Yep. You have a" — he plucks something out of my hair — "blackberry in your hair. Ripe too." His fingers linger on my face a second longer than necessary, but then another thunder-like noise erupts, rattling my knees through the earth.

"What *is* that?" The sky above us is black and clear. I can see every star, but the thunderous roar is coming closer. "A plane?"

Jake stands up, offering me a hand. "It's the herd." His voice is tense.

"Cows? But it's so loud." I have to raise my voice to be heard. On instinct, I step a little closer into Jake's chest.

He's looking over my head and keeps a protective arm around my shoulders. "Not cows, horses."

Horses? "Where's Blue?" I'm suddenly worried.

"Probably halfway down the mountain by now." His voice sounds light. "He spooks easy."

The crescendo of approaching horses hits a high and as they finally come into view. It's so loud, I press myself back into Jake's chest. "They won't run us over will they?"

"I don't think so. Hey, look who decided to pay us a visit."

I follow Jake's pointing finger and smack in the middle of the crowd of wild horses, Scout is running back and forth under the full moon in a wave of tails and hooves and beauty.

"Oh, that naughty girl."

"Seriously."

"She looks like she's having the time of her life, though."

Jake and I watch her—the wild beauty—running free under the countless stars.

"Hi, Scout!" I call out, which makes Jake chuckle.

"Like she's going to pay any attention to you."

But she does. She looks up, her eyes meeting mine, before neighing into the sky and thundering down the mountain, the rest of the pack dusting after her.

"Whoa."

"Wild, huh?"

"Yep."

I don't want this conversation to end. If I stop talking, Jake will likely get right to work. So I say, somewhat uninspired and obvious, the only thing I can think of that rings even partially authentic. "What a crazy day."

"Not any more eventful than yesterday was or tomorrow will be, I suppose."

I crane my neck and the side of my head nudges his jaw. He's that close. "Do you have to have the perfect one liner for everything?" I snap, and he laughs.

"How can I answer that without risking your condemnation? I swear you're just as bad as that horse of yours."

It's the ultimate compliment and my grin is so wide that he plucks a berry off the bush and pops it in my mouth. He watches my mouth as I chew in that careful way only Jake does. Heat crawls from the back of my neck. We lost our headlamps in the fall, and I'm glad he can't see me blushing in the dark. I finally let go of his hand, pretending I need to wipe sticky blackberry juice off my palms.

After the last sounds of the running herd have faded from the mountain and all is still and quiet again, I admit. "I don't want to go back."

He sounds surprised. "You want to spend the night up here?"

"Can we?"

He's smiling again. "I brought gear just in case."

"You did?"

"Sure. I always bring it along if I'm going this far in the evening." I love how he pronounces evening. It's like e-ven-ing: long and lyrical—a word with infinite potential.

"Did you bring other…provisions?"

He laughs. "I brought canned food and canteens of water, if that's what you mean, but I don't have your fancy coffee along this time. You'll have to make due with the good stuff. Genuine cowboy coffee. No more pampering if we're going to get you ready for that rodeo in time."

My eyes fly open. "You mean it, Jake? We'll try for the freestyle competition?"

"If you manage to get your wild 'stang back, we can try. Now stop your happy dancing and get over here and help me unload our grub." I do. Then, after, I ask somewhat sheepishly, "Where do you, uh, want me to roll out your bed?"

"Next to yours is fine."

I hope my face doesn't look as stirred up by the thought as my heart feels.

"Who else is going to protect you from bears and those mountain lions you city slickers are always talking about if I'm over there under the tree?"

I'm sure my blush is deeper than the flames of the fire Jake made in a center of rocks he found. "You make an excellent point," I mumble, hiding my grin.

We work together, easily. I'm keyed up but trying hard to keep it mellow. He hands me the can opener, and I flip the lids off two cans of chili. I hand them back to him—a little worried about the amount of beans we'll have to consume on this trip— and he spoons the contents into a small pot, holding it over the flames, just enough to warm it up. Jake leans closer, until our shoulders are touching, and shows me how to hold it perfectly over the flame. I'm eager and nervous and delighted, and for once don't try and resist these positive feelings.

"What about the horses?" I ask.

"Oh, they'll entertain themselves," Jake says, waving off my question in his nonchalant, joking manner.

"I wasn't suggesting we put on a puppet show for them."

His chuckle is low and genuine. "What'd you mean, then?"

"What are we going to do about them? Scout in particular?"

"Let her do her thing tonight. We'll rustle her up in the morning and try and convince her to come along home with us."

The flames rise and fall in the fire. Despite the heat, I shiver.

"Would you like some coffee?" he asks.

"It might keep me awake if I drink it this late." I'm going to have a hard enough time sleeping under the stars next to Jake. Nodding, he offers some herbal tea instead. Herbal tea. Jake the cowboy. He thought of everything. It was like he knew we were going to be up here for the night. Is he as flipped out over it as I am? If so, he sure hides it well. Ever the gentleman, he waits, patiently, until I say, "Sure. Thanks."

We drink out of little tin camping cups, making eye contact over our sips of lemon tea, and when we're finished, we watch the fire until its low flames fade to embers. We don't talk, but it's fine. Comfortable. After, he goes off into the woods; then I do, which is hilarious. I just try not to sit on poison oak, or worse, over a snake hole. I tell Jake this when I return, and we laugh about that, as he tells me a story about a rattler episode when he was a kid.

I watch him while he fusses around with more of the gear as I sit on top of my bedroll, just watching, watching, as he purposefully moves around the camp. I could watch Jake move around all day. He moves with such grace. When he finally sprawls down on his sleeping bag, I feel so nervous I unzip my zipper and jump, startled by its abrasive and awkward sound. "Jesus!"

He laughs. "What's got you so spooked?"

"Maybe the snake story. You didn't really need to tell me that one. Now I'll be worried every time I head to the bushes."

"Come on, you loved that story."

"I did."

Pause.

"I love all your stories."

His jaw moves back, surprised. "Well, that's nice to hear."

"It's true."

I don't let go of his gaze, and he holds mine. In front of us, the flames lick at the dry wood.

"This is nice," Jake says.

He's looking at me with those clear blue eyes.

"It is nice," I say.

Nice. It's more than nice. It's Jake and me spending the night together. But it also scares me to death. What if something happens between us and ruins everything? I came here to break free of toxic relationships. I'm not healthy enough to start a new one. But Jake is looking at me with those eyes of his, and all I want to do is fall into his arms and try and forget everything.

"Good." He lies on his back, and like last time, sets his cowboy hat over his face.

I'm wide awake.

Wide. Awake.

I bite my lip. Fiddle with my fingers. Is he really going to sleep? There's no way I can sleep now. He's so close to me I can practically feel his heartbeat.

"I took an astronomy class and had to memorize some of the constellations," I blurt out.

"Oh yeah?" he says from under his hat without lifting it off his eyes. "Tell me one."

"Well, that one right above us is Pegasus. See his wings? Jake. You're going to have to take that hat off your face." Chuckling, he does as he's told. "Better," I say. "Okay, see that? And that one is the Archer. Can you make out his bow and arrow there? They're only in the sky like this during the summer. In the winter the constellations are different."

"I like that. The shift."

He's looking at me again. His gaze is steadier. Holding on to mine tight. So tight, I never want to let go.

"What?" I say, in a small voice.

"Nothing. I'm just glad you're here."

I swallow. I tell the truth. "I'm glad you're here, too."

He flips over onto his stomach, and still looking at me, reaches his arm toward me. I don't waste a moment before wrapping my hands around his forearm.

"Jake?"

"Yeah."

"Thanks for bringing me up here tonight. This is exactly what I needed."

"The ladies seem to like my tea."

"You know what I mean."

"I know." Somewhere close by, a horse cries into the moon. "And you're welcome."

"Jake?"

"Yeah."

"Do you think…if it came down to it? To deciding to cut off the machines. Do you think he would've done it?"

He leans up on his elbow. "That stubborn ole' coot? No way."

My heart leaps. "Really? You aren't just saying that to make me feel better?"

"Two things you need to know about me if we're going to continue in this fashion. One, I won't ever lie to you. And two, I'm also a pretty damn good—how did you put it earlier? Bullshit detector? And your old man's as stubborn as you are."

"Meaning?"

"Meaning, he's not gonna give up on anything he loves without a fight. And this life?" His eyes shift to the patterns of summer stars—Pegasus, the Archer—back to me. "Sure is worth fighting for, don't you agree?"

"But what about the DNR. Isn't that giving up?"

"Think that's more about us than it is about him."

"You think he…" My throat closes. "Thinks he's a burden on us?"

"I think he doesn't want, in the state he's in, to live any longer than he should. Hooked up. If he's unable to communicate with us anymore, that's all he has left. If he loses that, that isn't really living, is it?"

I nod, a tear slipping down my cheek.

My hand slips down his forearm and my fingers tangle in his. Though my whole body is alive and pulsing in this close proximity to Jake, I don't move any closer, and neither does he, as if we both recognize the fragility of the moment, and how very small we are under the vastness of the universe. How one tiny move could ruin everything. How one tiny move could shift the order. How as much as I wanted to press my body into his, how I longed for his lips on mine, his large hands on my face, we aren't ready for that yet. I feel something on my face. Something warm and wool that smells like Jake. Smiling, I lift it off. Jake's cowboy hat. "Go to sleep, Cowgirl."

My dreams are not about death. My dreams are not about trains, or wheelchairs, or my father choking on baby food. They are not about a boy pressuring a girl into something maybe neither of them ever wanted. Instead, they are something else all together. My dreams are wild mustangs running on clouds. My dreams are hooves clapping thunder under a full moon's light. My dreams are Jake and me teetering atop the Tetons high cragged cliffs, questioning if we want to dive off together into the warm water pools below.

Chapter Forty-Nine

The next morning, Jake finally gets the rope bridle around Scout, but from the way she's tossing her head around trying to shake it off, it's clear she thinks of it more like a noose.

With each harsh toss of her neck, with each defiant neigh, I question my decision.

I touch Jake's shoulder. "Maybe we should just leave her here."

"She'll get used to it."

"What if she doesn't?"

"She will. We can't leave her up here, and we gotta head back."

"But she's so happy up here with her herd."

"They aren't her herd. She's only half mustang."

"Still. She fits in here."

Jake wipes sweat off his brow. It's only eight or so, but it's already hot. It took him thirty minutes to get the rope around her head, and now I'm suggesting he takes it off.

"Sorry. It's just that, what if this is where she belongs?"

"I get what you're saying, but her mama's a champion mare. If Scout here takes home a freestyle prize she can be worth two hundred k."

I stop and gasp. "Two hundred *thousand* dollars?"

"Yep."

"Wow."

"Yeah, you still think we should leave her to play with this herd?"

"I do think we should, and I also think we should bring her home."

"Too bad we can't be two places at once," Jake says, as always, meaning more than he says.

Though she's still a little miffed we pulled her away from her wild mustang friends, she lets Jake lead her down the mountain, and, like yesterday, she heads straight for the gate, but we shut it before Jake offers me a lift up on his conjoined hands.

She rears when she sees the gate is shut but surprises me a different way when I squeeze my thighs tight around her middle and she comes to an abrupt stop.

"How'd you do that?" Jake said.

"I don't know. I just squeezed my legs around her."

"Try and get her to get moving again."

"Just kick her sides like I would with spurs?"

"Sure."

I give her a little nudge with my boots, and she moves forward into a slow trot. I nudge her a little harder and she breaks into a canter, we're moving faster now and she's galloping. I lean forward, clutching her wiry mane. When we whip past Jake, he gives out a loud whoop, cowboy hat swinging like a lasso in the sky.

Chapter Fifty

"**P**aige and Scout are entering the rodeo in the Freestyle Without a Bridle event! They're already registered, so it's a done deal," Jake says as we burst into the kitchen.

It's a declaration, not a suggestion.

We're standing shoulder to shoulder in the strawberry kitchen, a wall of determination Anna can't bust through.

"Well, good morning to you, too," Anna says looking amused.

"Oh, right. Good morning." He tips his hat in greeting, before lifting it off his head and hooking it onto the hat rack by the front door. "We ended up staying on the mountaintop after we found Scout. It was too late to get home."

"That's what I figured."

"Where's Dad?" I ask.

"Still sleeping. He had a bit of a rough night." She takes a long sip of her coffee. "Ack, this is already cold. I got to daydreaming I guess and let it set too long."

"I'll warm it up for you," Jake says. Zipping past her, he sweeps the strawberry mug from where it was making a wet spot on the wood. After wiping the dampness with his plaid elbow, he disappears into the kitchen. I hear the trickle of the coffee as he pours it into the pot to reheat. They don't use a microwave here on the ranch.

"How you doing, Paige?" Anna looks up at me.

"Fine." I shrug. "Good."

"Have a good night?"

"Yes. Does…Dad know I spent the night with Jake up on the mountain?" I cringe waiting for her answer.

"No. Do you want me to tell him?"

"No."

She cocks her head thoughtfully. "I don't think he'd mind, though. He trusts Jake."

"Okay. Good."

"He's a good boy, Jake."

"Yep."

"Okay, then," Anna says, clasping her hands together.

"Okay?" Jake asks, reentering the room. "What, the Freestyle idea? Here you go, nice and scorching." He sets the mug in front of Anna. "It's going to be awesome."

"Awesome?" Anna cocks her eyebrow. "You're starting to sound like the City Slicker."

"That all bad?"

"Nope. Long as you're happy, it's all fine."

"We are. I am. I mean." I've never seen him flustered before. He whirls around, heads for the coat rack, and snuffs his hat back onto his head like he's trying to put out a fire.

"Well then, I suggest you start studying Stacey Westfall's moves and get to it."

"That's what we're doing," Jake says. He shoots me a quick *follow me* look and we slip through the door, out of the darkness and back into the sun.

We have work to do.

Later that afternoon, Jake and I sit side-by-side on Dad's cracked leather couch in his den, which still smells of cigars and peppermint, eating freshly popped corn with real melted butter, and watch videos of rodeo's past on his flat screen TV. After studying previous entries, we make up our own routine.

We practice all evening. I get Scout to back up, walk forward, spin. I ask her to move to a canter, slow to a trot…and she does. We are a good team, she and I. I'm beaming when we finish, all dusty sweat, and Jake is all smiles on the fence.

He runs into the corral, and I slip off Scout into his arms. He swings me around, howling, "You got this! Hot damn, Cowgirl!"

I'm laughing and holding on tight as he spins me. When he sets me down, he looks at me with a full heady grin, "Let's celebrate!"

"What do you have in mind?"

"Anna and Gus are in town for the evening, out to dinner, so I was thinking how about me, you, a couple of brews?"

"Sounds great," I say. But a red flag pops up, flying high. Beers? Drinking? This could lead to something else…something I know I'm not ready for. What if we screw everything up? I won't do that with Jake. I can't risk it. But we've come so far with Scout… "Or, something else? A picnic maybe?" Picnics are fine. Picnics are safe.

"That sounds good," he says.

"Where?" I ask. The where matters.

"How about the hayloft? You seem to like it up there."

So he's noticed my time in the hayloft, too. I'm both flattered and flustered.

"Sounds good," I say. Actually it sounds great, but I don't want to appear too excited. I don't want to lead him on, either. As much as I like Jake, I can't let him think anything romantic will happen between us.

"I'll make us some sandwiches." Grinning, he adds an enthusiastic clap like it's a punctuation mark.

"I'll take a shower." I match his enthusiasm, and we laugh.

"See you in a bit," he says. Then he adds in a weighty voice, "Have a nice shower."

I flush. Why did I mention taking a shower? I can see in his eyes he's thinking about me showering. Oy. We part, and I'm one part flustered, one part dismayed. All parts worried as I take my time showering.

I can't mess things up with Jake.

I cannot mess things up with Jake.

I'm leaving for college soon. I won't be here anymore. I want us to stay friends no matter what. I *need* us to stay friends. Dad needs him. Anna needs him. He's my lifeline here on the ranch. If something we do gets weird, or worse, goes *bad*...that just can't happen. So we'll have this picnic—as friends—and maybe I'll talk to him about it. Maybe it's time to talk to him about stuff at home.

Stuff with Ty.

But the thought of bringing Ty into this safe atmosphere feels all kinds of wrong. I don't want to tangle these two webs of my life together, so instead, I step out, towel off, and twist my hair into a loose bun. I dry off carefully and pull a clean white tank top over my lacy bra. I step into my nice skinny jeans from California, with the buttons on the back pockets. The ones I wore the first day that hung loose, but now fill out in the places where they are supposed to. A fitted button-down shirt goes over that, and I tuck it in. I barely recognize myself in the antique mirror—this pink-cheeked girl who doesn't look gaunt and hungry, but who looks satisfied and full.

A girl who looks happy.

Chapter Fifty-One

"Going, going, gone," I say, feet dangling over the hayloft as the rose sun dips over the mountains. "My dad used to say that."

But I'm not sad. I'm smiling. It's a good memory. Everything is good right now. No, everything is perfect right now.

Our denim legs swing side by side over the open-air hayloft ledge, Jake's and mine. Our thighs touch. Our boots occasionally clang in a fun, purposeful manner.

We're licking barbeque sauce off our fingers from Jake's chicken sandwiches when he uncaps two root beer bottles. "Now, this isn't your first beer, is it?"

"Hardly," I laugh. "I'd have the other kind, but I'm not sure that'd be okay with my dad."

"Oh, I understand that. I respect Gus very much."

"I know you do."

"I don't drink much myself, mostly because we have a sober environment around Gus, but also because of my mom. She's on the 12-steps, too."

"And because you're only 19?"

He laughs. "That, too. Though that hardly stops us in Wyoming. Must of us have been drinking since we were twelve."

"In your well-equipped kitchen?"

"Anywhere." He shrugs. "We grow up fast. Everything comes early. We ride at six, drive at twelve, drink at…well, damn if I can remember the first beer I had, but it was a long time ago."

"I bet some of the girls I went to first and second grade with are already pregnant by now," I say, remembering some of my old friends from my early days here on the ranch.

"Some of 'um, I'm sure, yep. Marry early, have kids early… just how it goes. If you're lucky enough to finish high school, you got that, but forget about college."

I nod, listening. I wonder why Jake isn't attached, married. He seems like the ideal husband for some lucky Wyoming girl. My heart twinges with jealousy imagining him married to a ranch girl, and I have to shake the thought away. "We grow up fast back in California now, too," I say. "Academically, at least, but maybe not in the other ways. Most of my friends have never even done the dishes, never mind cook or anything. They can speak three languages and code but have no idea where the recycling bin is in their house. We had to be beyond our years in some ways, while in other ways, we lacked the skills of most twelve-year-olds."

"City slickers," he says.

"Yep. And we're all too immature, or maybe clueless, to know some choices can't be undone." I swallow, remembering all the suicides. "Some bad choices are permanent."

I flash on Ty wiping out his character's motorcycle on that stupid video game. The way he looked at me, his young eyes already so old.

Game over, he had said.

I rub the chills off my arms.

"I guess no matter where you grow up, you have problems. Here I'd be worried about getting knocked up before I had my driver's license."

"Yep. And forget your fancy college plans. You'd be working at a diner or a resort if you were a townie. If you'd stayed on here, you'd be working the ranch."

I scan the land. The vast and beautiful country I've grown to love all over again. "Would that have been so bad?"

"It would've narrowed your opportunities, that's for sure."

"I don't know... I kind of like it here." I scan the pinkish landscape still fresh from the sunset, both raw and comforting.

"You might not if you'd been raised here. All the town girls want to do is leave. Sick of the tourists, sick of the fancy pants movie stars who fly in for a few weeks each winter and summer, sick of the cold winters and the too-hot summers. Sick of the dead-end minimum wage jobs. Sick of horse crap."

I laugh, imagining myself...this alternate version of Paige. Would I be one of those girls dying to leave? Begging to move to the big city? Talk about irony. Maybe that's why mom took me. To save me from that. I was going to college in the fall. A good college where I could study creative writing. Pursue my dreams. I'd worked hard in high school, and I got into the college of my choice. If I'd stayed on here, I'd be working at the ranch, teaching city kids how to ride horses, maybe waitressing at a local diner.

As if Jake could read my thoughts he says, "Grass is always greener, you know the phrase."

"Indeed," I say, taking a long sip of root beer. Was this the first time I had a soda since Jake handed me one on that bumpy Jeep ride when I first arrived? I could barely remember that girl—so broken and sick and hungry and shaky. She was an absolute mess. Was Jake right, though? If I had stayed on all these years, would I have resented it? Was living most of my life in California beneficial, even with the horrors of the past year?

The sun was bright, and everything from my vantage point gold.

"I've been here over a month, and I've trained a wild mustang. Does that mean I'm officially on the ranch timeline now or, in the very least, old enough to have a genuine beer with a genuine cowboy?" I lean into him and give his shoulder a little nudge with mine. His plaid shirt is soft. His muscles under it tight.

He nudges me back. "Ah, so you're a genuine cowgirl now, are you?"

"Getting there."

He pulls two dark bottles out of the little cooler. "I brought some real ones if you'd like. I wasn't sure."

"Sure." It suddenly seems like a fine idea. So naughty. So deliciously normal to sneak a beer in your daddy's barn with the boy you're crushing on. I let myself enjoy it.

He pops the bottle caps, and I take a long sip of the beer. It's light and wheaty with a taste of something…fruity. "Did you bring me a girly beer?"

"I did."

"Why do you have girly beers in your cabin?"

"Never know when a genuine cowgirl might propose a hayloft picnic."

"Good answer," I say.

Jake is so freaking cute.

I love the way he's looking at me.

I love the way he's talking to me.

I love how he is. How we are with each other.

I love the dimple tucked between his cheek and his jaw, his neck, his arms, his chest — the whole of him.

The moment is quiet, but it isn't awkward. "Do you really think we have a chance of winning this thing?" I ask him after another long sip that tastes of a sun-warmed apricot.

"If anyone does, you do."

My chest feels light and fuzzy. I'm sure he can hear my heart pounding. "Thanks for believing in me, Jake. It sounds cheesy but I mean it."

"You broke me in," he says, quietly. His Adam's apple moves as he swallows. I think he's going to look away, but he doesn't. I feel myself sway into him.

His face is close to mine, so close, and I'm spinning. I'm lost in the moment because the air smells like hay and my childhood: fresh and clean and good. Things I'd forgotten.

But I can't do this. I can't. It'll ruin everything, and I won't survive if I don't have Jake and Anna and my dad.

Sucking in a breath, I pull away.

"Paige?" His voice is soft. Confused.

"I-I can't Jake."

"Why not?"

"Not because it feels wrong, but because it feels right."

"How can something that feels right be wrong?"

"I'm leaving soon. I—I was in a bad relationship back at home, and I just don't want to ruin this thing we have, which, to me, is perfect."

He inhales and takes a sip of his beer, his hand shaking. When he sets it down, it falls over, froth seeping into the hay, and he curses under his breath. "Here," I say, I take off my outer shirt and, leaning over him, mop it up, ignoring his protests to use his, or just leave it. It's only hay. It's only a barn. "It's fine, it's old," I say. But when I realize I'm now sitting there in my quite possibly see-through tank top, I jerk back upright, hugging my arms around my chest, worried he'll be like Ty—accuse me of teasing him. Leading him on and then rejecting him.

I remember Ty's cruel words: *You're a tease. You know you want to, Paige.*

I shudder.

Jake is nothing like Ty, but Ty is still here, haunting me, lurking in the cool breeze, in the night's shadows.

"Hey," he says, sweetly, looking up from the sopping shirt, and touching my shoulder. "What's wrong?"

"It's not you, Jake. I adore you. If I were staying…if things were different…"

He nods solemnly, his eyes conveying words he doesn't say, things he wishes were different. It's a look I see Dad give Anna twenty times a day. The look she returns. It's a look I'm beginning to hate for its weakness, for its morose emptiness— good intentioned but ultimately worthless, like the stupid things they all said at the funerals trying to make the now childless mothers and fathers feel better about losing the person they loved most. *I'm sorry you've had your heart ripped out of your chest. Good luck surviving that.* Right. Like words could even dent that kind of pain. Like a pound cake smothered in whipped cream and strawberries from the organic GMO free bakery or a dozen white lilies could make you forget losing someone you've loved for all your heartbeats.

It's a look I give Jake in return until I can't meet his eyes anymore because it's too sad, too hard.

Nibbling my lip, I face the hayloft's splintered wall so he can't see the tears in my eyes. I feel his warm hand scooping mine up, cupping it in both of his. He lifts it up and kisses it and I don't pull away. I let it rest there in his, hoping this sand-sized bit of hope, of safety, of promise, will become a pearl.

When I lean back into his waiting arms, I tip my head against his flannel shoulder, sinking into his warm chest. I feel his lips press against my hair, hard and soft, tough and gentle at the same time. Just like Jake. And we stay like that for a while, as close as we can, touching as much as possible without quite crossing that imaginary line between temporary and forever.

That night I write in my journal for the first time in what feels like forever.

But I have to finish the story of Then. The story of Before. So I can have a future of Now.

Chapter Fifty-Two

Then

Two knocks.

Two more knocks—louder this time.

"That's four knocks," I said, opening the door. "What do you want, Ty?"

He eyed the *Alice in Wonderland* T-shirt I bought at Disneyland a few years back. "Nice shirt."

It was more like a half-shirt now—a half-shirt that used to come to my knees. After our talk, I wasn't expecting any more late-night visitors. I hug my arms around myself, concealing the parts I don't want him to see. "What's up?"

"Is that an innuendo?"

My voice hardened along with my firm stance in the doorway. There was no way I was going to allow him in. I eye the blue and white Italian vase on my dresser. If I had to, I'd use it on his pretty face. "It wasn't meant to be. What do you want?"

"Mom and Dad aren't home."

"So."

"So? I was thinking…" He tried to nudge past me with a little sashay like we were dancing.

I reached out my arm, palming the wood along the door opening, blocking him from entering. "I meant what I said, Ty. We need to move past the…other, and reestablish our relationship as stepsiblings, or just don't talk at all. Honestly, I'd prefer the latter."

"Reestablish. You sound like the shrink now."

"I'm serious, Ty."

"I'm serious, too. Seriously *horny*."

Ugh. "You're disgusting. Are you drunk?" I leaned in just close enough to smell his breath. Pretzels, not alcohol.

"No."

"Stoned?"

"May-be."

I folded my arms. "On what?"

"Why should I tell you?"

He was definitely on something. His pupils were dilated, and his body was all mushy, like Gumby. I could take him if it came down to it. Not that I wanted my parents to arrive home with Ty's blood on the carpet surrounded by broken pieces of Italian ceramic, but if he came one step closer… "This is my final warning. Get out of here, Ty."

I eye the vase. It would take only a second to grab it and smash it over his head. In fact, I kind of wanted to. *Go ahead, Ty. Take a step closer.*

He leaned in. Tried to kiss me. I shoved him forward, and as he fell against the hallway wall, I slammed the door shut and locked it.

Heart pounding, I grabbed my cell and called my mom.

"I'm heading into the tunnel, Paige. What do you need?"

She sounded bothered. Like I was disrupting something more important. "Oh, n-nothing."

"What? I can't hear you. You're breaking up."

"It's okay. Are you coming straight home?"

"Yes. If traffic isn't too—What are you doing, you jackass? A Prius just cut me off. And they say BMW drivers are the assholes. I'll be home as soon as I can, okay?"

"Okay. See you in an hour or so," I said, my voice cracking.

Click.

I slumped against the wall. Maybe Ty would leave me alone long enough for Mom to get home. Maybe if we all sat down together, he'd—

My phone pinged.

You're such a tease.

Shit. He wasn't going to leave this alone. Worse, he could easily open my door with a bobby pin. I'd done it myself once. I tossed my phone on the bed and shoved my dresser in front of the door.

You can't open your door dressed like that and expect me not to want you.

I know you're reading these.

Answer me.

You're never going to believe me about that girl, no matter how many times I tell you it wasn't true. You see me as a monster. So just do it. Tell me you hate me and I'll leave you alone. I'll leave you alone forever.

He was never going to listen.

He would never respect my "no."

So standing there shivering in my *Alice in Wonderland* shirt, I dredged up his slobbery kisses and his mushy condoms and his cheap-beer breath on my face, and I shoved down everything that used to be good, the parts of Ty that I loved.

I told him something I meant at the moment. The three words I'd live to regret, live to churn over and over and over again, words that haunted me night after night. Words like the sound of a hysterical train.

I hate you, I typed, and then I pressed send.

Chapter Fifty-Three

Now

I know my time in Jackson is running out, and I hate it, but the truth is, summer's almost over. When Mom emails me a return ticket to San Francisco, I ignore it. But Anna (wisely cc'd—smart move, Mom) sees it. She prints it out and brings it to my room. I tuck it into a drawer like it's a fortune cookie warning of impending doom.

After the time with Jake in the hayloft, I've been going over and over in my head what we said, what passed between us. I don't know a lot, but I know I'm not ready to go. I don't want to even think about leaving or moving away from here.

When I arrived, I couldn't think of anything worth living for. Everything felt numb, tasteless. I felt frayed, broken. I wasn't sure the jagged pieces of what was left of my life were worth putting back together, but Jake, and Anna, and Dad— they felt otherwise. Together they helped move around the pieces, reshape the edges.

They were starting to fit again.

And I was so grateful to feel myself healing.

Every smile, every sunset, every time I tip my head back and catch a glimpse of this blue, blue sky, I am thankful to be alive. And I owe it all to them.

Being here with Dad, getting to know Jake, even Anna's careful watch and healthy meals that relentlessly came at me until I accepted them, changed me.

I'd be lying to myself to say they weren't. To be totally honest, I was tired of lying to myself. It didn't work, anyway. I was scared to leave and face my mother again. To face the home I fled. To face the ghosts that waited for me in my old bedroom.

So I try to wish the return ticket away and focus on the time I have left. Savor it, because like all fleeting, beautiful, seemingly undeserved moments, ripped up pieces of a whole picture wafting on the wind, it would end soon, no matter what I wanted.

Three days before I'm set to return home to pack for college, pre-rodeo festivities envelop the town.

American flags hang in front of every storefront. Rodeo Jackson is more pro-cowboy than usual (if that's even possible). If you've entered the rodeo, then you get half off at most of the eateries in town and are basically treated like a celebrity, so when Anna and I drive into town that afternoon to shop for my rodeo costume, we get the royal treatment, too.

"If it isn't Gus Mason's daughter! Back to win the Freestyle competition I hear?" The owner of the Buck-N-Bronco greets us at the steakhouse entrance. We're blasted by the smell of charbroiled meat so sweet, it makes my stomach growl. "How's it feel to be back in the saddle after all that time in the big city, sweetheart?"

He puts a hefty arm around my shoulder and pulls me into a bear hug.

"That's why I decided to bypass the saddle. Too tricky," I say. He laughs, his big eyes sparkling like fireworks. His laugh booms similarly.

"We've got a live one," he announces to everyone within

hearing distance. "Just like her daddy." When he turns to Anna, his expressive face shifts to one of sorrow. "How is ole' Gus?"

"Hanging in, Pete. It's not easy for him."

"I reckon it isn't," he said awkwardly, like the conversation shifted to an unpopular president when you don't agree on politics. "We miss him around here. Bring him by soon, will you?"

"You can come visit anytime. You're always welcome at the ranch, and he'd love to see you." Anna's tone is clear and concise.

"Patty and I plan to get out there, we sure do, but with the business and the kids and all this—you know how it is."

Pete grabs two menus and, avoiding Anna's eyes, leads us to a table by the window.

"Thanks," I say, scooting into the brown vinyl booth. You could cut the tension between Anna and this guy with one of the steak knives sitting on the red, white, and blue paper napkins. As soon as he rounds the corner, I lift an eyebrow at Anna.

She sighs. "Pete is, was, one of your daddy's best friends. When Gus was first diagnosed with ALS, Pete and his wife Patty came around a lot, helping out on the ranch and visiting for supper. But about a year ago when Gus lost most of his physical faculties, their visits tinkered off. Gus doesn't say anything about it, but I can tell it hurts him."

"Why don't they come?"

I'm asking a question I already know the answer to. They're freaked out. They can't stand to look at him like that. They're in denial. Like Mom was, maybe. Facing things head on for exactly what they are is hard. Like looking in a Windex-clean mirror when you're used to a steamy reflection.

"You learn a lot about a person's character when something like this happens. You see Pete, he's larger than life and a good ole' cowboy, one of your dad's oldest and dearest, but he can barely look at your dad."

"Was Jake ever like that?"

"You know he wasn't. Not for a second."

I smile. I can't help it. "He's amazing."

"He's a good kid, that's for sure."

"The best."

We both sip from our water glasses, my throat thick with feelings I'm losing a fight with. We look over our food-stained menus. When the waitress comes over, I order a mixed greens salad and a half turkey sandwich on wheat bread. Anna orders a tuna sandwich with sprouts on pita bread. She spoons three tablespoons of sugar into her tall glass of iced tea.

"I don't want to leave, Anna. Can I stay? Please. Please can I stay?" I blurt out of nowhere. I have a ticket home. I'm going home to pack and then I'm leaving for college. But I can't help it. I don't want to go and Anna is my only hope.

"This is your daddy's ranch, Paige. This is your home. You can stay as long as you'd like. Forever if that's what you want."

Forever.

My anxious lungs deflate. I'm hungry again. "If my mom calls, can you tell her that?"

"I sure can, or you can tell her yourself. You're eighteen, and as far as the law of the land states, you can make your own decisions."

Anna. All knowing and all wise. No wonder my dad fell in love with her. I can stay. The choice is mine. What if I could stop running from ghosts, stop chasing the future, and just stay in this…comfort? It seems like the obvious choice. I can't wait to go home and tell Jake.

Our sandwiches arrive and we eat in silence until Anna orders two floats. The root beers arrive in the original Sarsaparilla bottles. After we topple the scoops of vanilla ice cream with foamy soda, Anna raises a thick glass mug to mine and we cheer to Scout and Daddy and Eight Hands Ranch, but what I'm really toasting is the hope of forever.

"Are you sure about this?"

After lunch, I'm playing fashion show and literally dressed head to toe in silver: A silver button-down bodysuit complete with silver sequin stars on the shoulders, and shooting stars on straight collars, cuffs, and back, is tucked into silver flared-bottoms riding pants.

"Try them with the boots!" Anna says, obviously delighted with the results.

I tuck the flared-bottoms into silver cowboy boots.

"Seriously?" I repeat when Anna's response is tucking here and snapping there. I wiggle around. In the full-length mirror, the body suit looks and feels ridiculous. *I* look and feel ridiculous.

"It's perfect," she says, her word muffled by the safety pin between her teeth. "You don't want your shirttail flying out behind you on the course."

I tug on the crotch. "It's like one of those baby things."

"A onesie? Yes, I know. It's a very practical design."

I groan. "I look like—"

"A cowgirl? Good that's what you're supposed to look like."

I squint at my reflection. I don't want to ride Scout into the arena in this outfit. I don't even want to exit the dressing room in it, but I also don't want to disappoint Anna.

"Isn't it a bit"—How do I put this graciously?—"much?"

"Nope. Hot pink spangles on your chaps and hat ribbon, and a clown on your belt buckle might be too much. But this isn't. This is a classic look. Clean. Simple."

Simple? I look like C3P0 tagged with glittery silver spray paint.

But since I knew nothing about rodeos and the proper attire for participating in them, who was I to argue? It's a costume. I'm competing in an event, and I need to maximize my chances of winning. Like an Olympic ice-skating event, style counts. I'll think of it as a play.

"Everything fits okay? We don't want your pants splitting

during your routine."

"We certainly do not want that," I say, sucking in my stomach. Not going to lie, the pants are pretty tight, but they're a stretchy material and do fit. "I'll have chaps covering most of it anyway."

"Just the bottom half of your leg."

I check the price tags and gasp. The shirt is $330, the pants $120. The boots were at least $200. And we still haven't shopped for a (certainly silver) hat.

"Anna this is way too much to spend."

"It's average. Really. We'll…just put it on the card."

Heat crawls up my skin and spreads out like roads on a map. I can't let them invest so much into something I'll probably screw up. "I'll get my mom to reimburse you."

"That's nice, but I get the feeling she is less than enthusiastic about this whole venture of yours. Don't worry about the cost. If you look good, you feel good."

I know for a fact that's not true. I've often looked just fine but felt like the floor of Scout's stall before we've raked it out.

"We'll need a blazer, too. Do you prefer white, pink, or black leather?"

"Pink leather is a thing?"

Anna gives up and sics me on the sales clerk, who says, "Magenta, yes. It's very popular this season."

The "magenta" is tailor-cut to fit the female body, and with embroidered butterflies on the back and down the sleeves, it's very in-season, apparently.

The white leather is the least gaudy and the beaded sequins match my onesie, so I suggest that one. Anna is happy with the choice and barters a deal with the sales clerk.

As we exit the shop with giant bags, I'm so happy to be back in my jean cut-offs and tank top I'm practically floating through the air…until she suggests we better do something about my nails.

"What's wrong with my nails?"

"What's right with them?"

I survey my fingers, which, admittedly, have some dirt under the close-trimmed nails. "A lot?"

"Wrong. Come with me."

As soon as we get back to the ranch, I call my mom from the red landline in the kitchen.

"Mom?"

"Paige! How are you? Did you get the return tickets? You've been avoiding my phone calls. You haven't emailed... Honey, I've been worried."

"Sorry. How are you? How's Phil?"

"As good as can be expected."

I can feel the weight of what this means through the phone. "Yeah."

"How are you?"

"I'm good. I'm actually good." I twirl the old-fashioned cord around my fingers and stare at a particularly large strawberry cookie jar on the counter. "You were right about me coming here. I feel better in so many ways. And I...I want to stay."

"Stay?"

"Stay here and help Dad and Anna and the ranch."

"You can't stay, honey. You have to come home and pack for college."

"I want to postpone. Maybe just for a semester."

"Postpone? No."

"Mom. *Yes*. I need to be with Dad. He's not doing well. I want to be here. I don't want to leave them."

She pauses. "We can talk about it when you come home, okay?"

"No! You'll just say no." I pull out the big guns. "I'm eighteen—You can't stop me."

She sighs. "If this is what you really want, I'll think about it."

"Really?"

"Really. I love you, Paige. I just want you to be happy."

If only making someone happy were as easy as saying the words.

After the phone call, I fill in Anna about the possibility of me staying on. She tells me I should talk to my dad. He's napping after our long trip into town, so I promise to talk to him later.

Jake is outside working with Scout. I stand on the porch and watch him for a while. I can't wait to tell him the news. This will change everything.

My heart swells as I slowly approach the corral.

He looks up at me with a grin. "Hey there."

"Hi," I say, unable to shake my giddy little smile.

"You look like you had a good time in town."

"I did. And I might have some good news to tell you later."

"Oh, really? I like good news."

I chuckle. "What're you doing?

"Trying to get Scout used to weight other than you on her back. See this saddlebag full of rice? I'm trying it out. She loves it, as you can see."

She bucks it off before he can even tie the strap, then bucks into the air so hard and fast, Jake has to dive out of the way to avoid a rear-hooves-to-the-face scenario.

"I don't think she likes your idea, Jake," I say.

Snatching his hat off the dirt, he sets it back on his head. "I think you may be right. Want to give it a try, hot shot?"

"No thanks. I have to keep her in my good graces. With the rodeo coming up and all."

"Probably smart."

We head in for dinner. I think about Pete and wonder if Anna is going to bring up the fact that we saw him. She doesn't. She rattles on about this and that. Dad listens and she feeds him, wiping off his chin gently. The evening sun shines through the window as I tell Dad what I talked to Mom about.

"I'm thinking about staying on at the ranch for a while, Dad. Is that okay with you?"

Finishing his sip of green protein and vegetable smoothie concoction, he types, *For a few more weeks? It's more than okay, kiddo. I would like that very much.*

"I meant for even longer. Maybe even for the school year?"

Across the table, Jake's eyes widen.

I don't think that's a good idea, sweetheart. Summer, yes. But you have college.

"Yes, but I want to stay here with you."

We can discuss it again at the end of the summer, but for now, let's keep your plan on track. You're my little girl, Paigey. It's easy to get sidetracked by things, and I want you to stay on track.

On track.

The irony of his use of "track" is not lost on me, though there's no way he intends it. I'm not ready to enter normal society again. The thought of school, classes, strangers, chills me to the bone. But I can tell by Dad's words that I need to listen to him now. I can bring it up again later. For now, at least I have a few more weeks. I have Scout, I have Jake, I have the ranch. For now I am safe.

How's your training with Scout going?

"Good. She's such a rascal."

Like her rider. ☺

I laugh. He continues typing in his way.

Do you remember the time you entered the rodeo as a little girl? You were supposed to tie up the calf's legs and you couldn't do it. You kept untying them. You were maybe 6 or 7.

"Oh, God," I groan. "I completely forgot about that. On purpose."

You had a big heart then. You have a big heart now. The people with the biggest hearts hurt the most when bad things happen. But guess what?

"What?"

When those broken hearts heal, they heal stronger than ever.

I don't reply. Not with words anyway. I lean over and kiss him on the cheek, nuzzling into his sallow cheek, his day-old scruff. When I look up, Jake is smiling at me. He has no idea what Dad typed to me but it doesn't matter. I let myself feel hope in the moment.

Chapter Fifty-Four

Then

I liked to pretend, for a variety of reasons, that my mother didn't know. That she never found out about Ty and me. But that was a lie.

They'd be home late. That's what they said, anyway.

Early into things between me and him, we were watching movies in the den — an eighties movie marathon — old raunchy classics like *Risky Business* and *Porky's*. Ty was appalled I hadn't seen them. Apparently, as a latchkey kid, he watched whatever he wanted while he waited for his parents to get home from work. After we moved to California, Mom made sure I was always in activities: I was proficient in ice-skating, French, water polo. I competed on the swim team, gymnastics…you name it.

"OMG, gross," I said, watching between cracked fingers as a guy shoved his penis through a hole in the girls' locker room.

"You gotta watch! Check out the size of that thing!" Ty cackled, tossing a pillow at the TV. "They just don't make movies like they used to. This would get an NC-17 for sure now."

"Fifty Shades of Porky's?" I suggested wryly.

"Exactly." He plops next to me on the couch, throws his arm around me. "Let's get that and watch it together."

"Are you kidding me?"

"Hardly. Maybe we can make it a family activity: you, me, Phil, and Carol."

"God, you are a sick beast."

"I know. And you love it."

We started making out, because that's what we did then.

Ty liked to watch all his movies on surround sound full volume on our enormous big screen TV. Needless to say, we didn't hear the door open or the stilettos clacking into the room until it was too late.

"What in the world are you two...?" Mom's voice dropped off as she saw, clearly, what we were doing, and it wasn't watching TV.

I pulled back, pushing him away, diving to the opposite side on the couch and focusing on the TV—a couple making out in a steam room—like it was the most enthralling thing in the world.

"Do we need to get a nanny for you kids?" Mom's voice lilted like she was joking, but I could feel the ice in it and it chilled me to the bone.

"No, ma'am," Ty said, saluting her. "We have everything under control. Sorry I'm exposing Paige to eighties pornography, however. We'll change the channel to something more age appropriate." He pointed the remote at the TV and switched it to the BBC news where we watched a foreign country killing citizens of another foreign country. I counted the casualties.

"Garbage going in, garbage coming out," she said pointedly.

"Yes," Ty agreed. "From here on out, we're going to aim for compost."

She laughed sharply. Her faux Nothing-Is-Funny-About-This laugh rivals most women's screams. I'd rather she just yell. Ground us. Threaten...something.

"This is why I read all my news online. Would you mind turning that off please, Tyler?"

"Sure thing, ma'am." The salute again. How was Ty unfazed by this? Wasn't he worried my mom would tell his dad and our home would turn into a prison camp of no electronics, home right after school, and worse, us being separated for life?

"Paige?"

I didn't turn around. "Yes?"

"Look at me when I'm speaking to you."

I turned around and looked at her. As soon as her eyes caught mine, they narrowed. Her nostrils flared. Oh, she was pissed all right. She just didn't want to let us see her faux fur flustered.

I stood halfway up expecting, "Follow me into my bedroom, we're going to have a little chat," but instead, she said, "Don't stay up too late."

I sank back onto the couch, confused and maybe, though it sounds weird, a little disappointed. This was okay with her? I was making out with my stepbrother, her stepson, *her husband's son*, on their living room couch.

"Okay."

Ty switched the channel to *A Few Good Men*, the eighties movie starring Tom Cruise as a softball tossing lawyer who gets Jack Nicholson to confess a major secret.

"You want the truth? You can't handle the truth!" Ty blurted out in his best Jack Nicolson impression. He looked at us over his shoulder, an innocent expression on his face. "What, too soon?"

Behind me, I felt Mom flinch. I could practically read her mind. *Would it be worth it to confront them? To open this enormous can of worms, and get Phil involved?* It would complicate things to the point of Nothing Being Perfect Anymore. The suicides were bad enough. Our years of being single, just the two of us while she worked her way up in a male-dominated world (her words) dating CEOs and VCs and finally settling down with her sweet Phil. Phil, who she golfed with, who she introduced on her arm at charity functions. Phil, who was positive and light and her best friend (again, her words). She wasn't going to risk losing Phil—even if it meant helping me out of a serious mistake.

Ignoring Ty's jab, she said instead, "I've always loved this movie. Demi Moore looks great with a bob cut."

"Right?" Ty said. "Want to watch with us?"

"No thanks, Tyler. Your father has a headache. That's why we came home from the event early." She looked at me pointedly. "I think I'll call it an evening, too. Goodnight, kids."

"Goodnight, Carol," Ty said in a singsong voice. How did he know? How did he know she wouldn't confront us? He was always flirting with the edge of disaster, that's how he lived. That's what he loved. I didn't. I wasn't even sure I'd make it to our shared bathroom before I threw up.

Chapter Fifty-Five

Now

Whether the sun is pushing up into the world or slipping over the mountains for the night, training with Scout and Jake is the best part of my day.

Dad and Anna watch our last training session before rodeo from the porch; Jake's animated gestures, Scout's neck beading with sweat as she responds to the commands my voice and thighs make. Like always, small successes and little failures define our practice: Jake catching my eye before pointing out an eagle's winged shadow in the dirt as he chews on straw under pinking blue skies, Anna's hand resting on Dad's leg. She's smiling and I'm guessing he is on the inside though I can't read it on his mouth.

I'm in the moment appreciating every single heartbeat, because this is it. This is where all the clichés like Carpe Diem and YOLO (You Only Live Once) spring from, and I get it and it's real and I'm fighting tooth and nail to keep it, though in the back of my head, that gnawing guilt never stops trying to fight its way back in. I almost think I can tell Jake the full truth, tell Anna, tell my dad—and they'll love me anyway. They'll still want me to stay.

Staying here would be hiding, though—hiding from my

past, hiding from my mistakes, mostly hiding from the truth—
and I don't feel right staying if I'm a lie. I can't stay if they don't
know the whole truth. They don't. And they need to. (Heather:
Like that?)

"You look great up there," Jake says after we go over our
routine. The music blasting from his little speaker set up on the
corral rail winds down to its final, beautiful end notes, and it's
all so dramatic and inspiring and hopeful I almost think I can
do it.

"You think?" I ask.

He nods appreciatively. "I do."

He means it. Jake doesn't say things he doesn't mean.

"And Scout's ready," he says, patting her moist neck. "You
were right about her. You two make quite a team."

I'm going to do it. After rodeo I'm going to tell him the
truth. I swallow away that last bit of doubt, swing my leg over
Scout's back, and jump down into Jake's arms. He gives me a
little spin before I slide down the length of his body and give
him a little kiss on the cheek on my way to touching the dirt.

"What was that for?" He cocks his head, happily surprised.

"This." I hug him tight. "No matter what happens in the
show," I whisper into his neck, "thanks, Jake."

"You don't have to thank me, you know."

"Yes," I say. "I really do."

Two days later I'm dressed again in the crazy silver bodysuit
tucked into silver spangled cowgirl boots.

My recently manicured nails now have American Flag
decals (true story) and I have on more makeup than a Miss
America contestant. My hair's been blown out and curled. I
have more foundation on my face than I did at my freshman
musical, bright red lipstick, and so much mascara I can barely
keep my eyes open.

I don't recognize myself in the mirror, which I'm okay with.

In my head, I go over and over my routine. In my heart, I go over and over what I'm going to say to Jake. How I'm going to tell him about Ty, about everything. It makes the rodeo far easier in comparison. As far as the competition goes, I'm performing a role and I'm out to win a prize. But the personal stuff between Jake and me is all me. It's all hard truth and blind faith.

But first, I have to survive the rodeo.

When Jake walks through the door, letting in a bit of sun to the shadowed hallway, he lets out a low whistle, stopping short when he sees me.

I tug on the bottom of my blazer, embarrassed. "Weird, right?"

With slow, roaming eyes, he checks out my whole situation with a deep appreciation. "I wouldn't say weird."

A flush crawls up my chest. Closing the distance between us, I slug him in the shoulder.

His eyebrows raise, a smile plays on his lips. "What was that for? You round the corner dressed like that expecting no reaction?"

"I don't know," I mutter. "I forget you're into this whole cowgirl thing."

He nods. "You can say that, yes."

"Oh my God, let's just get this over with. I'm going to need to borrow paint thinner from your toolbox to scrape this makeup off later."

Grinning, he springs one of my curls born from Anna's curlers. "Cute."

Groaning not entirely unhappily, I grab his hand and pull him toward the van where Dad and Anna are waiting. He pushes the front door closed, though, blocking my exit, keeping us in the dark hallway. It reminds me of Ty in my doorway and I'm suddenly scared, but Jake is looking at me like he both wants and admires me.

I know Jake would never hurt me.

"I forgot to tell you something."

"What?"

"Don't undo your hard work out there."

I laugh, suddenly at ease. "The untying the calves thing? Did you remember, or did Dad remind you?"

"Remind me? How could I forget? That's a Mason Family Legend."

"Ugh, how embarrassing."

"Nah. It was cute as hell." He squeezes my forearm affectionately. "Out there today, though, don't let your emotions take over. The crowds, the other competitors, don't let them distract you. It's just you and Scout out there, okay?"

I nod. "Okay." *And later it will be just you and me, Jake. I don't want to screw that up either. I* can't *screw us up.*

"Break a leg, Cowgirl."

He kisses me square on the lips, leaving my eyes blinking and my heart racing as he opens the door and slips into the sun.

Chapter Fifty-Six

Jake is right about the crowd. It's intimidating to say the least. I think about the Xanax I stuffed in my pocket in case of emergency and wonder if I'll need it. I almost threw the bottle out a couple times. I never wanted it at home, but I'd use it if I had to.

I hug Anna and kiss Dad on his cheek and get even more nervous when they wish me good luck, knowing what this win could mean for them, for the ranch, for our medical debt. Jake escorts me to this back area where the competitors wait. The majority of cowboys are sitting on long wooden benches, spitting into cans. A few are pacing on the dirt, spinning their ropes around in the air. The boys are generally quiet, in that way boys get when they are nervous.

"You okay?" Jake asks me as we find a corner to stand in.

"Yeah."

But I'm not.

This leather jacket feels like Dolly Parton's version of a straight jacket. The pants are riding up my butt, making me feel all twitchy. Suddenly, the bottom of my foot itches.

"Take your boot off and scratch it, then," Jake says.

"Here?"

A gaggle of girls in sequins and $300 cowgirl hats walk by

and flash me one of those Mean Girl glares under their heavily made up eyelashes.

"Where else?"

"It's fine." A flush crawls up the back of my neck. I don't want to appear anything less than professional in front of these locals.

"Come on, you don't want to have itchy feet riding Scout. She'll cue into that and get all itchy hooved and then it will all go to hell."

I shake my head but can't help smiling by Jake's oblivious confidence. "Okay."

Jake, in his speedy take-charge way, identifies a plastic chair, grins at some ladies who are using it for a place to stack their bags, and after a quick tip of the hat, carries it over his head, sets it down next to me, and extends a hand for me to sit. I do. Then he squats down in front of me…and slips off my boot.

Cradling my foot in his hand, he lightly scratches the bottom then rubs his thumb down the center. I don't even bother containing my sigh, but I *am* grateful for this long-sleeved costume covering my goose bumps.

"Jake." Fires burn my cheeks, but my smile erupts, too.

"What? Can't have you all stressed out there, can we?"

We.

He rubs. The Mean Cowgirls glance over and glare.

I notice. Jake notices me noticing.

"Don't mind them."

Frowning, I bend over and slip my foot back into the boot.

"Who are they?"

He shrugs. "Just girls."

"Do you know them or something?"

He shrugs again. "This town has a few thousand year-round locals. I've lived here my whole life."

"You know them, then."

He stands back up, stretching his whole body in the process. "Don't mind them, Paige. They're just staring because it's rare to see someone new in this town, someone not a tourist. Especially someone that stands out."

"I stand out, do I?"

He grins, his eyes full of meaning. "Yes, you most certainly do."

I play with the fringes on my pants. "This outfit is 100% Anna's fault."

"I don't mean the outfit. You look great. It's just that you're back from the city, and a lot of these guys and gals dream of going to California. They think of it like the shows they watch on TV—you know, all the bikinis and fast cars? They think you're *that* girl and now you're coming here to maybe take away their prizes and maybe even…"

"Their cowboys?" I say, and then immediately wish I could take it back, but Jake is grinning ear-to-ear.

"Maybe even their cowboys, yes. So expect a stink eye or two, but don't let it bother you in the least."

"I'll try my best to ignore them."

"Good. Remember most of them are here to cut horses. That's the traditional rodeo sport for girls, and, of course, they've all heard of this style Stacey Westfall mastered, but no one thus far has been willing to try it in rodeo here."

"I certainly don't want to step on any toes."

"You aren't. Come on, let's go."

Jake takes my hand and pulls me over to the snack table where I grab a bagel and a cup of decaf coffee and spend the rest of my wait watching cowboys and cowgirls do their best to wrangle bulls and horses and velveteen calves to the thundering applause of a wild crowd, ear-blistering country music, and an MC so loud they can probably hear him in Palo Alto. I'm so nervous, the plain bagel tastes like sawdust. The coffee is cool and bitter, and my foot is tapping so fast on the dirty floor, Jake grabs my thigh to stop it.

"Here we go," he says, and sure enough, it's my turn. "You ready?"

"Ready as I'll ever be."

He gives me a quick kiss on the cheek, and over his shoulder the group of rodeo girls glares even harder. I avoid their eyes. We cross the room and enter the tunnel linking the waiting room to the open stadium where Scout is waiting for me. She looks as nervous as I do, her hooves pound into the dirt, anxiously. Jake has her by her rope and she sort of whinnies up at him. "It's okay, girl." I stroke Scout's neck to calm her. "It'll be quick and easy. Just do what we do back at the ranch." I keep talking to her in a calm, soothing tone as the announcer continues.

"This will be draw four, exhibitor number 9, from Jackson Hole, Wyoming, Paige Mason, daughter of local legend and rodeo champ, Augustus "Gus" Mason. She's back at Eight Hands Ranch after some time away and we're pleased as punch to re-welcome her to the Jackson Hole Rodeo in the challenging Freestyle Without a Bridle competition. Paige would like to dedicate this ride to her father and inspiration, Gus..." The announcer's voice cracks as he continues my dedication, "who taught her to never give up on what she started."

I keep my eyes on Scout's velvet neck.

Don't cry.

Don't cry.

Don't cry.

Sucking in a breath, I hold my emotions back. *Focus on the ride.*

I thought about riding to "Live Like You Were Dying" a heartbreaking song Stacey Westfall chose and dedicated to her father. But there's no way I could do it. I'd be crushed. So I chose something upbeat, yet sentimental. Something that would make Dad smile instead of cry—"Mamas Don't Let Your Babies Grow Up to Be Cowboys." Daddy sang it to me when I was a little girl, strumming his old acoustic guitar, substituting "Cowboys" for "Cowgirls," and swinging my mom around the room. She'd laugh and duck out of the way and I'd giggle, "More!"

Since Scout isn't wearing a saddle, there are no stirrups. Jake gives me a lift up with conjoined fingers. "You got this, Paige," he says.

I flash him a nervous smile. "I hope so."

"You do."

I glance up and spot Anna and Dad in the sea of strangers' faces as the music starts. Anna waves for both of them. A soft flinch of my thighs moves Scout into the center of the arena. I move her sideways, left first, then right. She moves easily and fluidly, then like Stacey's routine, we do a full spin to the right, then to the left.

The crowd goes nuts. I hang on to her mane, combing it with my fingers. We stride forward slowly at first then break into a trot. As her pace builds from a trot into a smooth canter, my hands tangle in Scout's mane. Hot wind tumbles through my hair, my hat flies off and smiling, I try to catch it but miss and the crowd goes crazy again.

We break into a gallop, flying around that dusty ring until I don't know the difference between Scout and me, where she ends and I begin. I lean back and she slams on her breaks, coming to a fierce stop, which causes the crowd to erupt in even more uproarious applause.

The lyrics boom through the arena "They never stay home and they're always alone…" It's invigorating and uplifting and nostalgic. I squeeze Scout again, and she moves into another trot, and from there, progresses into a swift canter.

"Don't let them play guitars and drive old trucks, make them be doctors and lawyers and stuff…"

The crowd begins to sing along as we zoom around the arena.

I have chills all over my body, the familiar notes blaring from huge speakers into the arena. My quick kick stops her short. Dust swirls around us, and I wait for the applause to die down before nudging her backwards. She goes 10 paces, stops, and then lurches forward, breaking into a wild gallop. Finally the music slows and we stop. I don't dare try the Stacey Westfall trick of standing up on her back. She'd buck me the hell off. I mean, she's a good sport, but she isn't a saint.

But we do manage the little trick we've been practicing. Not even Jake's seen this one. I fall to my knees, and next to me Scout bends her front legs and does a little bow. I run into the center of the ring, where I find my white hat and toss it into the crowd.

They go nuts, screaming and whistling.

The metallic stutter of the announcer belts into the arena. "Now that was one heck of a ride out of Miss Paige and her pony Scout! Not sure if you remember her last performance ten years ago, but let's just say this was a major improvement." The crowd laughs, obviously remembering the damn calf story. "We're proud of you, Paige Mason. Welcome back to Jackson Hole, Cowgirl."

This time I don't bother fighting tears meant to fall.

Chapter Fifty-Seven

"Whoohooo!" Jake runs into the staging area, scoops me up, and swings me around. Then he kisses me soft and hard and perfect, right in front of everyone. "How'd it feel?" He cups my face in his hands, his blue eyes wild with excitement. "Huh? You were amazing out there! Just amazing!"

"Incredible. Unreal. Insert every adjective you can think of?" I'm smiling, crying, totally exhausted, and elated, and everything all at once. When a girl walks over to take Scout back to her stall, I'm reluctant to let them go.

"Let her go. She'll be fine," Jake says.

I nuzzle into Scout's neck. "You did it, girl. I knew you could." She shakes out her mane and gives me a look that says, *Like I had a choice, but yeah, I did*. Then she smacks her lips against my shoulder. I laugh. "I'll bring you a treat later, promise."

The girl leads Scout away and I turn back to Jake. He's smiling so big, I think his face might break.

"Damn!" He pounds his fist into his jeans. "Unbelievable. Did you hear that crowd? They were going nuts. Come on, let's go check the scores!"

He pulls me back into the arena where we look up at the scores. He doesn't let my hand fall, just keeps on holding it tight, talking in a fast, passionate voice. We were the last entry, so this is it.

"Stacey Westfall is a wizard, but she uses wheeled spurs. You did this with just your connection to Scout. Do you get how rare and special that is? Damn!" Jake pounds his thigh again.

"You're going to hurt yourself if you keep doing that," I tease, leaning into his shoulder, wrapping my arm around his waist.

But I'm beaming, too, swiping tears of adrenaline and relief off my cheeks. I did it. *We* did it. Jake, Scout, and me.

He ruffles my hair. He paces. We wait for the score.

We're clutching sweaty hands when we finally hear the crackle of speakers and a metallic voice. "Two hundred and sixteen points for Miss Paige and her horse, Scout."

"That's…" Jake calculates the points, which, like the Olympics are based on individual aspects of the performance I don't particularly understand, in his head. "That's…second, no third place. Third place!"

My heart falls to the floor, and I think my knees might give out.

Third place.

That's only $10,000.

It's not enough. It's not enough to save the ranch.

All of this was for nothing.

"No, no, no. Don't look like that. Third place is fantastic! Paige, come on."

"It's not enough, Jake."

He cups my face in his hands again, this time peering into my soul with those too blue eyes of his. Forcing me to stay with him. To stay happy.

"You listen to me. You did good. No, you did great. Third place is *fantastic*."

I break away from his gaze and try to swallow the Teton-size lump in my throat. Glancing out at the crowd where Anna and Daddy are sitting, I see Anna clapping. Dad is sitting there, not moving, like always. I close my eyes and will him to move. I will him to clap. *Just this once, please, Daddy, please. Move, Daddy. Just this once, please be okay.*

I look down at my scuffed cowgirl boots. I wonder if I can take them back. Can I take this whole outfit back, or, if not, sell it to a second hand shop? It was such a waste of money, all this sparkling suede of a charade. I'm so stupid for letting Anna stuff me into it. I feel like a clown. I want to rip it off and toss it the trash. "It's not enough to save the ranch, Jake."

"We'll think about all that later." He puts his arm around me, and pulls me in close, a devilish look in his eyes. "Right now, we're celebrating."

"I don't have an ID, Jake. I can't go into a bar."

I stop in front of the dusty steps of a loud saloon, complete with the kind of swinging Old West doors Wyatt Earp and Doc Holiday used to fall out of. My proclamation stalls Jake for less than a millisecond. But then, as if he's already thought this through and arrived at a reasonable enough solution, he says, "Trust me."

Grabbing hold of my hand, he tips his hat at the cowboy door guy who, dressed in a red plaid shirt, dusty blue jeans, and black cowboy boots looks not much older than Jake. The bouncer guy sort of checks me out without letting Jake notice he's checking me out, which of course Jake notices (because he notices everything) and flashes the guy a look as he dabs our admittance ink on our overturned wrists.

The stamp is a lovely image of a big buxom bikini-clad girl joyriding a cactus — charming — and just like that we're in.

The opposite side of the swinging doors is chaos, country music blaring from huge speakers on either side of a little painted black stage. And when I say "blaring," I mean ground-shaking-can't-hear-a-thing blaring. Thick clouds of cigarette smoke, the scent of tangy spilled beer, and the crunch of peanut shells under our feet, tells its own story as Jake pulls me through the shoulder-to-shoulder post-rodeo crowd to the long bar. He waits until I sit down to do so himself. His lips move, but I can't hear what he's saying so he leans in, the side of his face almost grazing mine, and I lean in, too. Before I know it, my hand is pressed on his thigh and his mouth is so close to my ear I feel the heat of his breath as we struggle to communicate in a way that is hardly a struggle at all.

"Beer?"

Um. I'm not sure if I should, but I nod.

He nods. Grins. Flips my wrist over and his fingers linger on my stamp much longer than they need to simply point it out. "Any kind in particular?"

I shrug again, and tell him anything is fine.

We hung out with Dad and Anna after the rodeo. They were both so happy, so proud. I knew if I let on how disappointed I am, it would take away from their moment. I'm damn proud of Scout. She couldn't have done any better. After spending some time with her, cooling her down, giving her a nice drink, some sweet oats, and then heading back to the ranch to shower and change, I feel a bit better. The relief of it just being done has left me in a state of cool, mellow exhaustion. The ride to the bar with Jake was nice, too, though I haven't let go of my other goal of the night: to tell him what happened back at home. A beer or two might help with that.

He hollers our order at the bartender, a very pretty woman I'm guessing to be in her late 20s or early 30s. She has two-toned layered hair—black underneath and light bleach-blonde on the top. She fills them and then sets the frothy glasses down in front of Jake, smiling at him in a way that makes my previously admiring hackles stand on questioning edge.

How well does he know her?

They chat for another minute before she says something in a very flirty voice while shooting him a little wink. Her zebra hair floats into the air when she spins back toward a group of rowdy guys and says in a sexy drawl, "What can I get you, cowboys?"

Their tongues practically drag on the bar as her cleavage pops over her tight pink tank top and she scribbles their order.

I peek at Jake to see if his tongue's wagging, too, but he's watching me.

"She's pretty," I say, gesturing over his shoulder.

"Yep," he says. Honest Jake is honest even about this, but then again the fact that she's pretty is not really a question.

"Do you know her…well?"

"I know her a bit."

Define "a bit," my head asks, but that's awfully pushy, so I just shrug and bounce my knee to the music. I need a plan for tonight. It's not like I can just charge into a conversation about everything that happened in California. In the hayloft I mentioned a bad relationship back home, but he'd obviously translate that into a regular high school kid with a regular high school kid. Someone as wholesome and honest as Jake knowing the full story of Ty? What happened with us and what happened after? How could he look at me the same way he's looking at me now if he knew the whole truth? Telling him the truth risks losing him. I know that. But I have to tell him. That was tonight's plan as much as the rodeo was today's. I would not chicken out.

I cup the tall glass stein, looking at it like it's the Holy Grail of liquid courage. I feel the cool moisture dripping down its side, before holding it to my lips and sucking down half of it in one long sip. I rarely drink, and I'm so small that it's not long before my legs numb, my brain lightens, and the song I swear they have on repeat is not the worst song I've ever heard. I can do this. I'll tell him.

"Um, Jake?" I start to say.

"You have a…" Jake reaches out his fingers toward my lips. My eyes flare open.

"Beer mustache."

"Oh." I look down shyly, wiping my mouth on my short sleeve.

Jake hands me a napkin. "Why do you keep using your pretty shirts for beer rags?"

I love his reference to our picnic in the hayloft at sunset. I was too scared to get close then, but now I don't feel scared. I feel the opposite. Jake feels it, too—I can tell. We exchange a knowing smile. Today has been the best yet, and it's getting better by the second.

"Hey."

"Yeah?"

"You look good, by the way."

"Thanks." The slow flush crawls up my neck again. It's hot in here. The beer is making me even warmer—not to mention the close proximity to Jake. I did put extra effort into my outfit for the night. I chose a lacy short-sleeved shirt, a swirly white skirt, and lace-up sandals.

He touches my elbow. "You were great in there today, Paige."

I don't know if it's the beer or if I've adjusted to the level of sound in here, but I can suddenly hear him—really hear him— like we're the only two people in the bar and the music playing is soft as a breeze. I zoom in on his face and it sticks.

"Thanks."

"Really. And I'm not just saying that."

"No, I know. You wouldn't mean it if you didn't mean it. I mean, you wouldn't say it if you didn't mean it."

His eyes widen, light, listening.

"That's why I like you, Cowboy Jake. You aren't full of shit. Sorry if that's not very lady-like."

A soft smile plays on his lips. "You know I don't care about any of that."

"Another reason I like you."

"So you like me, huh?"

"For someone smart, you are pretty daft sometimes."

"But you said…" He swallows. "In the hayloft, you said that it wasn't a good idea, you and me."

"It's *not* a good idea. But that doesn't mean I don't want it." Shit. I know where this line of reasoning is heading. I have to talk to Jake. I have to. But we're here, together, at a Jackson cowboy bar. What if Jake hates me after I confess everything? I need to have this memory.

So while he looks at me quizzically, I gulp down the last of my giant beer, before setting down the glass hard. Then I grab Jake's hand and shout into his ear, "Let's dance."

He's looking at me in that half-amused way of his, but he lets me pull him through the crowd to the slippery dance floor that's packed with cowgirls and their cowboys, dancing in this jovial swing-dancing style of dipping and swinging and twirling. And suddenly we're doing the same thing, and it's not awkward or jarring at all. In fact, Jake and I are in perfect stride with one another. We're laughing and he's swinging me around and I'm just going for it until the music changes, slows, and the cowboys are pulling their girls in close.

Jake pulls me in tight until I feel his belt buckle — and what's *under* the tight stretch of his jeans — dig into my hipbone. I don't back off. I don't back off at all. It's dangerous and I know it and I don't care. My inhibitions fall to the floor to play with the peanut shells. My fingers nestle in the wisps of hair on the nape of his neck, and soon my head is on his shoulder and his mouth is brushing the back of my neck and we're swaying back and forth, back and forth, our hearts beating fast. I'm thinking about dances before this and how this is different. How this is a dance for grown-ups, or for people like us who may not be officially "grown up" but who feel like they've lived a few lifetimes enough to be up for consideration.

I never want this dance to end. I want to dance with Jake until the end of time. But the slow song ends, as all songs end. Jake leads me by the hand back toward the bar, and we get another drink. And another. And we're leaning into each other and he's telling stories, animated, his hands flying through the air with inflection. On the bar stool, his legs are spread in that cowboy casual way and my sandals rest on the lower rung of his chair and I'm moving closer, listening—listening and laughing and we're both laughing. For storytelling emphasis, he rests his hand on my thigh. For storytelling emphasis, I squeeze his forearm where his denim shirt is rolled up, exposing one badass forearm…until, suddenly, I'm pulled from the moment by the bartender's unfriendly stare.

Who are you? her expression asks. *How did you manage to capture Jake's attention in a bar full of cowgirls?*

When he follows my eyes to her questioning face, she smiles at Jake, then gets back to rubbing down the bar with a wet dishrag.

I don't want to share him with her. I don't want to share Jake with anyone.

Suddenly I'm way too brave.

"Let's go."

"Where?"

"To your truck."

His forehead crinkles. "You ready to go home?"

"No." I lean in closer. "I'm ready to go to your truck."

The booze. It's making me say things. Want things. Want things I shouldn't.

He raises an eyebrow like *oh* and then *ohhhhh*. He spins back toward the bartender and holds up two fingers.

Two dripping bottles of beer arrive. She pops the tops. "Careful with this kid," she warns Jake. "This is the last one she gets."

He puts a twenty-dollar bill on the counter. She presses it back toward him. "On the house, Jake. You know that. Y'all need it more than we do."

Then she leans forward and says, "Don't think Gus and Anna would like you bringing her home all liquored up. You can bring her out back to sleep it off in the cabin if you need to."

Cabin? Jake's cabin? Whose cabin?

I suck down the new beer in this state of panic. Am I really that drunk? It's true I haven't had more than a couple beers at a party at home. I never liked the taste much and besides, at home I always felt like I had to be the good girl. Keep a watch out for Ty, who was always the bad boy. I had to be the responsible one.

But here with Jake I feel safe enough to scoot out of my comfort zone if only for a little while. He'll take care of me so I can relax and breathe for more than a moment.

"She hasn't had that much," he says, glancing at me. "But thanks, I'll keep the offer in mind. Maybe we can get some burgers?"

Food is a good idea.

Our hamburgers arrive, and we eat them in silence. Well, as silent as a bar blasting country music gets. I'm aware of sauce running down my chin and wiping it away with my napkin. I'm hyper aware of my chewing. Swallow. Chew. Dip French fry in ketchup. Eat. Wipe lips with napkin. Repeat. Hot damn, this burger is delicious. When I'm done, I feel way better. The alcohol buzz is still there but not as all encompassing.

"Yum," I say to Jake.

"Hmm?"

He leans closer to me to hear but now our body language is more like two buds eating burgers. I feel full and sort of groggy.

Jake excuses himself for a second to use the restroom and when the woman next to me turns away from the counter to talk to her friend, I grab her shot glass and pour it down my throat. Burns like fire. The second Jake gets back I stand up. "Let's get out of here."

I grab his hand and he doesn't resist as I pull us through the crowd. I elbow the swinging door and leave the steamy bar air, pressing into the cool mountain night.

Jake's truck is parked in the first row, tires pressed against a log. Nobody else is out there.

"You feeling okay?" he says.

"I'm feeling fine. I want to talk to you about something," I say.

But he looks so cute standing there with his head cocked and his eyes slightly red and suddenly I know what I need to do first. After I tell him about Ty, after I confess everything, he may not want me anymore, so I do what I wanted to do since I first saw him sitting in that Jeep with the hat over his eyes.

I slam him against the passenger door and kiss him for real. Like I mean it. Like I'm in it all the way. I kiss him like I'll never let him go.

He kisses me back, long and deep and so melty and perfect I feel like I'm going to float right off that dirt and into the black speckled sky. His hands are on my hips, pressing into the fabric of my skirt, grounding the soles of my sandals into the earth.

Before either of us can second-guess what we're doing, I open the truck door and jump up onto the fabric seat. I scoot backwards into the cab, pulling him along with me, and I can feel that he wants me. Wants me like I want him. It's so different. *So* different than what I've experienced before. We're like this for a long time. Touching. Tasting. Feeling. Then he pulls away and wraps his arm around me. "So what do you want to tell me?"

"It's…remember the guy back home I told you about? The bad relationship?"

"Yeah?"

"Well," I start to say when my cell phone rings. My ring tone is the song I practiced to, "Mama's Don't Let Their Babies Grow Up to be Cowboys."

Jake laughs. "It's Anna. You better get that."

"No. I'll call her back later. I really want to talk to you about—"

"Anna? It's Jake."

I sigh. Cowboy Jake, always the responsible one.

"What's that? I can't hear you; it's a bad connection." He pauses, a frown creasing his brow. "I can't hear you, but I'm sorry I kept her out so late if that's what you want to know." Another pause. "I'll call you back when we're in range. I can't hear a damn thing you're saying."

He hangs up, still frowning.

"Is everything okay?"

"I assume so, but I couldn't hear her. She's likely checking up on you, making sure I get you back to the house in one piece. We should probably go."

He starts the engine. My opportunity to confess slips through the cracks of the window, and I'm equal parts relieved and disappointed.

"Are you okay to drive?"

"I didn't drink half as much as you. And I definitely didn't sneak a shot out from under a tourist." He laughs as he backs up the truck, and I put on my seatbelt.

"You saw that?"

"You think I miss a beat, Cowgirl?"

Chapter Fifty-Eight

He doesn't say anything after he turns off the ignition in his cabin's dirt driveway.

"I don't want to go home," I whisper.

"So don't."

He turns the headlights off, and it's just the two of us under the wide black sky sprinkled with stars, so many spinning stars.

"Jake."

"Yeah?"

Maybe he sees it in my eyes. This black hole so deep that even something like this, something so perfect, can't pull me out of it.

"If you don't miss a beat, do you know why I'm here?"

My fingers weaving into one another on my lap are blurry. I hold my breath while I wait.

"I know a bit."

"What do you know?"

"I know some kids killed themselves."

"Which kids?"

"A few."

"Okay." I hesitate. It's so much more than that. "Do you know anything else?"

He shrugs.

He wasn't helping. Shit. Shit shit shit.

"Well, things were crazy then. You know how I tell you how alive I feel here?"

He nods.

"There, I felt numb. And sometimes when you're numb, you do things you regret just to feel alive, do you get that?"

I'm still a little tipsy. This is good and bad, but at least it's getting me talking.

"Yeah, I get that. I felt like that after my dad died. And I was like that for a long time after. I think that's how my mom felt, too, why she used the bottle to wake up or numb out." He shook his head. "Doesn't work, though. Eventually you just have to face what's bothering you."

"I bet you never did what I did."

"Maybe," he says. "I did a lot I'm not proud of."

I look at him dead-on. Jake. Perfect Jake. "Somehow I doubt that."

He cocks an eyebrow. "That bartender back there? The one you were giving the stink eye to? Well, I slept with her."

"I figured."

"No." He chews on his lip, like he's embarrassed. "I slept with her while she was married."

"Oh."

"And had a kid at home."

"Oh."

"Yeah."

I look at my hands. "What happened?"

"What happened was her old man found out and threatened to shoot me if he ever saw me again."

I gasp. "But you were talking to her tonight!"

"Yeah, well, he's not around anymore."

"Where is he?"

"Jail."

"For what?"

He smiles, and it's the wicked one I love. "Doing some awful things."

I duck my head and jump out of the truck. The stars spin and spin above me like a crazy crown of light. Maybe I'm more than a little tipsy. Suddenly Jake is in front of me. He's holding onto my elbows, grounding me into the earth so I don't float away.

"I feel like I know you so completely, Jake. You make so much sense. Your life makes so much sense. How do you do that? How do you make everything make sense?"

"I don't. And I'm not as perfect as you think." He cups my face in his palms. "Truth is, Paige—you're holding Jackson up on a high pedestal right now because things are crappy back at home, but we're not perfect. We make mistakes. We drink too much. Most of us are uneducated. There's no one place that holds all the good things in life and another place that holds the bad stuff. We're all human, and humans fuck up. I do. You did. Whatever you did at home, no matter how tragic or bad you think it was, I believe you, but you aren't alone in this." He smoothes the hair from my face, keeping my cheek cupped in one of his palms. "You aren't alone now."

His last line is a whisper. It's a promise. If I hold on to Jake, if he lets me, I might not crumble away all together. He looks me in the eyes and scoops me up. My arms are around his neck, and my face is buried in the soft sweetness of his neck. His kisses are snowflakes and I dissolve like the softest first breath of snow.

I don't want to talk anymore. I'm done talking. In fact, I can't even form words anymore. His kisses are so soft and his skin wonderfully hot. As he carries me inside, I see a fireplace and bookshelves and a comfy looking couch. There's a hallway, and then there's a bed in the middle of the room. On it rests a worn patchwork quilt and a white pillow. A square window that looks out to so many stars.

Jake's face is swimming over mine. His eyes bright blue pools I want to jump up into. But the alcohol feels like it's souring in my stomach, and I feel a little sick.

I pray this cabin has a toilet.

"Jake?"

"Yeah?"

"Are you going to sleep with me?"

He cocks his head. "Do you want me to?"

"Yes."

"Okay." With typical Jake efficiency, he whips off his hat, pulls off his boots and my sandals, hops into the bed next to me, and tucks me under his strong arm.

"Jake?" I mumble.

"Yeah?"

"Thank you."

"Stop thanking me."

I kiss his flannel-covered chest, and the last thing I remember is nestling my cheek against its comfort.

Chapter Fifty-Nine

Then

I woke up in my California bedroom with a chest full of dread. It wasn't from a nightmare. I always remember those. As a little girl I often remembered my dreams in such vivid detail that my mom asked a professional about it. The doctor told Mom that the more creative a child is, the more of the dream she remembers. At the time, I remember her saying it was a good thing.

Mom looked at me a little differently after that. She'd say things like, "Oh, Paige, head in the clouds, so creative!" She was always one to like an official, professional opinion on something to validate (or create) her own.

I loved remembering acute sensory details like flying above the sea, stars above dreaming-me bursting through the darkness like my old Lite-Brite peg colors found only in a six-year-old's imagination—mauves and lavenders and starburst orange.

Downside? Recalling my nightmares just as acutely.

Most often, they'd start with something real: a concrete memory of Dad holding a glass of "stinky drink" (what I called his hard alcohol), the ice cubes rattling as he yelled at Mom and she yelled back, exchanging ugly threats and cruel insults. In real life, I'd run down the hall and flop on my bed holding hands over ears until they quieted and moped in separate rooms. But in my nightmares, the yelling turned monstrous. Dad sprouted horns and grew hooves. Mom's eyes projected unnatural, horror-movie eye colors, and, as they argued, the ranch house crumbled around us until all that was left were piles of dust and dry wall rot and me, curled up as small as I could get on the last thing standing in our house—my bedspread, stained with tears that pooled to a flood and carried me away from the yelling and the rubble on its black river, like in *Alice In Wonderland*.

That night in California, I remembered nothing. So this sense of dread wasn't from a nightmare, it was real. Aside from the dim red light shining from a chili pepper shaped nightlight, my room was dark. The house was quiet. Not even the hum of the dishwasher that Mom ritualistically turned on as she was heading to bed every night, so I knew it was late. A glance at my phone on the bedside table told me I was right. 2 a.m.. If everyone was sleeping, what could be wrong?

Pushing aside the lump of dread squashing my insides, I went to the bathroom and splashed water on my face, hoping to wash away the gnawing feeling, but it lingered like the stench of spoiled food.

Just check his room, a voice inside me insisted.

No.

I didn't want to.

You have to.

No.

With shaky hands, I turned Ty's doorknob and gently pushed the door open.

His room was so dark, all I could make out was ruffled sheets and blankets and his scent. But it wasn't the noxious smell that disquieted me—it was the dark. Since the suicides, he'd insisted on sleeping with his lights on. I paused in his doorway, my pulse pounding. What to do? After what happened between the two of us earlier, I didn't want to move closer to his bed. At this point in our relationship, just a small gesture of touching his shoulder to see if he was okay could give him the wrong idea, and I knew what happened when Ty had the wrong idea.

I shuddered, hugging my arms over my chest, instinctively covering up and protecting myself. Swallowing, I moved closer on tiptoe, my steps so light I almost glided across the wood floor like in those long-ago dreams when my toes skimmed across the starlit sea.

Ty wasn't in his bed.

I ran back to my room, grabbed my cell phone out of my drawer, and flipped it on. The message I saw made my blood run cold.

Missed call
TY

Chapter Sixty

Now

The smell of bacon frying normally fills me with joyful breakfast bliss. Not today. Not after that nightmare. I leap out of bed, flinging covers onto the ground, and yank open the first door. But instead of finding a toilet, I find a row of plaid shirts, blue jeans, and on the floor, four pairs of cowboy boots.

A man's closet.

My eyes fly to the rumpled sheets and my mind whirls over last night's events, how I ended up here. Which is…where, exactly?

Then I remember.

Jake's bed. Jake's cabin.

"Jake?"

Glancing down, I'm startled to discover I'm wearing a plaid button down flannel shirt that must be Jake's. I must've puked on mine. I have a memory of puking.

"Jake?"

The tidy cabin is flooded with natural light. Framed photographs hang in rustic frames on the knotty pine walls. A wooden chair sits in the corner.

"You finally up, lazy bones?"

My heart and stomach compete for the biggest reaction to

Jake's playful voice.

When I round the corner, I know I'm still passed out and dreaming because Jake's standing in front of an antique cooking stove in an unbuttoned plaid shirt and jeans. His eyes linger on mine a second too long and grease leaps up from the pan, snapping his wrist. He flicks it off his skin and, with a spatula, flips the egg frying in another cast iron pan. "Over easy, if I remember correctly?"

I nod. Blinking. I felt sick before, didn't I? Now I was hungry. Starved, even. This whole scene left me wanting, wanting, wanting. I blink again, hardly able to trust my eyes. It's too good to be — "Oh, God. Do Dad and Anna know I'm here?"

"I'm sure they know I'm taking care of you. I couldn't hear her on the phone last night, but I let her know I had you. Post-rodeo things tend to get a little wild."

Wild? I look down at my naked legs. How wild did things get with us? The last thing I remember was curling up on Jake's arm, snuggling into his chest. I remember feeling his heartbeat pounding through his shirt. I remember starting to confess everything and then getting interrupted. Starting to tell him, and then him confessing to me. Everyone had dark secrets, even Jake. Maybe this would be okay after all, because what I'm looking at right now, how I felt like last night, were moments I never want to give up.

"Good to know there are post-rodeo exceptions for drunken debauchery around these parts."

"Debauchery?" he asks with a sly grin, glancing back at me. "Don't know if I'd go that far."

How far would you go? I glance back down at what I'm wearing. I tilt my knees in toward each other and gaze at my bare thighs. What happened between us last night?

I remember kissing. I remember a whole lot of kissing.

The way Jake's looking at me tells me he remembers, too. "Coffee?"

"Please."

I plop onto a chair and tuck my legs under the little wooden table.

Sauntering over, he sets a mug in front of me and then, from a pot, pours the black liquid. "Careful, it's hot," he says. "And strong, just how you like it. Cream and sugar right here along with a couple ibuprofen." His grin is devilish—if the devil was the most thoughtful and attractive cowboy on earth.

"You're a gem."

He narrows his eyes, his way of shoving off the compliment, but I can tell he's pleased I think so.

"A gem I couldn't afford even if I won All Things Rodeo," I add.

"You *did* get third place. Maybe that's me."

I grin, but it's shaky. He's worth more than any dollar amount, but my feelings for Jake, his feelings for me, aren't going to save the ranch.

"Speaking of rodeo. Where is my shirt from last night?"

"Didn't want you puking on it."

"So you…helped me out of it?" We exchange a look. "How very practical of you."

I catch the side of his smile as he turns back to his hot stove.

I lock this moment away like it's a photograph: me sitting in Jake's kitchen watching him cook, the feel of my bare feet on his cool, chipped wood floor, wearing a shirt that smells like him.

I scan the cabin, taking it all in. I've wanted to see the inside for so long, and now I'm here. How people keep their space, or what they choose to keep, tells their story: the knotty pine bookshelves look homemade—Did he build them himself? The spare kitchen where everything has a place, the thick red blanket folded neatly over the back of his worn, leather couch. "I like your place," I say. It's tidy and warm, like Jake himself.

"Thanks."

He moves the bacon around the cast iron pan with a fork. "I don't have a lot to make a mess with," he says without turning around.

"But what you have seems to count."

Now he looks, quick and over his shoulder—no more than a glance into my eyes. "Suppose that's how it should be, right?"

"I suppose."

Moseying over to his bookshelves, I pore over the mostly paperback titles. The classics are widely represented: a couple of Hemingway's—*The Old Man and the Sea* and *The Sun Also Rises*; Steinbeck's *East of Eden*, *The Pearl*, *Of Mice and Men*; a very old leather covered copy of a St. James Bible; a thick, multiple dog-eared paperback copy of *Lonesome Dove* (my favorite mini-series ever, which Jake knows); and…a few business books? Louis L'Amour I'd expect, sure, but business books?

"I'm taking a few classes at the local community college." His head peeks around the corner before disappearing again.

Does he ever miss a beat? "Oh, really?"

"Just things to help the ranch run more efficiently."

I round the corner, closing the space between us, padding barefoot back into the small kitchen.

"That's awesome, Jake."

"No big deal."

I hold up the book in my hand. "No, it's a really big deal. You've invested so much of your time helping Dad and Anna and…the ranch." *And me.* "I appreciate it, Jake. We all do." I'm glad he's facing the stove. Glad he can't see the honesty, the naked truth of this confession, cross my face. "You have no idea how much."

He glances over his shoulder, and there goes my attempt to appear casual. I suppose it's too late for that anyway. I'm walking around his cabin in his plaid shirt and my underwear.

He cooks the way he drives, the way he rides, the way he listens, the way he sets up a mountain camp: mindful of every detail, his brain two steps ahead of his body. In a flash, two white plates are filled with crispy bacon, eggs over easy, and whole-wheat toast topped with melty pats of butter.

This is easy, Jake and me. I could see us doing this every day. Every morning. Every evening. I could see us doing this forever.

"Do you think I should stay?" I ask him.

"Instead of going to college?"

"Yeah."

He shakes his head. "You have an amazing chance, here. I would've killed to go away to school. The only college we have is a two-bit community college with mostly older ladies. That's not for you. You need to get on out of here and do your thing."

"I—I thought you'd be happy. Especially after last night."

He squats in front of me and sets his palms on my thighs. "I'm happy you want to stay. You know I like you a helluva lot, but I'll be damned if me or your daddy will stand by and let you not get your education."

"Oh."

He stands and plops a plate of food in front of me. "Go on now, eat up. You want some jam? I have some of Anna's good stuff, the canned strawberry." He flips open the refrigerator door. The appliance is red and stocky, a foot shorter than him, and usually I'd laugh at how ridiculous he looks rooting around inside.

But I'm not laughing, and I sure as hell don't want to eat anymore.

Jake doesn't want me to stay, and he doesn't even know about Ty yet.

Chapter Sixty-One

Jake and I have barely finished our eggs when he mentions the offer to buy Scout.

I set my fork down. "Wait, what?"

"He approached Anna and Gus after your performance and offered two hundred grand cash for her last night."

"Who?"

"The guy who wants to invest in the ranch."

"That greasy developer approached you, and you didn't tell me last night?"

"He approached *Anna*, and she told me while you were showering to go out."

"Why didn't you tell me?"

He leans back in his chair and laces his hands behind his head. "I knew you'd be upset and I didn't want to ruin your night."

"At least you're honest," I say unhappily. "But you should've told me. Is that what last night was all about, Jake? Kissing me and tucking me in and making me breakfast and being so…" I growl at the frustrating blanks. "Were you trying to butter me up so I'll agree to sell her?"

This was worse than him not wanting me to stay on the ranch. This was betrayal.

"Of course not. You're misinterpreting what I'm trying to do again. I wouldn't do that. I'm telling you now because, A. you're sober, and B. it's something we need to discuss before we give Anna and Gus our answer."

"*Our* answer?"

"You broke her in. We consider Scout to be yours, too."

I folded my arms. "A. I didn't break her in. She agreed to let me ride her, and B. good, I'm glad you consider her to be mine, because the answer is a resounding no. No way in hell to be exact."

"No?"

"No. I'm not selling Scout—especially to that assclown."

"I'm not saying you should." He sits back up and holds out his palm calmly. I sort of want to stab it with the runny-egg fork. "I'm just saying the money…Paige, it's enough to save the ranch."

Fuck.

Fuck fuck fuck.

The eggs churn in my stomach. "So I risk everything to train her, enter her in the rodeo, wear that stupid outfit, and not only do I not win, but I lose—twice?"

His mouth opens, but I talk over his almost-words.

"If I don't lose her, I lose the ranch. It's a lose-lose."

"But if you lose—*sell*—her, you get to keep the ranch, Paige. Keep it. Forever."

"But what about Scout? This is her home."

He takes a deep, deliberate breath. "She's just a horse."

"She's not just a horse and you know that."

The tears I've been fighting brim over my eyes. I swipe them off my face as I see her up running in the moonlight with her herd of wild mustangs. The family she lost and only recently found again. It's not fair. "If this was going to be her fate, I should've just left her on the mountain in peace."

"I'm not saying you have to sell her."

"But just like me leaving for college, you're saying it's the best thing to do."

"For the whole of life? Yes, I do."

I get up and walk over to the fireplace so he can't see me cry. The framed pictures are mostly of Jake in various rodeo-themed shots: young Jake tying up his first calf at rodeo, Jake riding a bucking horse, Jake bull riding...and then one that surprises me—a couple of kids, a floppy haired boy and a blonde girl in pigtails, fishing over a stream.

"That's us," I say.

"Yes."

"How long have you had that?"

He shrugs.

"A long time, or since I've come this summer?"

"I found it when I was going through your dad's pictures. That's the girl I remember. Fearless. A girl who would untie a calf's legs because she was scared it was hurt—not caring what people thought about you—like you were last night."

I can't stop the tears this time. "He won't treat her well."

Jake's hands smooth over my shoulders. "He will. He's gentle with his animals. I've seen him. And he has a rider who is great. Accomplished. A nice girl who will treat her right. Scout'll get to tour rodeos. Now that she's got a taste of this, she'll want to keep it up. It's in her blood. You'll be off to college, not touring the U.S. doing rodeo."

"But...I could."

He sighs. "Yes, you could. But is that what you want from your life?"

"But I love her, Jake. I love that beautiful, stubborn horse. I—I-don't want to lose her."

"I know," he says. He pulls me in close, our hearts beating as one as his fingers run through my long, tangled hair, my wet cheek rubbing against the soft flannel of his broad shoulder. "I love her, too."

We talk for a while longer. I'm not happy, but I'm not as angry and hurt as I was at first, either. I even consider that it might be smart, if it means saving the ranch. I agree to meet the girl who would ride her and show her in the rodeo circuit. Then, together, we decide to go talk to Dad and Anna. As soon as we walk through the door, hand in hand, I know something's wrong.

There's no breakfast smells coming from the kitchen, no quiet chatter as Anna talks to Dad about the day or rehashes the daily newspaper's current events, no country music from her CD player as she sings along in her perfect pitch.

"Jake," I grip his hand hard and stop short in the doorway.

He senses it, too.

He moves past where I'm frozen in the doorway. "Stay here."

I'm sick. I fear the worst. Or course I fear the worst.

Last night's events, this morning's, flood my mind, turning love and light into guilt. I should've come home and I didn't come home.

Jake re-enters the room, waving a piece of Anna's notepaper. "They're at the hospital, come on."

"The hospital?"

Grabbing his hat off the hook—his keys are already out—he dashes out the door and I chase after him. He flings open the passenger door of his truck for me before running around the other side and starting the ignition. I hop in, slamming the door behind me. I've never seen him this rattled. Something is really wrong.

"What happened?" I ask in a shaky voice.

He hands me the hastily scribbled note written on Anna's personalized strawberry design stationary.

Meet us at the hospital ASAP.

Hospital.

The breath I've been holding slowly leaks out. At least he's alive. At least he's still alive.

"Why didn't they call us?"

I see the two of us last night, drinking and dancing in the loud bar, kissing under the stars, this morning waking up in his bed, breakfasts and bookshelves and…

"That may have been the call in the truck outside the bar. I couldn't hear her. Damn. Dammit." He slams his fist into the steering wheel.

I pull my phone out of my back pocket. The screen is black. It won't turn on to retrieve messages. "My cell is dead. I didn't even think to charge it at your place."

"Why didn't she—" His mouth snaps shut. I follow his eyes to his cell phone, which is lying on the floor beneath my feet, a flashing light indicating missed calls or messages or both. He slams his fist into the steering wheel again.

"Here I was worried about college, worried about Scout when Dad could've…" I choke back sobs. Jake drives so fast down the long dirt drive that gravel and swirls of dirt twist into the air behind us. He doesn't turn on the radio. I cross my legs. My foot twitches in a nervous rhythm for the whole of the ride. *Hurry. Hurry.*

At the hospital, he pulls into the first open spot he sees and grabs my hand as we race through the automatic doors. "Gus Mason?" I ask an older volunteer in a pink uniform at the information desk. In a slow voice, she points us to the elevators, third floor, ICU.

"ICU. Shit."

Her eyes widen.

"Sorry," I say. "It's my dad."

"I hope he'll be okay, dear," she says and her kindness is worse than if she was judging me.

Silently, we watch the floor numbers go up. At three, we jump out, walking fast down the waxed patchwork floor through a sterile hall. At the nurse's station I ask again for my dad, and we're pointed to a room, 113 bed B.

We screech to a halt at his door.

There's a man in the first bed, Bed A. An oxygen mask fits over his nose and mouth, tubes flow from his arms, and his stomach rises and falls. The slit in his light blue and white floral gown is open, exposing boxer shorts and more tubes snaking from his inner thigh.

A thick, mustard-yellow curtain separates us from my dad. Two pairs of medical personnel clogs, one black and one brown, are visible in the exposed inches between the curtains bottom and the hospital flooring. Doctors.

"Come on." I grab Jake's arm and quietly walk through Bed A's area, careful not to disturb the sleeping (unconscious?) patient. I peek through the curtain, my ear grazing the cool, white wall. Anna waves us in. I can tell right away from her face, red and puffy, her watery eyes, that something is really, really wrong.

"I'm so sorry we weren't there," I spit out. "We couldn't hear what you were saying over the phone. We were in Jake's truck and we couldn't hear you." None of this even matters but I keep going on about it.

"What happened?" Jake asks, cutting me off.

"He c-choked on dinner and aspirated. I couldn't clear it."

"Oh my God." My worst nightmare happened and I wasn't even there to help.

Jake's looking at her funny, which is…odd. Why doesn't he look as horrified as I feel?

"Jake, I…called 9-1-1. The ambulance got him here just in time."

Jake looks at the wires, the mask, the IV with a strange look on his face. "He's on life support," he notes.

Something that looks a lot like guilt rolls across her features. A foreign mask on Anna's confident face.

I'm genuinely perplexed and kind of annoyed at Jake for reacting like this instead of being apologetic. "Anna, it's okay. He's alive! You saved him!"

She touches my dad's hand, then like the cords are live

wires, recoils. "You don't understand, Jake. In the moment, I just couldn't…"

Jake doesn't say anything.

Why are they acting so weird? Maybe she's just in shock. I rush over to her. "You saved him, Anna. I'm so sorry we weren't there to help you."

I see Jake and me dancing and laughing again. The bar. Drinking. The truck. Oh God, and the cabin and breakfast this morning. Arguing over the horse. Guilt is cancer spreading through my cells. How could we be so *selfish*? We never even thought to call Anna back.

Maybe he felt bad about being with me? Taking me back to his cabin instead of back home? "We…I…got a little tipsy. And Jake let me spend the night. Don't worry, nothing happened, but we didn't think to call you."

I meet Jake's eyes, pleading with him to finish the confession, and when he does, his voice is clear and guiltless. "She stayed with me at the cabin. I'm sorry, we should've let you know."

She shakes her head. "I figured as much. It's not your fault, kids."

She's Anna. She doesn't care where I was. She accepted that I wasn't there and she's already over it. Moving on to the here and now and what's important to her.

"But your dad may have a different opinion when…if…he wakes up. You're his little girl after all."

Tears pool in my eyes. I'd give anything for him to sit up and yell at me for staying out too late, for drinking, for spending the night with a boy—but he's lying there with tubes and an oxygen mask and he has no idea what I've done. He has no idea we're even here.

Anna bites her lip and looks much younger when she says, "If you'd been there, Jake, things might've ended differently. And I can't say I'm unhappy about that."

Avoiding my questioning eyes, Jake nods. He looks at the wires. The IV.

"What do you mean if Jake was there, things would've ended differently?"

Neither of them looks at me. It's like with the story of Scout. It's like the story with the bankruptcy of the ranch. There's something else they aren't telling me. And by the look of their exchanged glances, this one is bigger than the others.

"He's alive. Obviously Anna did the right thing." I try to make them look at me. "What is it you're not telling me?"

Anna sighs, her eyes filled with tears. "Your daddy has a DNR, Paige. You know what that means."

"Do Not Resuscitate. Of course. But that doesn't mean that's what we're going to do. I'm his daughter, and I'm not going to let him die just because of what some stupid card says."

Now she's sobbing. Tough as chain-link Anna is sobbing, and I'm scared—really scared—because this is foreign, her vulnerability, and this whole situation is so screwed up.

"I went against his explicit request, Paige. I thought I could do it. I told him I could, but in the moment, when it was actually happening, him gasping for breath and looking at me with these scared eyes…I couldn't sit there and watch him die. No matter what he said, no matter what he told me before, over and over, that he wanted… In the moment, I just couldn't."

She collapses into an orange vinyl chair in the corner, and in an instant, I'm back in that sterile counselor's office sitting around the round table with Ty and the other kids, talking about all the people we couldn't save. The peers I couldn't help. The peers I didn't help, and the stepbrother I pushed too far. I learned my lesson with Ty. I wasn't going to let that happen again. I had to do everything in my power to save my dad.

Kneeling beside her, I hold her hand. "You did the right thing, Anna. You love him. You can't just let someone you love die. You have to do everything you can to help them, everything you can think of to save them."

I wasn't just talking about Dad anymore.

She shakes her head, pushing away my words. "He's going

to be so angry at me."

"For saving his life? That's ridiculous. He loves you. He'll understand. You can't just...he can't expect you to make that kind of choice. He can't expect you to play God."

"I'm not sure it's that dramatic."

"Life and death? If that's not dramatic, I don't know what is!"

Images from California funerals flash through my mind, lives that might've been saved if only we'd have known what to do to save them. Dad has another chance. Maybe he'll wake up. Maybe he'll sit in the kitchen with us again and I'll hold his hand and read to him and we'll email/talk together and make jokes.

"I would've done the same thing if I were there," I say. "No question."

She looks at me sadly and pats my hand. "That's why you aren't his caretaker, honey. The hospice nurses warned us about this. When a caregiver is also a loved one, they don't always carry through with the patient's wishes. I thought I was strong enough. That I respected Gus enough to see his wishes through, but in the end it's not about respect, it's about love. It all comes down to love, and I couldn't let him die."

"I don't understand, if he's DNR, why is he keeping himself alive, day to day then? With the tubes and the respirator?"

"Natural causes. He wants to die of natural causes."

"Okay." I sigh. I find myself wanting to think like Anna. Be logical and strong and deal with this new set of information in a rational, How-Do-We-Move-On-From- Here manner. I suck in a long, deep breath. Close my eyes for a second and wash away the images in my head of a woman unplugging the man she loves and waiting for him to die. That's not going to be us—at least not today.

"Well," I say in a calm, clear voice, "you did what you did, and it's done. So we have to move on. Dad's not going to hold this against you. He's going to understand."

I'm not sure this is true. For all I know, Dad will be livid, but I say it anyway.

He won't have a choice to be angry. He'll have to pack away his selfish notions that put Anna in this horrible position of choosing whether or not to let a man she loves die. And he'll have to listen to his own advice: "Suck it up, and move on. It's done."

Jake is on the other side of Dad's bed watching his face as he lies there, an oxygen mask tight over his face, too, but unlike Patient A, his covers are pulled high over his body, tucked in below his neck. What's left of his hair is neatly combed to the side over an oily forehead, slick with ointments that keep the devices from sticking to his skin. The day-old stubble is the only physical difference between today and any day.

Anna strokes his cheek, gently. "I was planning on shaving him in a few minutes—after the doctors left. He doesn't like stubble. You know him, clean-shaven or a full-grown beard. No in between with Gus."

Life or death: not a coma, not brain-dead waiting to be unplugged—no in between with Gus.

She's looking at Dad with such love. Even at their best, my mom never looked at him that way. Anna accepts him exactly for who he is—flaws and all. "He's so lucky to have you, Anna."

Her eyes lighten like she really needed to hear those words. "You think so?"

"I know so."

She swallows, eyes tearing up again. "Thank you, honey."

I put my arms around her and hug her tight.

Jake, who's been quiet for so much of the visit, says much more with his actions and gestures than with his words. He stands near my dad and rests his hand on Dad's wrist, in a comforting way—protective, strong. And even though everything is wrong, this moment is somehow exactly right.

Chapter Sixty-Two

We stay all day at the hospital bringing cup after cup of stale vending machine coffee to Anna, who won't leave Dad's side. I decide we need food to soak up some of the caffeine, so around 4 p.m., Jake and I pick up deli sandwiches in the cafeteria. We eat ours on a vinyl couch in the lobby because the cafeteria smells like sick flesh and vinegar.

"What a mess," Jake says, limply pulling lettuce from a sandwich roll and setting it on the side of his plate.

"I know." His eyes hold mine and what I see in them frightens me. "What?"

"If we'd been there, Paige…things…"

"What?"

He looks away. "Nothing."

"Come on, it's not nothing. What are you saying? That things would've been different if we'd have been there? I know that's what you've been thinking all day."

"I don't want to upset you. I just…I know what your dad wants, and I'd want to honor him."

I set my sandwich down, panic rising in my throat, the earlier calm of shock gone, replaced by pure emotion imagining the worse. "You would've sat there and watched him die?"

His Adam's apple bobs like this is hard to admit, but his

eyes hold mine in a steadfast gaze. Like admitting to Anna that I slept over in his cabin, he might feel bad about upsetting us, but he doesn't feel guilty about his choice.

"It's what he wants. I gave him my word. I signed the DNR agreement stating I would…" He breaks eye contact and moves the lettuce around on his plate. "But in the moment, who knows. Maybe I'd have done the same as Anna."

I don't know what to say. I don't know how to feel. Not letting him die is breaking a promise. He can't move. The only thing he has left is his wishes via the computer. He can't talk. He counts on us. Not that I want him to die, I absolutely do not, but suddenly I can hear what Jake is saying. I understand what my dad wants. There is no right or wrong answer when it comes to choosing to live or deciding it's time to die and once again, we're swimming in murky gray waters.

I cup my forehead, pressing into my temples.

"I think we need to hire a nurse, Paige. Someone without blood ties, someone…"

"Who doesn't love him?"

"Yes."

"I agree. How could Anna live with herself if she let him die? Let him choke on his baby food and not even call 911? It's not right to force her to make that kind of choice. To force you to make that kind of choice."

He nods, once, appreciatively.

"I don't know how we'll find the money, but I'll think of something." As I say it I know exactly how we'll find the money. Scout. We'll sell Scout. We'll have to.

I search Jake's eyes to see if he knows what "we'll find it" means. He does.

"I don't want you to have to do that," he says.

"If it means saving one of us from making this choice about Dad? If it means giving him what he wants? Honoring the one thing he still has control over? I'll do it, Jake. As much as it'll kill me to, I'll sell Scout to save Anna or you from having to make that kind of choice."

"Okay. If you're sure?"

I nod.

"We'll talk to her about it tonight. Or tomorrow. Or whenever Gus gets discharged."

He sets his plate down on the ground and takes my hand. "I'm so glad you're here." His blue eyes glisten with emotion, and I squeeze his hand back.

"I heard someone say once the right thing isn't always the easiest thing. I'm glad I'm here, too, but even if I wasn't, Jake, I know you—you'd do what's right."

"The problem is, in this case and with…" He looks at me. "And with you, I don't know what's right anymore."

"Yes, you do."

I'd had no idea how to deal with Ty.

I knew how volatile Ty was—how near the edge—and I didn't go to my mom or his dad to tell them because telling them would be me admitting how close we were, and so I protected my own pride over protecting Ty.

I made that choice and I've been living with it each day since. I had to tell Jake.

I should just tell him now.

But how do you tell someone you love that you're responsible for the death of someone who claimed to love you?

Chapter Sixty-Three

Then

I drove as fast I could down to the tracks.

Holding the phone in one hand I winced as, on speaker mode, I listened to his barely coherent voicemail ramble on words that made me barely able to focus on my driving.

I know you don't love me and it doesn't matter anymore just have a nice life and no I'm not sorry for you or for anything or maybe I am who the hell knows whatever goodbye.

I threw the car in park and jumped out into the darkness. "Ty!" I screamed his name into the cold windless night. Fog-thick air filled the empty space between the chain link fence and the tracks.

Warning signs have been hung in several places now. ACTIVE RAILROAD, with a crossed out cartoon of a person walking on the tracks. THERE IS HELP, with holding hands and a suicide hotline help number. Bright lights pooled on the tracks from newly installed lights. All cautionary measures the school took to dissuade railway suicides at our high school.

"Ty! Are you here?"

No answer.

I heard the message. He was going to do something. I knew it.

Shaking from both cold and fear, I wrapped my arms around myself and called his name over and over.

A crow grazed by me, landing on the tracks six feet away. I screamed.

Come on, Paige. Keep it together.

"Ty! If you're here, please. I'm sorry about what I said earlier. I…"

Just say it. Out loud. Just in case he's here and it could save him.

"I didn't mean it."

"You sure about that?"

Behind the crow, on the tracks, stood Ty.

He was wearing a gray hoodie, jeans, Converse. His hood covered his eyes. All I could see was his mouth.

Worry faded into anger. He was waiting for my apology. He knew how anxious I was, how scared, and yet he waited, lurking in the dark. "What the hell are you doing?"

"Seeing what they saw."

"What?"

"Those last moments. The lights coming toward them. The sound. It must be louder than waves, you know? And I've been way out, you know that, caught in the barrel, when the wave comes like this, from deep in the sea, after traveling so far, it overwhelms you. Louder than thunder." He looked at me. "Louder than screams."

My knees started to shake. "Get off the tracks, Ty."

"I wonder if when they saw it coming they thought about changing their minds, you know? If they thought, what the hell am I doing? But then when death really faced them, when they looked straight in its face and dared it to remove them from this life, I wonder if they chickened out, but it was too late and they were toast anyway."

I stepped through the hole in the fence — a hole Ty made? — disobeying the signs to stay away from the tracks. "Come home with me."

He pulled off his hood and looked straight into me with eyes that weren't Ty's. They were still the same beautiful green color, but something about them was dead inside. Hollow, like a crow's. Like the Ty part of him was gone, the funny, hopeful part, and what was left was just this angry, vengeful side. The side I hated.

"Why, Paige? So you can reject me over and over and over again? So you can remind me day after day that you think I'm a fucking rapist and make me feel like the most pathetic asshole on the planet? No thanks. I'd rather be dead then feel you look at me that way."

Shit.

Shit.

I scrambled. He was still standing on the tracks. I didn't know the train schedule. Did Ty? "Why? So you can live a normal life."

"Normal?" He laughed too loud. Chills ran down my spine. "You know as well as I do, there is no normalcy to this life of ours. Especially mine. Once you're accused of something like that, even if you get off, it always follows you. It always haunts you. Who knows, maybe the others—maybe they had stuff to run from, too. Maybe they were right to just check out."

He turned away and faced the northern tracks.

"*No*," I insisted. "They weren't right. They had families that loved them. Friends who are devastated. You can't just 'check out' because things get rough!"

He looked at me again with those purgatory eyes. Half here. Half already gone. "Who says?"

"Me."

"Oh, you say, so that's how things go, right?" His hands flew into the air and made swooping, sarcastic gestures. "Whatever Paige says goes. Don't worry—when you said you hate me, I heard you. You don't need to backslide and pretend you didn't mean it, because I saw the look in your eyes when you slammed the door in my face. I've seen it before. I saw it when my mom told my dad to fuck off and then disappeared forever. She might as well have told me the same thing, because she's gone, gone for good, just like you'll be gone for good soon, too."

I stumbled away. My back hit the fence, blocking any chance at escape. "No, that's not —"

He lunged forward and grabbed the chain links on either side of me. "DON'T LIE TO ME, PAIGE. If you think lying is going to get me off these tracks, you're stupider than I thought. You'll leave for Wesleyan and hook up with some polo player like that asshole at the dance and go to his parents' house on weekends and drink in the gardens. I'll be a blip on your radar. The creepy, drunk, pervy, rapist stepbrother you fucked whenever you needed to forget."

I slipped out from between his arms, scared to death.

I needed to call my mother. I needed to tell his father. I needed *help*. My hands shook as I got my phone out to dial, but he screamed at me so loudly I nearly dropped it. "Don't call them! This isn't about them! It's about us!"

I started to dial them anyway, but his words stopped me.

"Call them and I'll be dead before they get here."

I stuffed the phone back in my pocket.

"Smart," he said. "Good." He looked back at the tracks. His green eyes looked red in the lights. "I'm not trying to scare you. I just want you to understand. You have an escape hatch, Paige. You have one. But guess what? Not all of us do."

Maybe I could dial my mom without him seeing? I slyly tucked my fingers back in my pocket. If I could just get to my favorites, I could call her, and she'd hear what was happening. She'd piece it together and help me before it was too late. I tried stalling. "You're going to college, too, Ty. That's your escape hatch."

"*Whatever.*" His arms flew up and smacked down at his sides. "We won't be together! You won't visit! You can't wait to get away from me, from all of this." He gestured to the tracks, to the sign. Then he tucked his hands in his pockets and faced the direction I assumed the next train would come from.

"Stop it! This isn't funny anymore."

He looked at me over his shoulder. The lack of gestures. The lack of expression on his face made my heart stop. "Was it ever funny?"

"You know what I mean!"

He turned back around, and I took the opportunity to dial Mom. It rang once, twice, before being completely replaced by horrific sounds. Dooming sounds.

The train's horn bellowed through the night like a man's scream. The roar of the train engine closed in on us. Closed in on Ty.

Two headlights preceded 64 tons of steel that headed straight for one hundred and forty pound Ty.

"Ty! Move!"

I ran onto the tracks. I had no choice. If I didn't, the train would kill him. I missed the first grab of his sweatshirt sleeve. As I tried for a second time, he ducked out of my way, jumping to the right.

The train was too close. We weren't going to make it.

Bright lights blinded me. The screech of brakes overrode my shouts for him to jump. I fell out of the way just in time, smashing onto the dirt.

The train roared by, horn blazing and brakes screaming, but unable to stop.

Chapter Sixty-Four

Now

Jake makes me a cup of herbal lemon tea. I watch his back as he swirls a bit of honey into the boiling water. He catches me watching as he re-enters the room and smiles the sad smile of a long, hard day. I mirror his gesture. He sits down beside me on the worn leather couch that used to belong to my parents. My hair is damp, hanging loosely over my shoulders that are covered in the green flannel shirt he handed me when I was toweling off from a shower. I stood under the hot water until my fingers wrinkled and my cheeks pinked from heat, scrubbing away the institutional smells of the ICU, wishing the steam, the dull roar of the spray, would cover up the jarring beeps of the machines, the hum of the respirator that keeps my dad alive, the screeching train, and Ty's screams.

We talk quietly on the couch. I lean into Jake's chest, loving that he smells like soap and the comforting beef stew he warmed up for dinner. We stay like that, our hearts beating against each other, for a long time until the quiet soothing becomes something else. My skin burns wanting him. My soul wants the same. The flannel is soft under my palm as I let it slide over his shoulders and onto his chest, onto his heart. I make a fist with the fabric and bend my head, resting my forehead on the fistful of Jake. At first I just kiss the material. It's soft and rough, like him.

He lets out a little sigh.

I kiss him again.

This time I bypass his shirt and let my lips graze his bare chest instead. It's a little kiss, small, daring. Something I can still back away from. Something he can ignore and we'll pretend didn't happen. That I slipped. That it was just an accident. We haven't talked about what happened after the bar—we could blame those kisses on silly drunkenness—but this is something else entirely.

If he accepts it.

Stroking his shoulder with my thumb from left to right, I find that tender spot under his collarbone and kiss that, too.

"Ah, hell, Paige…"

He lifts my chin and takes my lips with his. Strong hands run through my hair, over my face, smoothing, clutching. One of us moans, a low sound of *want*. The other answers with a sigh. My hands smooth over all the parts of Jake I've been starving for since I arrived at the ranch. The bend in his arm, the hard ripples of his muscles, feel just like I've dreamed. Better, even, because there's softness to them, a gentleness.

"Are you okay?" he breathes.

"Yes," I whisper. "More than okay."

My skin is on fire, and I'm about two seconds from melting into the ground when he sweeps me up off the ground and carries me into his bedroom.

When he lays me gently on his bed, his need turns to patience.

Slowly, gently, with the skills of a guy in a romance movie, he tenderly unbuttons each of the buttons on the plaid shirt I'm wearing, and with a sweep of his long fingers, slips it off my shoulder, kissing every piece of now-exposed skin. I shudder with impatience while at the same time never wanting him to stop. This is nothing like Ty's urgent, sloppy insistence.

"*Jake*," I moan. I tug on his hair, pulling his face back to mine, kissing him with everything I have, everything I was, everything I am.

I kiss him like there's only this, and when he asks me with his eyes, when his hands wait to explore areas I've been dying for him to explore, and I answer with a tilt of my hips that *yes, yes, please, I've been waiting for you*, he pulls down my panties. After grabbing a condom out of his bedside table and rolling it on, he sinks gently into me. At first he's cautious, kissing my face, my neck, not wanting to hurt me. I'm not hurt. I'm in love. And I want it all. We move in a rhythm so natural, so perfect, so beyond expectation it blows my mind, and as my insides explode, I realize this is how it's supposed to be. *This*. And I don't want it to ever end.

After, he pulls me into his arms. I stroke his damp head as he lies on my heaving chest, both of us catching our breath.

He gently rubs my cheek with his rough thumb. "Why are you crying?"

"I don't know."

With Ty it was all about me comforting him. Me letting Ty have what he wanted to avoid someone else hurting. With Jake, I want it to be the opposite.

With us, I know it's not a mind game. A battle to see who will give in, who will get pushed away. I don't want sex to be a healing tool we're using to erase the pain of seeing my dad like that. Sex isn't a Band-Aid to cover other pain.

With Jake, it's just about the two of us. "I want it to be about the two of us," I say.

"Me, too," Jake says so quietly it's almost a whisper. Almost as softly, he pulls me in tighter. I press against his warmth and breathe in his comfort.

With Jake, I hope it's not about me being broken. I want it to be as real as it feels.

I want it to be about love.

Chapter Sixty-Five

Then

Ty jumped that first time.

He jumped when I told him to.

Maybe he was going to jump anyway, whether I was there or not, but of course I piled so much of it onto myself I didn't know the answer anymore.

The train still hit him.

It knocked him in the legs as he was jumping off the tracks, which fractured his left leg in three places, and left him with a serious concussion. When he was stable enough medically, they checked him into the psychiatric unit.

"I'm not suicidal," Ty said when I visited him, standing a few feet back from his bed, limply holding a yellow round balloon with a painted black smile.

"You were standing on the tracks, body full of pills and booze, a train hit you, and you wonder why they'd think you were suicidal?"

"Ever the comedian," he said with a wry smile, though his eyes were still that distant, zombie-green they were that night on the tracks that made me feel sick.

"I have to tell you something." I cleared my throat. "I need to go visit my dad. He's sick and my mom says I need to go, so before I leave for college I'm going to go see him."

I avoided his zombie eyes.

"Ty, did you hear me? I'm leaving."

"Oh," he said, nonplussed.

"Oh?" I was pissed. "That's what you have to say? Never mind then. Maybe I shouldn't have come."

"I don't care either way. You don't matter to me anymore."

"You know what? I hope you get help in here and you're able to deal with your disappointment in me in a healthier way from now on."

A slow mocking smile appeared. "A healthy way? Jesus, they've gotten to you, too, huh, sis?"

"Who?" I asked, irritated with his tone. His behavior was killing me, slaying his poor father, and my mom was a wreck. Yet he was smiling?

"*All the shrinks*, of course. Listen to yourself. Listen to what you just said to me—*how* you said it to me—like you don't know me. Like we're *strangers*."

"I did not," I said. The smell of this room was making me sick. "I'm just saying you tried to kill yourself, your behavior is psycho, and this is exactly where you should be. A psych ward."

"Boy, did you turn into a bitch."

"A bitch that saved your life," I snapped. "Maybe I should've just left you to die on those tracks, you asshole."

My chest tightened in disgust. I was disgusted with myself. With my hateful words. But I was beyond disgusted with Ty. Did he not want to be saved?

I wanted out of this room. Out of this stink of day-old sheets and drippy medicine.

He saluted me. "Okay, Captain Ahab, school counselor."

"You know what, Ty? You were once a pretty cool guy. Somebody I was stupid enough to actually care about. I don't know what happened to you, but this is all on you."

"Have a great life. Have fun in BFE or wherever the hell you're going," he said flippantly, picking up a skateboarding magazine and stuffing his face into it. "Don't forget to write."

Oh, hell no. He wasn't dismissing me. Not after everything we'd been through together. "You're an asshole, you know that?"

He didn't bother looking up. "Yep."

"You could've died."

He shrugged. "You could get hit by a car in the parking lot."

I put my hands on my hips. "If you meant to kill yourself, you wouldn't have called me. You would've just done it."

"So?"

"You *wanted* me to come find you. Wanted me to beg you not to do something you weren't ever going to do."

His silence was his confession. Even though I'd guessed it all along, it still pissed me off.

"So what was that all about then?" I asked. "Was it a game? A manipulative stunt to make me stay? To make me sleep with you again? Do you know what this is doing to your dad? I heard him crying the other night in the den. You have no business being in this ward, tying up this bed when someone else out there, someone who really is suicidal, could be getting help."

I glanced at the call button dangling from his hospital bed, wondering if I should report him to the nurse, to his doctor. But they already knew how sick he was. The psychiatrist told mom that just because someone who makes a suicidal gesture doesn't necessarily want to die, it doesn't mean they won't accidentally fuck it up and die anyway. We needed to take this seriously.

But that didn't mean I understood Ty.

I didn't understand if it was the pain of his mother leaving and his dad remarrying mine, if it was something about the present or the past. But I did know, in retrospect, that it wasn't about me. I was just who he centered all of this pain on, dumping it all over me so he didn't have to deal with it himself. Being in California, being in this hospital room, was probably just as bad for his recovery as it was for mine.

I handed him the string of the balloon. He clutched it in his fist.

I couldn't be responsible for whether or not he was happy or sad. His mind games, making me feel like sex was keeping him on or off the tracks? I couldn't fall for it anymore, or soon, I'd be as sick as he was.

"See you, Ty."

Chapter Sixty-Six

Now

When I call mom to tell her about Dad's accident, she gives me another week's reprieve. Offers to come help, but I say, no, no it's okay. What will she think about Jake and me? That I've moved on so easily?

We interview a bunch of potential nurses while Anna clangs pots and pans around in the kitchen. I stand in the doorway watching her scrub the crap out of an egg-laden frying pan until the bottom shimmers in the morning sun streaming through the strawberry curtained window.

Her face is flushed, and when she hears me pouring a mug of coffee for the most recent interviewee, her eyes are watery, not with sadness, but with indignation. "I don't understand why you two feel you need to replace me." She wipes sopping hands on her apron, leaving two handprints. "I made a mistake. It won't happen again. It should be me caring for him. Me."

"Anna…we talked to Dad about it. He doesn't want you to go through that again."

Huffing, she spins around on her bare feet and attacks another pan. As she battles the bacon grease, I set my hand on her shoulder. "You'll get to be with him for what matters. You'll still live with him, love him. You just don't have to handle all the feeding, all the caretaking. Or the medical…" *Choices. The life and death choices. You won't have to decide if you let him die or force him to live a life he's done with.* "…stuff."

"I understand."

"Do you?"

"I understand, but I hate it."

I understand my father. I understand his philosophy. But he should know by now that life isn't black and white — it's red. And in that color is where we spend the whole of what matters, the vibrancy of life, the bloody mess of death, and the pulsing heart of love. It was always red with Ty. My feelings for him were a twist of emotions, twining around and around, one never ruling the other, never taking over until the end. Relationships are always messy, but the ones that start wrong out of the gate are quicksand.

"I hate it, too. It sucks. It all sucks. But it's what we've got."

"When did you get so wise, kid?"

I blink.

"You think I'm wise?"

"Wise and brave. I sure do." She smiled. "But don't make me say it twice. Now go on and get that lady in there a cup of my coffee so she can't help but accept the job." She hands me the mug. "Scoot," she says with a playful grandma-ish swoosh of her arm.

Anna thinks I'm brave, and she's the bravest woman I know. Anna, like Jake, doesn't say something she doesn't mean.

Now I need to do something even more frightening.

The roar of a familiar oversized golden pick-up truck with gold-rimmed tires pulling a sparkly clean horse trailer climbs up the rocky driveway as if it doesn't want a splash of dirt mucking up its shimmer.

I hated this guy the first time I met him and I hate him now. Not because of him — Jake's right, I don't know him at all. I hate him for what he represents: power over the weak, power over me, Jake, Anna, Dad, and Scout, all because he has money and we're desperate.

Jake squeezes my hand as my nemesis steps out of the driver's seat in his two-hundred-dollar cowboy hat and brand new poser boots. Everyone knows a real cowboy's boots are never clean.

I wipe the sweat off my brow and suck in a breath.

"So I see you've changed your mind about that pretty little filly of yours, eh?"

Every instinct in my body wants to look away: at the dirt, at the sky, at Jake, but I don't. I hold strong and look right into his watery eyes.

"I'll sell her to you, but it's not because I've changed my mind."

His chuckle is as faux as his cowboy look. The fact that this jerk gets to walk and talk while my daddy is lying down inside in the hospital bed we rented after his ICU visit—the fact that he will never sit up in his wheelchair again, will never type a funny Dad-ism, while this prick breathes the air of Dad's ranch—makes me want to hand pluck the flaps of suede off his coat that he's wearing (even though it's 90 degrees out here) and light them on fire.

He hands me a manila envelope of cash.

I swallow when, peeking inside the flap, I see bundles of hundred dollar bills lined up and rubber banded together. I hand it to Jake who flips through it making sure it's there—all two hundred grand of it. This exchange feels so western, so gangster.

My legs shake, the result of never seeing this much cash in one place, or from what it all means. If it feels wrong, it is wrong—a Dad-ism.

"It's all there," the man says.

"I see it is," Jake says.

"Where's my prize-wining filly?" He says it proudly, like he had anything to do with how awesome Scout is.

"In the stable," Jake says, a resigned tone in his voice. His jaw clenches. He hates this, too.

The man takes a step toward her, toward Scout, and I jump in front of him.

I can't let him do this.

I can't let him take Scout. I know he's probably not a bad guy, and even though I never got to meet his daughter because of Dad's hospitalization, she's probably a perfectly nice girl. But I hate him. I hate him for buying my horse. I vilify him like he's a Disney character.

It's too much. My heart is pounding. Blood pulses in my head.

"I change my mind. Jake, give the money back." My voice wavers, and I'm seconds from a full-blown panic attack. Thoughts blur together. I'm thinking irrationally and I know it, but I can't stop. Everything is thick with meaning. This was supposed to be my chance to start anew. This was my fresh start. And now it's my fiery Scout who has to pay the price for my soul as I sell her to the devil? Unacceptable. No. No. Not Scout. *Take me. Take me instead.*

"Paige, it's fine. She's going to be with that great girl, out on the rodeo circuit. Are you okay? You're really pale. Do you need to sit down?" Jake's hand is on my shoulder, but it's not helping. I can't breathe.

"Paige." I spin around and see Anna and hear the message in her voice. I remember what she said to me in the kitchen. About me being brave...and wise.

Sucking in a shrill sound, the worst I've made since I screamed for Ty to get off the tracks, I head into the barn, take my girl by the lead, and prepare to hand her over to a man I can't stand.

"I'm so sorry, Scout. I'm so, so sorry." I hold onto her head, and my tears wash over her face. "If we had any other choice, you know I would never sell you, but we don't. It's for Daddy and Anna and Jake. I have to." And then I can't speak anymore, not with decipherable words, anyway.

Her nose presses into my shoulder and instead of fighting me, she lets me lead her to him. It's like she knows. It's like she understands everything, and the fact that she forgives me makes it so much worse.

Chapter Sixty-Seven

Then

Graduation day. Matching caps and gowns. Smiling for snapping cameras. Despite everything, I got caught up in the pomp and circumstance of it all.

Ty was allowed to walk through ceremonies after the lengthy hospitalization plus completing a rehab stint for drugs and alcohol because, due to all his AP classes, he already had enough credits to graduate. He opted out. "There's no fucking way I'm walking with those hypocritical tools," was his exact response to our parents, who had been acting like skittish coyotes ever since he'd come home.

I was glad he wasn't there.

But he was right about one thing: the ceremony itself was pretty awful.

They did this PowerPoint of the Lives We'd Lost with this weirdly upbeat song playing, like we were supposed to find inspiration in the dead teenagers or something and then followed it with a keynote from an affluent tech company CEO—a nerdy young billionaire types everyone worshiped.

When he finished, the crowd gave a rousing standing ovation, and we all released blue balloons into the air as a symbol of life moving on, moving ahead, moving forward, which was weird because our school colors were red and gold. Maybe red was too bloody and dark? Who the hell knew. Anyway, my peers clamored toward the CEO guy hoping for internships, and I took the appropriate photos with my smiling mom and stepdad, hugged my classmates. And went home to change. Ty's door was shut. I didn't bother knocking. He never came out.

That night, I attended a couple graduation parties (avoiding white golf-shoes Matt, the polo player from the unfortunate night after that dance).

The fact that I didn't run into Ty at any of the various parties didn't faze me. If he hadn't walked through the ceremony, he wouldn't want to come out to party.

I also assumed our parents made him stay home so he wouldn't be tempted to drink or do drugs.

My phone rang twice while I was out. It was him, but I ignored both calls. He ruined my entire year. I wasn't going to let him ruin grad night, too.

Screw you, Ty.

I powered down my phone, tucked it into my jeans pocket, and joined my classmates in a toast.

Chapter Sixty-Eight

Now

Through blurry eyes, I watch the bowl of soup Anna set on my nightstand lose its steam. When it's cooled to an almost chill, I cry myself to sleep.

The next day I don't get out of bed. Everything aches.

I can barely make it to the bathroom to dry heave in the toilet.

I can't stop thinking of her face—this terrible acceptance in her eyes.

The slack was loose on the rope. When I led her toward his trailer, she could've jerked away from me and galloped up the mountain to find her herd, but she didn't. She knew and she did it for me. What makes it so horrific—what makes it so unforgivable—is that in the end I did the very thing I fought so hard against. I made her trust me and then I let her go.

Chapter Sixty-Nine

Then

The next morning, I had six "Missed Call – TY" notifications and a text.

This is me running away. Game over. We both lose.

My stomach sank, and I knew this wasn't a joke. Wasn't a warning. I knew there wasn't anything I could do.

Mom and Phil got the call from the police that Ty stood on the tracks as the last train of the evening roared by the stop closest to our high school. The one that took Cornell, Elena, Elliot, and the others.

The train killed Ty, whether he meant for it to or not.

The autopsy showed that he had both drugs and alcohol in his system. I don't know where he got them.

His body—identified by his hoodie and the cell phone that had flown off the tracks—was so mangled, they had to cremate him.

I stayed in my room for two weeks. I was a murderer and a victim.

Ty was right. The game was over and we both lost.

Or had he won?

Because he'd killed me, too.

Chapter Seventy

Now

I'm completely despondent and depressed.

The combination of my dad's hospitalization and selling Scout cracked open everything I'd buried deep inside. As if almost losing him and then losing her wasn't bad enough, I'm now having PTSD because of Ty. I get so bad I have to call my mom and talk to my therapist on the phone.

She assures me Ty wasn't my fault. None of this is my fault.

I try to believe her but I can't.

Chapter Seventy-One

Eventually, I pull myself together. Mostly.

I figure it's selfish of me to waste my last few days with Dad holed up in my room, so despite how shitty I feel, I sit next to Dad's bed and—what else?—fight with him about college.

Like Jake, he still wants me to go, but after everything we've just been through—after everything I'm still going through—I want to stay here on the ranch. I argue with words, he argues with type. So far, I'm losing.

"Hey, Paige?" Anna calls, peeking through the door with a basket of dirty clothes in her arms. "You have any darks for this load?"

"No, I'm okay. I'll do my laundry later."

She squints. "You said that yesterday and the day before."

I shrug. "It's fine. I have plenty of clean clothes."

"You have plenty of clean clothes because you haven't stepped out of those stretch pants all week."

I shrug again.

She looks back and forth between us. "Don't tell me you finally got out of bed just to argue with your daddy over college again?"

"Yep."

"What's he saying?" She walks over and reads the computer

screen. Her smile grows bigger as she reads our conversation.

"Looks like your dad makes a good case for school."

"Whatever. He didn't go to college, and he's done great."

Dad's words flood the screen. *Which is why you're going, young lady! You want to make the same mistakes I made? You aren't giving your future up for me.*

Touching Dad's shoulder affectionately, she looks over at me. "You're never going to win this, you know."

"I know," I say. I'm so mad at myself for falling in love with this place, and I know I'm acting like a baby but I don't care. I don't know how I'll survive this new tidal wave of emotions without them to lean on. Without the safety net of the ranch. I don't want to be alone in a dorm room across the country while they're here. My heart wants to stay with Dad, with Jake, with Anna, even without Scout. This is my home now. It's all I have. I can't say that without getting into everything else, though.

And I won't bring up Ty.

I won't look like even more of a mess.

"You leave tomorrow for San Francisco," Anna insists. "We need to pack clean clothes."

"I'm not going," I try again.

Bullshit, you aren't, Dad types. He's extra ornery today.

Anna smiles again.

I scowl at her. "Anna told me at the restaurant before the rodeo that I could stay."

"That was before your dad and Jake convinced me otherwise."

Grrrr. "I can just take a semester off? Start again in the winter?"

Longer you stay the less likely you are to leave.

"How do you know?"

I just do.

If you don't go to college, I'll never forgive myself, Dad writes.

He's laying it on thick. I don't want to go. I really, really don't.

Jake said the same thing and he never left.

Oh. So this isn't only about me. Dad feels guilty for Jake staying on to help with the ranch, and he's not going to let the same thing happen to me. But at least *this* is an argument I can make a decent point in breaking.

"Jake's happy he stayed on here," I point out.

He may not say he regrets it, but he's wanted to get out of town since his daddy died, Dad types. *I should've made him go, but instead I was selfish. I was selfish and I let him stay when he offered, because after losing you and your mama I couldn't lose anybody else. I won't make that same selfish mistake again. I may be locked in a body that can't move, but I can still speak, and I want you to listen to me and listen good. You get up, take a shower, pack your bags like Anna says, and get on that plane tomorrow to say goodbye to your mama and close up that lid on California, you hear me?*

Close that lid on California. I wasn't only going back to pack my bags for college. I was going to say my final goodbye to Ty.

Because if you don't, you won't be able to start over here or anywhere, and that's what I'd like you to do. Consider it my dying wish if you'd like.

He puts a smiley face by that and Anna slugs him gently, "Gus!"

I swallow back tears. This is too much.

The ranch is the first place I've been happy since Mom dragged me away as a kid. This ranch restarted my heart. This ranch is what's keeping it beating.

Now he's pushing me away like I pushed away Scout.

I won't survive another loss.

I can't lose Dad, Anna, and Jake, and say goodbye to Ty all at once.

He starts typing again. *Listen, kid. I know I say a lot of things, and most of them you can ignore but one thing I've learned: We cannot control the wind, but we can adjust our sails.*

Chapter Seventy-Two

"I hear today's the day," Jake says the next morning. "You ready to head back to California, Cowgirl?"

I can't see Jake.

I can't say goodbye to Jake.

It's Scout all over again, but worse.

It's not like Ty, because I didn't love Ty. Ty didn't love me. Jake is pure and good, and I can't lose him.

Rolling over, I face the wall. Face the lavender buds that refuse to bloom. I decide to be angry instead of sad. It's easier.

"You win. You and Dad—the bromance from hell," I say, my voice strained. I don't want Jake to see how upset I am.

"Oh, come on." He pokes my back playfully. It's obvious he doesn't want me to know how upset he is either and is doing his best to keep things light, but I can hear it in his voice. The sadness. "Don't pout now. You know it's the best thing. You'd end up hating us if you stayed on, and you'd hate the winter. It's very *Shining*-esque, you know. Lots of people acting crazy. None of that fancy food you like, just canned beans and no electricity. Really. Anna will probably get a knife and chase me around the kitchen threatening to put me in her stew. Truly, you're better off up at your fancy-schmancy college. For safety reasons alone."

I sit up and face him. "You're very funny. You and Dad ought to hit the comedy circuit together." I swipe a tear off my hot cheek. Sad is winning. I can't be angry with Jake.

He pulls me in close and kisses my forehead, and I snuggle into his neck. "I'm going to miss you most of all," I say into his soft skin.

"I know."

He strokes my hair, clinging to a handful.

"I'll visit," I whisper.

"You might," he says in a funny voice, like a dare.

"And you'll call?"

"I could."

"And write?" The tears are really welling now. It's a lost cause, me fighting these back.

"I'm not much of a writer. More of a reader, really," he says, still trying to be funny. Still trying to make me feel better.

I pull away, my eyes pleading a case I've already lost. "Or I could just stay?"

"Nope." He kisses me. He kisses the tears off of my cheek. He hugs me tighter.

"I hate you, you know."

"I hate you, too." Grinning, he kisses me again, and then I bury my face into his chest the way Scout did with me. This is the thing about goodbyes, both the permanent and the temporary kind—they all really suck.

I open my nightstand and hand him the journal I've been working on all summer with the note I left in the front for him. "So since you're such a voracious reader…"

"That I am."

"So. You know that thing about my past I keep trying to tell you but never did for a variety of reasons? This is it. I never wanted anyone to read it. I mean, it's pretty awful, and I'm not proud of it, but it's real and true and anyway… And anyway, it's for you."

He starts to open the cover and I slam it shut, my hand

lingering on his for emphasis. "To read *after* I leave. Long after my plane has taken off and to possibly never discuss in real time."

"Okay," he says and sets it on the flower patch of my quilt. I tug at a loose yellow thread and sweep the tears off my cheeks that are starting to flow yet again. I hate goodbyes so, so much.

"Take care of him, Jake. And call me right away if something happens."

"You know I will."

Ask me to stay, Jake, my eyes plead. *Tell me you love me. Beg me not to go.*

He avoids my eyes, ignoring my pleas. "What time does your plane leave again?"

"Five."

"So we should leave for the airport around two."

"Three hours early?"

"Well. I wanted to stop off somewhere on the way."

"Where?"

"I don't know. Somewhere."

He looks coy. I'm intrigued.

But unfortunately… "Anna and Dad said they wanted to take me, so…"

"Oh." He looks disappointed, and my throat tightens.

"I know," I say. "I want you to take me, too. But maybe it's easier this way. Airport goodbyes are the worst."

"*All* goodbyes are the worst." Jake kisses me softly on the lips and tucks the journal under his arm as he stands up to go. "You need to shower and pack and stuff, so I'll let you get to it."

"Are you…leaving?"

"I got to feed the horses and get to a few things."

"Now? But you were planning on driving me, so I thought you'd maybe have a little more time to hang out."

He looks at me one more time—a familiar look, but one I can't place right away. His sky eyes are red and stormy.

"Okay. Just say…g-goodbye before I go, okay?" I manage

to choke out.

He looks at the antique door handle. He looks down at the journal. He looks anywhere but at me.

This is it. I'm not going to see him again. I dive out of my bed and throw my arms around his neck. We hold each other tight. "Thank you, Jake," I whisper into his neck.

"Do good, Cowgirl."

Chapter Seventy-Three

After a tearful, terrible goodbye with Dad and Anna, who promised to call and Skype, who I promise to visit, I fly back to San Francisco as planned. As much as I hated not seeing Jake again, I sort of appreciated it. I couldn't say goodbye to Jake in front of my dad and Anna. I just couldn't. I'd be a basket case, and I probably couldn't get on the stupid plane.

I wonder where he was planning on taking me. Maybe I'll never know.

SFO is so different than the morning I left. First of all, the sky is bright and sunny. "Looks like you brought Wyoming with you," Mom says, cheerfully pulling me into her arms. "You look fantastic, honey."

"Thanks," I say, "I don't feel fantastic."

"Well, goodbyes are always hard. I don't have to tell you. But I'm glad you're back home." She squeezes me again.

She looks good, too. Happier. Less severe. Maybe our break was good for the both of us, and time does have a way of healing things on its own, somehow. Look at me sounding like a genuine cowgirl. "How's Phil?"

"He's okay, considering. I think the ceremony will be good for him. Closure, you know?"

"That's what Dad said, too."

"He did?" She arches a perfectly sculpted eyebrow.

"Yeah. He said he wanted me to come here and close the lid on my past so I could move freely into the future."

"Jesus," she shock-laughs. "When did he become a philosopher?"

"Probably when he began dying?"

She sobers at that.

"I think he's made peace with it," I say. "We all have. Saying goodbye to him was rough, though. Especially when I'm not sure I'll see him again."

I swallow back emotion. I miss him already. Miss them all. Being with Mom, being back in California, feels foreign now. This airport is so big. So busy. I miss Jackson. Jake.

"I wanted to stay, you know. I begged," I admit. I need her to know.

"I heard."

"But in the end Dad wouldn't let me."

"I know." She patted my arm. "Your Dad's been emailing me...if you can believe that."

"Wow. Though I'm not totally surprised. He wanted a united front on Team Get Paige To College."

"Yes, well, he wants the best for you. We all do."

"I know," I said. "It was just so hard to leave. I was...I was happy there."

She smiles at me, her eyes shiny. "I'm so glad, sweetie. You needed it. I'm so glad you were able to reconnect with him. And you know? He apologized for past...mistakes. With me. And I forgave him."

"Wow."

It looks like I wasn't the only one who changed on the ranch.

"I know," she says. And it seems like she does.

Chapter Seventy-Four

The next morning, shortly after dawn, we bury Ty at sea.

They have these funeral boats on the coast, just regular boats, but you're allowed to sprinkle ashes off of them. We invite a few of Ty's friends from school, some family. Ty's mother flies in from New York to attend. Instead of dresses and suits and ties, we wear black sweaters, pants, and shoes with soles that won't slip on the wet deck. We all wear black sunglasses like Ty's to fight the glare off the sea.

The morning is cool and foggy. I read a Lord Byron poem that Ty liked. The irony of Ty admiring Lord Byron when he was alive doesn't escape me. When I finish, a seagull flies over the boat and lets out a horrible squawk. I jump along with the rest of the passengers, then spend the rest of the funeral trying not to toss my cookies.

A few days later, I'm on the couch sifting through boxes of photo albums and framed photographs when Mom comes and sits by me.

"I brought you some tea," she says.

"Thanks."

It's not Anna's or Jake's tea, but I take it. She sits beside me in white flowing yoga pants and a long, silky cardigan sweater. After a few quiet sips she points to a photo. "I like that one."

It's our holiday photo from last year: me, Mom, Phil, Ty. We're on the beach in Hawaii where they got married. We're all wearing white and smiling.

"Maybe we got married too soon," she says, stroking the photo.

"Why do you say that? I thought you and Phil were happy?"

She keeps her eyes on the photo. "Putting two teenagers, virtual strangers, under the same roof. It wasn't smart. I should've been smarter. If I had, maybe—"

"Me and Ty weren't your fault. It was our fault."

"I should've said something. Done something to stop it. I'm the adult. I'm your mother for god's sake. I'm so sorry, Paige."

I stare at the photo. At Ty in his open necked Polo and white flowered *lei*. "One of the things I learned on the ranch is that things happen. Bad things. Good things. And we can't do anything to stop them. Sometimes life just has to play itself out."

She starts to cry, then. Really cry. Deep, terrible sobs. I know she's crying over so much more than Ty. It's me, too, and Dad—and maybe blaming oneself for all of life's storms is something I inherited.

"He never…hurt you, did he?"

"He did. But I'm okay. I really am. Turns out between you and Dad, I'm made of pretty tough stock."

Her crumbling face pulls itself back together. Nodding, she straightens out her silk pants, running her palms across the wrinkles.

"If I believed it about that girl in Brooklyn, I never would've let him move in here."

"I know."

"Doubting the innocence of a dead boy. Does that make me a bad person?"

"It makes you human, I guess," I say.

"Some secrets go with us to our grave," is her reply.

Chapter Seventy-Five

Even though I haven't heard from Jake, Wesleyan itself is exactly as I'd hoped.

Under looming brick buildings with a history that has nothing to do with me, leaves melt from thick waxy green to blood red. Umbrellas crowd rain-soaked sidewalks as summer fades into fall. It's easy to disappear in this atmosphere of bright eyes and new books that creak when you open them.

Mom escorted me to the East Coast not long after Ty's burial, and we spent a few days in a hotel, shopping for matching sheets and comforters for my dorm bed, fluffy towels for the communal shower, and textbooks for my first semester classes. My roommate is Karen, a quirky, quiet girl from the Midwest, who reads a lot and raises rabbits back on her farm.

"The classic odd couple," Mom said when she met Karen and eyed the wall full of bunny posters. "That's the beauty of college."

When Mom left, we both cried, but it was different than the other goodbyes. It felt normal. Mothers drop their daughters off at college every fall. Something about the normalcy makes me feel better about it all.

Life here is simple: I get up each day, shower, eat breakfast in the dining hall, go to classes, eat lunch, go to classes, go back to my dorm room, eat dinner, study, watch a little TV (Karen and I like those *When Animals Attack* shows), and go to bed—rinse and repeat.

Karen's a nervous talker and babbles on and on about her bunnies when we run out of things to talk about: Florence the Brave won a blue ribbon in the state fair, she's worried about the upcoming winter because her mother won't let them inside until it's actually freezing so she's saving up to buy them an outdoor heater, et cetera. She doesn't ask me much about myself, and aside from a few easy comments—I'm from Wyoming (sort of true), I'm an only child (technically true)—I keep quiet.

Classes hold my interest. African-American women's literature and creative writing are my favorites. I'm on a major Toni Morrison bender and recently developed a healthy green tea addiction. My life at Wesleyan is purposefully simple and exactly what I need, ironically what I assumed my ranch stay would be. Aside from the literature, which I'm scarfing up like cows on fresh grass up on the mountain, my new life is intentionally, forcefully, drama free. I like being only responsible for myself. For getting myself up, to the dining hall, to class, and completing assignments. I don't party. I don't socialize much at all outside of Karen, but that's fine with me. I want quiet.

Busy quiet.

If I keep myself busy, I won't have time to think as much. With my nose in heavy books, reading about characters suffering bigger problems than mine, I won't have as much room for regret. That's what I tell myself anyway, as I watch the rain streak across windows that block all the life I'm missing outside. All the time with Dad I'm missing on the ranch, the sunrises and sunsets and everything in between with Jake.

"What a beautiful horse," Karen says, looking at a photo I've recently added to my bulletin board. "Is she yours?"

"Used to be," I say. Anna found the photo in a magazine. Scout has gone on to be a champion with her new rider, just like

Jake had prophesized and the greasy new owner had counted on. The fire has gone out of her eyes and she looks content, healthy—like she's being treated right. It still hurts to look at her, but knowing she's happy hurts a hell of a lot less. Seeing the return address from Eight Hands Ranch had sent hopeful shivers across my body, which, like always, was met with a lame sense of disappointment when I saw the note wasn't from Jake.

I really regret giving him that journal.

Karen nods. "Meetcha at the cafeteria for lunch? Same place same time?" We sit by ourselves in the corner every meal. I wonder if she'll tire of me and look for new friends after a while.

"Sure," I say.

As she smiles and slings her backpack over her shoulder, I question if Karen is the Universe's idea of a gift.

One day fades into the next until it's finally the end of crisp November, and I'm in a fluster of nervous excitement, packed and ready to take a cab to the airport for my first trip back to the ranch since I left. I'm ready to see Dad, find Jake—re-enter life—when I get the call from Anna.

"Honey, I'm so sorry, but they just closed the airport. A freak storm passed through and it's coming down like crazy out here. We were so looking forward to having you for Thanksgiving."

I swallow back the disappointment. "That's okay," I say. Though suddenly it's anything but. I want to be around people who love me who I love back. I didn't realize how lonely I've been, how each day I was just getting through, how much I want to go home. Holidays make it worse.

"Are you there, Paige?"

"Yeah."

I'm afraid I'll start crying if I hear her voice another minute. Imagining the smells of roasting turkey wafting from the old oven, the thought of Anna's homemade gravy on the stove, the snaps of the roaring fire…

"How is he?"

"He's okay, hanging on. Disappointed you can't be here, of course. Here, talk to him."

"Hi, Daddy," I say. "I'm so sorry about the snow. I really wanted to see you."

My voice cracks.

"He says you'll be out here soon enough, and 'Love you, Paige-y.'" Anna responds for him.

"Love you, too, Daddy."

I hang up and flop onto my bed, sobbing like a kid left at camp for the first time, like I haven't cried since I said goodbye to Jake in my purple wallpaper bedroom.

When my mom calls—Anna told her about the storm—I tell her I'm going home with Karen. Mom and Phil are going to Hawaii and won't be home anyway. She says the thought of spending a holiday, Phil's first without Ty, at home without me would be too depressing.

Since Karen left yesterday and our dorms are pretty much a ghost ship, I walk through the snow to the 7-11, the only shop open, and after buying saltines and a jar of peanut butter, I eat Thanksgiving dinner in my dorm room, watching movies on my laptop and wishing I were home.

Chapter Seventy-Six

December moves along swiftly enough. The sky darkens and days shorten. I'm working on my final short story for writing class. I changed all the names, but it's about Jake. I still haven't heard from him, and it's been so long now that I don't expect to. I guess he decided to move on, and even though it hurts like hell, how can I blame him? But I'm not over him. Not even a little bit. So I write him, or a loosely guised likeness of him, into one of my stories. My creative writing professor, an eloquent, brilliant blonde woman, Professor Diana Klein (we call her Diana), says it feels "real and alive," which is the best compliment she could give me. In a previous workshop, she asked if I could expand it into a bigger piece. That while she felt "all the bones were intact, it could be fleshed out, deepened."

I'm working on the Fleshing Out and Deepening, which is, essentially, reliving all my moments with Jake, leaving me in this sad, sick, euphoric state of nostalgia as I pound away at my laptop, when I get a frantic phone call from Anna.

"He's taken a turn for the worse."

"I'm coming," I say into the phone. "How bad? I mean, how long?"

"They don't know, but he's asking for you."

"But he's been so stable." We talk or Skype at least once a

week, and I email Dad daily. "What happened?"

"I'm not sure. Maybe it's just...his time."

After we discuss travel arrangements and hang up, I run into the bathroom and throw up.

I'm not ready. I'm not ready to lose my dad.

Twenty-four hours later, hugging my arms around the pea coat which hardly puts a layer between my skin and a Jackson winter, I'm a chilly island of frost among swarms of heavy-jacket tourists carrying ski gear and meeting relatives. Upbeat Christmas songs pelt us from the airport speakers. It's a happy, joyful time of year, which makes what we're about to face that much sadder.

Shivering, I tug my blue scarf tighter around my neck and pace back and forth on the icy sidewalk, half-expecting Jake's Jeep like that first day so long ago. No Jeep. I check my phone. No missed calls from Anna. She's probably on her way, but flakes are falling fast, thick and determined. She's probably driving slowly. If she doesn't show up, maybe I'll call Jake. I stare at his contact.

No. No. Don't even think it. If Jake wanted to talk to you, he'd have called.

It's been three months since we said goodbye in my ranch bedroom. I never see him in the background of our Skype chats. Anna hadn't mentioned him at all. I haven't asked, but it's the constant bear in the room. *Where is he?*

My heart leaps when I see the Eight Hands Ranch van pull up to the curb. When the door opens, I'm stunned to see my dad, who most *definitely* doesn't look like he should be out of bed, propped up in his wheelchair. He's thinner than before, his skin even more sallow and waxy. I'm so happy to see him, though, so I dive inside and cautiously wrap my arms around his neck.

"He insisted on coming," Anna says. "And you know your

daddy when he sets his mind to something."

I hug her, too, and she holds on longer than normal. "I'm glad you're here," she says when she finally pulls away, eying me up and down. "Miss Preppy Pants."

I grin. "So am I."

"You look like you walked off the page of a catalog, doesn't she, Gus?"

"Yeah." I blush, smoothing down my long skirt over thick sweater tights and tall leather boots. "A visit with Mom and her Nordstrom card will do that to a girl."

Anna grins. "You look beautiful. Miss College."

"A. Y'all are the ones who made me go, and B. they're just clothes. But yeah, they do fit the part at Wesleyan. Don't tell me you miss my Cowgirl shirt?"

"Ha! Never." She rubs my arms. "Ooh. This sweater is soft as butter!"

"It's cashmere."

"And here I am suffering in all this scratchy wool." She glares down at her thick purple sweater with, what else, strawberry decorations weaved into the pocket. "We have it all wrong here, I'll tell you, Gus."

She looks at him and his eyes are smiling.

Sitting next to Dad so I can hold his hand while we drive, I glance out the window, watching the falling snow against the gray, stormy sky, trying not to wonder how much time he has left.

I stay for the whole of winter break, and ours is quiet routine, watching light snow falling on tall pines from the huge windows next to the roaring fire. I tell Anna and Dad all about school, my classes, my dorm. They love the stories about Karen and her rabbits and want me to bring her out to the ranch sometime. I have so much to say now that my life is only about the positive things I'm doing and none of the bad things I was running from last summer.

They don't ask about California. That was in the past. Connecticut is my present. And the ranch. Of course, the ranch is my omnipresent center.

Dad and I watch the whole mini-series of *Lonesome Dove*. I sit next to his bed and hold his hand while snowflakes fall and fall and fall outside, piling up in soft, untouched pillows.

When Robert Duvall's character, Gus, (how did I forget he shared a name with my dad?) visits Clara and they sit under their favorite apple tree, I think that's me. No matter where I end up, when I'm old and done, the person I'll want to see most of all will be Jake, and I'll do like Gus did with Clara. I'll come to him wherever he is and maybe by then he'll have forgiven me for dumping my secrets on him like I did. When he tells me about his sweet, sane cowgirl wife and three healthy strapping ranch kids, he'll thank me for pushing him away, because I gave him a chance at a normal life without a bunch of baggage. Or, maybe he won't even recognize me. Maybe I'll be only a distant memory, but he'll finally remember and maybe, maybe, he'll hold my hand by the creek and I'll tell him it was always him. Always.

I'll tell him that when it's time for me to be buried, like Gus, I'll ask to be brought here, to Eight Hands Ranch, and have my ashes scattered on our camping spot where we watched Scout run with her herd and slept under a million stars. Where I was alive and free.

Helluva movie, Dad types. *Hellava story*.

"The best story," I say out loud.

No, Dad types, *this is the best story. You and me right here. You gave me my happy ending, Paige-y. Don't ever forget it.*

"I love you, Daddy," I say, and I lean into his weak, broken body and tell him he gave me my happy ending, too.

Chapter Seventy-Seven

Dad begins to fade quickly. One night, he falls asleep and doesn't wake up. He's still alive, but he's not coherent. The ranch gives way to quiet time of waiting for the inevitable.

The still quiet of a long grieve.

I read to Dad, but I'm not sure if he can hear me anymore. I tell him I love him. I sing him Christmas songs. Mostly I just hold his limp, cold hand and cry.

Outside, I take long walks in the snow. I stare at the empty corral. The horses have moved to warmer land for the winter, and it's so quiet without them. Quiet without Scout.

I see Jake everywhere. Everywhere and nowhere. I long for him to climb the porch stairs and sit with me on the swing, or smile at me from the corral, flicking snow off his hat. They're silly, these fantasies, but they're what keep me going on the long, sad days of waiting.

Anna must know where he is, but she doesn't tell me and I don't ask. We are kind and careful and gentle with each other. Like two war widows trying to make it through another day, grateful for warm food and a roof to keep the freshly fallen snow off our heads. The denial tactics I use at college don't work here. Faced with the reality of what I've lost and will surely lose soon, I'm dreading it. Dreading the inevitable. I can't wait to get back to school, and I never want to leave the ranch.

The only bright spot is an email with an attached photo of a white sand beach with a bright blue sky. It's from Greece where Mom and Phil are on a month-long cruise.

"I'm actually relaxing, Paige. It's a minor miracle. Inspired by you, honey."

I write back that dad is in decline, but I'm so happy for her. That I'm happy they made peace with each other, that I hope she has a wonderful trip. (And I mean it.)

After Anna falls asleep beside Daddy, I snag the spare key out of the kitchen drawer and crunch through thick, icy snow to Jake's cabin. My shaking hands take a minute to unlock the door, but I do. I press it open and slip inside.

It's only when I close the door behind me that it becomes too much. I burst into tears in the bitter cold living room where he once swept me up into his warm arms. Gingerly, I touch the leather chair where I imagined him having his morning coffee, the arm of the couch where I pictured him reading at the end of the day, his feet hanging over the other end. He'd be reading Hemingway or Steinbeck, or like me and Dad, *Lonesome Dove*.

It's wrong on so many levels, invading his privacy like this, but the dusty smell of the air tells me he hasn't been here for a while. I need to be with Jake, if only among his things. I check the fridge. A chunk of moldy cheese and some condiment bottles are the only contents.

Where is he? Did he move away? Travel? Neither sounds like Jake. If something happened to him, Anna would tell me. The quiet way she's acting, I feel in the silence that he's fine. That his distance is on purpose. And it's a punch in the gut.

I open the bedroom door, stalling a bit before I push it open and peek in. I half expect (want) to find him there sleeping.

But the bed is made neatly. I press my palm on the quilt and it's cold. So unlike Jake and his constant warmth. I go back into the living room and light a fire. Jake has a little basket with kindling, newspaper, and matches on his mantel place. I wrap myself up in the blanket that smells like him, lie back on the couch, and watch the flames dance.

Chapter Seventy-Eight

If this were a novel instead of real life, I'd end it like this: I'd be hiking along on the mountaintop and I'd see Scout's herd, with Scout in the center of it all. I'd call for Jake who would be unpacking our gear. From within the warmth and safety of his arms, I'd watch her frolic in the snow with her family.

In the city, they'd discover a cure for Lou Gehrig's disease, and by next Christmas, Dad would be walking again, telling jokes with his real voice, wearing jeans and eating steak. He and Anna would ride off into the sunset, the back of their covered wagon reading JUST MARRIED. Jake would squeeze my hand, and we'd exchange a look, knowing we're next.

Ty wouldn't have died. And he wouldn't have raped me or raped that girl in Brooklyn. Wouldn't have stalked me or blamed me for his screwed up life. Maybe his mom wouldn't have left his family at all. Maybe Phil would never have met my mom and maybe my dad wouldn't have been an alcoholic and Mom wouldn't have left him. Maybe Jake's dad would have lived and his mom never left him and he'd never have needed Dad.

If all of these things fell into place as fate, I never would've met Ty.

But this isn't fiction.

And Dad died the night before Christmas.

I was by his bedside, holding his hand as he took his last, shallow breath, and so was Anna. By that time, he'd withered away into no more than a wax doll of himself, just skin and bones, light as feathers. I kissed his cool skin and, later, we had him cremated.

Just when we were about to leave on our mounts and head up the mountain to scatter his ashes, I hear a truck rumble up the driveway.

The conditions are nowhere near perfect — in fact, they're downright fucking tragic — but the truck rumbling up the driveway is Jake.

We don't talk on the ride up the snowy mountain, Anna, Jake, and me.

When he climbed out of his truck, he'd greeted us, gave me a hug, and said he was sorry about my father's passing. I clung to him, desperate for him to wrap me in his warmth and let me yell and cry and fall apart. It broke me to look at him. It broke me to hear his voice. More than that, I was angry. Angry that he not only left me, but Dad, too.

When he let me go, eyes averted and a pained expression on his face, I wanted to slug him. He might think the worst of me — he might find me vile and reprehensible — but the fact that he left Dad without saying goodbye was unforgiveable. Had his years with my dad meant nothing to him?

We'd had three days to get used to the idea of Dad being gone. Anna folded up his wheelchair and tucked it away, but his stuff was still everywhere and we both missed him so intensely it was like a crack ran through the wood floor, so deep and cragged we were both about to fall into the grief of it all. Jake showing up is at least an emotional distraction, and I find the anger comforting.

I try my best not to dwell on Jake, but it's hard not to as

I watch him in his brown duster on horseback in front of me, his horse stomping through the thick snow. Fortunately, it isn't storming. It's all blue sky and fresh powder—a blue bird, the skiers called it.

"Here we are," Anna says when we come to the top of the hill. "You guys ready?"

Not unlike scattering Ty's ashes over the side of the boat into the open sea, we, per his request, are set to scatter Dad's over the snowy mountain cliff where Jake and I once sat on that warm, summer night ages ago.

The three of us stand side-by-side staring out at the frozen lake, the place where Jake and I found Scout running with her herd. I glance at him and find him watching me. This was Dad's place, this was our place—it's the best place.

"This was your spot."

Anna nods. "We came up here all the time moving the cattle."

"The second I saw it I knew it was special."

"You can just feel it," she says. "We felt it."

I squeeze her gloved hand. "I'm so glad he had you," I say.

"You coming back to him made him the happiest of all," she says to me, her voice firm and true. The toughest woman I know has the softest heart.

As Anna slips the ashes over the icy cliff, I worry the tears will freeze to our faces.

That night, we have to sleep in tents. It's too cold for open air. We only have one. Even though I catch him watching me like he wants to come closer, he rolls his bedroll far away from mine, so I roll mine out beside Anna's.

I take care of the horses before turning in. Like Jake prophesized long ago, they've grown used to me. They are so beautiful in the moonlight that's reflecting off the newly fallen snow.

When I return, the tent is filled with an awkward, nervous tension. It's clear Jake and Anna have been talking, but the conversation ends the second I slip inside. Jake's antsy, like he's spent the day bottling up all his never-ending energy and doesn't have an outlet. I get it. I can't begin to relax with Jake so close, with so much unsaid, never mind freezing temperatures so cold we can see our breath. Eventually, Jake slips out of the tent. Once Anna falls asleep, I jump out of my sack, pull on my tall winter boots and heavy, faux-fur thick winter coat, and stumble out in the deep snow to find him.

Enough of this.

I find him standing on the edge of our cliff looking out. His thick brown coat is slick with snow. His cowboy hat keeps the moon's glow off his face. His long legs look like they are made for dusty, snow-crusted jeans.

"Jake?" I call out tentatively.

He turns around, not at all startled to see me. There are tears on his face and he doesn't wipe them away. Expressionless, he turns back toward the wide expanse of valley.

This isn't going to be easy. Nothing worth having ever is. My dad's words echo in my head. "Jake?"

He doesn't turn around.

I close the distance between us. I want to put my hand on his shoulder but don't dare.

"Did your daddy ever tell you about Crazy Horse?" Jake asks in an even voice. "He asked his warrior cousins to, after his death, paint his body red and plunge it into fresh water to be restored back to life. He said otherwise his bones would be turned to stone and his joints to flint in his grave, and this way, his spirit would rise."

He stares out at the snow-capped mountains, the deep canyon of the frozen Snake River. "But when Crazy Horse was killed, the warriors were in such a state of mourning that nobody remembered his request. I used to worry about that all the time as a kid. That Crazy Horse's spirit was stuck somewhere because those who loved him were so busy with their own pain that they forgot to do what he asked."

Reaching out tentatively, I touch his forearm with my mitten-covered hand. "This is what he wanted, Jake. His ashes spread here. By us. Exactly this."

"It's not enough."

"I know."

"I'm so sorry, Paige." His voice cracks into the distance. "He was a great man. As good as they get. Better, even."

I wipe a tear off my cheek. "I feel like…this sounds morbid, but it might be better for him now, you know? He hated living like that, trapped in that broken body when his spirit was so strong."

"Shouldn't have happened."

"I know."

Jake nods. His Adam's apple bobs. He turns his face away from me because a cowboy like Jake would never want me to see him crying.

We stay like that, Jake and I, quietly mourning both individually and together, until the sun rises over the horizon.

I open and close my lips several times, trying to get up the courage to say what I need to. What I've been rehearsing for when I finally had him alone, if I ever had him alone again.

The timing couldn't be worse.

"Jake, I know this isn't the best time, but I need to talk to you before you run off again. Or before I do. Did you…did you read the journal I left you?"

"Of course."

"Why didn't you…try to get in touch with me?"

The five seconds between my question and his answer last a lifetime.

"I was doing something Gus wanted."

"My dad?" I blink. "It wasn't because you were disgusted by me?"

"Disgusted?" He wrinkles his nose. "No. Why would I be

disgusted? I felt awful for you. The guy—I don't want to speak ill of the dead, but I'll make an exception in this case—sounded like a real asshole. I would've kicked his ass from here to infinity if he was still alive."

My eyes freeze open. "He was just screwed up."

"Well, I didn't know him, but I know you. You were the girl who felt badly tying a calf's legs up. I don't think you'd hurt a fly, Paige. Whatever you did to keep this guy away from you was done as self-preservation only. And where was your mom in all this? If your daddy had any idea… He owns several rifles, as you know."

Jake doesn't hate me.

Still I feel the need to explain. "It just happened. It was stupid, and we were desperate. All these kids at school kept dying, kept standing on the tracks—kids we knew, kids I grew up with. Our parents were so weird and never talked about anything, and it's just… Jake, it's so different there. Nothing felt real. All I wanted was to feel real and alive. We wanted to matter to someone, so we decided to matter to each other. It was only a few times and I knew it was wrong so I put a stop to it, but he couldn't accept that it was over and when I finally ended it…"

"I know. I read your story. The whole thing." He finally looks at me. His watery red eyes are almost too much to bear and I feel like I swallowed a stone keeping myself still. "Shit, Paige, things happen. It's not like I've been a monk my whole life. What you did before you came back here is your business. What I don't get is why you didn't tell me about the mess back home? I could've helped you. Or helped you find someone who could."

"You're not mad?"

"How could I be?" His eyes are furious passion. "You are a beautiful, strong, challenging girl—no, *woman*. You deserve this." His arms spread out at the expansion of the valley—wild and free and lit with morning. "You deserve everything."

"Do I?" I'm not sure I do.

His eyes are hard. I know he's waiting for me to change my answer.

"I do," I amend. "I do now."

"That's right."

"Where were you, Jake?"

He sighs and looks at the ground. "After you left town, I ended up in North Dakota working on an oil rig. Cash job. I wanted to save up for when you came back for the holidays. I wanted to surprise you."

"You were working on an oil rig...to surprise me?" That is not the answer I expected.

"Yeah," he says, looking shy. "A buddy of mine was heading up there and asked if I wanted to go along. It was right after you left, and I just...couldn't stick around anymore with you gone. It was just..." He lets his voice trail off.

Jake missed me. It was as hard on him as it was on me. My heart swells.

"It was hard work," he continues. "Good work, though." He grinned. "And I made out with a lot of cash."

"I thought you didn't care anymore." My voice cracks.

"Didn't care? Of *course* I cared! I told Anna I was leaving to find work, and I'd be back for Christmas."

"Jesus, Jake." I crouch down. Hug my cold knees. My butt touches the soft snow.

He reaches for my elbow and pulls me back up. "I couldn't be in touch. There was nothing. Just a shanty of a town. Men everywhere. Oil. It was crazy. But I promised your daddy I'd watch out for you. And I needed something of my own to get us started."

I'm pretty sure my jaw falls to the ground. It takes me a few seconds to recover. I'm happy and sad. Elated and confused. I feel everything. "Get *us* started? As in, you and a pathetic city slicker?" It's a poor attempt at a joke, and sure enough, his face is still. He won't let me berate myself even if I'm joking.

"Pathetic? Yeah, right Ms. Straight A's at Wesleyan. Congratulations by the way. I hear you're killing it, Cowgirl."

I choke out a laugh. Anna and her gossip. But more importantly, "What did my dad say? After I left?"

Jake smiles. "He said, 'Find your way. Learn all you can. Be someone my daughter deserves.'"

"He did not." I'm part proud, part embarrassed.

"He did. You know Gus." The corner of his mouth starts to rise, remembering.

"What did you say?"

"I said okay, though you're perfectly capable of taking care of yourself, on the condition he not tell you what I was up to. When he agreed, I skipped town with my buddy, made a shitload of dough, and then signed up for fifteen units over a full load at the community college next semester."

I scrub my face with my mittens, just to make sure I'm not dreaming. "I'm speechless. This whole time I thought...I thought you weren't even thinking about me."

"You nuts?" He cups my face in his big, strong hands, looks me right in the eyes, and tells me exactly what I want to hear. Tells me what I've been dying to hear all these months apart. "I think about you all the time, Paige."

He pulls me into his arms, holds me for a long time and then, still holding my hands, lets me go a little so he can tell me something else face-to-face. "I've been thinking...this is terrible, but has to be said. Your dad's life insurance policy was a good chunk of money. If we work hard all year, we can open her up next summer after you finish up your school year. You can come back for summers, right? I mean, if you want to? Eight Hands Ranch. You, me, your dad, Anna. I want to honor his death, really honor it. He'd want this. What do you say?"

Sparkly rainbow-colored unicorns have nothing on the joy I'm feeling. "I say yes."

"Yes?" His eyes brighten. "Truly, yes?"

"I love you, Jake." The truth tumbles out, and even if I

wanted to, it's too late to take it back in so I just go for it. "I love you. I want to be with you. Forever."

I exhale a frosty breath into the dawn and wait.

He doesn't make me wait long.

"I love you, too, Paige Mason."

"You do?"

"Hell yeah." He grins broadly. "I've loved you since you showed up in those pigtails calling me a ballerina fisherman. And when you showed up again in that sparkly cowgirl shirt, I thought I'd died and gone to heaven. It's always been you."

When Jake wraps me in his warm, strong arms, his kiss is as real and true as the mountain air that lightens my heavy head and stitches my broken heart.

Epilogue

The following June, under a wide, blue sky, a gathering of fifty or so crowd around stretched yellow tape at the base of our new sign.

HEALING HANDS RANCH

I'm holding a pair of Dad's old scissors, the ones he'd opened envelopes with in his study for as long as I can remember. I'm using them to cut the tape. I glance up at the sign.

We transposed our handprints from the yellow stone mosaics leading up to the porch, and Jake carved us a new one out of some fallen wood from our favorite spot on the mountain. With my mom and stepdad's help, we got venture capital funding from California to turn this place into my dream. Anna runs an organic kitchen. We have two counselors on staff. We built handicapped-equipped bunkhouses and have a physician and psychiatrist on staff, as well as rehabilitation folks.

Our ranch isn't just a vacation destination anymore. It's a place where we help lost kids get found. A place where sick adults seek refuge on our wide, welcoming porch, where the sweet tea never runs out. A place where miracles aren't in the form of tumors disappearing overnight, or a mental illness dissipating into the air—none of us are naïve and that's just bullshit—but it is a reprieve, a mental rest. And we see progress.

Freshman year, I earned mostly A's at Wesleyan, and a couple B's. I volunteered my time at the counseling office shadowing therapists who helped depressed freshman, about half of who had eating disorders. The counselor, Dr. Scott, a lovely lady who wore all black, said I was a natural. I filled her in on why.

I didn't have to miss any school helping set up the ranch program. I even got Dr. Scott to commit to helping us out in June and July. Turns out I'm pretty persuasive when I have an idea I want to bring to fruition.

It turns out Mr. T from high school was right. I am the only one who knows how my story will end, and for the moment, the ending is here where healing isn't always visible on the outside, it's something we catch a glimpse of and hope it makes a difference. It's a depressed girl's eyes as she watches the birth of a newborn foal, an abused kid catching his first fish, a teenage girl with scars up and down her arms learning to cut horses, rodeo style, instead of herself.

We don't always succeed. I'm not going to lie—that's hard. It's like losing them all over again. Slicing open bandages, re-exposing wounds. But when we do succeed, we gather those moments like precious stones, and save them, each one, for when it becomes too much.

At the end of that first summer, Jake and I parked down by the airport and, under tossed blankets in the back of his truck, we looked up at the stars and watched the planes fly away and I wondered if I should leave, too. If I should go back to school or stay with Jake for the winter. We watched the planes fly in and out, we stared at the infinite stars, and at the end of the night, we drove back to the ranch. I slipped into his bed beside him, and wrapped my arms around his sleeping chest, feeling full of everything that matters.

The summer sky is wide and blue as we work, as we try, as we fail and try again. As summer leaves burst into reds and yellows and fall from trees, and I know my time is running out.

Though leaving is hard, I love my life at Wesleyan, hanging out at the coffee shops, listening to live music, and writing. Always writing. I even attempt a short-story reading at Open Mic night. My piece is about Scout and everyone said it was awesome.

Jake comes out to visit in early fall and gets a kick out of it, and my friends get a kick out of him. You'd think he'd be so out of place, but Jake manages to fit in wherever he goes, even in a crowded café full of college hipsters in their beatnik wools and college colors.

When heavy snow begins to fall outside my classrooms' tall glass windows, I know soon enough, I'll be back home. We'll be watching it snow together outside Jake's cabin window under thick blankets, brainstorming plans for next summer and making stew from scratch. We'll cut down a tree off our property and haul it into the big house. We'll hang Dad's stocking along with ours, and celebrate. That first anniversary winter, Mom and Phil joined us, too. Anna and Mom cooked together in the big strawberry themed kitchen, and it was the best Christmas I'd had since I was a little girl.

Then one April day, I'm home for spring break, and, after filling in Jake and Anna about my spring classes, Jake runs me up the slushy mountain on our snowmobile across snow so high it feels like we're floating on marshmallow. He's in front of me, driving, and my arms are wrapped tight around his stomach, my cold cheek buried into his back, and he drives crazy on purpose to make me laugh, to remind me I'm alive, or maybe just so I'll hold onto him tighter. On the top of the hill he points out hoof prints and in the meadow I think I'm hallucinating when we see her, we see Scout, back with her herd. "I knew eventually she'd find her way back," Jake says, kissing a snowflake off my nose. "I can't believe it."

I take a closer look, shielding my eyes from the glaring sun. "That's not Scout, Jake."

He takes a closer look. "You know you're right. Damned if she doesn't look just like her though."

He sounds so disappointed. I squeeze his forearm and say what I believe is true. "She is here. She never left this valley, not in the way that matters."

"I'm going to get her back for you one day."

"She's a star now. What would she want with us boring old ranchers?" I tease him but the moment is richer than my joke. It might sound cheesy, but I do feel them with us—in the fading patches of snow that will soon give way to spring blooms—Dad and Ty and the others we lost. The ones we loved so much, but lost anyway. I feel them in the breeze. I hear them in the eagles' cries. I see them in every hard-earned smile when our guests return summer after summer, when I go back to school in the fall and say goodbye to Jake and my heart breaks all over again, and then, when I see him next, the pieces melt back together.

Most importantly we live. We live like crazy.

And I know my story is far from over: My story's just begun.

Need Help?

If you're experiencing a crisis or having suicidal thoughts, please call the National Suicide Prevention Lifeline. We're here 24/7. You are not alone.

In the U.S., call 1-800-273-TALK (8255).

In the UK, call 08457 90 90 90.

In Australia, call 13 11 14.

Visit www.suicide.org to for a complete list of International Suicide Hotlines

For more information on ALS, visit:
www.alsa.org
www.alsfoundation.org

Author's Note

When I first had the idea for a novel inspired by a series of horrific, "contagious" teen suicides in my hometown of Palo Alto five years ago, I wasn't sure I could write it. The topic sickened and disheartened me. I had two young children at home. Why was I raising them in this suddenly dangerous town? Furthermore, what would make a kid—a healthy, affluent, brilliant, talented kid with seemingly everything going for them (this was the word on the street; I never researched specifics about the victims in order to keep the story purely fictional)—step in front of a train and end it all?

I had to find out why. Or at least hypothesize as to why. So I could help. So I could try and protect my own children and my students from bleak futures. So I created the character of Paige, with her semi fish-out-of-water backstory, who barely escapes the fate of her peers. I created the character of Gus, a hardass cowboy trapped in his own shell of a body suffering from ALS, to honor my Uncle Mike who died after gracefully suffering from symptoms of the terrible disease for years. Gus, like my uncle, would do anything to live: to walk, to talk, to hug his family, while five kids in one of the richest cities in America, students at one of the best high schools in the nation, wanted to die. Why? I wanted to understand. I needed to understand.

I had to do something…because doing *nothing* felt like I was on those tracks with a train rumbling toward me, too. So I did what I do: I wrote. It broke my heart. It frustrated and scared the crap out of me, but I wrote this story.

But then, once I finally finished it, I wasn't sure I could *sell* it: Rampant teen suicide in the Silicon Valley that this famous, wealthy community—home of Steve Jobs and Google and Facebook—was trying to brush under the rug? An alcoholic cowboy with ALS trying to save his decrepit Wyoming ranch? A broken girl trying to find herself after a harmful relationship a sociopathic teen boy who happens to be her stepbrother? These are two novels at least. Maybe three. But I knew it was one. It *had* to be one. All these characters all had to fit into one story because they needed each other. (They just didn't know it yet.) Their stories spooled out of my head in delicate, intrinsic threads, swirling together, weaving like scenes in a movie. "This is two separate novels," said many NY editors. "I love it. It's so well written. But it's two books. At least. Revise?" But I couldn't. I *knew* it was one book, and besides, I had the title ready to go. A perfect Crazy Horse quote I stumbled upon. I was stubborn and stuck, but I felt their story. It may sound crazy, but they felt real to me. I needed to tell this story.

Months passed, and when I was about to give up on *Paint* and all these flawed characters I'd fallen hard for, one night when I was lying with my young daughter before bed, an email popped into my inbox. It was from my agent Sara Crowe, who championed this novel from its initial spark. The subject was "Great news!" and the letter was a forward from my brilliantly gutsy editor Heather Howland at Entangled. I skimmed it lightning fast, blinking away excited tears. It said she loved the book. That she could relate to it. That, while it needed work, she saw, no she *felt* the story I was trying to write. As one story. One book. And she wanted to publish it! And with that, she brought this story to life, so all who tragically inspired it, in my small way, can live on. This one is for you all.

About the Author

Heidi R. Kling writes novels about contemporary teen girls set in fantastic situations. She's the author of the acclaimed novel SEA, bestselling fantasy series Spellspinners of Melas County, and more. A native Californian, she currently lives with her husband, two children, and scruffy Sailor pup in Palo Alto, California, where she also teaches self-esteem building classes for kids. She earned her MFA in Creative Writing from The New School in NYC. Visit Heidi @ http://heidirkling.com or on social media. She loves to chat with her readers!

CPSIA information can be obtained at www.ICGtesting.com
Printed in the USA
LVOW11s1009191115

463313LV00001B/1/P